JUDE TURNED TOWARD AURORA TO FIND HER LOOKING UP AT HIM.

Ten years disappeared in an instant, and they were back at this same lake, two teenagers, crazy in love.

She looked almost the same. Her face was a little slimmer, her hair a little longer, and there was a lot more wisdom and experience in her eyes. But she was still Aurora, and he was as attracted to her as he had been years ago. Arguably more.

He still cared about her too.

Deeply.

"Jude," she said, his name falling from her lips like a question.

The notion was insane, inappropriate—he wanted to kiss her.

Right here, right now, with fireflies dancing across the field and into the trees, the sun so low it was an orange sliver in the distance.

Her breath quickened, as if she knew. As if she'd let him, or even wanted him to.

Aurora swayed toward him and he acted. Not another thought in mind [illegible] woman and this night, and all the time they'd [illegible]

Also by Heather McGovern

Something Blue

Second Chance at the Orchard Inn

Heather McGovern

Includes a Bonus Novella by Jeannie Chin

FOREVER

New York Boston

Forever
Hachette Book Group
1290 Avenue of the Americas, New York, NY 10104
read-forever.com
twitter.com/readforeverpub

First Edition: June 2023

Forever is an imprint of Grand Central Publishing. The Forever name and logo are trademarks of Hachette Book Group, Inc.

ISBN: 9781538737460 (mass market), 9781538737453 (ebook)

Printed in the United States of America

OPM

10 9 8 7 6 5 4 3 2 1

For the Wild Women:
Amanda, Jenni, Jennifer, Keri, and Reagan.
You're the best sisters an only child could ever have!

Acknowledgments

Thank you to Lee, Sean, and ReyRey. Without your love and support, none of this would be possible.

Second Chance at the Orchard Inn

Chapter 1

The scent of sweet cinnamon lured Aurora Shipley down the hall and up the stairs to the main level of the Orchard Inn. The smell grew stronger, pulling her into the kitchen.

"Morning, Sleeping Beauty." Her sister, Beth, bright-eyed and with a big smile across her face, leaned against the counter, drumming her fingers on the back of her tablet.

Ugh. Morning people. "How much coffee have you had?"

"None. It's still brewing."

How? Aurora could barely make coherent words happen and her sister was already working on that blasted tablet of hers.

Aurora plopped down in a chair at the counter and propped her chin on her hand. "Wake me when it's ready, 'kay?"

"Will do. Sawyer made cinnamon rolls for us too. They should be ready in about five minutes."

Years of working in the food service industry did not a morning person make, and being the current, temporary chef for her family's inn hadn't changed that. The inn might serve breakfast at 8:00 a.m., but Aurora kept late hours, prepping food, creating menus, experimenting with recipes, and anxiously contemplating her path in life and what her future may hold.

Y'know, normal one o'clock in the morning stuff like that.

The coffee pot beeped its completion and Aurora poured a big mugful.

She focused on her coffee; hints of caramel laced through every sip. She needed the caffeine to function, but she was particular about a coffee's flavor profile. Nutty, hints of sweetness, warm notes, and nothing too overpowering. Miss her with blueberry pecan or coconut coffees. No thank you.

Half a cup down, her brain began to function. She'd been up even later than usual, reading over an email from her boss in California. Her time here in Texas was coming to an end. He'd sent her the menu for next month, which was only two short weeks away, and asked when she'd be free to talk about her return.

Beth refilled her mug and floated over to sit next to her. "Late night?" she sang.

Aurora pulled the mug closer. "You need to go somewhere with all that morning cheer."

But then, Beth was always cheerful nowadays. Apparently, love did that to people.

"Pssht." Her sister patted her head, more than a smidge patronizing. "Drink your coffee. You'll be fine."

Free to talk about her return.

Aurora sipped her coffee.

A couple of weeks into the leave of absence that allowed her to return home and help her sisters with the floundering inn, all Aurora had wanted was to get back to L.A. She had a career to pursue, people to impress, ladders to climb. Her goals were in Los Angeles, but she couldn't leave her sisters in the lurch. So she'd worked with them at the inn the past two months and, together with Beth and Cece, they'd turned the Orchard Inn around.

In doing so, they'd all grown closer, arguably tighter than they'd been as kids.

Now, the notion of leaving her sisters again—like she had at eighteen—was more unsettling than back then, or even how it would've been two months ago.

"Smells like breakfast is almost ready." Sawyer strolled into the kitchen like he'd been up for hours too.

He rubbed his hands together and took a deep sniff as he opened the oven door. "Oh yeah. We're in business now."

A cinnamon scented fog filled the kitchen, and Aurora's salivary glands came to life.

Sawyer cooked only about five things, but the rolls were now his specialty.

He set a plate of ooey-gooey cinnamon rolls on the counter and dropped a kiss on Beth's temple. "This ought to help get the day going."

Beth turned to kiss him before sliding the plate closer.

"Hey, don't hog the goods. Sawyer made them to share." Aurora tugged the plate toward her.

Sawyer sat small plates in front of them. "Someone feed this girl, quick."

He'd recently leveled up from boyfriend to fiancé, and he was a regular Saturday-morning staple at the Orchard Inn. Her sister had never been happier. Then again, with treats like this, who wouldn't be?

Aurora reached for a roll, taking a bite and letting the

warm sweetness melt in her mouth, while the glaze stuck to her lips.

"Shut your mouth," she said with her mouth still full.

Sawyer chuckled as he joined them at the counter.

"These are too good." She took another bite. "Are you trying to take my job? Because I'd happily let you have the Saturday-morning shift. Let me roll out of bed around ten, as long as you save me leftovers."

Sawyer laughed fully then, the rich baritone sound oddly soothing, even in the morning. "I cannot run a kitchen. Filling a request from my sweetheart is one thing." He shared a smile with Beth. "But multiple things, for multiple people? No way. Besides, I only know how to make these and a steak dinner. Pretty sure your guests prefer a star chef, not a cowboy."

"Oh." Beth set her coffee down with a clunk. "That reminds me. Aurora, the couple who checked out yesterday—here for their anniversary—they went on and on for about ten minutes about your brunch. I thought the husband was going to cry when he started talking about the quiche."

Well, in all honesty, her quiche *was* worthy of tears.

She'd shed a few of them while trying to impress her then-boss, years ago.

At first, she'd cried tears of frustration, the head chef being unimpressed with any and everything Aurora did, yet still tapping her to create and prepare the feature menu item for the restaurant's Mother's Day brunch.

Nothing like the mind games of a demanding, brilliant, narcissistic head chef to riddle Aurora with self-doubt and then throw her on center stage and demand perfection.

Wanting to do more than just a typical quiche Lorraine

or veggie, Aurora had tried variations on spinach, artichoke, and even lobster. None of them were just right, none of them up to the level of expectation she held for herself. Finally, she'd found the perfect combination of sundried tomato, spinach, and goat cheese. It wasn't a ground-breaking combo, but the concentration and quality of each ingredient was what made the quiche perfect.

It resulted in the first compliment her head chef ever gave her.

"Not bad," he'd said.

Might as well have been skywriting and a parade to Aurora. Later that day, tucked away in the janitor's closet, she'd wept tears of joy.

"I bet they leave an amazing review on Tripadvisor." Beth pulled a small bite of her cinnamon roll off with a fork, having no idea of the emotional roller coaster one quiche had caused.

"Good." Aurora's brain began feeling less fuzzy, her mind fully kicking into gear with thoughts of cheese, heirloom tomatoes, and kitchen trauma.

Her goal, in returning to the Orchard Inn, was bailing her family out of having no chef after a disastrous wedding reception. Then, helping her sisters rebuild the inn's brand into something sought-after and admirable. But she'd also gotten a break from the pressure cooker of being a chef in one of Los Angeles's most popular, and demanding, restaurants.

Aurora had never, and would never, admit she needed a break. But taking a couple of months to return home and work at the slower pace of the family business had restored some balance to her life. She felt more centered, and she remembered she was darn good at this chef gig.

Rebuilding the inn's reputation was well on its way—some might even say complete—but admitting her work here was done meant going back into the fire and facing her future.

Was she ready for that?

"Where's Cece?" Sawyer asked after their youngest sister.

Aurora turned her thoughts to the here and now. "Sleeping in, probably. We went for a long walk yesterday. She did great, but I think it wore her out."

Cece had fallen on a solo hike and hurt her ankle about a month before. She was out of the boot and cleared to get some activity but was wisely taking it slow. Yesterday was the longest walk so far and, while she'd done great, the effort had to have been exhausting.

Not to mention, she'd stayed up late in the kitchen with Aurora, catching up on gossip and taking dibs on when Beth would marry Sawyer, and how much of a control freak she'd be about the event.

If their late-night session prevented Cece from getting this breakfast, they'd all be in trouble.

Motion in her peripheral vision caught Aurora's attention.

"What in the— What are you doing to that poor roll?" She stared Beth down.

"What?" Beth haphazardly stabbed the roll with her fork again, tearing off a jagged bite.

"Stop. You're mutilating it."

"Don't tell me how to eat my breakfast."

"You're not eating it. You're torturing it. Sawyer, tell her she's doing it wrong."

Sawyer was too busy licking his sticky fingers.

"See? Sawyer knows."

"I don't like my fingers getting all gooey," Beth argued.

"Then at least cut into it like a piece of cake. Don't stab at it like you've got a pickax. You're killing me. Next, you'll be putting ketchup on your steak."

"No." Sawyer shook his head dramatically while chewing. "Don't blaspheme at breakfast."

Aurora grinned. "What are you going to do when you serve steak at your wedding reception and some guest asks for ketchup?"

Sawyer threw his hands up in outrage. "Absolutely not. There will be no ketchup at our wedding."

She chuckled at his reaction, and Beth joined in.

"This is not a laughing matter," he insisted. "There is nothing we're going to serve that should need ketchup. Not the steak, not the potatoes. Not with your cooking. It will be perfection exactly as is. Maybe we'll allow some salt and pepper, but even that's questionable."

Beth stopped laughing and her gaze shot toward the window.

Aurora set down her coffee. "What's wrong?"

"Nothing."

Beth was a terrible liar. She was thinking about Aurora leaving for California.

She and Sawyer had been talking about Aurora a lot lately. Several times, Aurora entered a room only for them to hush immediately, and then awkwardly begin blabbing about the weather or going horseback riding. When really, they'd just been mid-discussion about Aurora, their wedding, and the future without Aurora nearby.

They'd probably get married in about six to eight

months and, by that time, Aurora was supposed to be long gone.

Back to L.A., back to her dream and the hard work of someday being named head chef at one of the premier restaurants in the country.

She wouldn't be here to prepare their wedding feast. Heck, she'd be lucky if she got a couple of days off to fly in and be a bridesmaid, then leave again, not to be seen for months, maybe even years—given a chef's schedule.

"I could maybe take some time off and come back long enough to help with the wedding," Aurora fibbed.

There's no way she'd get that kind of time off. She'd used up all her favors by taking this current leave.

Beth turned to face her. "We both know that's not realistic. Not if you're back in California."

If.

That was Beth's way of saying, "But if you aren't in California, you could stay here with us and we'd all live happily ever after, so do exactly that, okay?"

Honestly, Aurora had considered it.

She'd lie in bed at night, wondering what life might be like if she stayed in Texas and remained the chef at the Orchard Inn.

But, while the past two months had been a blessing for her and her sanity, being a bed-and-breakfast and wedding chef was not her happily ever after. She didn't want to be a caterer. Being the inn's chef wasn't her culinary dream, and she couldn't stay home forever.

Home was the place of her dreams. The past lurked around every corner and reminded her of *him.*

The only thing scarier than returning to L.A. and

fighting for her future was staying here, letting her dreams die, and having to deal with the past.

No thank you.

"I can help you find another chef," Aurora offered. "I'll get Cece to help me put something online. We'll line up interviews. I'm not going to leave y'all high and dry, sis."

"I know, I know." Beth nodded and swallowed hard. "But they won't be you."

Aurora stared down into her black coffee.

Her sisters had made no secret of their wish for her to stay. They'd been supportive when she left for school and remained supportive during her years of striving and hustling in kitchens across Southern California. Now that she'd returned for a couple of months, and they'd bonded again, sharing the love and challenging one another as only sisters can, they were less enthusiastic about California being the place to make her dreams come true.

"It'll all work out in the end." Sawyer walked up behind them and squeezed them both with an arm over each of their shoulders. "You'll see."

"I hope you saved me one of those cinnamon buns or heads will roll." Cece joined them in the kitchen, moving better than she had in weeks.

"You know we did." Sawyer hopped up and grabbed her a plate. "I'll even warm it up a little."

"You're my hero." Cece smiled at him. "I don't care what Beth says about you."

"Hey," Beth protested.

Sawyer and Cece had been thick as thieves since the day they met, and it warmed Aurora's heart. Sawyer was the big brother Cece had never had but had probably always wanted.

Cece would hate it if she knew, but Aurora worried about their little sister.

Not the kind of worrying Beth did, but still, she loved the idea of Cece having someone else around who cared. She'd been diagnosed with a very mild case of cerebral palsy when she was born, but Cece had undergone surgeries and therapy, and worked hard to be an independent, capable young woman. She was stronger and more determined than all of them combined.

Nevertheless, it was always good to have people around who cared.

The same went for Beth. Sawyer was there for her, supportive and steady.

Aurora did feel a bit better about leaving with Sawyer there, but only a bit.

Somebody needed to be there to referee when Beth and Cece butted heads. It didn't happen very often nowadays, but it would happen.

Cece grabbed her warm cinnamon roll with both hands and dove right in.

"See?" Aurora lifted an eyebrow at Beth. "Cece knows how to eat."

Sawyer cracked up at the expression on Beth's face.

"Okay, fine. Y'all go on, eating like heathens and judging me. But one of us won't have to wash her face after breakfast. Just saying."

They wrapped up breakfast and Aurora and Cece did indeed need to wash the tips of their noses.

Aurora washed her hands, popped two breakfast casseroles in the oven, and made another pot of coffee while her sisters finished getting ready.

"Why don't you let me fix the fruit and put out the

casserole while you and Cece go to the market?" Beth offered when she returned to the kitchen.

"Seriously?"

"Yes, I'm serious. I know you like to peruse the veggies and you should enjoy going before you leave town. Do you not want to go?"

"I didn't say that, but—"

"Sawyer is here to help me. You've fixed breakfast. We can serve it. Plus, if you don't go to the market early, all the good produce will be gone."

This was true.

She could get in one last trip to the Saturday farmers' market before it was time to buckle down and find the Orchard Inn its new chef and get ready to head west. Maybe she'd find some good corn, tomatoes, and okra. She could make an old-fashioned southern supper for her sisters and Sawyer. A family meal before their family had to split up, again.

Aurora shook her head. Her time in Texas was winding down and making her downright sentimental.

She was taking a trip to the market with Cece, not a walk down memory lane.

Chapter 2

"Am I good?" Jude carefully made his way to the back of his pickup truck, attempting to see around the three boxes stacked in his arms.

"If by good you mean about to have an on-the-job injury, then yeah, you're good." His youngest sister, Bonnie, stopped him with a hand against the middle box. "I'm taking this top one."

With the top box gone, Jude could see the giant pothole a couple of feet ahead. "Thanks."

"No problem." Bonnie followed him to the back of his truck, and they loaded the boxes of dried lavender for the Saturday farmers' market. They'd already loaded pallets of fresh, potted lavender, rosemary, and fennel, along with sprigs of thyme, sage, basil, and oregano. If they were lucky, they'd sell out of everything, same as last Saturday.

"I thought we were going to get this fixed." Bonnie toed at the loose gravel and dirt around the pothole.

Jude swiped his brow with his bandanna. "I'm working on it. I made the mistake of trying to get Dad to sign off on paving at least the beginning of the driveway, up to the parking lot, instead of constantly filling in potholes with more dirt and gravel."

Bonnie huffed a laugh. "How'd that go?"

"About as good as you'd expect." Jude shook his head. "He's not okay with spending the money for paving right now, so I'll just fill these in myself next week."

"But we've got the money to at least pave the driveway and make it nice. We're busy and all the traffic—"

Jude moved one of the pallets in his truck bed, arranging the boxes so they were more secure. "You're preaching to the choir, Bon. I told him exactly that. Folks don't need to dodge potholes as they're pulling into the farm. We get all these retail shoppers now. They don't want to bump around in their Benzs and BMWs and pop a tire on their way to get their lavender and oregano."

"Should I try talking to him?" Bonnie asked.

"You're welcome to try."

They walked back to the shop, using the part of the driveway nearest the store as their loading area so as not to take up any parking spots. The farm's retail shop was bustling on a Saturday, and they tried to stay out of the way while preparing to go to the market.

Before they reached the store, Bonnie stopped him with a hand on his arm. "Is Dad going to the market with you?"

Jude considered his words before speaking. The last thing he wanted to do was stir up concern with his sister and have her going back to their mom and dad to inadvertently open a can of worms with his father knowing his children had been discussing his health and ability to work. Jude could just hear it now.

Jude is worried about Dad. Dad doesn't go to the market anymore and his energy gives out so quickly, and Jude said he had heart palpitations the other day and…

"I don't think so. Not today," Jude said instead. "He's going to stay here and help you and Mom and Meredith at the store."

"Oh." Lines formed between Bonnie's eyebrows. "He's not up to it, huh?"

Jude started walking. "I'm not getting into this again."

"Maybe we should try talking to him about it." Bonnie followed.

"We tried that. He got angry and didn't talk to me for two days."

"Maybe if Jenna talked to him." Bonnie volunteered their middle sister, as if she had the magic wand that would make John Jones open up and discuss his vulnerability or admit any signs of weakness.

Jude stopped walking and turned to face Bonnie. "I think you need to accept that Dad isn't the kind of person we can reason with, using things like logic and general concern, okay? Mom knows he needs to go back to the cardiologist, and she's trying to get him to eat better. If anyone can get through to him, it's her. I think the best thing me, you, and Jenna can do is leave it be. Unless you want him to ice you out for a few days, I suggest you let it go for now."

Bonnie sighed and rolled her eyes. "I know, but..."

"It's aggravating to ignore the obvious? Frustrating to not be able to speak freely about family issues?"

His sister nodded, looking deflated.

"I know." He pulled her into a hug, hoping he could ease some of her worry. Their dad was a bullheaded man, but they loved him. It should be okay to say, "Hey, we want you to live a lot longer, and maybe you should do a few things to make sure that happens, because we love you and don't want to lose you." But that wasn't what their dad heard when they showed concern. He heard some nonsense like he was failing as their patriarch and they wanted him out of the picture. "Listen"—Jude stepped back and met Bonnie's gaze—"we're in this together. We'll figure something out when it comes to Dad, but let's give it a few days. Let me at least get through the weekend in peace."

"Fine." She shrugged.

They began walking again.

"So just you and Jenna are running the booth today?"

"And Wyatt." Jude included his one-year-old nephew in the staffing lineup.

"Oh, Wyatt. He'll be a *huge* help."

"Hey, he's our salesman. Don't underestimate the power of a cute baby when it comes to luring in customers. He gets them in the booth, and we sell our wares."

Bonnie laughed as they made their way around to the back of the building to the workroom of the store.

"So, you going to be okay with Dad today?" Jude asked as they stopped inside the door.

"He's not an invalid."

"I know. I mean are you going to be okay—not getting annoyed with him?"

"I'll be fine." His sister closed her eyes and held out her hands as though she were meditating. "I'll be the picture of inner peace and zen."

"Uh-huh."

"Hey." Her eyes flew open. "Do you think *she* will be at the market today?"

Jude narrowed his gaze before walking away. "I don't know who you mean, but no."

Bonnie quickly followed. "Her sister Cece came by

the booth last week. You don't think she'll bring Aurora along this week?"

He tried to focus on the last three boxes of lavender that he needed to load.

Aurora. His high school sweetheart. She of the golden hair, blue-green eyes, prettiest of smiles, sharpest of minds, and quickest of humors. Part of him would love to see her again, while the other part would rather twist an ankle in one of those potholes.

He'd broken her heart way back when, she'd run off and headed west, and there was a big, gaping hole where their relationship used to be. Friendship and love—now an empty space.

If he did see her again, what was he supposed to say?

Hey. Sorry about breaking your heart and being a selfish prick ten years ago. Friends now?

He'd like nothing more than to make peace with what they'd left unresolved. But how?

Aurora Shipley hated him, no doubt. The last thing she'd want to do is swing by the Jones's farm tent and browse their lavender and herbs.

"Hello." Bonnie waved her hand in front of his face. "I said, now that she's back in town, you don't think Aurora will ever drop by?"

Jude met Bonnie's gaze before hoisting up the three boxes of lavender. "No, I do not."

Perhaps he should prepare himself in case she did.

How was he supposed to do that exactly? He counted the end of their relationship as one of his biggest regrets. Sure, he was just a silly teenage boy at the time, but regardless, Jude had always held himself to a higher standard. He should've handled things better, *been* better.

He hoisted the last three boxes in his arms and made his way out the store. If he did run into Aurora Shipley, he had no idea what he could say to fix the past. Still, the more he thought about it, the more he realized he wanted to see her again. He wanted to say the things he couldn't all those years ago, and maybe finally make things right.

Chapter 3

Aurora drove them into town. She and Cece debated—some might say bickered—about who would take the wheel. Cece, in typical fierce independence, insisted she should, but Aurora won on principle. Her car was still in L.A., so she hadn't gotten to drive anywhere lately.

A bribery of blueberry scones from the Great Bakery booth had also helped Aurora extract the keys.

As she drove, the winding rural roads turned into the wide streets of the residential area near downtown. The streets were shaded by the trees lining both sides, and they passed in and out of light, as if playing hide-and-seek with the sun.

Closer into town, the streets became more commercial, with the stone and brick buildings of business, retail, and gift shops. Restaurants. The settling of Fredericksburg by German immigrants showed up in flags on storefronts, the variety of German restaurants and bakeries, and the architecture of the landmarks and churches.

People strolled the sidewalks, milling about in common spaces and outside shops.

"Take a left up here and park behind the fabric store.

You won't find any parking closer to the market, and they close down part of Main Street on Saturdays, so pedestrians don't have to worry about the cars."

Aurora did as she was told and parked behind Cece's favorite store. They took a ten-minute detour so Cece could pop in and see if they'd gotten any new fabric since the day before yesterday.

They had not.

"Nothing yet," Cece declared, leaving the store as she hitched her bag of reusable bags higher on her shoulder. "I keep hoping they'll get some bolts of autumn-like fabric. Something with orange and yellow. I want to make new pillows for the seats in the gazebo. Freshen it up for when fall comes."

"That would be pretty."

"Maybe get some pumpkins out there. Decorate it a little for photo ops and stuff."

Fall was Cece's favorite season. Like most addicted hikers, she was drawn outdoors by the changing leaves and cooler temperatures.

Of course, in Texas, it took a little longer for said cooler temperatures to show up.

Today, even before noon, it felt like they were living on the sun.

Aurora grabbed one of the fashionable ties off her wrist and twisted her long hair up into a messy bun.

"People are all about the photo ops and videos now," Cece continued. "Between Instagram, TikTok, Snapchat, YouTube, and whatever comes next, we need places where guests will want to take cute vids and pics, and post them. It's free advertising, really."

Cece wasn't wrong, that was for sure. Aurora wasn't

a huge social media fan herself, but she was guilty of watching a few travel and foodie YouTube channels.

"That's actually a brilliant idea, Cece."

"I know. I'm full of them." She smiled as they walked toward the market, the live music slowly growing louder. "Like, we need to do more with our branding. We have an IG account, but I'm the only one who posts. You need to start posting images of your food."

"We post a lot of the wedding food."

"No." Cece shook her head and whipped out her phone. "I'm talking about the stuff you cook outside of events. When you mess around, creating new recipes. Post them. See this account?" She held the screen up in Aurora's face. "This lady cooks using only old-fashioned kitchen utensils and old-school methods. She has *thousands* of followers. You come up with incredible combinations and unique ideas, and you should post them. You'd help your branding and its content for the inn."

"Branding and content for the— When did you become such a marketing genius?"

Cece tossed her hair good-naturedly. "Since forever. Plus, I haven't been able to go hiking, so I've spent a lot of time online. I mean *a lot* of time."

They reached the closure of Main Street and walked another block to the Marktplatz in the center of town. Tents circled the Vereins Kirche, the octagonal building in the center of the market, and dotted the green space around it.

Produce, baked goods, wildflowers, honey, spices, paintings, pottery, jewelry—you name it, someone probably had a booth for it at the farmers' market. Originally, it'd begun as a true, produce-only market, but the popularity and draw for tourism over the years helped it grow into so much more.

Aurora first stopped at a booth with corn and summer squash. She picked up an ear and peeled back a corner of the husk to reveal the kernels beneath. Golden yellow and plump, the corn looked perfect. But did she really want to buy it now and haul corn around the market all morning?

"You could wait and come back to get some later," Cece suggested.

Corn this pretty wouldn't last until later though. The farm's booth would sell out within the hour.

"No, I want to get it now and not risk losing out."

"You're going to make me carry sacks of corn around, aren't you?"

"No." Aurora began picking out the best ears of the bunch. "I'm going to make you *help* carry sacks of corn around. I'll get two and you can just carry one."

A few minutes later and they were both loaded up with two bags of corn each.

Aurora scored a deal by buying in bulk, and this was some of the prettiest corn she'd ever seen.

Better to have too much than not enough.

"I guess I could take these back to the car while you look around some, and I'll just find you."

"I don't know, I quite enjoy being strapped down with produce like a pack mule," Cece quipped.

"Ha ha, fine. Gimme."

"Oh, wait though." Cece hurried ahead to the next booth down.

Aurora glanced at the banner stretched across the top of the tent:

Stonewall Peach JAMboree & Rodeo

And a sign on the table in the tent read, Pie-Baking Contest.

Nope.

"C'mere." Cece beckoned her into the tent. "They're going to have a baking contest this year."

"I see that. But I'm all good. Give me your corn. I'll be right back."

"You better get your butt in here right now or I'll make a scene."

She wasn't bluffing either. No one could pitch a fit like the youngest of the three sisters.

Aurora dragged her feet into the tent.

"You should enter," Cece stated, like Aurora would have no idea this was why they were in the booth.

"I'm not entering a pie contest," she murmured.

Cece smiled at the lady behind the table before turning to Aurora. "Why not?" she asked through her teeth, without dropping the smile.

"You're seriously disturbing when you do that."

"Answer the question."

"Because I don't want to."

"You'd win."

"Cece." Her sister was going to make her say it. Make her have the same conversation she'd already had with Beth earlier this morning.

"What?"

"I can't enter. I probably won't even be here when the contest happens."

Cece's face fell. "Oh."

Aurora sighed, her corn-induced joy fading.

"I keep forgetting you have to leave."

"I know. Let's just enjoy the day, okay?"

Cece nodded, but a slight pout remained.

"Cece."

"I'm fine. Really. Let's enjoy the day. Here." Cece took the bags from her shoulders and shoved them toward Aurora. "You take the corn and I'll go get our blueberry scones. Just stay around here and I'll be right back."

"I thought I was buying the scones since you let me drive."

"I changed my mind. You're buying me lunch." Cece grinned as she strolled away, leaving Aurora in her wake.

She smiled to herself, shaking her head.

No one made her laugh and smile as much as her sisters.

She didn't have this dynamic with anyone she'd met in L.A., except for her roommate, Sloane. Not that she expected to bond with people the way she did with her sisters, but she had expected to meet more like-minded souls.

In truth, she'd found only Sloane and one of the guys who'd waited tables at the restaurant forever. They got her humor, and they were genuine, laidback sorts.

Genuine and laidback didn't describe most of the hospitality scene in Los Angeles.

Aurora wandered over to the next booth.

More like pretentious and tense, she thought with a smirk. The staff wasn't all bad, but so many of them were vying for the same thing. Everyone had their own agenda and looked out for themselves. She rarely let her guard down, because it could come back to bite you.

A display of homemade jewelry caught Aurora's eye and she paused to browse, shifting three of the bags of corn to one arm.

"Hey there!" The lady who ran the booth greeted her. "Let me know if you need anything, okay, hon?"

"I will, thank you." Aurora eyed a pair of wood-cut dangling earrings, stained a deep teal that would be set off beautifully against her reddish-blond hair.

"Good morning," the lady said to a pair of customers.

An ache that shouldn't exist clenched Aurora's heart. A longing she couldn't define, beyond knowing it shouldn't live inside her, tugged at her soul.

The day was so lovely. Peaceful. The slow cadence of people talking, the jovial sound of the crowd weaving through the banjo being played on the main stage, she and Cece laughing earlier, the distinct scent of funnel cakes being made somewhere in a half-mile radius—comforting, yet it left her wanting.

The ache in her heart shifted and changed. It spread to her chest, tightening.

Not quite anxiety but getting alarmingly close.

Her heartbeat quickened as her face grew warm.

She could *not* long for this place, this town, this life. All this peace and loveliness was fine and dandy, but it came with a lot more baggage than corn and country music.

This place came with broken promises and a broken heart, memories of a blue-eyed boy who'd meant the whole world to her, before he'd thrown her away.

She didn't want to live in this world anymore. She wanted to be Aurora Shipley, world-renowned chef and independent woman. Free of baggage and making a name for herself.

Aurora took a deep breath and let it out slowly.

Nostalgia. That's all her little panicked moment was about. These were the sights and sounds of her childhood.

Funnel cakes and hanging out with her sister on a Saturday. Nothing more than that, no reason for alarm. She didn't want to come home permanently.

The nostalgia would pass, it always did, and when she made her way back out west, back to the life she'd left behind, the small strands of longing that remained would fray and wear away, and she'd be free again.

"There's one more bushel in the truck. I'll get it," a man called.

Aurora stiffened. She'd know that voice anywhere. The lilt of it filled her ears, like a song she knew by heart.

She turned, following the words to their source.

Jude Jones.

He stood maybe fifteen yards away, working at the booth for his family's farm, as though thinking of him had conjured him from thin air. But some part of her knew he might be here. His family owned a farm. This was a *farmers'* market.

She'd managed to avoid running into him for a couple of months now, and she'd hoped she could keep the streak going. So many years had passed and now there he was. She still wasn't ready.

There'd been a time he was the love of her life, and she'd spent her nights wondering if he felt the same. Then a time she knew he didn't love her, and she wondered if she'd survive the pain.

"Yeah, I've got it. You run the register," he said to someone.

Ten years disappeared in an instant. She was seventeen again, waiting for him after baseball practice. Joyfully taking crumbs of his time, especially during playoff season. She didn't have all the after-school activities he did, the pressure of perfection or the expectation to be exceptional.

Aurora had been just the ordinary girl next door.

Until she wasn't.

"Miss?"

"Huh?" Aurora snapped back to the present.

"The earrings in your hand. Would you like to buy them?"

Aurora had wandered out of the tent with the lady's goods and hadn't paid.

"My goodness. I'm so sorry. Yes." She juggled her bags of corn around to dig some cash out of her pocket.

"Would you like a bag?"

"No thank you." She had enough bags.

Jude hoisted a crate and carried it around to place on top of one of the booth's tables. His white T-shirt stretched across his broad back, tan arms tense under the weight of the crate, sunlight catching in his sandy-blond hair.

The last decade had been unfairly kind to Jude Jones. He'd aged perfectly, developing from boyishly handsome to, if she was completely frank with herself, smoking-hot grown man.

What would he think of how the years had treated her?

Jude had been her everything in high school. All she thought she wanted in life.

But he hadn't wanted her.

At least half a dozen priorities had come before silly little Aurora. He hadn't chosen her or the future they'd dreamed about, the one they'd talked about until the wee late hours.

So, Aurora had chosen her other dream. She chose herself and let him go.

Shaking off thoughts of the past, she shuffled the corn around and tucked her new earrings into a side pocket of a bag, nearly dropping everything.

Naturally, that was the moment Jude turned around, his gaze locking with hers.

Chapter 4

Jude froze in place, a giant bundle of lavender in his hands.

Aurora Shipley. Right in front of him, just a few yards away. Pretty as you please, in the middle of the Marktplatz green, standing all alone.

Except for the sacks of corn.

Aurora couldn't wave with her hands full. Instead, she gave him a little smile.

A smile that, even after a decade, was still as familiar as his own.

He'd spent years missing that smile. But only after a year or so of resenting it for leaving him behind. He'd heard she was in town, albeit temporarily, to help at the Orchard Inn. The idea of her being so close had crossed his mind many, many times.

He'd thought of visiting her, but only once.

Common sense had corrected his wayward thoughts, reminding him his presence would be neither needed nor appreciated.

Better to let the past stay in the past.

"My word, is that Aurora?" His sister Jenna appeared beside him.

Jude played dumb and immediately busied himself

with sticking lavender in a large, empty pail. "I don't know. Maybe."

Jenna put an arm under her son's baby wrap and did the bouncing thing she did constantly. "You don't know? Mmm-hmm, sure. Because you barely know her?"

He ignored his sister, which was never easy.

"That has to be her. Look. She's got it up in a bun, but no one has hair like that except Aurora."

This truth jarred him more than it should.

With golden hair that could look strawberry blond in the right light, fair skin, and a sprinkling of freckles, he'd never seen anyone who looked quite like Aurora.

Then again, he was biased.

No one else was Aurora Shipley, and no one else ever would be.

"I don't know," he lied.

"Fine," Jenna bit off in that tone she used, and he winced.

Nothing good ever came from that tone.

She turned away from him, waving frantically. "Aurora? Aurora Shipley? Hey! I thought that was you."

What were the chances he could crawl behind their tent and hide? Now was not the time for some half-cocked reunion with Aurora. Not after how they'd left things. Time didn't heal *all* wounds.

Ten years be damned, there was no way this wasn't going to be as awkward as a dog in socks.

"I can't believe it's you!" Jenna's voice drifted as she went down the street to greet Aurora. "I'd hug you but between your corn and little Wyatt here, I don't think we'd make it."

Aurora's bright laughter tickled his ears.

"Wait a sec. Jude? Jude!" Jenna called to him.

He clenched his back teeth together and turned to face his past. "Yeah?"

Aurora looked like summer sunshine in yellow shorts and a white top, strands of her golden hair falling into her eyes. She followed Jenna toward the booth, juggling four or five bags of corn, one of which was in imminent danger of falling.

"Hey, Aurora." Jude held out his hands in an offer to take the corn before realizing it looked like he was offering a hug.

Aurora would not want to hug him.

"Let me help you with that corn," he quickly added.

Let me help you with that corn. That's what he'd chosen to say when seeing his high school sweetheart for the first time in a decade?

Smooth, Jude. Real smooth.

"That's okay, I've got it," she insisted.

Now it was awkward, because she clearly did not have it.

"How are you?" he tried. "I'd heard you were back home for a while."

"I'm good. Just picking up a few things for the inn. We've been wanting corn on the cob." She lifted the bags a little to indicate them.

Then, silence.

Somebody put him out of his misery.

"Is that Old Man McGregor's corn?" Jenna asked. "Though, he probably doesn't like being called Old Man McGregor, huh? But now he really is! Remember when we used to call him old man, when we'd sneak through his field on the way to swim? He wasn't but maybe fifty years old back then. At least now he's in his late sixties or seventies, but even that's not as old as it used to be."

Thank the good Lord for Jenna and her tendency to ramble.

"Yes, it's his corn." Aurora finally got to answer when Jenna paused to come up for air.

"Good. His is the best."

Jude just stood there, praying someone would need his help with something so he could bow out gracefully.

"So, things are good?" Jenna asked Aurora again.

This was going to take a while.

"Yeah, great. Busy. But more importantly, can we talk about this little one?" Aurora pointed to baby Wyatt, who was currently chewing on his fist.

Yes, baby Wyatt, coming through in the clutch.

They could talk about Wyatt and this whole exchange could be cute and pleasant, and painless.

"That's right, I haven't seen you since. This is my son, Wyatt."

"Aww, Jenna." Aurora's gaze softened and Jude looked away.

"Here, come to our tent. I'll let you hold him." Jenna urged them all forward.

Aurora went to their tent but protested holding Wyatt. "I haven't washed my hands and I've been handling money and corn."

"Are you kidding? He's a farm baby. He crawls around in dirt half the time, it's fine. Put those bags down. Jude, do something with her corn for a minute."

Aurora and Jude shared a silent understanding. There'd be no arguing with Jenna on this matter. Better for everyone if they simply complied.

Jude cleared his throat and took the bags of corn, refusing to acknowledge the familiarity of this whole exchange.

"Hey, Wyatt!" Aurora's sister Cece joined them. "I thought you were taking the corn to the car."

"I didn't get that far. You've met Wyatt already?" Aurora asked.

"A few times."

Truth was, Cece came by their booth almost every Saturday. She'd chat and pick out some herbs. Every time Jude had considered asking about Aurora, and every time, he'd held back.

Their time together was so long ago, but that hadn't made their breakup any less severe or painful. That time in his life had changed him, irrevocably. Aurora left him and left Texas, making it clear she wasn't interested in having anything to do with him. He'd never had anyone leave him like that.

Asking her family about her felt like prying. She'd had her reasons for cutting him out of her life. He could just imagine the conversation between Cece and Aurora if he'd nosed into her business.

"Guess who asked about you today at the market. Jude."

"Ugh. Why does he even care? It's been years. Move on already."

"I didn't know you'd been by here." Aurora's tone with her sister sharpened slightly, holding the faintest bit of edge.

"You didn't ask," Cece replied, while Wyatt was clutching her finger in his chubby wet fist.

"Don't worry. I have wet wipes and hand sani a'plenty," Jenna assured everyone.

The local musician providing this weekend's live entertainment chose that moment to start strumming her guitar on center stage.

While they were all distracted by the music, hand sanitizing, and Wyatt, Jude slipped behind their tables and through the back of their tent.

He took a deep breath to steady himself. This was fine. He and Aurora were water under the bridge, yeah? Ages ago. They were different people now. Once he was done setting up the farm's selection of herbs, he would make small talk.

No problem.

He busied himself with the basil and rosemary they'd brought to sell. He worked quickly, not wanting to come across as rude, but the Jones family's herbs weren't going to sell themselves. Besides, Aurora would be put much more at ease without him hanging around.

The last of the herbs were in the cab of his truck, including some Mexican tarragon he'd been working with and had finally grown into something worth selling.

"You really think you can hide back here?" Jenna popped her head out the back of the tent.

"I'm not hiding. I'm retrieving the tarragon."

"Really? Because it looks like you're avoiding your ex, like a big ol' chicken."

"I'm not a chicken." But that's exactly what he was doing. "I'm trying to get everything set up in the next five minutes, because we were running behind and got here late. We're missing critical sales right now. All the serious buyers are in the early crowd."

"I know that. Have you heard anything from Dad?"

In the past, their father was the first one here for setup.

"His back is at him today. He's a little slow going this morning, but he'll be by later."

Unlikely, even if Jude wished it were true. Their dad

had pulled a muscle in his back only two days ago and was struggling to get around, never mind lift anything.

Jenna rocked on the balls of her feet. "You don't have to cover for him with me. I know he's not coming."

"But when people ask where he is"—and they would—"tell them he's on his way or something."

"You need to talk to him. It's not the first time he's overdone it and hurt himself. He's ill as a hornet right now, but he's got nobody to blame but himself. Trying to move those boxes all alone. What was he thinking?"

"Who knows? But I'll talk to him. I just…I need to find the right way to broach the subject." Jude grabbed the last of his tarragon and returned to the tent.

Aurora was holding Wyatt in her arms as he stuck a little bundle of lavender up to her nose.

Wyatt, the future lavender salesman, and Aurora, the cover of *Town & Country* magazine. Fresh-faced, even more strands of hair falling out of a haphazard knot on the top of her head, cheeks warmed pink. Behind her, a canvas of flowers and herbs. Greens and purple, a little yellow, a smattering of orange.

She'd always been pretty, but the years had turned the cute girl into a stunning woman.

"How much?" She looked up at him, her gray-blue eyes like steel.

"What?" He didn't remember her eyes ever being that cold before.

"For a large bundle of lavender."

"Oh, um, eight dollars."

"That's it?" She looked at Jenna to confirm. "I'm used to paying almost fifteen for this."

"You're a long way from Los Angeles." Cece plucked

the sprig of lavender from Wyatt's hand. "Now, gimme that baby. It's my turn."

Aurora handed over Wyatt and gave Jude a ten.

As if he would take her money. "It's on the house. Let us know what you create with it."

"I insist." She held the money out farther.

She could keep stretching that arm all day, he was not going to charge Aurora for a little lavender. "*I* insist you take it as a friendly gesture."

"A friendly ges—" An expression, completely foreign to him, crossed Aurora's face. She clenched her jaw, her pink lips pinched together, her eyes shaded impossibly colder.

As if on cue, to stop whatever storm was gathering inside Aurora, a noise exploded from the neighboring booth. Something that could be described only as a holler, then a cacophony of crashes.

"Dang it, Roscoe!" someone yelled.

The Wattersons' seventy-pound German pointer barreled out of their tent, hauling off down the street, followed by a stream of at least a dozen tiny yellow chicks.

"Oh no!" Cece flapped her free hand toward Jude. "Baby chickens are loose."

Jude blinked twice, taking in the full situation before him.

"Stay here," he told Jenna, his brain kicking into gear. He grabbed the nearest empty basket and took off after the chicks.

"Y'all go that way, we'll go this way." Cece waved him on and followed Mrs. Watterson in the other direction.

He hurried down the walk that circled the center of the Marktplatz, scooping up a straggler as he went. He wasn't as fast as when he was eighteen, but he still had more speed than most.

"Grab those two!" Aurora ran a few feet behind him, a baby chick in each hand.

He nabbed the two on her radar and slowed down so she could gently place her escapees into his basket.

"Some went this way." She headed between two tents and he followed.

"I saw some headed toward Main Street too."

"We better go after them when we catch these. Mrs. Watterson will never be fast enough."

They scooped up several chicks that had run into the obstruction of a curb. The spacing between tents was intentionally tight, and they jostled one another as they tried to turn around. Aurora's arm rubbed against his chest, and his hip bumped her side.

He was diligently ignoring all of this, of course.

"Okay, this way," she directed.

He turned, a tight grip on the basket of baby chicks as they moved swiftly into the crowd.

"Hurry!" Aurora urged.

He was already going as fast as he could without bowling people over.

"Hurry," she repeated. "They might get stepped on."

She was no longer the quiet, meek girl he'd known in school. The Aurora of his youth never shouted directions or commanded him to do anything. This development suited her. He'd always wished she would've spoken up more back then, but he didn't want to admire changes in her. What good would it do to like things about Aurora now?

He'd had his chance. They'd had their moment as a

couple, and it hadn't worked. Their time had come and gone, and he'd be smart to remember that fact.

"I see them." He spotted a cluster of chicks by a tent where cookies were being sold and hurried ahead.

He needed to focus on finding the baby chickens, and not worry about the past. His hasty immaturity had put the nail in the coffin of their relationship, but there was nothing he could do to change what'd happened between them. He'd promised himself, long ago, to move on.

Aurora caught up with him and gently picked up a chick as he set the basket down. He scooped up another two and placed them inside.

"I don't know if that's all of them," she said.

"Yeah, I think I saw more than this scurrying out of the Wattersons' tent. Let's get on Main Street and look around."

They reached Main Street, his basket of wares cheeping and chirping delightfully.

"They're adorable." Aurora peered down to check on them.

"Cute little fugitives," he agreed. "Did you happen to see which way Roscoe went?"

"No."

They began methodically making their way past the outer market booths, peeking under tables, but finding nothing.

Jude was about to give up hope when someone behind them screeched.

As he turned, a lady lurched in their direction, all but diving past Aurora and shoving her toward the ground.

He couldn't drop the chicks, but he couldn't let Aurora fall either.

Jude kept the basket in his left hand and reached for

Aurora with his right arm, wrapping it around her and pulling her close.

She stumbled, but his body blocked her fall. Aurora bumped against him and ricocheted off just as quickly.

"Oh!" She tottered on her feet, trying to hold her balance. "Sorry."

"It's oka—" He barely had the words out as Roscoe barged past, skidding into Aurora's calves.

"Oh!" she said again, her hands flying out to brace against Jude.

He caught her. Not in an embrace, because he knew better, but in a hold.

"What in the world?" She pulled away again, her hair now in a side bun, as about half of it fell loose.

"Roscoe is on the run. Must've seen more chicks."

"More chicks," they repeated in unison.

They turned together and ran after the dog.

Sure enough, up ahead, three little chicks wandered innocently into a green space at the end of the market.

"Here." Jude shoved the basket at Aurora. "I'll catch Roscoe, you get the chicks."

He was the faster between the two of them, and had experience hemming up rambunctious dogs.

"Roscoe!" he yelled, the dog barely looking back as he cleared a hedgerow, closing in on the chicks.

There was nothing for it but to dive for the leash, so that's what Jude did.

Like diving into home, he propelled himself forward, over the perfectly manicured bushes, arms stretched forward. He landed hard and skidded a little, the smell of earth and grass filling his nose, but, more importantly, the feel of nylon in his hand.

"Gotcha!" Jude exclaimed, his lungs protesting the words when the wind had just been knocked out of him.

For his part, Roscoe rounded on him and planted both front feet on his back, licking him eagerly.

Somewhere, off to his right, he heard giggling. Giggling that grew and grew until it was uncontrolled.

He knew that laughter. A laugh that had made his heart sing as he could only laugh in return.

God, he'd missed the sound of it.

Managing to dislodge Roscoe, Jude rolled over and sat up, only to receive more kisses.

"Enough." He tried to hold the dog back.

"At least he's lost all interest in the chicks. Now he only has eyes for you."

Jude glanced up. Aurora stood above him, surrounded and backlit by sunlight, her hair a lost cause and a basket of baby chickens in her arms.

She looked like someone's overworked guardian angel, or the rumpled patron saint of chicks.

"Lucky me." Jude pushed himself up and Aurora offered her hand to help.

The gesture surprised him, but he was glad of it.

"You're filthy," she said.

"Huh?"

"Your shirt and jeans." She pointed.

His once white T-shirt was now streaked with green and brown. "It's okay. I always keep a change of clothes in the truck. Getting dirty is part of the job."

"Yeah, I remember." Aurora smiled as she nodded, and their gazes locked.

Something in his chest twisted at the sight of her smile. He wanted to cling to this moment a little longer. Just the two of them—a crazy dog and a dozen chickens. They were standing there together, after all this time.

He'd often wondered if he'd ever see her again. Aurora was so different, but still so much the same. And one thought grabbed him.

He'd messed up.

He'd known Aurora was unhappy in their relationship near the end. They'd started bickering a lot, but she wouldn't talk about what was bothering her and he couldn't handle the angst on top of everything else he had to deal with. When he ended their relationship, she'd quietly accepted his decision—and then disappeared.

He'd never understood, and it made him wonder if he'd ever really known her at all.

Regardless, he'd gone about things all wrong back then. He'd handled their breakup awfully, but by the time he realized it, she was leaving town. Heck, leaving the state. She left their hometown for good, and that was it. They never spoke or had the chance to hash it out. She was just gone, and he wasn't about to intrude upon her new life.

Aurora deserved happiness, and it was best if he let her be.

"I should— Here." She handed him the basket and turned to go. "I need to get back."

Jude shook off the trail of his thoughts. "Yeah, I should get back too."

To his job, and many responsibilities. Back to the present, and back to reality.

Chapter 5

Did y'all get all of them?" Cece asked, passing Aurora her water bottle.

She took a long drink. "I think. I hope so. Jude is taking the basket and Roscoe to Mrs. Watterson."

"You're all flushed."

"It's hot."

Cece lifted one eyebrow.

"What?" It was already about a million degrees outside, and a stream of sweat trickled down her back.

Jude returned to the tent, glistening like a golden god in his dirty, clingy T-shirt and ruffled hair, damp at his temples.

"Sure is." Cece smirked.

"Zip it."

"That was crazy." Jenna bounced Wyatt as she finished twisting a wrap around her. "The market isn't usually this exciting. Must be you."

Jude dipped behind the tent and out of sight.

"I doubt it." Aurora ran her fingers through her hair before pulling it back and up into a bun again.

"It really has been good to see you. It's been forever. I know…" She waved both Aurora and Cece toward the front of the tent and lowered her voice. "I know I should've reached out to you weeks ago, when I heard you were in town, but I didn't know if things would be weird."

"Why would they be weird?" Aurora asked, as if she didn't know.

"Because of you and Jude." Jenna was as straightforward as ever.

"That was years ago. It's fine."

No, it wasn't, and they both knew that. She'd loved Jude's family like her own, but when they broke up, she felt like she had to break up with his family too. Teenage Aurora had no clue how to navigate the web of an ex-boyfriend's family, especially not once she decided to move away for culinary school. So, she'd talked to no one in his family about leaving for Colorado and hadn't reached out to any of them until years later.

Cowardly? Maybe. But she'd been reeling from the breakup, and the sudden decision to go to school in Colorado, instead of in-state. She'd done the only thing she knew how to in the moment. She ran away.

"I know. It was all a long time ago, but I've heard from you maybe twice in ten years—and that was online. It's different than in person. I was afraid it might be awkward if I reached out or dropped by. But now you're here." Jenna's smile was warm and genuine.

And Aurora felt like crap for not extending an olive branch weeks ago. "No, I should've called you. That's on me."

Jenna's smile widened. "Then how about we make up for the lost time?"

"Okay?" Nerves fluttered in her stomach.

"Come by the farm tomorrow. See what we've been working on and check out the full collection the farm has to offer."

"This isn't the full collection?"

"Are you kidding? Not nowadays. This isn't half of it. There's so much more since you were last out there. You'll see what I mean. We've even started supplying a few restaurants in town."

"Wow, really?" Aurora tried to temper her reaction, but she was impressed. Her family had done the same, taking their home and, first, turning it into a bed and breakfast, then expanding into weddings and events. They'd turned the scandal of their dad leaving into something beautiful.

"Yep. You never know, you might even find some inspiration when you visit."

"Can I come too?" Cece chimed in. "I haven't been by in a while."

"Of course. Tomorrow afternoon okay?"

"It's perfect." Cece answered for them. "We should probably get home now though. Beth will send out search and rescue if I miss our afternoon appointment."

Aurora should take the easy out and leave right now, without saying goodbye to Jude. Maybe it was guilt over not saying goodbye to Jenna ten years ago, or maybe it was because she wanted to see Jude one more time today. Whatever the reason—or complete lack of—Aurora went behind the Joneses' tent on her way out.

"Jude?" she called, wishing to simply be polite and prove they could be normal, neighborly people to each other.

"Yeah?" He popped up from behind several boxes. Shirtless.

"Oh." Aurora immediately stared at the sky, the side of the tent, anywhere except him.

"Sorry." He shrugged a clean T-shirt on quickly, but not quick enough that she couldn't get a look at him.

Jude hadn't looked quite like that in high school.

Sure, he was an athlete then. Baseball kept him fit and muscular. But farm work? Farm work did him justice. Manual labor was a good look on Jude.

"I just wanted to say bye." Aurora stared at the tent again. She shouldn't have come back here, and she probably shouldn't go by the farm tomorrow. What good could come of them spending any more time together? They'd both moved on with their lives, right? And the past should stay there.

"Y'all are leaving?"

"Yeah. We have a potential client coming by at one, and I smell like chickens."

"Okay, well, um. I guess I'll…see you around?"

"Sure. I'll see you."

"Aurora?" He paused after saying her name.

"Yeah?"

"I have my shirt on now. You can look at me."

"Oh." Her laugh came out all nervous and twittery. She hated herself for sounding like that. "I wasn't not looking—" Yes, she was. "Anyway. I will see you around." She waved and spun around, returning to Cece as fast as her legs could carry her.

"Okay, we can go," she said to Cece as she whizzed by.

"The corn," Cece reminded her.

"Crap." Aurora backtracked and grabbed the sacks of corn. "Bye, Jenna. Bye, Wyatt."

"Bye," she heard Jenna's voice trail off as she passed Cece on the way to her car.

"Good gosh, would you slow down?" Cece called behind her. "I'm not back to full speed yet."

Once she was a block away from the market, and safe,

Aurora stopped around the corner and waited. "Sorry. I know we need to get back, so I'm hurrying."

"You're all flushed again." Cece grinned.

Aurora made a face at her sister. "Just get in the car."

On their way home, Cece leaned her seat back a bit, reliving the morning. "How funny was that with the chickens?"

"Yeah. Funny." Aurora shifted in the driver's seat, trying to relax her grip on the wheel. "I wish you'd mentioned seeing Jenna and everyone at the market before."

"By everyone, do you mean Jude? You wish I'd warned you that Jude is usually at that farmers' market."

"Not *warned* me, exactly. It would've been nice to have a heads-up though, and to know that you've been in touch with them."

"I know. I should've said something, but I thought you knew he'd be there." Cece sat up, turning toward her. "They do own a farm, and it is a *farmers'* market."

"I know, but…" But what? She'd known chances were good she'd see Jude there this morning.

"And I should've mentioned I talk to them from time to time." Cece's voice softened. "But it's a small enough town, it'd be weird not to talk to people. Plus…" Her sister let the sentence drift.

"Plus, what?"

"It's a touchy subject to bring up. I didn't want to make it weird."

Too late.

"It's not a touchy subject," Aurora lied, denying the weight and impact of Jude Jones and his family upon her life.

Cece scoffed. "Who are you trying to kid here, me

or you? I'm not some casual California friend of yours. I'm your sister. The subject is touchy. Always has been, always will be."

Aurora took a deep breath and had to relax her grip, again.

Cece was right, and annoyingly so in that way only little sisters could be. "Okay, whatever, it's touchy. You still should've told me."

"Fair enough." Her sister leaned back in her seat. "I should've told you. I can tell you now though. Anything else you want to know?"

"No," Aurora answered too quickly. She wanted to know everything about Jude and Jenna, and their parents and Bonnie and—

"It's going to be okay." Cece's voice went soft again. "Going to the farm tomorrow? Might not be the easiest thing you've ever done, but it'll be fine. Everyone seemed fine today."

Fine. Right.

She and Jude had said maybe a dozen words to each other, while alternating between awkward proximity and careful politeness—a far cry from how they'd been years ago.

Back in the day, she and Jude had been so comfortable in each other's presence. She'd sneak off at night and drive around with him, talking into the wee hours. Sometimes they'd fall asleep while talking on the phone. She'd loved Jude with everything she had, and he made her feel the same. Even though he was the guy almost every girl wanted, he made Aurora feel like the only person in the world.

If not for biology lab, in the spring of their junior year,

they might not have ever gotten close. They knew each other, distantly, before, but ran in completely different circles.

Dissecting earthworms together made you fast friends.

Friendship flowed into flirting, and Jude had the kind of confidence that allowed him to ask her out within just a couple of weeks.

Even when jealousy brought out the cruel side of a few girls, Aurora weathered their snide comments with Jude's affection. And, when the school's queen bee, Erica Burr, started a nasty rumor about her, Aurora held her head high, knowing it wasn't true.

What Erica and those other girls thought didn't matter. All that mattered was her and Jude. What they had could survive anything.

Except it didn't.

"Are you going to stay in the car and roast, or what?"

Aurora looked around. She'd gotten them back to the inn and put the car in park, all while her thoughts were years and years away.

Cece was standing by her car with bags of corn, staring into the open passenger door. "We're home. Snap out of it."

Well, they were at the Orchard Inn. Could she still call this home?

She was a visitor here now. Her home was her apartment in L.A. All of her stuff was still there, her job that she'd worked so hard for, and, most notably at the moment, her car.

"I'm coming." She grabbed the last bag of corn and the small bag of herbs from the back seat. "I cannot believe I'm going to their farm tomorrow."

Aurora waited for her sister's quick retort, but Cece was already halfway to the house.

What if Jude's parents came around and wanted to talk to her? They had to hate her. She loved his folks, but she hadn't seen or spoken to them since the breakup. She didn't want to deal with any ill will from them. She'd always felt comfortable around Jude's family. Accepted.

With a grumble, Aurora plodded around the back of the inn, the door to their private residence hanging open in Cece's wake.

"Leave the corn on the table for now. I'll help you shuck it outside later if you want," Cece yelled down the hall.

Aurora set everything on their table and flopped onto the sofa. She could use a moment to relax before washing up for their appointment.

A few minutes later, her phone pinged from inside her purse, startling her from her impromptu nap. Hauling herself up, Aurora dug around her bag and grabbed it from the bottom as it pinged again.

The texts were from Sloane. Roommate, work bestie, knower of all gossip, and keeper of all confessions. Sloane was junior chef at Brio, the restaurant where they worked, and she'd been keeping Aurora updated on all she'd missed while away.

Aurora rubbed her eyes, forcing them into focus on Sloane's text.

> What's new in Texas? It is all going down out here rn. Jonah and Lark broke up and OMG the work drama. You're missing it! When are you coming back?! I'm boooooooooored without you.

I miss you too, Aurora messaged back.

Sloane responded. One of the restaurant group execs came in last week and asked about you. 😳

A partner of the restaurant group was asking about her. She replied to Sloane, Asking in a good or bad way?

I think a good way. He wanted to know when you were going to be back.

It was time to go back to California. Maybe past time.

Chapter 6

"Is the Holcombe order ready yet?" Jude's mom, Linda, pushed back her ever-present straw hat as she walked into the main store of the farm.

"Yep. Got it right here." Jude handed a box of half a dozen lavender bouquets to her.

He checked on Jenna in the back of the shop. She was quietly snipping and separating lavender into small bundles for retail sales, while his dad "supervised." His sister Bonnie and her friend Meredith rushed into the back room of the shop, disrupting the peace. "Logan is here for his order. If it's ready, we can take it to his truck."

"Ready." Jude tapped four boxes sitting on the outgoing table. "Invoice is inside."

"He wanted a double order this time," his dad chimed in. "Did you remember to fill a double order?"

"Yeah, Dad. I remembered." It was his job to remember.

As they took out the order, John Jones made his way around the worktable, eyeing the progress of the other orders like he was the foreman at a construction site. "I'm just making sure. No need to get defensive."

"I'm not getting defensive."

His dad peered at him over the top of his glasses. "That sounds an awful lot like your defensive tone."

Okay, maybe he was being mildly defensive, but he'd run the sales side of things on the farm for a year now and had been diving heavily into operations. Yet his dad still didn't trust him to handle any of it responsibly. Or without his supervision.

"Uh-oh, is there a family meeting I didn't know about?" Bonnie returned and joined them at the worktable.

His youngest sister knew how strained things had become between Jude and their dad, and she waffled between full support of Jude taking charge, and full insistence that he wasn't doing enough for the farm's future.

"No meeting." Jude went to work on the giant bin of picked lavender and the wrapping paper used to protect the bundles.

"Your brother is in a mood because I asked about an order."

Jude clenched his jaw to keep from taking the bait.

"Hmm." Bonnie grinned, leaning eagerly over the table to pick up some lavender. "Are we sure this mood is all about work?"

He flashed a look at his sister, knowing exactly where she was going with this.

"Because Jenna said you've been in a bit of a mood since the market yesterday."

Jude huffed through his nose. "Jenna's got a big mouth."

Bonnie smirked. "She said Aurora came by our tent."

"Aurora as in your ex-girlfriend Aurora?" his dad asked.

Jude grabbed several sheets of thin protective paper and wrapped a bundle of lavender with entirely too much gusto. "Let's all just get back to work."

"Quit picking on Jude." Meredith joined them at the table, probably to pick on him more. "He's outnumbered and he's going to hurt the lavender."

"I have so many questions though." Bonnie wrapped her bundle of lavender carefully. "Like what did she say? What did you say?"

"Go run the front of the store. How about that for an answer?" Jude put on a big smile.

"I'd like to know more too," John added, his tone far less playful than Bonnie's.

"Come on." Meredith took Bonnie's bundle and placed it in a shipping box before pulling her toward the door. "You can interrogate Jude later."

"Aurora Shipley was at the market?" his dad asked, as soon as the girls left the room. "At our booth?"

"In the flesh."

His dad's brow furrowed. "It's been a while since she was in town."

If that wasn't the understatement of the decade.

"She moved to California, Dad. By way of Colorado. I haven't seen her since graduation." Though she'd surely visited at holidays, they'd managed to avoid each other until now.

"Why was she at the market?" his dad asked.

"I don't know. I guess to buy produce and crafts, like everyone else."

"Mmm." John took off his glasses and polished them.

"She's coming by the farm today too," Jude added, knowing it'd bother his dad, but it'd bother him more if Jude didn't give him advance notice.

Aurora had been close to his entire family, except for Jude's dad, but her absence affected them all in some way. His dad had always insisted she was a distraction for Jude—their relationship something that took his attention off baseball, his grades, and his responsibilities at the farm. But when they broke up, and Aurora left, the change in Jude wasn't what his father had anticipated.

John paused with his glasses halfway up his nose. "Tell me you're kidding."

"Nope. You can ask your daughter."

"Jenna?"

Jude nodded. "She invited her when Aurora and Cece visited our booth."

"Well, that'll be . . . interesting."

Jude's mom chose that moment to join them, still fiddling with her too big straw hat. "What's interesting?"

"Aurora Shipley is coming to the farm today," his dad blurted.

His mom's eyes went wide. "I'd heard she'd moved back here, but—"

"Not moved back. She's here temporarily to help at the inn," Jude corrected her.

"That's right. They had to fire that caterer or whatnot, who gave those people food poisoning."

News traveled fast around town, and everyone had quickly learned of Aurora's return to help her sisters get their inn back on the rails. Details like Aurora's moving back permanently versus her being here only temporarily didn't matter when it came to local gossip.

His mom shook her head. "That was some bad luck indeed. It will be so good to see her though. Where was she working in California? Do you know?"

As it so happened, he did know. When he'd heard she was back a couple of months ago, he'd googled her. She had a public Instagram page, so he'd had a scroll. He'd told no one about his little investigative jaunt on social media though. All he'd heard for months after Aurora left was that it was time to move on. He should get over her, get over the two of them and what they'd had, and live his life. Mostly this came from his dad, but no one else ever jumped in to argue otherwise.

For a while it'd felt like an impossibility, but finally, he'd managed to move forward.

If he ever mentioned to his family that he'd looked her up, he risked their deepest concern—again. They meant well, but Jude didn't want to go back to the place, ten years ago, with their worried glances and apprehensive questions.

"I don't know," he answered instead. "Some restaurant."

"Is she in town for much longer?"

"I have no idea," he answered honestly.

"Quit quizzing the boy, Linda." His father rescued him, surprisingly.

But Jude knew why she was asking. His mom had adored Aurora while they were dating. And why wouldn't she? Aurora had always been kind and respectful, funny and endearing.

From what she'd shared with him, and what he'd seen, Aurora had had a rocky relationship with her own mother. Not unusual since she was a teenager, but Jude got the feeling it was more than that. Aurora often commented how easygoing and accepting Jude's mom was with her.

Jenna popped her head in from the front of the shop. "Someone is here to see you."

His stomach twisted into a knot. Aurora was here.

He tried to pace his steps to the front of the store, not to seem overeager or dreadful. Just calm and relaxed.

Any old day, business as usual. His parents followed right behind him.

Jude pushed open the swinging door and found two ladies at the counter. He recognized them from the farmers' market the day before.

Decidedly not Aurora.

"Well, hey! Good, the gang's all here. I'm Maureen and this is Doris, we're on the Planning Committee for this year's jamboree and rodeo, and we noticed that no one from Edge of the World Farm signed y'all up for the big pie contest."

"Or for anything for the jamboree," Doris added.

Maureen nodded as she spoke. "Y'all are planning to participate in the celebration, aren't you?"

Bonnie and Meredith slowly made their way over to join everyone at the counter.

Jude's mom looked to him to answer, but his dad spoke up. "You bet we are. We wouldn't miss the big celebration."

"Wonderful. What kind of pie can we sign you up for?"

His dad looked at Jude.

So *now* he had to answer for the family?

"Or is it a secret?"

"Secret," Jude answered quickly. "Naturally. We want it to be a surprise. Put us down for surprise pie."

His family hadn't discussed the first thing about the Stonewall Peach JAMboree. With everything going on at the farm, along with his dad's health, they hadn't gotten around to even acknowledging the annual event was coming up. The whole tri-county area participated in the jamboree each year. It was a big deal, had gone on for decades, but this year, it'd snuck right up on them.

"I can't wait to see what y'all do," one of the ladies exclaimed.

"Are you the baker in the family?" Doris asked Bonnie.

Jude burst out laughing, then tried to cover it by clearing his throat.

Meredith slapped him on the back. "Bonnie doesn't bake," Meredith explained. "Or cook things. At all. So no, she won't be entering the contest."

"I am available for judging though." Bonnie smiled.

The ladies laughed. "Wonderful. We'll just put the farm's name next to your pie contest entry. And give some thought to anything else you might like to do for the celebration."

They made some more small talk and eventually the ladies left with a few bundles of lavender.

"You don't bake either," Bonnie pointed out as soon as they left.

"Which is why I didn't sign us up for a baking contest," he murmured to her while checking his phone. So much for getting out of it though.

"We've participated in the jamboree every year, son," his dad grumbled.

"We've got a lot going on this year, Dad. It's okay to sit it out one year."

"Pssht." His father dismissed him with the wave of one callused hand. "We ain't missing a year. And if they want to do a cake contest this year, we're doing a cake."

"Who is going to bake the cake?" Meredith asked.

"Pie. Not a cake," Jude corrected. "And heck if I know. Mom?"

His mom shook her head. "I don't enter contests to have my food judged."

"We can figure out the pie later." Jude checked his phone again. "We also need to decide what else we're going to do to participate in the jamboree. Can you two find out what that includes, what are our options, etcetera?"

"Sure. Are you late for something?" Meredith asked. "You keep checking your phone."

Bonnie grinned. "That's because Jenna invited Jude's high school girlfriend to come by the farm today."

"Oooo, nice." Meredith tapped her fingers together like some cartoon villain. "I'm so glad I'm here for this."

"I don't need an audience, thanks. Don't you two have something you could do in the fields?"

Behind them, his mother gasped.

Jude spun around, expecting to see a snake, a giant spider. Something. Anything other than his dad about to fall under the weight of several wholesale boxes.

"Dad!" Jude grabbed the boxes as Bonnie grabbed his dad.

"They're overweighted," his father claimed.

Jude put the boxes back on the counter. They were not overweighted. They packed each box to a specific weight, and Jude was a stickler for compliance. But arguing with his dad over the weight of boxes was a fool's game. He'd never win, and in the end, everyone in their general area would be brought into it, and all would end up feeling a little bit worse than they had prior.

"Let us move the boxes," Bonnie tried. "You and Mom can go back to the house and relax."

"I'm not going back to the house." He shrugged her off and pulled away.

Bonnie shared a look with Jude. They both knew their

father was aging out of the manual labor required on the farm, but you couldn't tell him that.

His cardiologist had told him, told the whole family, no red meat, more vegetables. No heavy lifting, more walks around the farm. Less fats and cheese, and—worst of all—start taking a statin.

Well, John Jones was not going to stop eating steak or cheese, he was fine with a daily walk, but he was absolutely never going to take heart medication.

I've never taken so much as an aspirin my whole life was the man's mantra.

Jude and his sisters knew their father needed to retire, just like they knew he never would.

"I'm fine." He stomped toward the door to the back room. "Besides, don't we all want to be here to see Aurora?"

The way he cooed her name grated across Jude's skin. For as much as his mother loved Aurora, his father resented her. The way he saw it, their relationship had threatened Jude's performance. When they'd started to have a little dating drama during playoffs, Aurora had become the worst in the world.

"That girl is messing with your head," his father had fussed. "Get your mind back in the game and forget about her. Girls are a dime a dozen, but championships come once in a lifetime."

In the present, Jude rolled his eyes. To think he'd ever bought into such garbage. Aurora wasn't one of a dozen. She was one of a kind. And sure, he could've focused more on his education and baseball career than he had on her, but he should've been able to do both.

"C'mon Linda," his father summoned his mom to

follow him into the back, probably to complain about their children and their disrespect for daring to have any concern over his health. "You need to watch how you're packing them boxes."

His mother gave them a sympathetic look as she passed.

"We have to do something about him," Bonnie insisted as soon as they were gone.

Jude dug a hand through his hair and tried to relax his jaw. "What would you suggest we do, Bon?"

"Those boxes aren't overpacked. He just can't lift stuff anymore."

"I know that."

"He needs to retire. He can't keep up anymore."

"I've already tried talking to him about stepping down and letting me take over. He won't hear of it. Mom has tried to get him to take his medicine. Should we just tie him down and force him to stop working, shove pills down his throat?"

"No!" Bonnie paced, as aggravated as him. "I'm not saying that, but…you're going to have to talk to him again. He'll listen to you."

"Since when?"

"I don't know, but he's got to. It's time for you to run the farm. He can't do it anymore."

"You don't think I know that?" Jude shouted. He knew it better than anyone. He wanted it more than anyone.

His whole life, Jude had longed for and prepared for taking the reins of Edge of the World Farm. That was the dream. Take over the family business, expand and improve, bring the farm into the next era, make sure they could all provide for themselves, secure the family's future and make them proud.

"Hey." Bonnie scowled, her brow creased and eyes wide with hurt. "I'm on your side."

Jude's shoulders dropped and he reached for his sister. "I know. C'mere. I'm sorry."

They shared a side hug.

"I just…dealing with Dad fires me up. I get so aggravated, but I have to be calm. He can't get too mad or, I don't know, he might have a heart attack. He won't listen to reason. It's exhausting."

"I know."

"I don't know how to get through to him."

Bonnie's mouth tugged down in the corner. "We've got to figure out a way, or he's going to get himself killed."

Her words echoed the thought he'd had every day for the last few months. It was time for John Jones to retire. Jude was ready. He wanted to run the farm, he wanted to lead. And he'd be the kind of leader who actually listened to others. His sisters were smart and skillful, and better than him at certain things.

Together, they'd grow the farm into the kind of business they'd only dreamed of.

But not if their father wouldn't let them.

Jude took a deep breath and let out the longest sigh of his life. "I'll talk to him again. I'll take care of it."

"You will?" Bonnie looked up, her blue eyes wide with hope.

"I need to figure out how to get through to him, but yes, I will."

"Um, I think the old girlfriend might be here." Meredith's words jolted him to attention.

A sporty little SUV was parked in front of the shop.

Aurora climbed out of the passenger seat, her hair wavy and falling to her shoulders.

"Is that her?" Meredith glanced back at them and Bonnie nodded.

"Wow, she's really pretty. Hmph. This ought to be interesting."

Jude's chest tightened, and his feet refused to move as he watched her through the front windows of the store. The sight of her made him want to run to her and away from her, at the same time.

They'd broken each other's hearts, and now they were going to—what? Explore the farm together? Just make small talk, casually coexist and pretend like they'd dealt with each other and made peace with the past instead of diligently ignoring it for ten years?

Sure.

Interesting.

That was one way to describe it.

Chapter 7

A sea of purple and green greeted Aurora as she got out of the car at Edge of the World Farm. The soothing scent of lavender covered her like a favorite cozy blanket, the sights and sounds of the farm taking her back through time, back to an early summer evening after her junior year of high school.

A crown of lavender had circled her head. She and Jude smelled of sunscreen and a late afternoon spent wandering the lavender fields. She'd been officially dating Jude for almost two months, and he'd insisted on bringing her to his family's farm.

He'd shown her to the biggest field of lavender she'd ever seen. Rolling waves of flowers, the breeze making them rise and fall.

"I want to kiss you," he'd said.

"I want you to."

His lips were firm but inviting. Warm and wanting. She wanted so much. Like nothing she'd ever known. No one else existed. Only the two of them and their ocean of flowers. Her heart so light, she could've floated away with him.

"Aurora!" Bonnie exclaimed, pulling her into the

present by almost knocking her down with an embrace. "Cece! I can't believe it. Oh my god you both look amazing. I was basically a kid last time I saw y'all. How are you so gorgeous?" She said everything fast enough for it to be one run-on sentence.

Aurora's gaze met Jude's as she hugged his baby sister, and Aurora quickly looked away.

Jude's mom, Linda, and a young woman she didn't recognize walked out the front of the farm's store.

"Aurora." Linda opened her arms. "How long has it been?"

"Too long." Aurora's throat tightened.

"I'm Meredith." The new-to-Aurora lady waved.

Perhaps she was Jude's girlfriend. And, if so, good for them. Aurora should have no opinions on the matter.

"Meredith is a good friend of mine. She works here sometimes," Bonnie clarified, as if reading her thoughts.

"Nice to meet you."

"It's really nice to see you again." Linda gave Aurora a smile, melting away some of the anxiety.

Jude's mom had been a second mom to her during her senior year of high school. Between the stress of life after her father left, and the inability to find some kind of common ground with her mom, Aurora had grown to feel like the odd sister out.

She'd often butted heads with her mom about culinary school and her future, and their relationship had become argumentative and tense. Aurora felt like more of a chore than a child, but with Linda, she could simply exist.

"It's good to see you, too, Cece." Linda gave her sister a squeeze. "I know I've seen you at the booth from time to time, but it's been a while since you came out here."

"Yeah." Cece smiled, nervously tucking her hair behind her ear.

"I need to have you girls over for dinner sometime. Or something. It's been so long, and I don't want to seem inhospitable or like we can't, you know—"

"Mom." Bonnie patted her mom on the shoulder to stop her jittery jabbering.

This situation was new ground for all of them, and everyone was a bit uncomfortable—except for maybe Bonnie.

"We can talk about maybe doing dinner later," Bonnie offered.

Linda loved to cook for her kids. She was an old-school comfort-food cook, a feeder of souls. Her big Sunday dinners were legendary, and Aurora had had a standing invitation when she dated Jude.

Being from Mississippi, Linda's generous use of seasonings and spices had secretly inspired some of Aurora's most popular dishes. The Jones family loved a good shrimp boil and fish fry, too, and Aurora would eat a Cajun shrimp boil until her nose ran and she was too full to move. She'd created something similar at the restaurant and it'd been a huge hit. The entire dish was basically an ode to Linda Jones.

She didn't want Jude's family to be uneasy around her, any more than she wanted to be uneasy with them. The time had come to make whatever amends she could.

"I think that's a great idea, Bon." Aurora used the family nickname intentionally. "It's really good to see you all. I'm sorry it's been so long."

When Aurora and Jude ended things, she'd lost her connection with his family. His family was an extension of her own, and she'd missed them more than she'd thought possible.

Her first few months of school in Colorado were some of the most difficult of her life. She'd been homesick and heartsick, missing her sisters and Jude's family and everything she knew. But leaving her hometown was a must after their breakup, and eventually, she'd found her way.

Burying herself in culinary school had helped.

"Ahh!" A squeal of delight came out the front door of the store. "Aurora." Jenna ran down the store's porch steps, holding Wyatt tight in his baby wrap. "You showed up!"

"You didn't think I would?"

Jenna shrugged off the question as they made their way toward the store, coming face-to-face with Jude.

"Hey," he said.

"Hey."

A beat of dead silence passed.

Jude shifted on his feet. "I'm glad you could make it out here today."

"Me too." Aurora nodded. "It's been a long time."

More silence, and Aurora wanted to jump out of her skin. Being this close to him, having no choice but to look him in the eyes, was too much. She wanted to avoid his gaze, but that'd be weak. She could do this. She could stand here, everything too quiet except for the sound of their breathing.

"You still wear that honeysuckle perfume, huh?" he asked, shocking Aurora to her core by noticing, let alone commenting.

You're still devastatingly handsome, huh? She'd never say it, but she needed to say something. She opened her mouth and "It works the best with my body chemistry" came out.

Aurora cringed inwardly. Body chemistry? She didn't need to talk about chemistry with this man.

"Y'all back up and let the girl breathe." John Jones's gravelly voice saved her from embarrassment. It was a first.

"Hello, Mr. Jones." Aurora's smile felt tight on her face as she stared at the man still standing on the porch.

While Jude's mom had always been Linda, Jude's dad remained Mr. Jones.

"Aurora. How are you?" Mr. Jones dipped his head.

Mr. Jones was not her biggest fan. While Jude had always insisted otherwise, Aurora knew the man saw her as an unnecessary distraction at first, and a downright dream-wrecker in the end.

"Okay, okay. Enough gum flapping, everybody." Jenna graciously broke the moment of tension. "I invited Aurora and Cece here because I want to show them around."

"You give the tour," Mr. Jones announced. "Everyone else can get back to work."

Jenna gave Aurora an exasperated look. "Come on in." Jenna corralled Aurora and Cece through the front of the store and toward the back. "We'll start back here before they get into loading boxes again. Big shipping day today."

She guided them through the door to the workroom, past long tables of fresh-cut lavender, dried lavender, and other aromatic herbs that Aurora didn't have time to inspect.

"Wow, look at all this stuff. You guys are really busy," Cece commented.

"More and more so every year."

"Is it just the lavender industry in general or something different that your farm is doing?" Aurora asked.

Jenna stopped once they reached the depths of the back room, surrounded by boxes and fragrant lavender. She patted Wyatt while bouncing slightly. "I'd say both. The whole herbal remedy industry has taken off in the last decade, along with people making their own soaps and candles and stuff, but we've also done some new things business-wise to help catalyze client growth."

"Catalyze client growth. Listen to you." Aurora smiled.

"Well, after Jude finished ag business school, I thought I'd do the same. It's helped to have our background and then the business education. College wasn't for Bonnie, but she's so creative and free-thinking. She has all kinds of ideas, while Jude and I have the skills to make it happen."

"We're kind of the same." Cece nodded. "I'm more creative while Beth is all business and detail-oriented."

"And a task master," Aurora added.

"But the combination works," her sister finished.

Jenna picked up some dried lavender. "Exactly. I guess Jude is our task master. He's so organized and diligent. Like this stuff." She waved the dried lavender around. "It's our edible lavender. Bonnie said we needed to broaden our sales to retail and small businesses, because now lavender teas and lattes are a huge thing. More people want edible lavender, so Jude ran the numbers and we started offering four-ounce packets on our website. They sell like hot cakes!"

"Wow." Aurora was intrigued. She hadn't used lavender in her cooking lately, but maybe she should branch out.

"Have you ever had a lavender honey latte?" Jenna asked.

"No, but it sounds divine."

"It's so good, and I don't even like lattes. The smell is incredible and it's this soothing warm beverage that also caffeinates you."

"And now I want one." Cece laughed.

"Right? I've actually thought about adding a little coffee bar to the shop, specializing in lavender teas and coffees, but..." Jenna shrugged. "We just don't have the manpower."

"You could hire some people," Aurora suggested.

Jenna's laugh was dry as day-old toast. "That costs money, adds liability to the books, and it'd mean non-family members all up in our business. John Jones is not about to hire a bunch of strangers or listen to our next, great idea. We're lucky we got to hire Meredith, and that's only because she and Bon are so close."

Aurora couldn't believe she was about to bring him into the conversation, but it couldn't be helped. "Maybe when Jude takes over, you can explore these ideas?" That'd always been his plan, even when he was seventeen. Someday, *he* would lead the family farm. "He's forward-thinking. Would he be up for the idea?"

"Oh yeah. Jude is right there with me and Bonnie when it comes to ideas and plans. He'd love to expand. Unfortunately, it's not up to just us. Dad has the final say in everything and I don't see him letting Jude take over any time soon."

"Really?" Aurora pinched her lips closed. She didn't mean to sound so surprised, but Mr. Jones had to be well into his seventies. It seemed like a reasonable time to start letting go a bit and enjoying the fruits of his labor.

"Really. Listen"—Jenna lowered her voice—"Jude is

more than qualified and prepared to run things, but he refuses to push or go against Dad on this. I think he tried one time and...well, they didn't speak for weeks afterward. Suffice it to say, that convo didn't go well. Don't tell him I told you that though, okay?"

Aurora was unlikely to have the kind of conversation with Jude where they confided in each other about anything.

"Okay," she said anyway.

Their dad was bound to retire sooner than later, but maybe even then he'd prevent them from going in new directions. The notion wasn't completely alien to Aurora.

When she'd first told her mother and sisters about going to culinary school instead of traditional college, like Beth had chosen, her sisters were excited and supportive.

Their mom, Anita, however, was skeptical. Judgmental.

She'd insisted she was merely concerned for Aurora's future and prospects, but they all knew the truth. Anita wanted her daughters to stay close to home and have grounded, secure futures. Jobs in accounting and business, and husbands with money who would never lie and abandon them. Never leave them struggling financially and heartbroken, like their dear old dad.

Aurora shook off the shadow of her thoughts. "I bet, in time, the three of you could convince your father to try something new. Probably not a lot of new things, but pick one project and really get behind it. He'd be hard-pressed to say no to all three of you if you come together."

"Y'know, it's funny that you say that. We do have one idea we're all for, and I'd like to get your thoughts on it." Jenna sniffed the air. "But first, someone here needs a little tending to, if you know what I mean."

Aurora was intrigued by what Jenna wanted her thoughts on, but a dirty diaper took priority over almost everything. "Okay. You take care of Wyatt and we can talk in a bit?"

Jenna sniffed some more. "Yes. Let me grab Bonnie, and she can finish showing you around back here. I didn't even make it past the edible lavender."

Jenna left, and Bonnie returned in her place, still the same bubbly personality and dimples as when they were kids.

"How far did y'all get? Just the lavender tea packets?"

"And talks of lavender lattes," Cece said.

Meredith joined them, smiling as brightly as Bonnie.

Cece gave Aurora a look. How close to the family was this Meredith? And how awkward was it going to be when Bonnie inevitably blurted out personal details from the past?

"Oh, don't worry." Bonnie looked back and forth between the two sisters. "I already told Meredith about you being Jude's ex. *The* ex." She added big wide eyes for effect.

Heat rushed to Aurora's face as Cece gave a nervous chuckle.

"Jeez, Bonnie." Meredith poked her in the side.

"What? Too blunt?"

"Way too blunt." Meredith shook her head.

"Sorry."

"No, it's okay." Aurora shrugged it off with a chuckle. "I mean, it's true."

"Yeah, see?" Bonnie flicked her hand in the air good-naturedly. "Tiptoeing around it takes too long. Now, back to the tour. Over here is some more dried lavender, and here is the ornamental lavender that we've done for eons."

She dragged out the last word. "But I'm trying to get us into some new markets."

"Like?"

"I think we should get into a subscription service type thing. Have just a quarterly box, or even only annually, add in some of our other herbs and spices, delivered right to your door. Voilà!"

"I think that's a great idea."

"Right?" Bonnie's face lit up. "And if that went well, we could partner with vegetable farmers and do seasonable boxes. People *love* seasonable boxes." Bonnie flicked the open top of an empty box and Jude chose that moment to join them. "Dad hated the idea though," Bonnie added. "So that's as far as I got."

She lowered her voice and grumbled in a good impression of her father. "Our family has worked this land since before the Depression. We don't need some gimmick to be successful. We just keep doing what we've always done."

"Bonnie." Jude shook his head.

"And then he made you agree with him, even though you want us to branch out too. As much or more than I do."

Jude's gaze touched Aurora's, then darted away.

For as long as she could remember, he'd had plans and new ideas for the farm. Even as a teenager, he'd talked about running the farm after his dad. He'd thought about growing wildflowers in addition to lavender, expanding into herb gardens.

But Jude didn't go against his father, on anything.

"I know, but your impression of him makes him sound like Colonel Sanders."

Bonnie's mouth gaped in offense.

"It is pretty bad," Meredith agreed. "Mr. Jones is more Sam Shepard than Colonel Sanders."

"He's more like..." Jude cleared his throat and, in a raspy baritone, said, "We keep doing what we've always done."

"That was *not* Sam Shepard." Aurora laughed at Jude's expression before she could catch herself. "It's not."

"I wasn't doing Sam." He grinned. "I was doing John Jones. Badly."

Aurora returned his smile, until she caught Bonnie studying her.

"Bonnie? Bonnie," Linda called as she found them in the back of the store. "Come on. I need your help with something."

"But it's just getting good here."

Linda stared hard at her youngest child.

Meredith followed her cue. "Come on, let's give your mom a hand, and then maybe grab a snack. I'm starving."

"Fine." Bonnie dragged her feet as she followed her mom and Meredith. "Y'all can enjoy the fields without me, I guess."

Once they were out of the back room, only Cece, Aurora, and Jude were left. The three of them stared at one another for a moment. This was too intimate a tour group for Aurora's liking. She'd need a way to get out of this.

"We can just go out the back if y'all want," Jude offered. "Circle around to check out the new herb section before the lavender. It's up to you."

"Actually, I just got a text from Beth." Cece held up her phone as if it were state's evidence. "There's an issue with the Williams wedding, so, I've got to go."

Aurora checked her phone. "She didn't text me. We can go—"

"No, no," Cece spoke over her. "It's about their photographer. And the, um, the bridal pictures at the inn. That's a me issue…thing. You stay here. I'll go deal with this and I can come back later and get you."

Her sister was the worst actress ever.

"I can leave now, and we'll see the fields some other time," Aurora offered.

"No. Stay! You've earned a break from the inn anyway." Cece turned and hurried away.

Aurora watched her leave. Cece was already halfway to the front of the store, making the quickest of getaways. "I'll be back later. Bye!"

And like that, Aurora was stuck at the farm.

If she made a big deal about not staying here with Jude, it would be weird and rude. She'd come across like she couldn't stand being alone with him, and then it'd be a whole thing.

If she stayed, it'd still be weird, but surely, they could survive.

"Bye. I guess." Aurora lifted her hand helplessly.

"Wow," Jude said from behind her. "We just got set up."

"In the worst setup job of all time."

"The segue into the setup was okay. Not the smoothest, but tolerable. I give it a six outta ten."

The sound of their old ranking system coming out of his mouth twisted her heart. They used to rank everything. Friday night pizza at Tony's, nine out of ten if the crust was just right. Homework over the weekend, zero out of ten.

Kissing in his truck while parked by the pond, as it rained outside. Full ten out of ten.

Aurora wanted to melt into the floor right now, never to be seen again, but she had to face him.

She turned to Jude. He was standing entirely too close to her, his arms crossed as he stared down, blue eyes flashing. "How long you think they'd had it planned out to leave us alone together?"

"Since yesterday."

Jude nodded and tapped his nose. "While we were chasing chickens."

"Should've known." She shook her head. "It's not like our sisters are an unpredictable bunch."

"True. And they probably want to give us time alone, to talk. You know, if we want to."

Aurora stiffened, her nerves tingling. She wasn't ready for all of that. She might not ever be ready.

He glanced around and stuffed his hands in his pockets, the strong line of his jaw undeniably appealing. "But we don't have to. We can enjoy the fields and being outside. The weather is perfect, and I'm fine with showing you around."

"You sure?"

"Sure. You came all the way out here."

"And my ride just left me here like an unwanted UPS package."

He laughed, the rolling warmth of it making her smile before she could catch herself. "Yeah, she did. Cece bailed on you, big-time. But I'm game for a tour if you are."

She ought to be game. This was Jude. Regardless of their history, they knew each other, knew each other's families. They weren't bitter enemies, just old flames. She could spend half an hour in his presence, wandering the farm, and it wouldn't be the end of the world.

To refuse this time with him would be ridiculous.

Aurora nodded. "I'm game. Show me the latest and greatest at Edge of the World Farm."

They exited the back of the shop and were immediately surrounded by wave after wave of purple.

Jude walked between the two rows of lavender in front of him and she followed closely behind. The buzz of honeybees was so prevalent, it disappeared into white noise across the farm. Songbirds chirped and sang their approval of the warm midday sun.

Aurora extended her arm, letting her fingers dance across the tops of the blooms, stirring their fragrance even more. The fields were so familiar, comforting, even as her tour guide bewildered her.

"The fields are essentially the same as the last time you were here," Jude said.

Perhaps it was just her, but every time he mentioned—or even alluded to—their past, a pang hit deep in her chest.

She didn't hate him anymore, so why did thinking about them then cause such a reaction? Was that merely the default for all lost loves the world over? Maybe that's just how it was for everyone, and if you never saw your ex again, then you never had to deal with that feeling. Out of sight, out of mind.

But now that she was here, and around him, would exposure help it go away completely?

One could hope.

"We've extended growth several acres to add in more culinary lavender, but the biggest difference out here is the addition of the herb gardening section."

When they finally reached the end of the long row,

Jude took a wide left and led her over a hilltop to a separate area.

This garden was all green, with smatterings of yellow and orange here and there.

Jude's herb garden. He'd made that dream come true.

"We grow basil, thyme, rosemary, tarragon, sometimes cilantro successfully, though it's been fussy, and a lot of mint. Oh, and we're trying some lemon balm at Bonnie's request. Not sure what she plans to do with it, but I thought I'd be supportive."

"Did you ever branch out into wildflowers?" The question was out of her mouth before she could catch the words.

Growing wildflowers was a dream they'd once shared. Wildflowers for the bees to pollinate, then they could harvest the flowers for retail sale, gather honey to sell as well, then replant and start the cycle over again the next year.

He'd probably dumped that idea when he dumped her.

Jude paused and plucked some mint. "No, I... we uh, went with herbs instead. I guess." He ran his fingers up the frond of mint and lifted his hand to his perfectly straight nose.

He'd never been able to resist scents.

Jude had always been highly attuned to olfaction. He'd reveled in the smell of flowers, his mom's cooking, Aurora's cooking. Old books, new books. Aurora's perfume and hair.

She jerked her gaze away.

Enough reminiscing.

"Yeah, Bonnie was telling me about the herbs and her ideas for subscription boxes. And Jenna mentioned another project you're all interested in?"

Jude stared. "She did?"

"She said she wanted to talk to me about it later today."

He knew exactly what she was talking about, she could see it in his eyes. But when he opened his mouth, "Hmm, I don't know" came out.

He was as bad a liar as the rest of his family, and hers.

Jude started walking again and presented the rest of the farm like a pro, speaking of crop rotations and soil acidity like it was the most fascinating stuff on earth. He was in his element out here, doing exactly what he'd always dreamed of doing. Jude was made to farm this land, and his contentment was contagious.

His calm confidence was as disarming as ever, too, and slowly, some of her unease began to fade across the fields.

"We still have several dozen acres unused," he said, pointing beyond the herbs. "But for now, with our existing staff, we've got all we can handle."

The same message she'd gotten from Jenna. If they wanted to grow the farm, they'd have to hire more farm hands, which meant people other than the folks who'd worked here for ages. But, as Jenna said, their father had no interest in growth or new staff. Because of that, the farm was stuck, right where it was. Successful, but stagnant. Eventually, the stagnation would cause decline.

John Jones needed to listen to the next generation, or the farm would cease growing.

Then again, none of this was her business. Not anymore.

"Your family has done an amazing job here. You should be really proud."

"Thanks." His gaze swept to hers, then skittered away, and a small tick tensed his jaw. "I, uh, I appreciate that."

It was an old tell, but she'd recognize it until the end of time. Jude had two of them. When he was angry or frustrated, he clenched his jaw, hard. This wasn't that.

This was Jude, nervous and anxious. His jaw would tense and relax, tense and relax. He did it only when he had to talk to his dad, he overthought a question from a tough teacher, or he got caught in a sticky situation.

A smile tugged at her lips.

The habit was charming, always had been. Even steadfast, confident, dutiful Jude Jones could still be vulnerable.

He might seem like a stranger, the years changing them both, but the core of what made him Jude was still there. And she knew him, in so many ways. The curve of his smile, the way his eyes and nose crinkled when he laughed, the way his skin smelled warm and nutty after a day in the sun by the lake. She also knew how hard he worked—at everything—and how he got tunnel vision sometimes, even to the detriment of those around him, but that he meant well, most of the time, even if he was hard-headed and proud.

They returned to the rows of lavender, making their way back to the store.

"You should..." Jude stuffed his hands in his pockets as they walked, his air of confidence still taking a little hiatus. "You should be proud too. Of everything you've done. I mean, at Orchard Inn. I...I don't know about everything you've done, but I've heard business has really picked up because of you. Word around town is the inn is one of Fredericksburg's best places for an event or weekend getaway."

Aurora mirrored his steps, walking alongside him now.

"That's nice to hear. I think for smaller occasions, we'd be way up there. We haven't done one of those three-hundred-guests-style weddings or anything, but I doubt people come to Fredericksburg to do that anyway."

He chuckled. "That might be more of a New York or L.A. type wedding?"

Aurora stopped walking without realizing it. He paused as well.

She didn't know why she'd stopped. Something about Jude speaking of Los Angeles, knowing that's where she'd been all these years, combined with being here with him, doing something normal in a thinly veiled attempt to make amends…she couldn't continue not talking about it.

He was still Jude and he was standing right here.

While she didn't want to get into her feelings and past hurts, or deal with any of the messy, squishy emotions of their relationship, she also couldn't be around him and keep pretending they were just casual old pals. School chums who hadn't hung out in ages.

That was wrong in so many ways.

Aurora opened her mouth to attempt an eloquent explanation of her thoughts. Then, an unmistakable sting lit up her ankle.

"Ow!" she shouted. "Shoot. *Ouch!*" She swatted at her foot. She looked down, knowing exactly what she'd find and…Yep.

"Yellow jackets. Run!"

Chapter 8

Jude grabbed Aurora's arm and they took off down the row, running as fast as they could, and they didn't stop until they were halfway back to the store.

"You okay? Did one get you?" He knelt beside Aurora, checking her sock and shoe.

"I think two or three got me." She balanced with a hand on his shoulder and lifted her foot up into his grasp. "Geez, I forgot how much those things hurt."

"Let's see." He turned her ankle, carefully looking over her skin as her hand warmed his back through the old T-shirt. "They're gone but looks like they got you three or four times."

He looked up, and she scrunched her face in pain. "How can something so small hurt so bad? Did they get you too?"

Jude shook his head, still looking her over. "No, I'm good. We keep a pretty good check on the fields, but we must've missed that one. I'll spray them at dusk, when they all calm down and return to the nest. I'm sorry about that." He was still holding her ankle, for probably too long. "The stingers aren't in there anymore though."

"Good. I'll be okay." She moved to lower her foot and he let go.

As he stood, her hand brushed the length of his arm, pausing on his forearm. When his gaze met hers, she jerked away like she'd been burned.

"We need to get something on the stings." Jude ignored the moment. "Did they get you anywhere else?"

"No. I— I'll be okay until I can get home."

"You aren't allergic, are you?"

Aurora arched her brow. "I've never been allergic. We've been stung before, remember? A lot more than this."

"That's right." He shook his head at forgetting. "At the lake that time. I think I got hit, like, five or six times. Come on, I have a first-aid and sting kit at the barn. We can put something on it to ease the pain." He offered his arm as though she'd twisted her ankle and couldn't walk.

She could probably make it to the barn just fine, but she took his arm anyway.

He'd need to get some of the farm hands to check the fields carefully over the next few weeks. He didn't want any yellow jackets messing with people or the farm's honeybee population.

Jude hadn't always loved honeybees, but he learned to appreciate them, like all farmers.

"Remember our junior year biology project?" he asked Aurora.

"Of course. When I learned how much you hated bees?"

"I didn't *hate* bees. I just didn't like being close to so many of them."

When they'd paired up for a big class research assignment, he and Aurora had chosen bees and pollination.

They'd visited the hives at Jones's farm as part of their research.

Jude had given the colony a comically wide berth, and Aurora had teased him.

The guy who was tending the bees had misunderstood. "Without these bees, there'd be no farm."

"I know. I'm a fan of their work, just not the stinging and swarming part."

That's when the beekeeper explained, in detail, the symbiotic relationship between bee and farmer. Most of the information Jude already knew, having grown up on a farm, but that day they'd received a college-level course on bee behavior. Riveted, he and Aurora had decided to create an apiary for their project. And when they received an A and many accolades on it, Jude had been so proud.

"Who knows?" he'd said, a million years ago. "Maybe we'll even go into the bee business. Make honey and raise bees together. Jones Honey."

"Or Shipley Honey," she'd corrected.

"Yeah, but what if your name ends up being Jones too?"

That's where their wildflower honey dream began. He'd meant what he said too. Even at the ripe old age of seventeen, he'd thought about spending forever with Aurora.

When they first started dating, she'd talked about maybe moving to a big city after high school and taking culinary classes. She'd said big cities offered more opportunities, more chances to grow important skills.

Slowly, her plans had changed. They'd started dreaming of a future together, here in Texas. They were going to run the farm, expand into honey production, and Aurora could still take culinary courses locally.

Then, all those new plans, the dreams of a life together, were gone. He'd broken that dream, so Aurora went back to her original plan and left. Turned out, that was the best thing for her. She was thriving in her career and she must love living in L.A. because, as far as he knew, she rarely came home until now.

Jude took her to the renovated barn, as it sat a lot closer to them than the store.

Inside, there was a small kitchen area and a first-aid kit. Being himself, and given to overpreparedness, he kept first-aid kits in all the farm buildings and in all the family's cars.

Much to Bonnie's annoyance, he'd even snuck one into her trunk.

"Come in here and I'll get the anesthetic." He showed Aurora to the kitchen area and went straight to the cabinet with the first-aid gear. He found the sting swabs and had her hop up on the counter to treat her ankle.

"I can do this myself."

"I know, but I can see the stings better from my angle."

He gently wiped the red welts on her ankle and dotted the anesthetic on each sting, her ankle warm in his hand, her skin against his.

Aurora inhaled sharply when he touched the angriest-looking sting but relaxed as the swab took effect.

"Just sit there a second and let it soak in." He let her go, resisting the urge to blow on her stings the way his mom used to when he'd stumbled upon a nest.

"Thank you," she said after a moment, slowly rotating her ankle and looking a lot more comfortable.

His heartbeat thumped in his ears.

Years ago, a part of him had wondered if he'd ever see

Aurora again. She might never come back, happy to be away from him and the pressures of home. Now here she was. At first, it was just as awkward as he had imagined, but their togetherness was getting easier. Being around her still felt…natural.

He cleared his throat and began packing away the first-aid kit.

"What do you do with this barn now?" she asked, easing herself off the counter. "Anything?"

"Some storage right now, but mostly it sits empty."

"When did the renovations happen? I remember this used to be in rough shape."

"Over the last couple of years."

But the renovations didn't just *happen*. He'd done them himself, mostly by himself. At the end of each day, for many days, his way of unwinding was to renovate this old barn. His dad kept such tight control on any changes at Edge of the World Farm, there wasn't much Jude could do that wasn't under the watchful eye of the patriarch.

This barn, however? No one gave two hoots about the old barn.

Jude had worked out his frustration and pent-up energy by sanding, scrapping, hammering, and painting. Eventually he'd worked his way into new flooring, and for that he'd called in a buddy to help.

His friend's advice had turned into plumbing the place out and adding a small kitchen.

After two years of chipping away at the project, they had a fully renovated barn.

"What's all this for?" his dad had asked, or, rather, demanded.

"It's not for anything. Just a project."

John Jones had grumbled while inspecting the finished product, but Jude's mom and sisters had gushed.

The barn had turned out amazing, and he'd be lying if he said he wasn't proud.

"Well, it looks really good." Aurora wandered across to the windows. "Adding windows was a nice touch."

She walked toward the front, where the doors still hung open from their arrival. "Who did you get to do the remodel?"

"I did it." He fought not to grin.

Aurora turned, her eyes wide. "Seriously?"

"Thanks for the vote of confidence. I am capable of some carpentry, you know?"

"I know, but this is a tad more than carpentry work. You plumbed it out and fitted the barn with a kitchen."

"A friend of mine is a contractor. He helped me bring everything to code and make the upgrades. Took a while, but it was a nice project for weekends and after hours."

"I'll say." She went to one of the windows and opened it with the roll bar, leaving just a screen in place so a breeze could come in. "I'm impressed."

It shouldn't matter that he'd impressed her. But it did. Her opinion of him had never ceased to matter.

"What do you want to do with it?" She approached him with an expectant expression and his muscles stiffened. He stood a little taller, a zip of joy shooting up his spine.

No one understood quite how his mind worked like Aurora had.

For all his practicality and preparation, he also loved making big plans. Some plans had never gone further than talk, and some, like his herb gardens, had come to full fruition. But his favorite part was the birth of an idea.

"I don't know, really. I have a few ideas?"

"A few ideas like the coffee and tea shop Jenna mentioned?"

"Something like that. Or something more food focused."

"Like a restaurant?" Her gaze focused on him, her sharp eyes burning through his skull as though trying to read his deepest thoughts.

"My sisters and I have talked about it, but it's just been talk."

Aurora began walking the open room again. "You'd need more than just a small kitchen if you do full-service dining. That means additional renovations and then the deep rabbit hole of starting up a restaurant. It's an unimaginable amount of work."

Jude frowned. His family was in no position to present rabbit-hole restaurants to their father.

"Look at this view though," Aurora cooed, making him smile. "You couldn't ask for a better location for farm-to-table dining."

His thoughts exactly.

"And with a potential porch?" She gestured. "The fields, the wide-open acres, stunning sunsets. That alone would give you all the ambience and authenticity you needed."

She was on a roll now, so he let her go.

"Add, like, I don't know, maybe some quaint, but rustic, casual décor. Simple. Natural. A completely local menu."

"We wouldn't need to leave Fredericksburg for vendors

either," he added. "Everything can be sourced from right here on our farm or nearby."

"Exactly. Feature dishes from neighboring farms. Names that people around here know. Use your own herbs in the dishes."

"It'd generate buzz for our farm products and the products of other farms."

"Yes." Her smile turned wide and bright. "You list the names of farms by each menu item, have their locations and information on the back. It comes full circle."

Jude nodded, his mind whirling with potential as he fought not to match her smile.

"Wait." Aurora tilted her head. "This is what Jenna wanted to talk to me about, isn't it?"

He wasn't sure what to make of her tone. "No. Jenna and I have talked about it, but it's only talk. It'll never happen. Not for a long time anyway."

Her gaze locked with his. "Because of your dad."

"How did you—?"

"Your sisters told me that your dad isn't interested in anything new. Bonnie mentioned subscription boxes and Jenna talked about expanding the shop into new areas, but your dad is against it. I know how that goes."

Aurora knew better than most. She'd had her own experiences with the formidable John Jones and his control issues.

Jude tried to explain, for some reason. "He just doesn't like change or doing anything different than how it's always been done."

"Oh, believe me, I know, and—" She pinched her lips closed.

"And what?" he urged.

"Nothing. We don't need to get into it right now."

Get into the past. That's what she meant.

They both fell quiet. The weight of their conversation went far beyond a farm-to-table restaurant. He knew it and, clearly, she did too.

How could feelings still be raw after so many years?

"Aurora, I know how my dad can be. How he's always been. I know it better than anyone."

She looked away, out the open barn doors, into the distance. "Yeah," she managed, her voice shaky. "I should go home. For real now."

"I'll give you a lift," he agreed.

The ride to the Orchard Inn dragged with heavy silence. Too many unsaid words hung in the air. He turned down the driveway for the inn and slowed his truck to a crawl. "Aurora, I don't want the day to end like this."

She didn't say a word in response, or even look his way, but he had to get this out. They both knew what needed to be said, and he wasn't a teenage boy anymore. He was a grown man, who'd learned this lesson the hard way.

Jude took a steadying breath before opening his mouth. "I know, better than anyone, how my dad can be. And I know the role he had in how things ended between us."

She turned toward him, quiet, her expression unreadable.

"But I was the one who handled our breakup the wrong way. I was a stupid kid, but that's no excuse. I'm sorry. And I'm sorry my dad... was the way he was too."

Aurora blinked, still silent as he parked the car.

This Aurora was not the outspoken woman from the farmers' market or even from the barn a few minutes earlier.

She opened her mouth, then closed it. Opened again, but nothing came out.

"Thanks for bringing me back," she finally blurted, and fled the car like it was on fire.

Once she'd disappeared inside the inn, Jude rested his head on the steering wheel.

He wasn't sure exactly how he'd expected Aurora to react, but not like that.

Chapter 9

Aurora's phone chimed with an alarm, but she was already awake. She'd lain there, for the last hour and a half, refusing to move.

It was all Jude's fault. He'd apologized. Just said it flat-out, he was sorry, and he was sorry for his dad's role in pressuring him to break up with her.

And Aurora? Oh, she'd sat there, like a knot on a log, silent and dumbfounded. But that wasn't her fault. She had not been prepared for his apology. Nothing in their history had led her to believe he'd step up and take ownership of his mistakes and acknowledge his father's faults.

Teenage Jude had been prideful and stubborn to a fault, defending John Jones unflinchingly and ignoring his own personal flaws as though they were unthinkable. Actually, that described about ninety-nine percent of high school boys.

Adult Jude was the exact opposite. He listened and expressed himself. He didn't just shut down, and *that* is why she'd dreamed of him.

It was his fault.

"Ugh," she groaned, pulling the covers over her head, the dream still dancing through her mind.

She'd been back in high school, wandering down endless, empty halls, looking for Jude. She desperately needed to tell him something. She needed his support, his attention, and his reassurance.

It was all too real and too familiar.

She finally found him outside, near the baseball field, getting ready for practice. A pit opened in her stomach and her heart raced.

She was losing him. He didn't care about her anymore. Why would he? He was Jude freaking Jones, star pitcher of the baseball team, everyone's favorite golden boy, sure to be the future prom king and local hero, bound to bring home a regional title, if not state.

Who was she? Some quiet little girl who never made a stir and followed him around like a lost puppy. Half the school wouldn't know she existed if it weren't for Jude.

Maybe it was better when they didn't know.

Then, in the dream, Jude turned his back on her, ignoring her calling after him as he walked away.

She'd sat up in bed with a start, her room still dark. Who was he to invade her dreams? They were *her* dreams. Maybe if she just stayed here, under the covers, she'd fall back to sleep and forget all about the dream and yesterday.

She'd spent half the day with Jude and his family; they'd talked about the farm and the plans they wanted to make a reality. Then Jude had tried to make amends for the past, and she'd run away from his truck like her hair was on fire.

Aurora threw off her covers.

There'd be no distraction from that dream or yesterday or Jude if she just lay here. She needed to get on with her day and hope something in the kitchen would push all of this from her mind.

After washing up and getting dressed, she was in the kitchen by seven, yet her sisters had beaten her there, as usual.

"You look rough." Cece sipped her coffee while scrolling her phone.

"Thanks so much. The bedraggled look took me all night to put together."

"Didn't sleep well?"

"Nope."

Beth joined them, coffee in one hand and her tablet in the other. "That's weird. You usually sleep like a log. I'm the insomniac."

"Something on your mind?" Cece stared her down over the top of her phone.

Aurora cut her eyes at her sister. "Stop."

"What?" Beth jumped on the shift in conversation and poured herself some more coffee.

"Nothing," they both answered.

"Well, now I know it's something."

"We went to see Jude yesterday." Cece kept scrolling with a quirk of her lips.

"We went to see his family and the farm," Aurora attempted to correct her.

"That's right. How did it go?"

"How it went was Cece *abandoned* me at the farm in an attempt to force me to spend time with Jude."

Cece set her phone down with a plunk. "I did not abandon you. Beth needed me here."

"I did?" Beth asked.

"Ha, see!" Aurora pointed at Cece.

"I saw you two together at the market, and again yesterday," Cece argued. "There's stuff between you and Jude—and maybe it's just some leftover angst, I don't know—but something is there. You both needed a chance to really talk. Alone. I wanted to make sure you had that."

Aurora shook her head and went to the cabinet for a coffee cup. "It's not like we're going to make up and hang out together."

"You could," Beth said.

Aurora threw up a hand. "I can't with either of you right now. I'm barely awake and you want me to be BFFs with the boy who broke my heart? Don't think so." She focused on pouring her coffee, hoping that was the end of the conversation, but the heat of her sisters' stare scorched the back of her head.

"Just hear me out." Beth took a seat at the counter with Cece, urging Aurora to join them. "I know you two may not be best friends, but trust me when I say it's better to make peace with what happened *now* than to ignore it and assume it won't affect you for the rest of your life."

Cece nodded in agreement.

"Look at Sawyer," Beth continued. "He tried to bury how an old breakup affected him, and it almost ruined our relationship."

"And his brother's relationship, and his relationship with his brother," Cece added.

Beth nodded. "Exactly." Her eyes grew soft green, pleading. "If you haven't already, at least consider talking to Jude about what you went through. It's okay to open up and express how you felt. It will help. I promise."

Open up. To Jude? That was the most absurd thing

she'd ever heard, even if the idea did hold some merit—in theory.

Opening up to him meant seeing him again. That meant reaching out to him, as in she'd have to take that step. Make that move.

Alternatively, she could just ignore all of this and hope it went away. It'd worked for the last ten years. Kind of—but not really.

"I don't know about opening up to my ex. That's weird." Then again, still having dreams about him wasn't exactly the peak of emotional health.

Beth raised one perfectly sculpted eyebrow. "So, instead, you want to move back to California, never having spoken up, with nothing resolved? The Aurora you've shown me for the last two months speaks up."

"A lot," Cece agreed.

They had her there. She'd grown into someone unafraid to express her opinions and stand up for herself, especially at work. In big kitchens you had to speak up or you'd get run over. This was Jude though, and dealing with those feelings wasn't like dealing with a busy kitchen.

Cece got up and rounded the counter to give Aurora a one-armed side hug. "I'm sorry if I abandoned you. I was only trying to help."

"I know."

"It had to be weird for both of you. Blast from the past and all that."

"Honestly? Yeah, it was super weird." Aurora relaxed into her sister's hug. "But then it wasn't, and then it was again, even more so. It's hard to explain."

Cece squeezed her in support.

Maybe Beth was right. Maybe, if she really talked to Jude, they could put the past to rest. She could leave Fredericksburg with a clear mind and focus solely on her future.

"Fine. I'll talk to Jude," Aurora announced. "If for no other reason than to shut you both up."

Cece shoved her away from the hug good-naturedly.

Beth hopped off her chair. "Good. I'm proud of you, sis."

"Oh yeah." Cece bit her bottom lip, her expression suddenly sheepish. "I got a call from Mom yesterday."

Aurora held back a groan.

"She's back from her cruise and she wants to see us."

Their mom was retired and into traveling and looking out for herself full-time.

"When?" Aurora managed.

"I don't know, exactly. She just said she wanted to have us over sometime."

That could easily never come to fruition. Their mother was notorious for no follow-through.

"Well." Beth tapped her nails against her tablet. "I guess keep us posted and we'll go see her when she's ready. I have one nibble on our chef posting too. Aurora, I forwarded their résumé to you."

"Sounds good." Aurora hoped she sounded enthusiastic and fully supportive.

While she wanted her sisters to find a permanent chef, the idea of the wrong person working at their inn, with her sisters... She pinched her lips between her teeth. Aurora couldn't entrust her family to any old cook. They had to be just right.

"Oh, you guys will never guess who booked a small

ceremony for a couple of months out." Beth quickly changed the subject from their mother.

At this point, Aurora wasn't in the mood for guessing games. "No clue. Spit it out."

"Erica Burr."

Her stomach turned as Cece audibly gasped.

"What?" Beth's eyes widened. "Why are you looking at me like I cussed in front of the preacher?"

"Erica Burr." Cece held her eyes open even wider than Beth's. "You don't remember her?"

"Barely. She was younger than me, in Aurora's class. We never spoke."

"Precisely. She was in Aurora's grade and she spoke about Aurora. A lot."

Realization slowly dawned across Beth's face. "She's not the one who—"

"Oh, she's the one," Cece retorted. "She told everyone in school, Aurora's senior year, that Jude was only with her because she put out, and then that he broke up with her because he'd gotten what he wanted."

"And who was I to walk around like I was so goody-goody, when really, I was—apparently—easy," Aurora added.

"But that's not why you two broke up." Beth shook her head. "And I know Jude never went around saying that."

"Correct. But I couldn't stop the rumors, and Jude was too wrapped up in his own life to get in the middle of high school girl drama. Erica made all of it up, but people still believed her."

"I didn't believe her," Cece said.

"Me and Cece." Aurora quirked her lips. "And Jude.

An astounding point zero zero one percent of the school didn't believe her."

Beth's gaze softened even more. "I didn't know that was Erica. I am so sorry."

"You'd graduated. You were long gone. I don't expect you to remember." Aurora attempted to console her.

"I'm going to call her and cancel," Beth said.

"No, you are not!" Aurora put down her mug and closed in on Beth. "That was all years ago. Erica probably doesn't even remember it. Most people probably don't. I do because that was a really difficult time for me. But you are not going to turn away business over old high school drama. Erica's family knows everyone, word would get out. No way. You're a smarter businesswoman than that."

"Yes, but you're my sister."

Aurora met her sister's gaze with steely resolve. "I'm more than capable of facing Erica Burr. Like you said, I'm not that quiet girl anymore. I can take care of myself." She would have to leave her sisters and the Orchard Inn soon, with a new chef and without her support. She wasn't about to cost them a valuable client as well.

"If it's any consolation, I've heard Erica has changed." Cece refilled her coffee. "Word is she's toned down a lot. Maybe too much, because I've also heard her fiancé is a jerk."

"Cece."

"I'm just telling you what I've heard." Cece threw one hand up like she was on the witness stand, then added in a lower voice, "But from what I've experienced, I agree."

"You know him?"

"No, but I saw them out and about in town a couple

of weeks ago. I was trying to speak to her, you know, polite small talk, and he was completely overbearing and talking over her. The Erica of high school would've taken him *down*. No one talked over Erica Burr back in the day. But she let him do whatever."

Aurora wasn't convinced. One instance didn't mean she'd changed. Maybe she'd lost her voice that day or maybe she didn't want to talk to Cece.

"Well, whether she's changed or not. You're going to plan her wedding, and all will be fine. Now, I must start breakfast, so y'all get out of my kitchen." Aurora hit them with a wide smile.

Her sisters collected their coffees and devices and meandered out of her workspace, and Aurora began pulling out the prep work for breakfast. If she started working with food, maybe she could stop thinking about everything else.

She'd put a couple of quiches together the night before. Now all she had to do was bake them, cut up some fresh fruit, and put together a vegan option for a couple who'd requested it the night before.

Avocado toast was always a safe bet.

"Eh." She contemplated aloud. "Overdone." Especially in California. What if she did some sort of potato hash with avo on top? "Mmmm." She nodded to herself. "Savory flavor, add tomato, a little onion."

The potato-and-veggie hash was finished just before her quiche Lorraine came out of the oven. She served up the dishes at eight thirty—as scheduled.

Even after breakfast service, Aurora's brain still buzzed with thoughts of the past. Between her time with Jude, Erica freaking Burr on the agenda for a wedding, their mom wanting to see them, her sisters, their future at the inn—what had she expected coming back here, living in the belly of her history?

Of course she'd collide with her past.

When her mind got too busy, there was only one thing that would center her.

A new recipe.

And she felt like baking something.

She grabbed the flour, sugar, butter, salt, eggs, and vanilla, with no idea what she might make. Didn't matter, these were the base of so many options, so she started sifting.

Stirring and whisking acted as her therapy. Rolling and pressing were like meditative yoga. A crust came together mindlessly. She popped it in the oven and contemplated a filling.

She'd cooked enough with peaches lately. Strawberries were a little late in the season and she'd had plenty of them too. Actually, she wasn't in the mood for fruit at all. That left chocolate, custards, creams…

"Ooo, something gooey," she said to herself. Something sweet and comforting.

"Honey."

In a rush, she heated honey in a small pot. After digging around in the pantry for far too long, she settled on it.

Culinary lavender.

She threw the lavender in the pot and let it steep. After five minutes, she strained the honey and whisked in eggs, butter, and vanilla. A pinch of salt and "Voilà!"

Aurora poured in the filling and slid the pie back into the oven. Setting a timer, she sighed.

This was either going to be delicious and unique, a

stroke of genius, or it was going to be a disgusting globby mess. Either way, she wasn't going to read into why she'd chosen lavender and honey for this recipe. She'd write it off as inspiration from the sights and sounds of yesterday, and nothing more. Certainly not the man who'd set up shop in her dreams and woke her in the wee hours.

Half an hour later, her pie wasn't a globby mess at all. Golden across the top, a little darker near the crust, custard-like in consistency, and it smelled divine.

"What smells so good?" Beth returned to the kitchen, nose first.

"I'm trying out a new recipe."

Cece joined them, leaning over to inspect her creation.

"Back up off the pie. She needs a while to set up. It's a custard base, so let's err on the side of patience."

Something none of them had.

"How patient are we talking?" Cece asked. "Five minutes? Ten minutes?"

"Twenty to thirty."

Her sisters complained dramatically, but they dispersed from the kitchen and returned exactly twenty minutes later.

"It's probably still too soon, but fine." Aurora cut three pieces for them, serving the slices on dessert plates with sprigs of lavender as accents.

Sometimes, if the finished product wasn't perfect, a little presentation helped.

The pie was firm, but a few more minutes would've helped. This didn't seem to matter to Beth, because she dug into hers right away.

Closing her eyes, she hummed as she tasted.

Silly as it might seem, this being an impromptu recipe, tried by her nearest and dearest family, Aurora still got a pang of anxiety when someone ate her food.

Beth drew out her hum, which was a good sign.

Cece tried a bite of her slice and immediately went in for a second. "This is out of this world."

"Seriously." Beth nodded. "It's so different. Creamy and subtle. I taste the honey, but it's not too sweet. It's comforting."

Cece nodded. "This is what you should enter in the pie contest."

"Yes!" Beth clapped her hands together.

"I'm not doing the pie contest."

"Um..." Cece took another bite.

"Cece!"

"What? I know you didn't want to, but one of the judges is a publisher at Prescott Press out of Austin. She's going to feature the winning pie in a new dessert cookbook, so, in the off chance you're still here for the jamboree, why not enter?"

Because chances were almost certain she wouldn't be here.

"You have to do it." Beth leaned forward, with that wild look in her eyes she got whenever she wanted to accomplish something—whether it be for herself or someone in her immediate vicinity. "This pie would win. It's not the same old apple or peach."

"Do it," Cece commanded.

"I doubt I'll still be here for the jamboree. I don't know my timetable yet."

"Then if you aren't here, I'll cancel your entry. Problem solved."

"Haven't you ever thought about being in a cook-book?" Beth asked.

"Yeah." It wasn't at the top of her list, but every chef *thought* about it. "I've thought about a lot of things."

Beth's enthusiasm ticked down a few notches, her gaze growing somber.

Her sister wasn't just thinking about a cookbook now. She knew being at the Orchard Inn wasn't Aurora's life goal and, while they'd both enjoyed the last few months, and had grown as a result of working together, things wouldn't stay this way forever.

"Let's just keep the entry for now," Beth said. "What could it hurt?"

Aurora's phone rang on the counter, making her jump. "I better get that."

"And the contest entry?" Cece raised both eyebrows hopefully.

Aurora groaned, but she couldn't say no to that face. "Fine. But don't get mad at me if you have to cancel or bake a pie in my absence." She grabbed her phone and headed outside, needing some air.

"Hey, Sloane," she answered, seeing the ID. She didn't ask what was up, because her friend required no segue when it came to actual phone calls. Sloane was a texter by nature. If she was calling you, it was either an emergency or emergency-level gossip.

"Mark is opening a new restaurant in Malibu!" Sloane was basically panting with excitement.

Aurora blinked.

Mark was their boss, and a partner at their restaurant group. Aurora's current restaurant was his last project. There'd been rumors about a new place, but she thought it'd be next year before they picked a location. "I didn't think he'd choose Malibu."

"Did you hear what I said? A new restaurant, Aurora. And I've heard you are at the top of his list to open it."

"You think he'd choose me?"

"That's the word going around."

Sloane's gossip was rarely wrong.

"What's the cuisine? What's the style?"

"I'm still digging around for those details, but you've got to be a shoo-in. You're next up for the opportunity. Who is he going to have do it, *Jon*?" The disdain in Sloane's voice was almost comical.

"Mark could hire someone new. Depending on the direction of the menu, he could hire someone fluent in that area."

She'd seen chefs have the rug jerked out from under them before.

"No way he trusts someone new."

True. Her boss would need to have a lot of faith in someone to trust them with a new restaurant, especially his first venture in Malibu.

"Sloane, I've been gone for a while now. What if I ruined this chance because of my responsibilities here? He'll want someone who is married to the restaurant. Someone dependable."

"You're dependable! You told him you'd be gone no more than a quarter, and it's been two months. He knows the inn is an investment for you and your sisters. He'd do the same thing if it were his family."

Aurora was grateful to still have a job, never mind this kind of promotion.

"He'll probably be calling you in the next few days. When will you be back anyway? Next week or so?"

"Uh, yeah. Yes. I need to place a chef here, and then I'm back."

"Perfect. And mum's the word on what I told you too."

Aurora smiled. "Naturally."

"All right, I've gotta run. Post some more pics on Insta, okay? It's been a while."

"Will do."

Aurora hung up, her limbs suddenly heavy, her heart pounding.

"Hey." Cece popped her head out the front door. "Everything okay?" She came out onto the front porch when Aurora didn't answer immediately, walking over to join her on the porch swing.

After a moment, Aurora finally answered. "Yeah."

Things weren't great. Her head was all over the place.

Her life, her job in L.A.—they wouldn't wait. She needed to go back as soon as possible, if she wanted this window of opportunity to remain open. But she still needed to make sure her sisters were set up with a chef, and now she wanted to settle things between her and Jude, so they could both make peace.

Being head chef of a restaurant was the dream, so why were all these obstacles filling her mind? Why did she hesitate?

She needed to talk to Beth and Cece, let them know she had that timetable now. There would be emotions, maybe some tears, but they all knew this was coming. It'd been part of the deal from the outset. She could talk to Jude tomorrow, and settle the unrest of their history. Then she could go back to California free and clear. Nothing holding her back.

This thought shouldn't trouble her. It shouldn't twist her heart in a knot.

Her sisters weren't going to be mad at her. She didn't owe Jude any more than one quick chat. This was the plan. It had always been the plan, and she was being silly.

"You sure there's nothing you want to talk about?" Cece gently swung them.

"I'm sure," Aurora fibbed.

Her sister nodded. "Well, I'm here if that changes."

"I know."

Her sisters were always there for her.

"You want me to help you make that corn for dinner tonight?" Cece asked, still rocking them gently.

"I could use the help."

"Gladly. I'll even cut the tomatoes and cucumbers, but the fried okra is all you."

Aurora chuckled. "You know how long it's been since I fried okra?"

"Not a lot of okra fans in L.A."

"Not really." Aurora slouched down and relaxed into the sway of the swing.

A chirping came from Cece's vicinity. She dug into the pocket of her jeans and pulled out her phone. "It's Mom." She stared at the screen.

Their mom communicated mostly with Cece, occasionally with Beth, and rarely with Aurora.

"Hey, Mom," Cece answered. "Yeah, we're all good. Uh-huh. Yeah."

Their conversation went on like this for a minute or two, with mostly monosyllabic answers from Cece.

"Uh, I think we can do that. Sure, after checkout. Yes, we have other staff here to cover it. Mom, we got it. It's fine. Okay, see you then. Love you too. Bye."

Cece tapped her phone to end the call, and Aurora

refused to acknowledge any jealousy over how easily they could say they loved each other.

"We're having lunch at Mom's tomorrow," her sister announced.

Aurora sat up straight. "Says who?"

"Says me and Mom."

"Cece, I have things to do tomorrow. I have two chefs' résumés to review now." And a life to contemplate. "I can't spend all day at Mom's."

"It won't be all day. She sounded like it was something really important though, so we're going."

"We all have to go?"

Her younger sister did an amazing impression of Beth's firm stare. "Yes, we all have to go."

Chapter 10

"Stop fondling the rosemary." Jenna clipped her snippers in Bonnie's direction.

"But it's my favorite smell." Bonnie ran her fingers up the frond, stirring the scent, and held her hand up to her nose. "It's so fresh and clean."

"Then sniff and clip at the same time."

Jude held his freshly clipped rosemary to his nose. It was delightful. Not as good as lavender or mint, but it was up there in the top smell category.

He'd begun working in the herb garden as the sun came up, eager to dive into manual labor and forget about yesterday.

Finally, he'd worked up the gumption to address the past with Aurora and apologize—something he'd failed to do ten years ago. They'd made progress during their time together, wandering the farm. They'd walked and talked—and touched.

Jude shook off that thought.

They'd even talked business, and the future of the farm, both things he never thought they'd discuss again. But then, when he opened the door to address the elephant in the room, Aurora had taken off.

Wouldn't be the first time she ran away.

"Jude." His dad made his way down the row of herbs, swiping a cloth across his brow. "We probably have enough for tomorrow."

They didn't have nearly enough, but his dad was tiring out. "Why don't you go on up to the house, and we'll join you in a sec."

"I don't need to go up to the house."

"Mom is up there with Wyatt. She could probably use help with dinner."

"Don't use your mother as an excuse to get rid of me."

There he went again. "I'm not trying to get rid of you."

"Come on, Dad." Jenna stepped in. "I need to go check on Wyatt, and it'll give us a chance to talk about building his train table."

His sisters were so much better at managing their dad than he was.

"Okay, but only because you need me," their father grumbled.

Bonnie and Jude watched the two of them head toward the house.

"What are the chances he complains to Mom that we ran him off?" Bonnie asked.

"One hundred percent," Jude answered. "More, if it were mathematically possible."

"I don't get it. He's got three kids, perfectly capable of running the farm, but it's like he thinks we'll—I don't know—burn the whole thing to the ground, all in twenty-four hours."

"I know."

Bonnie moved across from him to pick mint. "Have you talked to him yet?"

"No. I have to find the right time."

"When's the right time? Just do it," she insisted.

"That is not how Dad works, and you should know it. If you want to handle that little talk, go right ahead."

"Oh no. You're the oldest, you're the one who wants to run things someday."

Jude moved his stool over to the next rosemary bush. "What about you?"

Bonnie busied herself with a patch of mint. "I want work and to help. I want to be involved, not in charge. There's a big difference."

"You don't want to just do odd jobs around the farm though. I know you have ideas. Plans of your own."

"Maybe."

"Maybe isn't an answer. I heard you told Aurora about your ideas."

Bonnie raised her head, her gaze locking with his. "And?"

"And I love your idea. We can't do it all at once and make half a dozen changes immediately, but—"

"You don't hate the idea of subscription boxes straight out of the gate?"

"Not at all. These expansions and the growth will take a lot of work though. Way more than what we're doing right now."

"I know. So?"

"So, working is all we would have time for, at least for a while. No social life, no vacation time or time off until we get the first project off the ground, be it subscription boxes or a coffee shop or—"

"Or a restaurant," Bonnie finished for him.

"Or a restaurant. That would take the most time of any project."

"I know that, Jude." She rolled her eyes. "I'm not afraid of hard work, and neither is Meredith. She can work more hours too."

"I know, but I want you to understand how it will take over all your time. You're both young. You may want to go out, go to parties, have fun and meet people. If I ever get Dad's buy-in and we start even one of these projects, there won't be any time for parties and boys."

Bonnie bristled and went back to her mint, snipping angrily. "Maybe we don't want to party and meet boys. Maybe we'd rather be working here, spending time together, and doing something that matters."

"Okay, sorry, jeez. I'm just trying to look out for you."

"I know, but I'm telling you what's best for me, what I want." Bonnie clipped at the mint, in danger of taking off a finger. "I'm not some party girl."

"Good. And be careful with those clippers." He decided to leave it at that, totally baffled as to why his sister had suddenly gotten her hackles up.

"Good." She kept clipping. "Maybe you need to worry about what you want. You're here working more than any of us. Shouldn't you be out, meeting girls?"

Not this again. "I don't need to meet anyone."

His sister's sharp laugh cut through the air. "You get so annoyed at Dad for being hardheaded, but you're just as bad."

"I'm not hardheaded."

"You're so hardheaded, you can't even admit it."

Jenna rejoined them, short of breath. "What'd I miss?"

Jude stared at Bonnie, across the herb garden. She stared back, silent.

"Nothing," he finally answered.

"Big brother here was just telling me I should be out partying and meeting boys, instead of helping the family."

"That's not what I said at all. I wasn't telling you to do anything. I was just making sure you knew what you wanted for your future."

"I know what I want, Jude. Do you? Because I want to be here, working with my family and Meredith."

"Of course you do." Jenna comforted her. "And naturally you want to include Meredith. I told you, the two of you have our support."

Jude looked back and forth between his sisters, suddenly keenly aware he was missing something. "Support with what?"

Jenna's voice was low as she huddled closer to Bonnie. "You didn't tell him? I thought you were going to tell him."

Bonnie's response was quiet too. "I tried. But I don't think he understood."

Jude stood up from his stool. "Understood what? What am I missing here?"

His sisters shared a silent look. He was clearly out of the loop.

"Bonnie and Meredith," Jenna eventually answered, "are dating."

Bonnie took a deep breath, her shoulders relaxing like a thousand pounds had been lifted from them.

Jude stood there, the coin dropping in slow motion—probably too slow, but thinking about his sister's romantic life wasn't something he ever did.

"Oh." He thought back on all the times he'd been around Bonnie and Meredith. How they did seem closer than friends, even closer than sisters. If he really thought about it, their connection was different than two buddies.

Deeper.

He'd seen the way they looked at each other, how familiar it seemed, but he couldn't put his finger on it.

Now he realized where he'd seen those kinds of gazes.

It was how Jenna looked at her husband, Max, how he caught himself looking at Aurora.

"*Oh.*" Jude said again.

He was an idiot. A stone-cold doofus, so wrapped up in work, himself, and the weird new developments in his personal life that he didn't recognize the obvious.

"Well...I...why didn't you tell me I was being dense sooner?" He grinned.

He liked Meredith. She was good people, and for him, that was all that mattered.

"We thought you knew you were oblivious." Jenna smirked.

Jude circled the herb garden. "No, I didn't. I'm oblivious to being oblivious. Come here." He reached for Bonnie and embraced her, smooshing her face into his chest in a bear hug.

He held her tight and didn't let go. "Hey. I'm happy for you. I'm sorry I didn't know, but I'm glad you told me." The hug drew out, but she clung to him, and he knew it wasn't time to let go. He pulled back enough to meet her gaze. "You know I love you, right?"

Bonnie nodded, her eyes misty.

"And I support you. In everything." He swallowed the knot in his throat. "Family *is* everything."

"You're a big softie." She smiled.

"Don't tell anyone."

They separated and Bonnie swiped at her eyes. "What about you though?"

"What about me?"

Both of his sisters stared.

"What about your love life?" Bonnie asked. "Or lack of one."

Jude cocked an eyebrow.

"You're not in high school anymore," she said. "You're a grown man and all you do is work and hang out with us."

He waved them off and picked at the mint. "I don't have time for all that. Besides, there's not really anyone who interests me."

A shrill laugh popped out of Bonnie's mouth. "Sure. Totes. I mean, definitely not the old love of your life who came by yesterday. She *definitely* doesn't interest you."

"Definitely." Jenna nodded.

"I don't even know if you can call us friends at this point, so don't go barking up that tree. That tree fell in the woods, years ago. *And*, she doesn't live here, in case you forgot. She'll probably be gone soon, hundreds of miles away."

"I don't know. I sense something there," Jenna insisted. "Bonnie?"

"Me too."

"Maybe what y'all sense is two people being polite after many years apart, and a history together." Even though she had run off when he tried to apologize. Not sure that counted as polite.

Bonnie crossed her arms, overly pensive to make a point. "Mmmm, no. That ain't it."

"The two of you have chemistry." Jenna began gathering

their snippers, deciding they were done gardening without asking for input. "You always have, and I think it's still there."

He shook his head and tried to deny it, but contrary to the way things had ended yesterday, he and Aurora had gotten along the rest of the time. They'd laughed, reminisced. She didn't seem to hate him, and he certainly had no ill will toward her. Maybe some hurt feelings, a little raw nerve, but he cared about Aurora. He always would.

He'd like for them to at least be able to talk about the past and be friendly, but spending time together was like navigating a minefield. All they knew of each other, and the hurts of their past, dotted the landscape, easily tripped and ready to blow up in their faces.

"I mean, sure, you blew it in high school, but you're older and wiser now." Bonnie smiled like she'd given him the greatest of compliments.

"If you want a second chance, this is your shot," Jenna added.

"First of all, I didn't blow it. I was immature and hasty, but—"

"You blew it," his sisters both insisted.

Jude tossed up his hands in surrender. "Fine. But I'm not gunning for another shot."

His sisters looked at him, expressionless.

"Though it would be nice, and probably healthy, to have a normal, functional friendship with her, at least for the remaining time she's here." And to have some sense of peace when it came to Aurora Shipley. Something he hadn't had for a decade.

"The two of you get along too well not to at least be

friends," Jenna agreed. "So, I guess friends is better than nothing."

There was a time when even offering his friendship felt like going out on too shaky a limb. She would've had every reason to wish to go the rest of her life and never see him again.

Yesterday gave him hope.

He wouldn't go so far as to hope they could ever be more than friends. Even if he did, putting himself out there, wanting something from her, needing her—only to be left behind again—he couldn't do it.

Yes, he'd hurt her before, but she'd hurt him too.

When she left after their breakup, never returning and never responding to him, he'd felt…unforgivable. Like the worst, rottenest creature in the world.

No, they didn't need to stay together and cost each other their dreams, their futures, but that didn't mean they had to act like the other person didn't exist. Like what they had together never meant anything.

Then again, maybe he'd deserved it. Looking back at his teenage self, he didn't know what to think. They'd both hurt each other, and he wouldn't let that happen again. If that meant only ever being friends, then friends was all they'd ever be.

Chapter 11

"Why do you think Mom invited us over?" Beth put her SUV in park and turned to them.

"She probably just misses us," Cece reasoned. "She's been gone on that long cruise and we haven't really hung out since right when Aurora came back."

"Mmm, I think there's another reason behind it." Aurora opened the passenger-side door and got out, another lavender-honey pie in her hands. She'd figured she might as well make use of the opportunity to practice her new recipe.

"Agreed." Beth hit the remote lock on her key ring. "She never wants to just *hang out* with all of us."

"Sometimes she does," Cece argued.

"With you maybe, but not us, and never all three of us together." From the time Anita Shipley moved out of the house in order to make it an inn, Aurora had never once hung out with her alone.

"Yeah, something must be up," Beth agreed.

"Y'all are so suspicious, and judgy. Lighten up."

"I'm not judging her for it," Aurora argued. "I'm stating facts. This is outside the norm. I think it's normal to wonder why, and why now."

While Cece sighed dramatically and rolled her eyes,

Beth led the way up to their mother's second-floor apartment.

After a gentle knock, Anita appeared at the door, with a tall, salt-and-pepper-haired man standing in the foyer behind her.

"See? Told you," Aurora muttered.

"Girls! Come in, come in."

Cece elbowed Aurora on the way inside.

They crowded into the foyer, each of them hugging their mom.

"You baked? Aurora, you shouldn't have. But this looks divine. And it smells so good."

Their mother's perfume fought with the pie, the weighty gardenia scent filling the apartment.

Anita had always worn the same perfume, the smell of it taking Aurora back in time. She was instantly a child again, curious about the stereotypical things that made her mother a woman. She wanted to play with the makeup, dabble in her perfume. Her mother had fussed, refusing to let her play or teach her how to apply any of it.

Beth had been the one to eventually teach Aurora about makeup, shaving, and menstrual cycles.

As a result of her mother's hands-off approach, Aurora had swung to the other end of the cosmetics spectrum, refusing to wear much makeup or perfume in high school. She was a college graduate before she ever owned more than mascara and lip gloss.

"Girls, I want you to meet Lyle. Lyle, this is Beth, Aurora, and Cece."

Lyle gave them all a smile. "I've heard a lot about you."

Aurora felt like she'd been kneecapped with a baseball bat. Who in the heck was Lyle?

"Must be nice," she muttered, and Cece elbowed her again.

"And this is Lyle. My boyfriend."

Boyfriend?

Aurora blinked.

Whatever happened to "all men are liars"? Swearing she'd never be in another relationship after their dad ran out?

What happened to "all you need are your sisters and girlfriends because they won't betray you"?

"Wow." Beth was the first to speak. "That's... great."

Their mom and Lyle smiled, waiting for more of a reaction.

"Yeah. Great," Aurora managed.

"We went on the cruise together," their mom added, "and decided to make it official while we were gone."

They all stood there for a moment, staring at one another. Their mom had gone away for almost two weeks, with a man, and they'd had no clue. Their complete lack of insight into their mom's new life shouldn't surprise Aurora, but it did.

"How did you meet?" Cece tried to fill the gaping silence.

"Here, let me take that." Lyle held out his hands for Aurora's pie. "And we can all sit down in the living room."

Numbly, Aurora gave him the pie and followed her sisters into the living room. They sat, lined up on the sofa, with their mom and Lyle on a smaller love seat.

Lyle settled his tall frame, his hands open, palms on his knees, and he rubbed them back and forth. "So... how I met your mom..."

He was nervous and hiding it poorly.

The knowledge made Aurora feel a bit better. She didn't want to be the only anxious person in the room.

"I was doing some work for your mom's friend Loretta."

"She had a new deck put in," Anita added.

"And your mom came over to see it. We got to talking and hit it off, so I asked her for her phone number."

"So I gave it to him." Anita laughed.

She gave it to him.

After years of bitterness and swearing off love, her mother just...gave some guy her number?

"We just went out for coffee at first," Lyle continued. "Then lunch, eventually dinner, and before you know it, we were dating."

"How long have you been dating?" Cece asked.

"Four months now," he answered. "Since I got her number."

Aurora sat there, blinking, and tried to digest this information.

For so long, all she'd heard from her mother about dating and men and relationships was that she shouldn't date. Disillusionment, disappointment, and distrust. All men were just like their father. They'd lie to suit themselves and walk out when the going got tough.

Then she'd met Jude and he was nothing like her mother's claims.

He was caring, supportive, and honest. He'd been a wonderful boyfriend, right up until his loyalties were really tested, and he'd failed at being able to have a relationship and balance it with the other priorities in his life.

She hadn't had the experience to recognize or label all

the problems at the time, but Jude needed to be all things to all people, and there simply wasn't enough of him to go around.

When the chips were down, and it was Aurora and a future together or his dad's approval and the farm, Jude had chosen the latter.

So, while Jude wasn't a liar, he hadn't exactly been loyal to her either. After their breakup, Aurora figured her mother was probably right, in general if not in every way.

Aurora had given up on finding love and someone to have forever and made do with finding someone for the moment. She dated a lot, never anything too serious and never for too long. Rarely intimate, and she never let anyone too close—she was happy filling her time with the distraction. Her career was demanding enough; she didn't have time for a real boyfriend.

Come to think of it, only one person had ever carried that official title.

"Aurora?" Beth looked at her, both eyebrows raised.

"What?"

"Lyle asked you a question."

"Oh. Sorry, what was that?"

"Your mom tells me you live in Los Angeles and you're a chef out there?"

"Yes." She didn't know what else to add.

"Are you planning to head back that way eventually or—?"

"She's going back soon. Aren't you, honey? She's made quite the name for herself out there. Tell him."

Made quite the name for herself? Since when did her mother keep up with her career, much less brag about her?

Had she slipped into some kind of alternate universe? Had her mother been body snatched?

"I'm, um. I'm the sous for—" Like this man would know a thing about the names of chefs and restaurant groups? "I'm assistant chef for a very popular restaurant in Los Angeles."

"Have you ever met any famous people?" Lyle's wide-eyed earnest gaze was endearing.

There didn't seem to be any guile or smarminess to him. He kept sharing warm looks with their mom, attentive to everything Aurora said. Perhaps he was a decent guy. Maybe her mom had changed her tune entirely because she'd met someone decent.

Stranger things had happened.

"I've seen a few famous people come into the restaurant. Not regularly or anything." Working in hospitality on Sunset though, it was inevitable to hear about some famous so-and-so in the dining room, as the waitstaff gossiped during and after shift.

Aurora rarely got to see anything other than the serving line.

"You'll probably be head chef soon." Lyle looked at her expectantly.

Aurora laughed. "I don't know about that."

"Don't sell yourself short, Aurora," her mom insisted. "You're always so hard on yourself. You've been with them a long time. They obviously see your value if they let you leave to help out at the Orchard Inn and then come back."

This was true. Look at her mom, talking sense instead of judging and second-guessing Aurora.

Maybe this Lyle guy was a good influence.

"Probably, but the head chef where I am now is very happy. I won't be replacing him any time soon."

She debated sharing her news, especially here of all places, but the eager enthusiasm from her mother was a refreshing change, and addictive. "I could be offered a role in a new restaurant in Malibu though."

Her sisters shared a quick glance at each other, then at her.

"That's great, honey!" Her mom beamed.

Aurora's heart clenched. Where had this approval been for the last fifteen years?

"I have to go back soon. Obviously. Just waiting to talk to my boss."

"When did this happen?" Beth's tone was more than a little accusatory, and Cece cut her eyes over at their sister.

Aurora girded her loins. "Recently."

"Why haven't you told us?"

"I just did. Besides, we knew this was coming."

Beth's stare was more than a smidge accusatory. "Then you're leaving really soon."

Aurora opened her mouth to respond, but Cece placed a hand on Beth's arm. "I think what Beth means is, first, congratulations, and we're going to miss you. Right, Beth?"

Cece stepped right into Aurora's peace-keeping role without missing a beat.

"Right," she managed to bite off the word.

"Head chef?" her mother encouraged. "That's an amazing opportunity."

Aurora fidgeted with the couch cushion, unable to fully process her mother's support. "It is. I love working at the inn, and being with family, but..."

"But?"

"I'm ready for the next step. Something of my own. And an opportunity in Malibu would be amazing and so generous."

"I know." Beth placed her hands in her lap and stared at them. "I'm sorry, it's just..."

"We've loved having you here," Cece blurted. "We love you being here and we really don't want you to leave."

"Cece." Beth jerked her head up.

"Well? It's true. We don't. You and I have talked about it."

Beth rolled her eyes with a sigh.

"You guys have talked about this behind my back? About not wanting me to go?"

"Of course we have." Cece looked at her like she was dense. "We're your sisters."

"We're proud of you." Beth smiled. "But we don't want some restaurant group to have you. Selfishly, we like having you right here."

Aurora's heart clenched again. She knew her sisters loved her, but they weren't a family that often talked about their feelings for one another. In action, she was often reminded, but it was still nice to hear.

"That means a lot," she admitted. "And we can talk about this more later. I'm sure Lyle wants to hear about more than just my job drama."

"There's so much I'd like to hear," he said. "Anita talks about y'all all the time. I feel like I already kind of know you. I want to hear the story about the last runaway bride y'all had."

"Oh my gosh." Cece slapped her hands together. "You heard about that?"

Anita laughed. “I didn’t get into all the details, so you’ll have to tell it.”

“Well, buckle up then. This tale gets wild!”

Aurora’s phone buzzed in her purse.

A way to escape the conversation and catch her breath. “I better get this,” she said, pretending it was a call.

She made her way toward a sliding glass door and stepped outside onto her mother’s balcony. She pulled out her phone, half expecting a spam text.

The message was from Jude.

I feel weird about the way we left things when I took you home. Would you be able to meet up tonight? Just for a quick chat?

Aurora sighed.

She wasn’t happy with the way the day had ended either. With anyone else, she wouldn’t think twice about a quick chat, but with Jude, every encounter was loaded.

They’d left things estranged before, and it still bothered her. Better to be grown-ups about their situation and find some peace. Rather than text back, she called him. Texts couldn’t emote, and if they were going to make amends, emotions were going to be involved.

“Hey.” Jude answered on the first ring.

“Hey. Yeah, I didn’t like how things went either. I can meet you tonight.”

“Good. That’s...that’s good. Why don’t I come get you and we can grab a coffee or—”

“Okay.”

“I want us to have a chance to talk. Alone. Not that I don’t love my sisters, but—”

"Yeah, same. Alone is a good plan. Seven thirty okay with you?"

"Perfect. I'll pick you up then."

Aurora stuffed her phone into her pocket. "It'll be fine," she tried convincing herself.

She peeked inside the glass door, watching her sisters talk animatedly with their mom. Lyle sat next to Anita, his hand on hers, smiling like he was having the time of his life.

Her mom seemed…happy. Not stressed.

She couldn't remember the last time Anita had been jovial, even kind. And paid Aurora a compliment? It'd been years.

Not to say she was a bad mother. Far from it. But she'd spent her daughters' formative years stretched thin with work and trying to deal with a man who refused to grow up and handle real responsibilities. It'd made their mom more hard than soft, more likely to push her daughters toward self-sufficiency and independence than to pull them in for a hug.

Seeing her mom this way was different. Nice. Perhaps Anita had finally found peace with someone who built her up instead of wearing her down. Aurora could only hope Lyle was the real deal. If her mother had found happiness in a healthy relationship, and Beth had found it with Sawyer, then maybe there was a chance such a thing still existed.

Chapter 12

Jude arrived at the Orchard Inn promptly at seven thirty. He went in the front door and found Aurora waiting in the main kitchen at the table with both of her sisters.

"Right on time as always." Aurora immediately got to her feet.

She still looked like sunshine in distressed jeans, sandals, and a white blouse. Her hair was down, windblown and wild, and he fought not to smile at the sight of her.

"Hey, Jude." Cece propped her chin in her hands.

"Hey." The scent of fruit and basil caught his attention and he glanced down at the two flatbreads on the table in front of him. "What's all this?"

"Aurora is trying something out." Cece pointed to each one. "This one is fig, goat cheese, and prosciutto, and this one is apricot, goat cheese, and basil. Want to try?"

"Cece," Aurora admonished.

"Of course I do." Jude already had a slice of the apricot and basil flatbread halfway to his mouth.

The sweet burst of apricot eased into the creamy richness of the cheese, and then the clean bite of the basil. "Oh, wow," he said, trying not to be rude as he chewed.

"So good, right?" Cece nodded.

It was amazing. "You made this?" he asked Aurora.

"Yeah. We should probably go."

"She's the best. And the figs and apricots came from our orchard." Cece tooted Aurora's horn for her. "And she got the basil from your farm and I got the cheese at the market. Can't get any fresher than that. Try the fig." Cece shoved a slice toward him.

"Where are y'all headed?" Beth asked as he chewed.

Jude shrugged, currently in tastebud heaven. He knew Aurora was talented, but the flatbread was out of this world.

"We'll figure it out on the way." Aurora grabbed her purse and started heading for the exit.

"Y'all are leaving right now?" Cece asked.

"Yeah," Aurora called from the hall.

Jude shrugged again. He'd thought they might visit with her sisters for at least a millisecond, but apparently not. Aurora seemed laser-focused on getting down to their talk, and he couldn't really argue. He considered a third slice for the road but decided against it. "Good seeing you both. Catch you later, I guess." He waved on his way out.

He followed Aurora outside and then led her toward his truck. "Aurora, that food was... I'm impressed."

"Thank you. I tend to cook a lot when I'm stressed."

She was stressed, huh? "Do you want to just drive around a bit then?"

"I would love to. I need to get out and get some air."

Jude popped a mint from the container in his cup holder and waited until they were in the truck and down the driveway before he asked, "Got a lot going on or just a lot on your mind?"

Aurora took a deep breath and gazed out the side window. "Both."

He kept quiet, giving her room to say more if she wanted.

"And you know how it is with siblings," she eventually added. "I love them, but everyone's got an opinion, and their opinions tend to weigh in on your life choices."

He chuckled. "Tell me about it."

She laid her head back on the head rest, turning her face toward him. "Sometimes I just need a little space from all the…I don't want to call it noise, but noise, in order to think."

"Yeah, I get it." He took a left and headed away from town. "I go for a lot of drives and errands, just to think. Keep my own counsel."

Aurora chuckled, and the sound of it danced across his skin.

"We can drive around and just listen to some music if you want."

She smiled, and he tried very hard to ignore how his body and soul reacted to making her happy. "That would be really nice. Thanks."

Jude steadied himself and found a station playing easy listening. He was happy to have the time to let Bonnie's news sink in and ponder how he'd been so blind. They drove around for a couple of songs without either of them saying a word. The sun hung lower in the sky, softening the light before a summertime late sunset.

He loved this time of day in the summer. Work was done, it wasn't quite a million degrees outside anymore, and the birds came out to socialize before nightfall. It was as though the day itself relaxed, taking a deep breath and winding down before the dark.

His family would all be together right now, everyone

taking it easy, entertaining Wyatt, probably watching or ignoring some singing contest on television. Meredith would be teasing their dad, playing name that tune. Her knowing the more modern ones, him knowing the oldies.

The thought made him smile.

"What are you smiling about over there?" Aurora asked.

Jude's gaze glanced off hers. "Just thinking about my family and..."

Should he say anything to Aurora? Was Bonnie's talk with him confidential or was being secretive an insult?

He was, once again, oblivious about what to do.

He settled on, "Bonnie and I had a talk yesterday—about her personal life. I was just thinking about it."

Aurora turned her face toward him. "What about her personal life?"

"Um..." he hesitated. "I'm not really sure I can say."

She shifted, so her body faced him too. "Was it, maybe, about her love life?"

"Yep."

She nodded, making a noise of affirmation. "About her and...?" Aurora let the question hang.

Jude glanced toward her, and immediately he knew she knew. The smile on her face, the recognition in her eyes.

He looked back to the road and again at her. "How did you know?"

"I mean, it's not hard to see how they feel about each other. If you pay attention."

He shook his head. "I guess I wasn't paying attention. But I'm glad she told me. I'm happy for her. For both of them."

"Has she told your parents?"

Jude scowled. He had no idea.

"Oh, Jude." Aurora giggled.

"What?"

"You didn't even ask her if your folks knew, did you?"

"I didn't think to ask!"

She patted his arm, humor crinkling the corners of her eyes as sparks fired beneath his skin. "Some things never change."

"What does that mean?"

"Nothing. I'm just saying, when you get home, maybe ask Bonnie if she's talked to your folks and Jenna."

He nodded, making a mental note. "Jenna knows. And I hugged her and told her I supported her. You think that was good? Was that enough?"

Aurora smiled softly. "I think that's perfect."

Her expression did something to his chest. Something painful, but pleasurable. It'd been too long since he'd seen that look on that face.

"Yeah?"

She nodded. "You're a good guy, Jude."

He tried to focus on the road, but his mind hummed.

"You want to settle somewhere? Or maybe get out and walk?" he asked.

"Let's walk," she quickly answered.

He headed west, in the general direction of some of the area's best parks and walking trails.

"Well." Aurora sighed. "Your sisters probably adore you right now. Meanwhile, mine are stewing in silence because I don't want to stay and work at the Orchard Inn forever," Aurora blurted. "They're supportive of me, but also a little mad and sad because I have to go back to L.A."

"But you just came back to help out while things were rocky, right? They knew you'd go back eventually."

"Exactly."

"And now things are good at the inn."

She nodded. "And they understand all of that, deep down. They always knew my time here was temporary, but we've had a lot of fun while I've been back, and we work surprisingly well together. I think they secretly held out a little hope I might change my mind and stay in town longer, if not indefinitely."

He couldn't blame her sisters. After only a couple of encounters, he found himself wishing Aurora would be around at least a little longer.

"They aren't mad at me or anything, but there's some tender feelings for sure."

Jude glanced toward her, trying to read her expression.

She shrugged one shoulder and kept talking. "I guess they think the hospitality lifestyle out there isn't good for me? The long hours, the grind to get to the top. I get it. Climbing the culinary ladder can be pretty cutthroat in a big city. It's just different from laidback Fredericksburg, you know?"

No, he didn't know. He'd never lived in a big city, but he could imagine.

"When do you think you'll go back?" he asked instead.

"That's the million-dollar question." Aurora let her hands flop, open palmed, in her lap. "I'm waiting to hear from the manager on a new opportunity. In that case, I'd probably leave next week or early the week after."

"And if the new opportunity doesn't pan out?" he asked, earning himself her side-eye. "Not that it won't," he quickly added.

"If I get passed up for this new restaurant, then I—" Aurora bit at her lip, and stared out the side window. "I don't know what I'll do. Go back to what I was already doing, I guess."

"Not thrilled about that second option, huh?"

She glanced his way with a smirk. "That obvious?"

"Very."

"I have to go back though. Regardless. My life is there, my stuff, my roommate."

She had a life, stuff, and roommates here in Texas, too, but he kept that observation to himself.

"It's just…I can't think that way right now, you know? I might've hurt my chances by taking this leave and coming here, but to be fair, I've worked at that restaurant *for years*. No one works one place for years in L.A. I've earned the chance to head up a new place, even after taking some family leave."

"Hey, you don't have to tell me," Jude insisted. "They'd be lucky to have you be their chef. They're idiots if they go with someone else. You could outcook everyone in town—don't tell my mom—when you were seventeen. Doesn't take a genius to figure you're three times as good now."

"Try ten times." She smiled.

"So, see?" He returned her smile. "Idiots if they don't hire you."

Her smile softened, and their gaze held. "Thank you for saying so. I guess I'm…I'm just at a crossroad with my career, and I'm ready to move forward."

Jude pulled his gaze away. "Yeah, I know."

"Thank you for listening. I don't mean to unload on you," she said.

"It's fine. I don't mind at all."

This was a huge improvement from their first interaction. He wanted them to be able to talk. They *should* be able to talk.

"I'm sorry for the other day." Aurora shifted in her seat to face him. "I know I freaked out when you apologized and then I jumped out of the car, but there's a lot of"—she motioned between them—"stuff here and I just, I didn't know how to react in that moment."

"I know." He nodded. "And it's okay. Ours is a very"—Jude chuckled—"particular kind of situation. I think it's okay if we don't know exactly how to proceed now, ten years later. But I would like for us to be friends, if possible."

Aurora studied him, her eyes scanning his face intently. "I'd like that too," she finally said.

"Good." He nodded, his heart doing backflips in his chest.

They had a ways to go, as far as friendships went, but this was a start.

He'd had Armstrong Park in mind, as a spot for them to get out and walk, but as they followed the winding road, they passed an old favorite of theirs from high school. McGregor's lake.

Aurora chuckled as they went by.

"You remember?"

"Of course I do."

"Do we dare?" Jude laughed too.

"I am *not* going swimming."

His laughter grew. "I don't mean swimming. I'm talking about the path around the lake. We can just walk and sit. Watch the sun go down."

"And trespass?"

"It's not trespassing when you're friends with the owner."

"You're friends with Old Man McGregor now?"

"He's not that old, and yes. He buys from the farm all the time now, and us from him. I can text him and let him know we're here. He's mellowed over the years, and I'm pretty sure kids come here regularly now, without all the sneaking and drama we had."

"Aw, the drama was half the fun."

He thought back to the time the two of them got chased off from an afternoon swim by the sound of McGregor's loud truck, barreling toward the pond. Jude had never seen proof firsthand, but rumor was, if he caught you swimming, McGregor would shoot. Turned out, that was all fable, and likely just his angry truck backfiring, but it made for good rumor mill fodder.

Jude turned around in the middle of the country road and went back to the driveway.

Old Man McGregor, whose real name was Tom McGregor, was in his late sixties or early seventies, far from being an old man when they were in high school, and a very generous gentleman.

Jude reached the lake, parked, and sent him a quick text. All he received in response was a thumbs-up.

"Okay, we're good to walk around," he told Aurora.

They got out and headed down a worn path. Wildflowers and grasses covered acres of fields on either side of the dirt path. Trees rose on the other side of the lake, as the path started its slow decline.

A small dock stood on the swimming side of the lake. Well, calling it a lake had always seemed generous. Large pond was more like it. On the opposite side, tall grasses and cattails dotted the lake's perimeter. It wasn't unusual to catch a heron cruising in for a landing.

"Can you believe we used to sneak onto this poor man's property? We were awful." Aurora fell into step beside him.

"We weren't so bad. We were kids. Aren't most teenagers a little selfish and stupid?"

"True."

They kept walking and reached the edge of the lake. "Let's go this way." He led her to the right, following the path that'd been worn around the edge.

"I was, um." He cleared his throat. "I was hoping we could talk. Like, *talk* talk."

Aurora nodded as she matched his pace. "Talk about the past."

"Yeah."

"I think we should," she said. "I don't want to not talk about it. We're both adults and, seeing you again, like this, I think it's..."

"It's time." He stopped walking and faced her. The sun sat even lower now, and in this golden hour Aurora glowed, her reddish-blond hair wavy, falling to her shoulders, angelic.

"I want you to know that I did love you," he said, and the hurt in her eyes broke his heart. "I don't know that you knew that, back then. I'm not sure I made it clear, and that's on me. But you can love someone and things still not—"

"Work out."

"We were in love, and then it was just—"

"Over," she finished the sentence for him.

"Yeah." He took a deep breath. "And I know I was the one who ended it. I broke up with you, but I didn't handle it right. We'd started having problems and rather than deal with them and take the time to sort things out, I got out. I was hardheaded and selfish, and I didn't think about your feelings. I thought I couldn't handle us and everything else on my plate. I was stinking up the mound in baseball, and my dad was riding my tail about that."

"I remember."

"And we were about to graduate. College was around the corner, and I knew I had to make good grades to keep my scholarship. Even though we were arguing more and more, you were still going to stay local for college, when I knew the culinary school here was not up to snuff. I mean, you needed to go to Johnson and Wales or someplace like that. Not that there's anything wrong with our community college, but you were meant for the big leagues. I knew that. But I got all caught up in being so sure I was doing the right thing, setting you free and focusing on my responsibilities, that I didn't think about what it'd mean long term. Not really." He shook his head.

"You never really told me why it was over," she said, her voice raspy. "Not back then. Not until now."

"I know." He swallowed hard, his heart aching enough to fill his chest. "And I'm so sorry. I thought it'd be easier if I just ended things. Cleaner. Not to mention I had zero clue about how to deal with my own feelings, let alone yours."

"And your dad," she offered the segue.

"And my dad was against us being together one hundred percent," he confirmed. "You were a distraction. I needed to play baseball, graduate, go to college, make straight As, and work the farm. He thought you distracted me from that path. One bad game, one D on a math test, a few nights of coming home late, a few normal, teenage spats, and you were the fly in his ointment."

Aurora nodded with a sigh. "I always knew he played a big part in our breakup. I mean, we'd started bickering, sure, but it was probably just a phase, and that was his opening. I was going to wreck everything."

"It was stupid, and if I could go back in time, I'd do things differently. I'd talk to you about things. The way I'm doing now."

She studied him again, silent. "I would do things differently too," she finally said. "I should've spoken up more. I would've made you explain yourself. I was so timid back then. I let you break up with me and barely said a word in my own defense. I just took it."

"You didn't deserve it. And I'm glad you speak up more now. I like it."

Aurora smiled sweetly, all the more beautiful now that they'd opened up. "I learned a lot from our breakup, and then from years in restaurants. There are a lot of things I'd do differently, if I knew then what I know now. Not just when it came to you."

Jude tilted his head, intrigued. "Like?"

"Well, number one, I'd deal with my mother differently. I don't know if it would've done any good, but I'd speak up for myself and let her know when some of her passive-aggressive remarks hit below the belt."

Jude and Aurora had talked about her mother a lot back in high school. Aurora always felt third best to her perfect older sister and her beloved baby sister. She also tired of her mom's criticisms and critiques. Their mom pushed all three girls hard, but none as hard as Aurora. While Beth flourished under the pressure and Cece rose to most challenges, Aurora focused only on her failings, and Anita wasn't the best at softening life's blows.

"Second, I'd confront Erica Burr about trash-talking me around school. I never confronted her when I should have."

Her last comment drew him up short. "Erica Burr talked trash about you?"

Aurora scrunched her face up. "Seriously? She totally trash-talked me, right up to when you dumped me."

Jude shook his head. "How did I not know about this?"

"Because you were a self-absorbed teenage boy?"

"True, but I normally heard some of the rumblings of high school drama."

"Erica and her little crew hated me, mostly out of jealousy, but I didn't realize that at the time. I was dating you and I wasn't supposed to be the kind of girl who dated a popular boy. I was supposed to stay in my lane. Always be the quiet little nobody."

"You were not a nobody," Jude argued.

"I flew under the radar. Way under. Dating you put a target on my back. I disrupted the social order, and I didn't have the experience with competitive girls to know how cutthroat they can be. I get it *now*. All of that drama had very little to do with me and everything to do with the dynamics in our school, but it sucked."

"I wish I'd known that was going on."

"It wasn't your battle. But then you dumped me."

He stared, unsure of what to say. "I still wish I could've helped you fight that battle. You're right though. I was so wrapped up in my own fights. My dad, his demands, the farm, the pressure of having a winning season in baseball—like it was life or death. Like I was going pro? You know how freaked out I was about the playoffs, how much it meant to me and my dad. At the time, it felt like my life depended on it. I was treated like the rest of my life really did depend on it, when really, the rest of my life had nothing to do with baseball. It was a time capsule. So important then, means so little now."

Looking back, he wondered if his slipping grades and one bad game was less about Aurora being a distraction and more about his feelings being a big distraction.

The truth was, he'd cared about her more than he had baseball or school. He recognized this now, but his dad had suspected it even then. That's why his old man had always been against their relationship.

"I know," Aurora said. "But back then, all I knew was your dad hated me and you dumped me like last week's trash. Everyone else thought it was because you were done having sex with me."

Jude thought his eyes might pop out of his head. "Wait. *What?*"

Aurora shrugged and continued like she hadn't just said what she'd said. "That was the running narrative."

"Because I was done having…? Where did— No. How am I just now hearing about this?"

She shrugged again.

Jude scrubbed a hand through his hair. "I…" He was at a loss. "Good lord, I felt crappy enough that our breakup went down so badly, but sex had nothing to do with it."

Aurora's gaze was soft, almost sympathetic, as she shook her head. "You lived in such a bubble back then. Perfect Jude Jones who no one ever said a cross word about. Clueless, never hearing all the usual gossip in school, all the crap swirling around him."

He shook his head and glanced down. She wasn't wrong. "I had no idea. I'm sorry."

"But I should've told you. I should've made sure you heard it and did something about it. Yelled and fussed, and made you open your eyes to see what was going on around you, besides your father's expectations and baseball, but I didn't. That part was my fault."

"No, that's not your fault." He placed a hand on her shoulder, hoping it was okay.

She didn't move or shove it away, so he continued. "You shouldn't have had to tell me anything. I should've seen. Plus, you weren't that kind of person yet. You still had growing to do."

Aurora leaned into his touch. "We both did."

They'd loved each other and had dreams together, but neither of them was ready for that kind of serious relationship. Looking back, he could see how much growing they'd had to do. Clinging to each other would've held them back, and they'd both gone on to pursue what they'd really wanted. He still should've talked to her before they broke up, included her in his thoughts and decision making. Maybe they could've ended things amicably and remained in touch all these years. It was his biggest regret.

"For what it's worth, I knew I'd screwed up by graduation," Jude admitted. "I'd ended things and you cut me out. I hadn't talked to you in weeks and losing you was like losing a limb. I wanted to reach out to you, I even tried a few times, but by then..."

By then it was too late. She'd refused his calls, and a man

had his pride. He couldn't go chasing after her. She was moving forward, going away to culinary school, he'd heard, and she might've taken all those steps back if they reunited.

His gaze locked with hers, hundreds of unsaid words between them and at least twice as many memories and emotions. He'd missed her over the years. He could admit that now. He'd missed her face, her smile, the way she made him laugh, the quiet comfort she provided by simply being nearby. He missed holding her in his arms, kissing her, the scent of her hair and the way she always wrapped her arms around his neck like he was her favorite thing in the world.

But most of all, he missed talking with her. Sharing and dreaming, being each other's sounding board and support.

"I know," Aurora admitted, her eyes sad. "I should've talked to you before I left for Colorado. Told you how I was feeling and what I was going through. I didn't have the courage then, but I should've sat you down and made you listen. I should've talked to your sisters too." Tears welled up in her eyes. "Instead, I ran. I was scared to face them, scared to face you. But not anymore. I'm sorry I left without a word."

He wanted to hold her so badly. Reach for her and take her in his arms, make sure she knew it was all okay. All was forgiven and he hoped she felt the same.

Aurora swiped at her eyes. "Do you think maybe we could have a hug now?"

Jude all but lunged to embrace her. "Thank god, I was hoping you'd want to hug it out."

She sniffed against his chest, burrowing deeper into the hug. "This has been a lot, but I'm glad we talked."

He brushed his cheek against her hair and closed his eyes at the smell of her shampoo. "Me too," he said with his eyes still closed.

They stood like that for a moment, until eventually she pulled away. "I have to admit, I like walking around out here, and talking, a lot better than fishing. Even with the crying, it's still better."

"I knew it," he said with a smile. "I always suspected you hated it, but you insisted it was great, and just went along."

"I know. I *hated* fishing." She returned his smile as they began walking again. "But you loved it, and I got time alone with you, so I just went. Stinky old bait and all."

"That bait was crazy stinky." He laughed.

They walked quietly for a while, stopping when a flock of geese flew overhead and landed in the lake for a swim. The evening air began to cool, only slightly, and the cicadas started warming up for their sunset performance.

Their time together out here had done him a world of good. His soul felt...lighter. More at ease. One thing she'd said still weighed on his mind though.

"I do have a question about something though," he started. "Where did anyone get the idea that I was with you only for sex?"

Aurora shook her head, looking as baffled as he felt. "Erica started a rumor and everyone at school believed it, except my sisters."

He blinked at her, attempting to compute.

"I thought you knew that was the running story."

"No, I never heard that. It's ridiculous." He scowled. "That Erica Burr was mean as a snake."

"You're telling me. Now I know she was being a

spiteful teenage girl, trying to put me in my place, but at the time it killed me."

He widened his eyes for effect. "We weren't even having sex."

"I know." She shook her head. "But that's too boring for the gossip mill. No one wanted to believe that."

He shrugged and ran his hand across a cattail. "I guess we went parking and made out enough to make it a little unbelievable." Still, he'd like a time machine to go back ten years and kick everyone's butt who'd spread that rumor.

"If I remember correctly." Aurora smiled. "A lot of that making out was right here at the lake."

"I believe you're right." The memories warmed his skin as the evening breeze blew cool. "I was way too nervous to take it any further though. I thought, What if I do it wrong? And I didn't want to upset you or pressure you. I didn't want to lose you if we did something we weren't ready for or because I didn't know what the heck I was doing."

She gaped. "Like I did?" Aurora shook her head with a smirk. "The Shipley sisters got no birds-and-bees talk from Mom, and Beth was as buttoned up as they got, probably well into college."

"Dad was the same. He didn't talk about puberty, sex, none of it. What I knew, I learned from the locker room, and turned out none of it was reliable. Some of my friends had started having sex, and they'd talk about it, which did *not* help me. At all. And with everything I had going on, and younger sisters at home—how they'd talk about guys pressuring them. I knew you weren't ready, and I didn't want to rush us, but I also didn't—y'know—I didn't want to have sex with anyone else."

"Aww, Jude." She batted her eyes at him, teasingly, and he thrilled at the realization they'd come far enough to joke with each other.

They could make light of things again, smile and laugh. The damage from their breakup wasn't irreparable. And man, he'd missed her.

"You know what I mean. Besides, I was perfectly happy with our marathon make-out sessions."

She elbowed him.

"What?" He shrugged off her weak punch to the arm. "It's true. Those were great, and I think we're old enough to talk about it without being coy."

Aurora stopped walking and considered him. "Fair enough," she said.

While it was a bit surreal talking about this with her now, it mostly felt natural. Like she was the one person in the world he *could* talk to about this.

Aurora reached out and placed her hand on his forearm. "Listen, thank you for initiating this. For the talk. I was really hurt back then and, even though I moved on, part of me always wanted resolution."

"And we never got it," he added.

"Exactly. Regardless of all the ins and outs, we did break up. It was over, and that's what made me realize I needed to start living my life for me. You had other stuff in your life. Priorities. Everyone had their own life, and I needed mine."

Exactly what he'd feared most back then. Their relationship, their love, was holding her back. Aurora was loyal to a fault, and she would've given up her dreams for him. He'd had to let her go, even after he knew what a mistake he'd made.

Aurora sighed, crossing her arms as if she were chilled. "Leaving the nest was good for me though. I wasn't exactly the picture of confidence and maturity back then."

"Eh." He waved her off. "You were perfect."

"Ha! That was my sister Beth."

"Oh, that's right." He tapped his chin dramatically, drawing up a memory. "I remember her tattling on us over Christmas break, because you missed curfew."

Aurora's eyes flew wide. "That's right! I forgot about that. She was home from college, the little snitch, otherwise Mom would've never known."

"And we weren't that late, but you woke her up sneaking in."

"She was just mad because I had a boyfriend, and she didn't."

Jude remembered how indignant Aurora had been. She'd gotten grounded and was so angry.

"I didn't see you again until the end of winter break," he recalled.

They mused at the memory, a stillness falling around them. He'd missed her terribly during their time apart. He remembered thinking he never wanted to be apart like that again.

Another memory came to his mind, of their reunion. A warm fire and even warmer embraces. Kissing and touching and talking about forever.

Once Aurora had been released from her house arrest, she and Jude had reunited on New Year's Eve. Beers and a bonfire and later, in Jude's first pickup truck, they'd almost gone all the way.

Aurora cleared her throat and glanced away.

She was, undoubtedly, remembering the same moment.

She'd asked him to wait, and he had been perfectly fine with that.

Then she told him she loved him, and his heart had soared higher than the fireworks that night. Her love was all he could've wanted and more. The rest would wait until they were ready.

Jude turned toward Aurora to find her looking up at him.

Ten years disappeared in an instant, and they were back at this same lake, two teenagers, crazy in love.

She looked almost the same. Her face was a little slimmer, her hair a little longer, and there was a lot more wisdom and experience in her eyes. But she was still Aurora, and he was as attracted to her as he had been years ago. Arguably more.

He still cared about her too.

Deeply.

"Jude," she said, his name falling from her lips like a question.

The notion was insane, inappropriate—he wanted to kiss her.

Right here, right now, with fireflies dancing across the field and into the trees, the sun so low it was an orange sliver in the distance.

Her breath quickened, as if she knew. As if she'd let him, or even wanted him to.

Aurora swayed toward him and he acted. Not another thought in mind except this woman and this night, and all the time they'd lost.

Jude kissed her. His hand on her cheek and then in her hair, he kissed her. And she let him. Parting her lips, sweetly, softly. They lingered, a gentle brush of her tongue, and he felt like flying.

The rumble of an automobile and the shriek of laughter jerked them from their moment. Aurora jumped back as Jude searched for the intrusive noise.

A van bounced over the hill and barreled toward the lake.

"We have company," Aurora murmured, a touch of pink in her cheeks.

The van rolled to a stop near the lake's edge and a gaggle of teens poured out, laughing and talking loudly, some hand-in-hand, towels draped over shoulders.

He knew this scene. He and Aurora had *been* this scene once.

"It's probably time for us to go," Aurora said.

"Yeah." But he didn't want this to be the end.

He wanted to kiss Aurora again. He wanted more time with her. More talking, more laughing. He wanted to turn back the clock and have endless days in her company, making her happy, sharing more of life. They'd missed out on so much, and he wanted to make up for lost time.

But he couldn't.

Aurora was leaving, maybe in a matter of days, and, like before, he'd have to let her go.

Except this time, he didn't know if he could.

Chapter 13

Beth was tapping the side of her tablet with her stylus, the sound creating a rhythm in Aurora's head.

Kissed. Jude. Kissed. Jude.

She'd kissed Jude last night.

Aurora pulled her knees up to her chest, adjusting her weight on the living room couch. Just kissing her high school sweetheart, all impulsively and thoughtlessly, like she didn't know better. Nothing to worry about here, folks.

She was certain the admission was written on her forehead for her sisters to see.

I kissed Jude last night.

She'd clearly lost her mind. It couldn't happen again. Correction. It wouldn't happen again, so there was no need to tell Beth and Cece.

Aurora eyed them suspiciously. Could they tell? Did they already know?

Beth studied the notes on her tablet, oblivious to everything except the plans in front of her face. "Okay, listen up. Erica said she wanted simple and understated when it comes to both menu and décor for the wedding and reception. It's going to be a small ceremony with a limited guest list."

Aurora bit her tongue, figuring the less she said this morning, the better. But the fact remained, the Erica she'd known was the exact opposite of understated.

"What's that look for?" Beth had stopped studying her notes and was staring at her.

Uh-oh. Had her face betrayed her? It was always doing that. "What look?" she asked, hoping she sounded innocent.

"You rolled your eyes."

"No, I didn't."

"Yeah, you did," Cece added.

Ugh.

She was trying to be the bigger person here, regardless of the past. Lift one another up, women supporting women, and all that. Besides, all their drama was ages ago. She should just let it go.

"I just... *understated* and Erica?" Aurora quirked her eyebrows. "Are we sure this is the same woman? Because the Erica I went to school with rented a pink stretch Hummer for homecoming. The dance where a few of our classmates wore denim, and everyone drove their own cars. It was at the Lion's Club for crying out loud."

"I'm telling you, I've heard she's changed," Cece insisted.

Did people change *that* much?

"Maybe. But I can't grasp her having thirty people at her wedding. She'd be more likely to have three hundred. She also would *never* have her wedding here."

Beth, bless her heart, looked offended.

"No, not because there's anything wrong with the Orchard Inn," Aurora clarified. "But that's how snooty she was. First, she would've never lowered herself to get married somewhere that involved me. Second, she'd want this huge ordeal at the finest hotel in Dallas. Or, better yet, a destination wedding in, I don't know, Hawaii. Then all of her guests would be expected to shell out thousands of dollars to see her on her big day because she's just *soooo* important."

Her sisters were quiet, staring at her.

"What?"

Cece whistled quietly.

Okay, maybe she wasn't quite ready to be the bigger person yet.

Beth stepped closer, sympathy all over her face.

"Don't give me that look." Aurora crossed her arms.

"You don't have to help with any of this, okay? I know it's weird and she was awful to you. You're being gracious enough by not insisting I tell her to hit the bricks."

Aurora chuckled despite herself. "I know, but I'm not *that* wounded."

Truthfully, she wasn't sure why all of this was spewing out now. Probably because she'd dug up old bones last night with Jude. And then kissed him.

Erica Burr had used Jude, and Aurora's relationship with him, to hurt her. Getting close to him again brought up a lot of old memories.

So this was kind of Jude's fault.

"I'm a grown woman and I'm a professional," Aurora told her sisters—and herself. "I just needed to get that off my chest. Please, continue with the plans for this intimate affair to remember."

"Hello?" a voice called from the foyer.

Aurora and her sisters stared at one another. They weren't expecting anyone to visit this morning.

"Hello?" Aurora called out.

"It's Jenna and Max." The voice got closer. "Oh, hey, here y'all are." Jenna and her husband, Max, rounded the corner into the inn's sitting room.

The sisters rose to their feet to greet the couple. Aurora had only heard about Jenna's husband recently, from Cece. He worked on an oil rig offshore and was often gone for weeks, even months, at a time.

"I hope it's okay that we came by."

"Of course." Cece hugged Jenna in greeting. "I told you y'all could come by."

"My mom is keeping Wyatt today, so we have a little time to ourselves. Thought we'd visit on our way into town."

"That's great. You deserve some couple time, just the two of you," Beth said. "Come on in. We'll show you around."

As Beth and Cece gave the couple the tour, Aurora went to work on her form of hospitality. She made fresh lemonade and little chicken salad and pimento cheese finger sandwiches to have ready for afterward.

You never left guests or friends unfed.

"Come on out to the gazebo when you're done," she called to the group.

She arranged the tray of sandwiches on the table in the center of the gazebo and set up five glasses full of ice next to a large pitcher of fresh-squeezed lemonade.

Her strengths might not include the attention to detail of Beth or the natural welcoming nature of Cece, but by gosh, she could put together some tasty food in a snap.

"My goodness, Aurora. You didn't need to do this." Jenna's delighted expression said she was glad she did though.

"I know, but I thought everyone might be getting peckish, and it's nice out here. An added touch for your day date." Aurora quickly filled each glass with lemonade before she sat down.

"You're so considerate. You always have been." Jenna sat down right beside Aurora, with Max on her other side.

Beth joined them, but it was Sawyer with her and not Cece.

"Look who showed up at the back door." Beth took her fiancé's hand. "Cece had a phone call, but she said she'd join us in a sec."

So, just Aurora and the couples?

Normally, she'd think nothing of it, but after yesterday, she wasn't feeling as fabulous about being the fifth wheel. She'd been single forever—it seemed—and that had never bothered her. Why did it matter now?

"How was the tour?" she asked, trying to wipe such thoughts from her mind.

"Amazing. You guys have such a great place here. We're so impressed."

"I've heard you put on quite the shindig too." Max picked up a napkin and a sandwich. "A buddy of mine came to the Silva-Meyers wedding and couldn't stop talking about how much fun he had."

Beth and Sawyer exchanged glances.

"That was a special night indeed." Sawyer grinned.

"That's right. You two got engaged that night. I heard your brother is very happy now too."

"He is. He takes Shelby riding now on the weekends. Easy trails only. They're doing great."

"Aw." Jenna tilted her head. "Good for them. Have you two picked a wedding date yet?"

Aurora took in the sight of Beth and Sawyer.

So obviously in love, happy, and content. Sure, they probably had their moments, like all couples, but the minor irritations, the tedious spats, were nothing next to the support, trust, and unconditional love and connection they'd obviously found in each other.

She'd never seen Beth so happy, so anchored, and yet so free to soar.

Her sister had found the kind of love people dreamed of, and Aurora was happy for her and so thankful that she'd found someone like Sawyer. Still, she'd be lying if she said there was no bittersweetness to seeing other people's happily ever after.

At eighteen, she'd been silly enough to think she'd found hers in high school. Life had taught her that people and relationships were way more complicated than teenage love. True, enduring love was hard won, and elusive, but she still believed in it.

When the time was right, when she was ready, love would find her again. And this time, she'd know how to handle it.

Aurora came back to earth and took a sip of her lemonade. "So, what's new with you guys?" she asked Jenna, ready to steer the conversation away from weddings and relationship bliss.

"Working, working, working. We're busier than ever." Jenna's smile appeared strained. "It's been... well, with a baby, it's been a lot."

Max placed a hand on her leg, patting as if to comfort. "Things are going well at the farm, but I've missed out on a lot on the rig."

Jenna nodded. "And we've been missing him. Today

has been nice, having some time together. But..." She shared a quick glance with her husband, before shifting to face Aurora. "I have a confession. Wanting to see the inn wasn't our only reason for coming here today."

"Okay...?" A sense of foreboding tunneled down to Aurora's stomach.

"I wanted to talk to you about what I mentioned at the farm. The thing I wanted to pick your brain about. Jude said y'all talked about it a bit."

"The restaurant?"

"Yeah."

Aurora sighed and fought the urge to shake her head. "We talked about it briefly, but he made it clear your dad isn't a fan of the idea. Plus, if you think you're busy now, a restaurant will only make that worse."

"I know but"—Jenna glanced at Max again—"we may get more help soon and this isn't just about what my dad wants. This would be for our whole family. I'd like to know what *you* think."

"I think it's a good idea. I told Jude as much, but he made it seem like, without your father's blessing, the whole thing is a nonstarter."

Jenna nodded. "Jude's stuck between a rock and a hard place. He's the one who has to deal with Dad, and that's never easy."

"Does Jude really want to open a restaurant?" Because he'd seemed noncommittal to Aurora. He'd always had a lot of ideas for the farm, but that's what most of them had remained.

"I know he does. Of all our ideas, having a restaurant is our favorite."

This time, Aurora did shake her head. "Jenna—"

"I know what you're going to say, but I definitely want to pursue this, and Jude does too. He only hesitates because of Dad. You know more about restaurants than anyone else I know, so I was hoping maybe you could talk to us sometime."

Aurora could help, absolutely. But was this the best idea? Encourage your ex-boyfriend's sister to consider something that he didn't seem to be one hundred percent sold on and their father was one hundred percent against.

They all studied Aurora as she sat there in silence.

"I just want to pick your brain a little." Jenna stared at her with big blue eyes like her brother's, but nowhere near as mesmerizing.

Aurora was not about to get between Jude and his father again. No thank you.

"Jenna, I'm not sure I'm someone who should get involved with this."

"I know what you're thinking and it's not like that. We'd just be talking. You don't have to be *involved* involved."

Aurora leveled a look at her friend. The line between talking and getting involved was thin.

"Okay, but we're just talking. I can spitball some ideas with y'all, but first, I suggest you find out if Jude is completely on board."

Everyone continued to stare, Jenna slowly lifting her eyebrows.

"Oh no." Aurora sat up straighter. "No, no, no. I'm not talking to Jude for you."

Jenna touched her arm. "Aurora, he'll listen to you. He loves the idea of a restaurant; I know he does. Talk to him and you'll see. He only hesitates because of Dad's naysaying, and because Jude doesn't know enough about the business to fight him on it. Jude respects you, and you *do* know the business. If you talk to him, it'll give him the push he needs."

She scoffed. "He isn't going to listen to me. Jude makes up his own mind about things."

Jenna shook her head, adamant. "He *always* listens to you. I came here today because he told me what you said about the old barn he remodeled, and how y'all discussed ideas for a restaurant. You should've seen how he lit up. I was ready to let the idea die a painful death, at least for the next few years, but when he told me how much you liked the barn and envisioned it making a great location…his excitement got me excited again."

Aurora frowned. Why hadn't he shared any of that excitement with her? "He told you about that?"

"He couldn't wait to tell me."

Aurora blinked back her surprise. Jude had listened to her ideas for the farm, even after that day ended awkwardly. Wonders never ceased.

"If you bring it up to Jude, he'll talk your ear off, I promise."

Aurora shook her head. She couldn't believe she was considering this.

Then again, she did know restaurants. She'd not only studied culinary arts, but she'd taken business classes. She'd helped her sisters develop their business, and then come back home and saved the catering and food service side of the inn.

Come to think of it, Aurora might be the perfect person to help Jenna—outside of the whole ex-boyfriend-whom-she-kissed-last-night side of things.

She could give Jude and his sisters information, inspiration, and some cold hard facts about what they needed to consider before going down this path. But these plans and getting involved wasn't only about logic. There were emotions here, a history. And plenty of both to muddy the waters.

Aurora took a fortifying sip of her lemonade and set the glass down. "*If* I talk to Jude, and to you guys about restaurant basics, that does not mean I'm involved when it comes to your dad."

Jenna tilted her head and scrunched her brow.

"I have to draw the line there. When it comes to John Jones, my involvement won't benefit anyone." Including herself. "Your father hates me."

Jenna's mouth fell open. "No, he does not."

"Might want to check your math on that. He didn't like me ten years ago, and it's obvious he doesn't like me now. I distracted Jude from his future, from the farm, from his obligations and opportunities. Your father wanted me gone so Jude could focus on what mattered."

The crease between her brows deepened, but she nodded. "Dad was way too tough on Jude. Still is, really. I think he figured Jude was so into you that he was going to screw up his future. But I thought y'all broke up because you decided to go to culinary school out of state."

Aurora shook her head. "We broke up weeks before I decided to go out of state."

"Oh." Jenna quirked her lips. "I…I didn't know that." She stared into her lemonade. "So my dad probably pressured Jude to—"

"Probably. But Jude made the decision to end things."

Aurora studied the top of Jenna's head and felt the heat of everyone else's gaze.

"That's all in the past, of course," she quickly added. "But you can see why it makes sense for me to not be involved when it comes to your dad."

Jenna glanced up, her gaze soft with sympathy. "Yeah. Still, you're the best person for us to talk with. You're smart and talented, you know the industry, and, more importantly, you'll be honest with us. There are always folks who tell you only what you want to hear. You'll give it to us straight."

This was also true. How was she supposed to say no? This was a childhood friend, asking for help. She couldn't refuse.

"Fine. I'll have a chat with Jude and tell y'all as much as I can about restaurants."

Jenna smiled like Aurora had just promised her the world. "Thank you!"

Aurora nodded and changed the subject back to weddings and the inn.

They all polished off the sandwiches and lemonade, and at the top of the hour, Max stood up to stretch and announce the end of their visit. "Well, thank you so much for showing us around, and feeding us."

Jenna thanked Aurora again, and they all said their goodbyes.

Once their guests were gone, Aurora retreated to her room, pondering when she'd see Jude again and have the opportunity to broach the subject of a restaurant at the farm.

She could simply call him up and ask him to hang out. Grab a coffee or something to eat.

Was that too much like a date?

If they were friends now, they could share a meal and it wouldn't be a date, right? Even though they'd just kissed each other.

Aurora sat on the floor by her bed and buried her face in her hands. How had that become a thing that happened? She couldn't casually kiss Jude Jones! She couldn't casually *anything* Jude Jones.

Yet, the sun had been low, the evening gentle, and the moment intimate. He'd had that look in his eyes and being near him felt natural. The kiss felt right.

But it wasn't.

There was no such thing as harmless flirtation when it came to him. There could be no trips down memory lane to see if the flame could still catch fire. No encore performance and no reunion tour.

"Don't be a glutton for punishment," she told herself.

Running her hands through her hair, she sat up straight and took a deep breath.

"Focus on the positives." She and Jude were on better terms now. They'd made huge progress. They were going to be fine. Friendly.

She could ask him for coffee. No big deal, just buddies catching up while they still could.

Staring straight ahead, a shimmering title caught her eye: *The Mesa.*

Her senior yearbook.

With a snort of laughter, Aurora crawled over and pulled the book from her bookshelf.

The yearbook staff had gone with a modern look that year. Geometric patterns and funky, bold colors, even a paint splatter look on the inside cover. Not their finest creation over the years, but it did stand out on the shelf.

Aurora opened it, flipping through the first section of color photos. Pep rallies and ball games. Homecoming and pageants. Kids on campus being…kids.

There were interesting fashion choices and lots of goofy faces. Evidently scarves had been a big thing, because they wore a lot of them, even though it was rarely *that* cold in Texas. There also seemed to be a tendency to layer tank tops.

"What were we thinking?" She shook her head.

She found the candid pictures from Home Economics, where she'd been a teacher's aide during her free period. The Home Ec teacher let Aurora lead the class when it came time to cook.

Those sophomores had so much fun cooking pizzas with Aurora that they asked for another cooking section at the end of the semester. Aurora had kept it simple enough, with pasta dishes, but they'd made homemade pasta and sauces for their final grade. The results of her pasta lessons became legend over Christmas break.

"Pasta princess." Aurora used the underclassmen's silly nickname for her and smiled, running her fingers across the black-and-white photos.

Some of her high school memories were good. Great even.

"You say something?" Beth popped her head into Aurora's room.

Aurora glanced up, still smiling at the images before her. "No, just reminiscing. And laughing at how cool we used to think we were. How many tank tops did you layer when you were in high school?"

Beth stepped in, glancing down at the open yearbook in Aurora's lap. "Oh, wow. So many." She laughed. "At least you missed the UGGs phase. We all wore UGGs in eighty-plus-degree weather. And bedazzled pockets on our jeans. It hurt to sit down sometimes."

Aurora snorted a laugh. "I forgot about those."

"So..." Beth straightened her blouse and fidgeted with her bracelet, clear signs she had something on her mind. "Are you going to call Jude and see him again?"

Aurora slouched under the weight of that question. "Looks like it."

"You said the last visit went well."

"It did." *I kissed him*, her mind echoed. "We talked, finally, and I think we're at a good place now. We made peace with the past, but I don't want to jinx it." Or end up kissing him again.

"You won't jinx it."

Aurora cocked an eyebrow. "If I get too involved or offer up too much advice, I might step on some toes. I can be a little pushy at times now, and Jude can be as stubborn and proud as his dad."

"Good thing you don't know anyone else like that."

"Hey!"

"I meant all of us. You, me, Cece. You have plenty of experience dealing with determined, prideful personalities."

"I guess I never thought about it like that."

"It's just my opinion, but I think your conversation will be the opposite of a jinx. He knows you're the best person to give advice on a restaurant and, sure, maybe they decide not to go through with it, but at least you offered your help."

Aurora stared at her old yearbook.

The idea of Jude needing her help and seeing her as any kind of expert on a matter did funny things to her stomach.

His opinion of her shouldn't matter as much as it did, but she'd never stopped caring what he thought. That's why the years after their breakup were so difficult. She didn't want him to resent her or view her and their time together as a mistake. She cared about how he felt. She cared about him, and probably always would.

"Okay." Beth backed toward the bedroom door. "I'm going to butt out now, but good luck."

Once her sister left the room, Aurora flipped to the back of the yearbook, to the next to last page, where Jude's inscription took up the entire page.

What really mattered was the last sentence.

I can't wait to spend forever with you,
making our dreams come true.

They'd had so many dreams, so many plans. Their lives had turned out okay without each other, yet thinking about what could've been made her heart ache. Maybe, even if they hadn't ended up spending forever together, she could still help Jude make his dreams come true.

That's what friends did after all.

Before she lost her nerve, Aurora picked up her phone and tapped out his number.

Again, he answered on the first ring.

"Aurora. Hey."

"Hey." She smiled at the surprise in his tone. "I was

wondering if you wanted to grab a coffee or dessert later?"

"Yeah, absolutely. How about Lucky's Diner?"

"Sounds good. Is after dinner okay?"

"Works for me. Just text me when you're leaving the inn. See you there."

Aurora hung up, her heart hammering like she'd just asked a boy to a Sadie Hawkins dance. She wasn't going to overthink her reaction *or* how long it took her to get ready to see him.

Chapter 14

Jude was already waiting for her when she arrived at Lucky's Diner. He sat facing the door at the last booth in the corner.

Their booth.

"You look nice," he said as she sat down.

She'd finally settled on a casual sundress. Yes, it was a great color for her—sage green—and yes, it accentuated her shoulders and neckline, *but* it was casual.

Just like the two of them.

Casual and friendly. Just two casual friends, hanging out.

"I went ahead and ordered two coffees and got menus," he said.

"Smart move. I might get some fries too. I had an early dinner snack thingie and I'm still hungry."

"Dinner snack thingie," he repeated with a furrowed brow.

"You know. Finger sandwiches. I ate a bunch of them, but it's not enough to count for real dinner."

"Well, I did have real dinner, but I can't sit by and let you eat fries without participating. Let's get the large and split it." He popped open his dessert menu.

Splitting a large fry basket was what they had done in high school. She couldn't eat all the fries in a regular order, so she wouldn't order any. But when she stole Jude's, she'd end up eating half of them and he was left with a gaping fry void.

Solution: split the large fry. With a side of ranch dressing.

The memory warmed her, and she bit back a smile, remembering the time she'd cross-contaminated his ranch with some ketchup from one of her fries.

She might as well have spat right in that little white paper cup of homemade ranch for how he reacted.

"What are you grinning about over there?" he asked now.

"Do you still order ranch with your fries?"

"Here I do, are you kidding? Best homemade dressing in the tri-county area. And you better not get your nasty ketchup in my ranch either. Don't think I've forgotten about that."

Aurora laughed.

"It wasn't a little bit either." He scowled. "Big ol' blob of ketchup right in my ranch. You turned the whole thing pink."

Aurora laughed harder. "Didn't you order a second cup?"

"I had to! You ruined it. They charged me for extra too." His laughter tangled into hers. "That's like getting cheese sauce in the salsa."

"I used to do that as well, huh?"

"All the time!" He shook his head good-naturedly. "Just dippin' all haphazard, cheese globs in the salsa. Ketchup in the ranch. It was chaos."

Her cheeks hurt from smiling at his outrage.

Spending time with Jude was so refreshing. There were no false airs about him. His genuine, down-to-earth personality and unpretentious nature were completely different from most of the people she'd met in L.A.

There were no guys like Jude in Los Angeles. At least, none that she'd ever met.

"I'm glad you called me," he said. He put his elbows on the table and leaned closer, as if confiding a secret.

His eyes, already ridiculously blue, were brighter in the lighting, and she was close enough to make out the gray around his iris.

She probably didn't need to be this close to him again.

"I know we..." He tilted his head to the side, conspiratorially. "You know."

Kissed. Jude.

"We kissed," she blurted what'd been repeating in her mind all day.

He had the grace to look a bit bashful. "But I hope that doesn't...I don't want to make it weird. You know?"

"Yeah." She did know.

"We got caught up in the moment. Maybe?" He offered them both a safe excuse. A way to make it okay and not threaten the progress they'd made toward amends.

"Yes," she said with a sigh. "The moment."

"Right. But it's okay. We're good, right?"

Aurora took a breath, alarms of self-preservation ringing in her head. He was still too good-looking, too charming, too funny and nice, and too familiar. Being on the outs with Jude Jones had been her only protection over the years. Now she was defenseless.

What if they had another moment like by the lake?

If he got that look in his eyes again, if he leaned in

to kiss her, was she strong enough to say no? Push him away and run?

No. Probably not.

"Right," she said. "We're all good."

The waitress arrived with their coffees. They ordered the basket of fries; Aurora ordered a slice of pecan pie and Jude ordered the apple. Same as always.

"You could branch out, you know? Try something different," she teased. "Do you ever get anything besides apple from here?"

"Why fix it if it ain't broken?" He held up his hand, ticking off his points on his fingers. "Apple is a classic, it's the only one you automatically get a la mode—unless you say otherwise—and it's their best."

"Agree to disagree there. Unless something has changed, their pecan pie is the best."

"Oh, really?" He leaned back, looking entirely too smug. "Because it's the apple they're entering in the big pie contest for the jamboree."

"Guess I'll have stiff competition then."

His eyes widened. "You are not."

She shrugged. "Don't laugh. I told my sisters I'd do it if I was still in town."

Those last three words bounced around her brain, a small knot forming in her stomach, but she wasn't sure why.

"Why would I laugh?"

"I don't know. Pie contests at local festivals aren't in my usual repertoire." But, since she'd made the lavender-honey pie, more and more recipes had come to mind. Ways to improve the base, new interpretations on old classics like pecan, peach, and, yes, even apple.

She was, dare she say, inspired.

"Oh, so you think you're too good for our lil' ol' jamboree contest?" he teased.

"I did not say that. It's just not what I normally do."

"Well, regardless, I wasn't going to laugh. I'm just mad I didn't act fast enough to get you to bake our pie for the contest."

"*You* entered the contest?"

Jude's laughter rippled across her skin. "No, *I* didn't do anything. My dad agreed to the contest, but no one has stepped up to actually make the pie for our entry. We're all playing this big game of Not It. Fun times, everyone avoiding the task until the last minute, and then I'll probably go buy a lemon meringue from the store and play dumb."

"You could make a pie."

He snorted. "I could make a mess."

"No, I'm serious. A real, legitimate pie. Pie recipes can be very forgiving if you keep it simple. I could help you find an easy recipe. An icebox pie or something. Very little skill involved."

"Little skill. That's my tagline in the kitchen."

Aurora gave up fighting how easily he made her smile and laugh. And on keeping any kind of distance.

"I could walk you through it," she offered.

Jude suddenly went quiet, no longer joking around. He leaned forward again. "You'd really do that?"

"Of course."

She wanted to help him, if she could. Part of her even needed to help. Prove that they could be friends and be good for each other.

"I will gladly take you up on the help, but what happens when I beat you in the contest?"

Aurora quirked her lips. "I don't think we need to worry about that."

"We don't?" He grinned as the waitress delivered their fries and cup of ranch.

"No, we do not. Eat your ranch."

They shared the fries and talked about what might be the easiest pie to make. In the end, they settled on a lemon cream icebox pie—a simple recipe with only a few ingredients, equally sweet and tart, cool and refreshing.

Their diner pies arrived, and they each cut into their own before sharing some with each other.

"Mine is better," she announced.

"I don't have enough time to tell you how wrong you are. Mine is better." He licked a smear of ice cream from his lips.

Aurora glanced away, and someone outside caught her eye.

Erica Burr. Walking up the sidewalk, into the diner, a man trailing behind her.

"Crap," Aurora muttered with her mouth full. She was supposed to have until tomorrow to deal with Erica.

"What?" Jude leaned toward the window, following her gaze.

The door jingled, announcing her arrival.

He looked at Aurora with comically wide eyes. "Guess her ears have been burning."

"Jude," Erica exclaimed as soon as she saw them. "Aurora. Hey. I heard you were in town."

"Hey," Jude said.

"This is crazy seeing y'all here." Erica brushed her long red hair back over her shoulder.

"You too," Aurora managed.

"This is my fiancé, Ted. Ted, these are some old high school friends of mine."

They all made introductions and Aurora pasted on a smile. High school friends? Since when?

Ted looked annoyed at his meal being delayed by their introductions.

"I guess I'll be seeing you tomorrow, won't I?" Erica tilted her head the other way, her hair swinging again.

"Sure will. Are you excited?" Aurora used a little too much inflection on the question, trying not to cringe at how forced she sounded.

"I don't have to go to that, right?" Ted huffed and crossed his arms.

"No." Erica feigned a laugh that was more forced than Aurora's enthusiasm. "Dear. Of course not. Just us girls, right, Aurora?"

"Right." A pang of inexplicable sympathy rose in Aurora's chest. Ted's attitude was . . . well, it sucked.

"Thank god." Ted restlessly looked around the diner. "You can deal with all of that."

All of that being *their wedding*?

"Well . . ." Erica pasted on a big smile. "I guess I'll see you tomorrow."

"See you then."

"Nice meeting you, Ted," Jude added, no doubt just being nice.

"Yeah. Likewise."

Jude widened his eyes as they walked away, taking a seat at the opposite end of the diner.

"Wow." He mouthed the word to her.

"Right?" she mouthed back.

He hunched his shoulders, whispering conspiratorially. "What was that about her seeing you tomorrow?"

Aurora realized Jude wouldn't know anything about that new development in her life. She leaned in, whispering back. "She's having her wedding at the Orchard Inn."

"Shut up," he hissed.

"As I live and breathe."

He shook his head and mouthed *wow* again. "That seems weird to me."

"You're not the only one."

"That guy had the personality of this saltshaker." He nodded toward the basket of condiments on their table.

"Not even. That saltshaker seems nice."

Jude grinned and sat back. "Well, Godspeed to both of them."

Ditto, Aurora thought. She couldn't imagine spending the rest of her life with someone like Ted.

To be fair though, it'd gotten pretty difficult to imagine spending her life with anyone. She'd yet to meet someone in her dating adventures whom she could tolerate longer than a couple of months.

Chefs were notoriously difficult to date, with long, late hours, a giant helping of stressful working environments, and sprinkles of neurosis. That wasn't the only reason though.

She couldn't find anyone who fit. Her partner needed to be patient, supportive, good-humored, and independent. And she wasn't about to settle for someone like Ted.

Jude dabbed his mouth with his napkin, the fries and his slice of pie gone. "Told you mine was better. You still have half of yours left. Thus, it is the subpar pie."

He grinned, teasing her—some might even say flirting with her—and Aurora felt it all the way down to her toes.

She shouldn't entertain this, but it was too fun to resist.

"Then I guess you wouldn't be interested in the rest of my subpar pie." She pushed her plate aside.

"I didn't say that." He tugged her plate in front of him. "Thank you very much."

He'd always been willing to finish what she couldn't eat. At seventeen, he'd been a veritable bottomless pit for snacks, leftovers, and treats.

Aurora shook off the past, willing herself to focus on the present. Broaching the restaurant topic was trickier than one might think.

This was Jude and his family. This was important.

"I wanted to talk to you about something."

"Sounds ominous," he said around a bite of pie.

"No. Not really. Your sister wanted me to talk to you about the restaurant idea some more."

Jude swallowed, then opened his mouth to speak.

Aurora held her hand up to make him pause a bit longer. "Before you say anything, *she* brought it up to me. Jenna showed up at the inn with Max and asked me to discuss the restaurant with you. Let me just say that straightaway."

He was quiet.

"She first mentioned something to me that day in the shop when I visited the farm. Then she said you told her about what I'd said when we were in the barn."

Jude nodded. "We've batted around the notion for months now, and I knew she'd want to hear what you had to say on the topic."

"And?"

"And?" His eyes sparkled as their gazes met. "We both think it's a viable plan, with a lot of potential. I...I think it's a great idea, but I don't see how we can make it happen. Not right now."

Jenna had asked her to talk to Jude about the restaurant and now, technically, she had. He'd plainly stated now wasn't the time, and the Aurora he'd known wasn't the type of person to poke and pry and pursue a matter.

But Aurora wasn't that meek girl anymore.

She realized *she* wanted to talk about the restaurant. Not because Jenna had asked, but because she knew Jude liked the idea. Those big blue eyes were dancing with unexplored concepts and options he wanted to discuss. He wanted to go down this rabbit hole, at least in theory, and so did Aurora. Why shouldn't they discuss a restaurant and share ideas again? She shouldn't let John Jones get in the way of that.

They weren't kids anymore.

"What are the obstacles if all you're doing is exploring the idea?" she dared ask.

"I...Nothing, I suppose. I know a restaurant will be a lot of work, time, and energy. I know Dad will hate the notion because it's new and different, and therefore bad. Not to mention it'd split our dedication—in his eyes—from the traditional roles on the farm. Oh, and we know next to nothing about the restaurant industry."

"But you still think it's a good idea?"

He studied her so intently, she thought she might melt into the booth. "What do you think of the idea?"

Aurora could hedge her bets and wait for his response before she really spoke her mind, but that's not who she was anymore. She'd promised herself, years ago, she'd live more boldly than when she was young. And, if she wanted something, she'd try her hardest to go after it.

"I think it's a great idea, Jude. With the potential of being very successful with the right people at the helm."

A smile formed on his lips, subtle at first, before it beamed.

"I'm not about to get into the middle of things with your dad though," Aurora quickly added.

"No, I..." He nodded. "Of course not. I get that."

"But we could talk about it, if you want. Talk ideas, plans. You can ask me anything."

The waitress dropped off their bill as they sat there studying each other.

It'd been years—a decade—since they'd dreamed of the future together. This was shaky ground at best, dangerous at worst. Was this too much like when they were a couple? Too much like when they promised to live out all their dreams together?

Jude reached across the table, past the bill, and squeezed her hand. "I would love to talk more. Let's go for a drive."

Aurora knew this would likely bring them closer, maybe too close, but she found she didn't care.

Chapter 15

He settled the check and they managed to leave the diner with only a wave in Erica's general direction.

Once outside, Aurora stopped dead in her tracks on the sidewalk. "Look at that."

Jude followed her gaze upward, where a huge full moon was rising into the sky. "I know where we can get a better view."

"You do?"

"I still have a few surprises up my sleeve."

An indecipherable expression crossed her face, but she climbed into his truck.

He drove the two blocks to Ridge Lane and turned left. He followed the road all the way to the top of the hill, where the old hardware store sat, past its parking lot, to a wide-open patch of land with no lights from town.

"Wow," she said. "I forgot about this place."

He'd brought Aurora here before, one moonlit night when they'd first started dating. His intention wasn't to reminisce about that night, though he was aware of how it might seem, but to remind her of all her hometown had to offer.

Sure, California was nice. He imagined a city like

Los Angeles had a lot going for it, things a place like Fredericksburg never could, but their hometown was special too. There was plenty here that nowhere else could compare.

"Can't see a night sky like this in L.A.," she mused.

Exactly.

He didn't want to inspect his feelings too closely or question why he wanted her to remember her home. Maybe it was merely their reconciliation that made him want to give her other positive thoughts of home. Something to take with her when she was gone. Or maybe he wanted her to be a bit homesick.

Selfish though it may be, he wanted her—or at least some part of her—to want to stay. He'd missed how many months of her visit? Now they were getting along, enjoying each other's company. There was nothing wrong with wanting more of her, more time with her.

"This is a better view," she said as they got out of the truck.

"I know." He let the gate down and they hopped up to sit.

"Wonder if the full moon is why Erica Burr keeps popping up in my life this week."

"Strange things can happen during a full moon." He smiled.

Aurora tilted her head back, staring up. "You know, you can't see any stars in Los Angeles for all the city lights. You have to go up into the hills, past the fancy neighborhoods, or out into the desert. Then again, I'm always working and all I want to do after work is go home and sleep." She took a deep breath and sighed. "But that's restaurant work. The reality of it. Long, hard hours. Worrying yourself into insomnia. And that's when you're only working at an establishment, not owning and running one."

They looked at each other.

She started to speak, but he stopped her. "I know it's not easy work. Nothing worth having ever is. My dad is going to take a lot of convincing, and he may not ever be convinced, but my sisters and I want more for our family. We're ready to grow and this excites them more than any other idea, so I want to explore it. See if it's got real merit. And I really want to hear what you have to say. I trust you."

"Thank you for saying that." Aurora smiled sweetly. "Okay. First, you need to think about the basic premise of the restaurant. What's your mission? Your theme. What do you want? Farm-to-table, bistro, southern fusion, etcetera. Do you want to focus more on lunch or dinner, or both? High end or accessible? Plated, family style, tapas?"

Jude nodded slowly. "We definitely want the place to be accessible. Quality food, but not too expensive or fancy. Nothing stuffy or pretentious."

"Agreed. That wouldn't fit with the farm and your family."

"Exactly. We want it to fit in with the farm. Casual, rustic, local ingredients, high quality."

"I think that's wise. You're thinking farm-to-table?"

"Yes."

"The next thing to consider is capacity. Small and intimate would be best, given the space, at least at the start. You don't want to go big and go bust."

"Agreed."

"That means fewer staff, less supplies, but also a lower

return overall. Again, at least at the start, but I think that's best since this is a brand-new venture. In the future, who knows? But start small."

"Hang on." Jude hopped off the tailgate and hurried to the cab of his truck. He leaned in and dug around in the glove box until he found a small notebook and pen. "I want to write this down," he called to Aurora.

If he didn't start writing stuff down, he'd forget something important—or miss it because he was too busy noticing her eyes in the moonlight like a big ol' sap.

"How are you going to see to write?" She laughed as he hopped back up with her.

"You're going to hold my phone and use the flashlight app." He handed over his phone.

"This is the epitome of professional." She turned on the flashlight.

He cocked an eyebrow at her. "You'd rather go sit in the office at the farm for a few hours?"

"No, I like being out here. You know I'd rather be outside."

"Then quit griping and hold that light closer," he teased.

She held the light so close it bumped his hand as he wrote.

"Smart aleck."

Aurora laughed as he jotted down some of the key words she'd used.

"What about time frame?" he asked. "From when we first really get started, beyond the ideas phase, to the opening of the restaurant. What are we looking at?"

"Depending on the number of people and how many hours spent working on it? Six to eight months. If resources are limited, a year? Since you have the proper space for it, that helps, but you'll need to work on making it a commercial kitchen."

He wrote some more. "Key employees to hire first?"

"Manager and chef. And you'll want someone with plenty of experience. They can help guide the process. A strong chef can lead the menu creation and head up the food side independently, since the Jones family isn't a bunch of restaurateurs."

"What about you?" he blurted, only half thinking.

Aurora went still, blinking at him in the dim light cast by his phone.

"Want a job?" He kept his voice light, even though he wasn't kidding. Not really.

He realized she'd come back to Texas only because her sisters needed her. Now her family was fine. She had no reason to give up whatever amazing opportunities awaited her in a big city. But his gut reminded him that in life, you miss one hundred percent of the shots you don't take.

Aurora opened her mouth and closed it. Opened and closed. "I..." She pinched her lips together.

An awkward silence grew, and he recoiled from the tension. "I'm kidding." He shook his head. "I know you don't want that kind of uphill battle in little ol' Fredericksburg. Not with L.A. waiting on you. But do you know of anyone?"

A crease formed between her brows. "Huh? Oh, um...around here? No. But I could, I can make some calls. Someone always knows someone."

"Thanks." He nodded and wrote down the words *Call around*, just to have something to do. "What about insurance?" He spat out the first thing that came to mind, even though he remained hung up on Aurora and having her as his chef. "Level of insurance and type. I know there's probably an entirely different type of coverage we'd need. Deductible."

Aurora stared off into the middle distance, nodding. "Yeah. That's good you're already thinking about insurance and mitigating risk. Then again, of course you are."

"So?" Jude followed her gaze, but there was nothing out there in the darkness. "Isn't that smart?"

"What?" Her gaze shot back to him and she shook her head. "It's very smart." She put on a smile. "But you're the only person I know who dreams big about whole new business ventures and branching out, but also about insurance coverage and little things like how many parking spots you'll need."

"Oh yeah, parking!" He made a note about space for parking as Aurora smirked at him for reinforcing her point.

They talked about the business for over an hour, even sketching out a dining room setup with table layouts. They'd made more progress tonight than he'd expected. Aurora had insights on everything from raw food costs to the best colors and fonts to use on a menu.

Jude smiled, despite the earlier moment of tension. He'd figured Aurora knew her stuff, she'd always been one of the sharpest people he knew, but the extent of her knowledge, the attention she paid to detail, impressed him. He shouldn't be surprised. She'd followed her dream and made herself an expert in the field.

Warmth filled his heart. "This has been a huge help." His gaze met hers. "Thank you."

Aurora held his gaze for a moment, but then looked away. "No problem."

He closed the notebook with the pen inside as a bookmark, refusing to let her brush off a compliment. "I knew you'd know your stuff, but this is... beyond. And your ideas. I mean, you've always been creative, and able to come up with stuff, but—"

"Thanks," she said casually, unfolding her legs and shifting on the tailgate.

"No, I'm serious. You could have your own restaurant. You *should* have your own."

Aurora sniffed a laugh.

"You should." He leaned forward until she met his gaze again. "I'm not talking about this restaurant." He thumped the notebook in his hands. "But *a* restaurant. You've got the experience and knowledge. There are plenty of places that open every day, and their food is nowhere near as popular as yours, they have no idea what they're doing. You could do whatever you wanted."

She studied him, her eyes dark and unfathomable. "Owning and running your own place is a process. It takes a long time."

"In a big city, I'm sure." But the truth was, if she were a big fish in a smaller pond, she'd have her own restaurant by now. Maybe even two.

He set the notebook aside, unwilling to let the topic go yet. If she was dead set on leaving for California in a week or whatever, fine. Well, it wasn't fine, but he couldn't stop her. What he could do was make sure she knew her value. *He* knew her value. He'd made the mistake of not telling her before, and he wasn't going to let that happen again.

"Aurora, everything you've accomplished is amazing. And I know you don't need me to tell you you're great, but I'm going to do it anyway. You should be proud of yourself. I'm proud of you. Everyone in my family is. I hated that you left Texas. I hated the way things ended, but I am glad you followed your dream and, I mean, look at you now. You deserve whatever you want in life."

Even in the dim lighting from his tilted phone light, he could see the mist in her eyes.

"Jude," she said his name, her voice trembling. "That's . . . dang it, why do you have to be so nice?"

They both chuckled as she wiped at her face.

"It's true," he insisted.

"That has to be the nicest thing anyone's ever said to me." She reached over and touched his hand. "Thank you. It means . . . that means a lot to me."

He turned his hand over to hold hers, tangling her fingers with his, and studied the way her long fingers still fit perfectly with his. "Your boss doesn't tell you how good you are?"

She sniffed again. "No. Head chefs and restaurant group owners aren't known to give a lot of praise. I've never been told I could do whatever I want or that I should be proud of my work. They're from the tough-love school of thought."

"Hmm." He squeezed her hand gently. "I don't know, but sounds like they might be idiots."

She smiled sweetly and brushed her thumb over the back of his hand, sending sparks of electricity up his arm.

He was not an idiot, and he was too old to play dumb. The other evening, at the lake, they weren't just caught up in the moment. They'd *had* a moment. And while they'd professed it was fine and no biggie, and he'd told himself not to overthink it or get too into his feelings about her, his heart and his soul argued otherwise.

Their kissing, their reuniting, their chemistry and understanding, it was a big deal. He couldn't deny he had feelings for her. This was Aurora. His wonderful, amazing, ever-changing, surprising Aurora. And even if she left again tomorrow, ripped his heart out and backed over it with his truck, he didn't much care.

He wanted to kiss her again.

He was *going* to kiss her.

Jude leaned forward and touched her cheek with his free hand, because he was not letting go of her. His intent clear, he waited for her to pull away.

She didn't.

He rubbed his thumb across the top of her cheek, wishing he could freeze this moment and keep it with him forever.

Then Aurora closed the space between them and kissed him.

Chapter 16

Aurora sat in the inn's living room with her sisters, but she was a million miles away.

She'd kissed Jude. Again.

She had kissed Jude.

Kissed. Jude. Kissed. Jude.

Sure, he was the one who'd started it. He'd leaned in and had that look in his eyes, but something in her snapped and she'd been the one to close the deal.

Perhaps it was her patience. Or maybe it was all those years of letting him lead their relationship, while she'd followed him around like a lovestruck little girl.

She wasn't a girl anymore, and sometimes she liked to take the lead.

"This weekend we have a group of ten ladies staying with us. A girls' weekend," Beth said, somewhere in the distance.

"Fun," Cece replied.

And what a kiss it'd been.

Aurora brushed her fingers across her bottom lip. Jude had always been a good kisser, and his skill had aged well.

Firm, yet soft. His fingers dancing along her jaw, then tangling in her hair.

Technically, it'd been more than one kiss.

A kiss that went on and on, turning into two or three kisses. Maybe five? Making her melt into him. Warm and solid, he fit around her perfectly. She'd wanted to stay there all night, until they'd pulled away, reality crashing down.

Zero regrets though.

They'd grinned like little kids as he dropped her off at her car, promising to call her tomorrow. They were going to see each other again.

And let her not forget about his blurted offer to be head chef of the farm's restaurant.

Aurora gripped the edge of the couch cushion with her free hand, digging her fingers in. He'd played it off like he was joking, but Jude didn't make that face when he joked. He was serious.

But she'd froze.

Her reason for freezing up though—very unsettling. Because her answer wasn't immediately no.

While most of her brain said that was not her plan, she had to get back to L.A. and get back in the game, some of her brain, and most of her heart, perked up at the offer. She'd rolled it over in her mind, tried it on for size.

Farm-to-table in Texas was not a bistro in Malibu though. And working with Jude... working on something that had anything to do with his father?

She couldn't. That'd be a recipe for disaster. She shouldn't even consider the offer.

So why was she?

And why did she kiss Jude? Again?

Kiss Jude. Kiss Jude.

"They're going to do some hiking and horseback

riding, visit some vineyards, do a little shopping." Her sister kept talking.

Aurora's heart danced in her chest, reminding her of the feeling from years ago.

Giddy anticipation.

She wanted Jude to kiss her again, as unwise as it may be. She could forget about his offer, the changes and choices coming her way, and simply exist in his arms.

"Hello, Aurora?"

"What?" Aurora dropped her hand from her lips.

"I said, the girls' weekend group. They want a hearty breakfast every day before they head out on their adventures, and they said family style works great. Is that good for you?"

"Yeah, sure. That'd be easy," Aurora said.

"Great. Thank you. Just let me know what you need as far as ordering."

"Mmm-hmm."

"Something on your mind?" Cece asked, cocking her head to the side.

"Nope."

"Moving on." Beth stopped the sidetrack before it could begin. "Regarding Erica's wedding. She'll be here in a bit, but there won't be much to go over with her. She's having an early wedding, with just cake and a champagne toast after. We need to make sure we have the cake request correct and show her the gazebo to go over the layout, but that's it. I think it's only immediate family coming."

"I'm sorry, I know I've said it already." Aurora held up a hand. "But I can't believe this is the same Erica. I saw her last night at Lucky's, but—"

"You did?" Cece leaned forward, eager for some dish as always.

"Yes, with her fiancé. He's...different. Anyway, she mentioned her appointment, and still has that passive-aggressive vibe about her, but I don't know. Something seems off with them. And this small, casual wedding plan seems way off from the Erica I knew."

"People change," Beth insisted. "Ten years is a long time."

"Do people change that much?" Aurora raised an eyebrow.

Look at her and Jude. Ten years apart and they'd drifted back together like two magnets. They'd changed, but so much remained exactly the same.

"I'm with Aurora. This wedding doesn't seem very her." Cece shook her head. "I know folks have said she's changed, but maybe she's also become a conscious consumer and has a less-is-best mindset. That's very popular nowadays. Reducing consumption and focusing on the people and memories."

"Yeah." Aurora shook her head too. "Not Erica. I don't buy that for a second."

"Regardless of what we think, this is what she said she wanted." Beth stood up. "So, let's stop talking about her in case she walks in on us."

Beth had gotten burned while planning her best friend's wedding, when an overheard conversation with the mother of the bride brought on a whole kerfuffle with the groom's brother.

But now, Beth was engaged to said brother, so it wasn't really a bad thing.

They heard a car pull up and moved to the foyer.

Sure enough, it was Erica. Right on time.

"Hello!" She made a show of greeting them, air kisses and all.

This was the Erica that Aurora knew.

"Welcome, welcome." Beth, the ultimate hostess, thankfully took over and gave Erica a tour of the place.

Aurora and Cece hung back, sharing their skepticism.

"This is so cute," Erica commented as they rejoined them in the sitting room. "And quaint. It's just darling."

Her compliment managed to come across a bit snide. It was quite the talent.

"Now." Beth had Erica sit on the sofa and sat across from her in a chair. "Let's go over the toast and cake."

The two of them spoke for a while, and Aurora contributed just enough not to seem rude. They were wrapping up the meeting and showing her out, and Aurora was just about to do a happy dance that it was over, when Erica turned to her.

"Could I talk to you for a second?"

"Um, sure." A pit opened in Aurora's stomach, but she followed Erica outside to the front porch and down the steps.

"I won't keep you long." Erica turned to her. "But I wanted to talk to you for a moment, alone. After seeing you and Jude together last night, back together after all this time—"

"Oh, we aren't—"

"I know what I did all those years ago. To you." Erica clasped her hands in front of her and fiddled with the business card Beth had given her. "I know how awful I was about things our senior year. All anyone could talk about was the two of you and I just... I guess I got sick of hearing it. I'm embarrassed, thinking back on it now."

She really didn't want to relive that part of the past with Erica.

"The two of you were just so happy together." Erica rolled her eyes. "It was kind of disgusting."

"Thanks," Aurora deadpanned.

Erica looked surprised that she'd said anything.

"Sorry. I...anyway, maybe I was a tiny bit jealous of how happy y'all were. But now *I'm* happy."

She sounded as though she was trying to convince herself.

Aurora nodded, uneasy about her insistence. "That's—I'm glad."

"Anyway, I just wanted to get that off my chest."

Aurora stood there a moment.

Was it an apology? Of sorts, maybe. Erica regretted the past, but Aurora wasn't sure any apologizing had happened. More like a polite, and a little patronizing, statement. Nice with a side of snide.

Quintessential Erica.

"Well, I have a lot to do." Erica stepped away.

"Sounds good." Aurora put up her hand to wave, but Erica had already turned her back and was on her way to the car.

She watched her drive off, still wondering what—exactly—had just happened.

Her phone buzzed inside her back pocket.

It was a series of texts from Sloane.

Hey good lookin! Whatcha got cookin!

I meant to text you the other day. The pic of you and your sisters on IG is gorgeous! You guys look amazing. Guess all that fresh air really is good for the soul. 😊

Aurora had posted a picture in the gazebo, showing off Cece's new setup in there.

Thank you, she texted back. Might be all the decent sleep.

Sleep? What's that?

Aurora tapped on her phone and looked at her latest picture on Instagram.

It wasn't only the fresh air and sleep that gave her a healthy glow and bright smile.

No longer being completely stressed out, day in and day out, working sixteen-hour days, did wonders for a person. The pressure of climbing higher, faster—she'd left all of that back in L.A., and now she could breathe.

Think.

About her career and ambition, the future. And her heart?

She'd made peace with Jude, and they were friendly again. Okay, more than friendly. This feeling was nice, even if it was dangerous in the long run.

What if she compartmentalized? Set boundaries, and made it clear their encounters were merely embers of an old flame. Comforting, yet thrilling. Maybe kissing Jude was for the here and now, not for her future.

The notion curdled in her stomach.

Aurora scrolled down to her pictures in L.A.

While the people were fabulous, she looked exhausted, a little gaunt, and unhappy.

And of all the people in her pictures, she missed only Sloane.

Funny, because she remembered every picture, and swore, at the time, she was living her best life. Fulfilling her dream. In the rat race, she'd felt full of purpose and drive. She'd told herself she was happy, but was she happy or merely insisting she was happy in the hope of making it real?

Now, being back in Texas, she felt more awake. Aware. Alive.

Was it possible she'd gotten so caught up in the idea of chasing big city success that she never stopped to make sure it's what she really wanted?

When she'd finished college and set her sights on California, she told herself a big city was the only way to go. Los Angeles, San Francisco, San Diego. No one cared about a brilliant chef in a midsize town. And it needed to be anywhere other than Texas.

Her family was in Texas, but so was her past. Jude. Her mother. All the emotions and unresolved issues. But now she was beginning to resolve them. Sometimes, she was even happy here.

She'd left Texas to live life on her terms, find out what she wanted in this world. She'd done exactly that, so why did it now feel like her traitorous heart was nudging her back home?

"What are you still doing out here?" Cece joined her on the steps of the inn. "We thought you'd left."

"Just thinking." Aurora climbed the porch and made her way to the swing.

Cece followed and sat beside her, swinging them gently. "Anything you want to talk about?"

"Not really." That was a lie.

Beth popped her head out the front door, wide-eyed and a little ruffled. "Is Erica gone?"

Aurora chuckled at the sight of her sister popping out like a ferret looking for its predator. "Yeah, she's gone."

"Okay, good." Beth joined them on the swing, squeezing in on the other side of Aurora. "She was nice enough, but…"

"She's a lot," Cece offered.

"Yes. Like handling a cute porcupine."

"I think she tried to apologize to me," Aurora confessed.

Beth shifted. "Really?"

"She didn't do a great job of it, but she did say she felt bad about all that stuff our senior year. I mean, I think she feels bad? It's hard to tell with her."

Beth nodded. "I bet. She kept complimenting the inn and commenting how much she'd heard about our weddings, but they weren't exactly compliments. They were more—"

"Backhanded," Aurora finished the thought for her.

"Yes. I feel like I've been tromped on, but politely."

Cece laughed. "That sounds about right."

"Honestly, I think that's just how she is," Aurora added. "I don't know that she can help herself. Her mom was like that and I remember her coming to middle school functions and talking to Erica that very same way."

"Goodness." Beth pushed off with her feet, swinging them a bit more. "Our mom was perfection in comparison."

"Mom isn't so bad," Cece said.

Aurora patted her leg. "No one said she was bad."

"She had a lot on her, raising three girls after Dad took off, and dealing with his fraud scandal. Maybe she wasn't the most attentive or affectionate, but she wasn't mean."

"No, she wasn't." Aurora closed her eyes, enjoying the back-and-forth lull of the swing. "Her priority was keeping a roof over our heads, food on the table, and us between the lines. She did a good job, considering."

"And we had one another," Beth added. "For the attention and affection."

A laugh burst out from Cece. "Sometimes too much attention. Remember when y'all went as chaperones to my middle school dance?" She used air quotes on the word *chaperones*. "Y'all just wanted to see the boy who'd asked me to the dance."

"Kyle Duncan," Aurora mused.

"He was so cute." Cece nodded.

"Whatever happened to him?"

"No clue. His family moved away our freshman year. Remember the drive home from the dance?"

Beth had driven them, but she wasn't that seasoned of a driver. Aurora had gone along out of a fear of missing out. On the way home, Beth had overcorrected the car to dodge a kamikaze squirrel, and they'd spun out on the side of the road.

"I thought we were going to die." Aurora sat up.

"We were not going to die." Beth huffed. "You two were so overdramatic. Cece wanted to call the cops."

Cece began giggling too. "Why did I want to call the police?"

"You swore we'd done something wrong." Beth rolled her eyes. "Meanwhile this one"—she stuck her thumb toward Aurora—"was all *Go! Go!* Like a SWAT team was about to pop out of a cow field and arrest us for a minor incident."

Cece swiped the laugh tears from her face. "That's probably the real reason Kyle moved away. He told his parents three crazy girls tried to kill him after the eighth-grade dance and they should probably split town."

"Remember the dresses we wore?" Aurora asked.

Cece hid her face behind her hands. "I don't want to! So poofy. So much taffeta."

"I think mine had holes at the shoulders." Beth snorted.

"It did! You thought you were so daring. Ohhhh, bare shoulders."

Beth shoved at Aurora's arm.

Her face hurt from smiling at the memories. She'd missed this so much over the years. Sloane was great, but no one was like her sisters. No one fought with her like them or understood her like them.

And while she had so much on her mind, she didn't have to handle it all alone.

Her sisters were here, with her. She could talk to them about everything that'd happened lately, and they would understand.

They might give her a hard time about it, too, but she expected nothing less.

"Listen." Aurora sat up to face them both. "I need to talk to y'all. I, um... well..."

Cece leaned in impatiently. "What is it?"

"I'm going to tell y'all something, well some things, and I don't want you to say anything until I'm done, okay?"

They both nodded.

"I mean it, Cece." She looked pointedly at her younger sister. Cece struggled with containing her commentary as much as Aurora did.

Cece mimed zipping her lips and locking them.

"I kissed Jude last night."

Cece gasped.

"I said no comments!"

"I didn't say anything! I can't help it if I breathe heavy."

Aurora shook it off. "Anyway, I kissed him. And... it might've been the second time."

Cece covered her mouth to hold in another gasp, but Beth studied her quietly.

"I don't know what happened. I don't know if we were caught up in the moment or if it means anything. The other big thing is, he and Jenna want to open a restaurant. At the farm. And he kind of offered me a job, but not really."

Beth's eyebrows creased together. "What does that mean, not really? It's an offer or it isn't."

"He kind of blurted it out and I froze, so he said he was kidding."

Cece's eyes asked why, but Beth did an amazing job of showing no reaction or emotion.

"Anyway, then we mainly talked about plans and ideas, and it's probably going to be a really great restaurant and dining experience. And—"

Cece dropped her hands, unable to contain herself any longer. "You might really want the job offer?" she blurted.

And there it was. The million-dollar question.

Did she? How could she? Why was she even considering this?

"I should be hearing from my manager soon. I'm supposed to leave for California soon. I have a life there. But, turns out, I still have a life here as well and it's just..."

"It's a lot," Beth finished.

"Yeah."

Beth nodded solemnly.

"So...what if you didn't go back to California? What if, instead, you stayed here and worked on Jude's restaurant?"

"If the job offer is legit."

"I'm sure it is."

"I don't think it'd even pay. Not at first. And it's *Jude's* project. This is my ex we're talking about."

Cece tilted her head to one side, seeing straight through her. "Is he your ex though? If y'all are kissing. And would the project really be all his if you're involved?"

Leave it to Cece to give voice to the questions inside her.

Jude would back the restaurant and fund it, but he'd need someone to lead it. He and his sisters weren't restaurateurs. They were farmers. They'd need someone to handle the table part of the farm-to-table.

"I'm not sure it's a good idea, us working together," Aurora voiced her concern.

"He kissed you," Beth stated.

"Actually, I kissed him the second time."

"I'm sure he protested bigly," Cece teased.

"Exactly." Beth shifted to face Aurora. "Look, I know you and I know Jude. If he's told you about this restaurant, and asked you to be involved, in any way, and now he's kissing you? Come on, Aurora. He doesn't just want your advice or your help. He wants you."

Aurora shook her head. "It's not like that. After all

that happened, and as far as he knows, I'm leaving soon. And it's not like Jude and I haven't been down this road before. We dated, we were in love, and it didn't work."

"You were kids."

"He broke my heart." Aurora choked back the surprising emotion in her voice.

Cece's arm went around her immediately, and Beth placed a hand on her arm.

"I can't go kissing the man who broke my heart and thinking about involving myself in a business venture with him. Can I?" She swallowed hard. "How did this happen? This is crazy."

Beth brushed back her hair and waited until Aurora breathed through some of her emotion. "Have you talked to him about all of this?" she asked gently.

Aurora shook her head. "No, not exactly."

"When Sawyer and I had to deal with his issues with Shelby, it would've been so much better if we'd just talked about it. Sooner rather than later. If I'd known all that was going on in his mind and in his heart, we could've avoided a lot of heartache. I think you should talk to Jude. You may not know exactly what you want to do yet, but it's okay to confide in him. Tell him that you're torn."

"If you had to decide right now, which would you rather do?" Cece asked. "Best-case scenarios all around, head chef in L.A. or head chef at Jude's new restaurant. Which would you prefer?"

Aurora sat in silence.

The truth was, she didn't know.

Chapter 17

Papers and boxes stood in stacks like towers on Jude's desk.

The business side of the farming industry was attempting to go paperless, like so many other businesses, but they had a long way to go.

"We need to talk." His dad burst into the office with Jenna in tow. Outside his office, Bonnie and Meredith stood wide-eyed.

Jude took in the expression on his dad's face, along with Jenna's chagrin.

Something had hit the fan, and he was about to find out what, and how much.

"Sure, Dad. What's up?" He kept his tone neutral because his dad could be fired up about any number of things.

"This." He slapped down an open notebook.

Jude's notebook from the truck, from his talk with Aurora, with pages of ideas about a farm-to-table restaurant.

"That is a notebook," he said blandly, his stomach tying into double knots.

"It's a book of plans. For a restaurant that you've told me nothing about."

Jude considered telling his dad they weren't plans at all. That he was merely daydreaming about something that'd never happen, but that'd be a lie. It'd be a betrayal to Aurora and to his sisters. That notebook was both a dream and plans, and Jude was tired of playing this game with his dad about the farm's future.

"It's brainstorming plans, Dad. Ideas. Nothing is written in stone."

"Ideas that you've left me out of. Jenna told me you've been thinking about expanding. Talking about it."

"True. But we didn't want to trouble you with something we're just considering and talking about."

Jenna stared him down, as if trying to speak without saying a word.

"You've been tired lately," Jude continued. "We didn't want to pile this on you."

Jenna's eyes were now about to pop out of her skull. Bonnie and Meredith had huddled closer, clearly wanting to know what was going on, while staying out of the line of fire.

"This isn't some problem that fell out of the sky onto the farm." His dad jabbed a finger toward the notebook. "This is a problem you're about to bring down upon us."

"I'm not bringing anything down on us."

"This concerns me, and you've left me out."

"I know, but whenever we've tried to talk to you about expanding and diversifying the farm's business—"

His dad scoffed.

"You do that," Jenna jumped in.

"Exactly. You don't want to hear about changes. You cut us off before we can ever start talking to you about it."

"That's a bunch of bull, and you know it."

Jude shook his head. "No, actually, it isn't bull at all. We've tried for months to discuss ideas with you, and you shut us down. You don't want to hear any of them."

"We can't discuss it with you, so we discuss it with each other," Jenna added. "We're not leaving you out intentionally. We've tried including you on everything."

"You shouldn't be discussing it at all." He spun toward Bonnie and Meredith. "Are you both a part of this too?"

To their credit, the two of them stood there, stone-faced, neither denying nor confirming the accusation. They weren't neck-deep like Jenna and Jude, but Jude appreciated their silent support.

His dad refocused his anger on Jude and Jenna. "You're all in on this together. You're going to open some restaurant without ever telling me?"

"No," Jude insisted.

"I'm the last one to know about anything. First about Bonnie and Meredith and now about this."

"Dad," Bonnie pleaded.

Jude moved closer to his dad. "We were going to talk to you about the restaurant. As soon as we had all the information and had decided it's what we really want to pursue. We're not *doing* anything to you. It's a family discussion. That's all."

"What do you even know about restaurants?"

"Not much," Jenna admitted. "That's why we brought in Aurora to consult."

Jude cringed. Dragging Aurora into this wasn't going to win their father's favor.

"We got her input. That's all," Jude explained.

"Why would you ask her for anything?"

A decade ago, he hadn't had the will to fight his dad

or his opinions about Aurora. Times had changed though, and so had he. "Aurora knows her stuff, Dad. There's no one I know with more restaurant experience than her. No one has her expertise. You should hear her talk. She knows what she's doing."

His dad sniffed at the notion.

Jude ground his back teeth together. "She's worked in restaurants for the last ten years. She's been in the trenches and worked her way up, seen what makes success and failure. Look what she's done for her family's inn. She knows a lot more than any of us."

Including you, he wanted to add. He was not going to let his dad bulldoze over the fact that Aurora was the best person to ask about and involve with this project.

"And she thinks this is a great idea," Jenna added.

"Well, lah-de-dah. Aurora thinks it's a great idea."

"That's enough." Jude stopped him. "Regardless of what you think about Aurora from back then or even now, she knows this business."

Jude picked up the notebook. He hadn't stood up to his dad ten years ago, but he could stand up for both of them now. "If she says it's a good plan, then it's a good plan. She said we could be profitable within a few years. It's a viable investment and I like the idea. In fact, we all like the idea."

"Where would you even put it?"

"In the barn Jude refurbished," Jenna answered quickly. "I've checked on building out some of the renovations and the cost is less than we thought, especially if we do some of the work ourselves."

"You've got it all figured out then, huh?"

"Don't be like this," he pleaded with his father. "This

could really work and be huge for the farm. We could use a boost to keep this business thriving, in the family, and all of us able to stay on full-time—for years to come. But we need to all be on the same page."

"Then you can forget it." His father looked them both in the eyes in turn. "It's my name on this farm, my name on the deed. I'm not opening a restaurant. And that's final."

Their dad turned on his heels and marched out of the office.

Jude didn't have the heart to point out that *he* wouldn't be doing much of anything to open the restaurant. They didn't expect him to take on that much manual labor. Their father could barely handle the responsibilities already on his plate. The plan never included their dad actively contributing.

Maybe Jude should feel bad about that, but it wasn't about leaving his dad out because of ill will. His dad had earned his retirement. He deserved the time to relax a little and let his children pick up the weight.

If only he'd let them.

Jenna balled her hands into fists, her mouth pinched tight as she watched their dad storm off. "He's being completely unreasonable," she hissed as soon as he was out of earshot.

Jude shook his head and tucked the notebook into the back pocket of his jeans.

"You have to make him listen," she insisted.

"You can't talk sense to him when he's like this." Jude tried to will his heart rate back down. "He's made up his mind and arguing won't change it. Problem is, I don't know what will."

Bonnie and Meredith joined them in the office.

"It's not just the restaurant," Bonnie said. "He's trying to process that his daughter has a girlfriend too."

"He's doing okay with that though," Meredith offered. "I mean, arguably, he handled our news better than this."

"Maybe Dad won't change." Jenna marched toward Jude. "But at this point, what could it hurt to push?"

"What would you have me do?" Jude asked.

"Stand up to him more. Push harder," she said.

"Great idea, Jen. Let me go chase him down and keep arguing. Turn this into a full-blown family fight and get us all kicked off the farm and out of the will. I'm sure pushing harder would really bring him around to our way of thinking, lickety-split. Have you met the man?"

"Don't use that tone with me."

"I can't help it, I'm frustrated."

"Well, so am I!" Jenna tossed her hands up.

Jude started to pace his office.

"Okay," Bonnie spoke calmly. "Let's all just take a deep breath. We can't take it out on one another."

"Yeah," Meredith agreed.

"No one needs to say anything to Dad right now. Let him cool off." Bonnie nodded.

"Maybe everyone should cool off before taking any next steps," Meredith added.

They were right. Jude kept pacing. Blood rushed in his ears; his muscles tightened. What were they going to do now? They could try to start moving forward without their dad's approval. Push ahead and let him wallow in his anger.

He and Jenna both had access to the business accounts.

But wouldn't that go over like a fly in the punch? If John Jones let it be known in town that his children were bowling him over at the farm, they'd lose customers right and left.

No.

"Do you think your dad would be more open to discussions once he calms down?" Meredith asked.

"No," all three of them answered at once.

Her eyes went wide. "Okay then."

But somehow, they had to get their dad's approval. They couldn't progress without it.

He wished he could talk to Aurora. Get her thoughts on what had just transpired, and where to go from here. And he just plain wanted to talk to her.

"I need to get some air." Jude grabbed his truck keys from the desk.

"You're leaving? Now?"

"I thought we were all cooling off. Besides, I can't think cooped up in here. I'll be back later."

The Jones family was at a crossroads, and somehow, Jude had to find a way through.

Chapter 18

With the kitchen clean, Aurora took a break. She was enjoying her iced tea when her phone buzzed on the counter.

The name Mark filled the circle on her screen.

Her manager in Los Angeles.

"Crap," she muttered, and set down her glass. This was it. This was the call he'd promised.

"Hello," she answered.

"There she is. Our long-lost sous chef. How are you?"

"Good. I'm good."

"Glad to hear it. Then I guess I'll cut to the chase, since I know Sloane has already told you about the Malibu venture."

There was no point in being coy. "Yes, she did."

"I know you took an extended leave and had some stuff to deal with back home."

And that was months ago, she filled in the unsaid portion of that sentence.

"But we'd like you back for the new restaurant."

Aurora's hearing went fuzzy, her stomach knotting up double. Instead of feeling the fireworks she'd expected, she felt numb.

"Chef Jon will be joining you. Both of you will head it up."

That was... different.

"So, we'd be creating the menu together or—"

"The menu is already decided." A pinging sounded on Mark's end of the line, like he was getting in or out of his car. Wait. Was he driving? Driving around, giving her this news like this wasn't her life they were talking about? "The restaurant is seafood forward, sushi, featured fish, and shellfish."

Not really where her talents shined brightest, but she could make it work.

"Hang on a sec." He rifled around for something. "And we need you back next week. I'll let you pick the day but make it before the weekend. We need to go out to the location on Saturday."

He hadn't even asked if she wanted the position—which, perhaps, was silly. Who, in her shoes, wouldn't want it? But she'd have no say in the menu? She'd be co-head and, essentially, do the restaurant group's bidding.

"Text me tomorrow and let me know what day you're back in town. Hang on again." Mark spoke to someone else in a muffled voice. Apparently, he was driving around, with someone else, while discussing her future.

Once upon a time, she'd wanted nothing but a head chef role in a big restaurant. No questions would've been asked. She would've dived right in.

But this wouldn't really be her restaurant, would it?

She wouldn't have just an investor or even business partner. This restaurant would be someone else's.

This place in Malibu would be someone else's dream. Not hers.

Their idea, their vision, their menu. Their everything. She'd be an employee, a worker bee, not a partner and not an owner.

And taking this job would mean leaving. Again.

"Listen kiddo. I have to go. Text me tomorrow."

Aurora opened her mouth, but the call had already ended.

"Thanks?" she said into the silence.

She shoved her phone into her pocket and glanced around the kitchen.

Normally, when her mind was filled to the brim and almost overflowing, she found solace and sanity in cooking. She'd start sautéing garlic and onion, without fully knowing what she might make. The creativity, the improvisation, the process, was what calmed her mind, and the world would slowly start to make sense.

Right now, though? The last thing she wanted was to be in a kitchen alone.

She needed to get outside.

Her feet took her to the front porch, but then she kept walking. If she stayed on the porch, her sisters would find her, and they'd want to talk. She needed to think.

She started down the driveway of the Orchard Inn, seeing that path like she'd never seen it before. Their driveway was beautiful. Lined with stone fruit trees all around. Green and vibrant. Alive. Breathtaking. The rolling hills beyond her home echoed more of the same.

Unsure of where she was going, she took a left and kept walking. She needed to move and be in the fresh air. It helped.

Aurora let out a long, suffering sigh. "Really?" she asked the sky.

All she'd wanted for years was the opportunity to head up a restaurant. Now the moment was here, and there were all these strings attached.

No input, no creative contribution, she'd be co-head at a place that served cuisine that left her feeling the least inspired. Seafood was great; but a menu of only seafood didn't light her creative fire. Actually, this new offer left *no* room for creativity. All the major decisions for the restaurant had been made for her.

She'd gotten her dream, but it was skewed.

"It's way off." She shook her head as she walked.

Now what? She could consult her sisters, but she already knew their thoughts on the matter.

They'd want her to stay in Texas.

But staying in Texas couldn't equal working at the inn forever. It'd mean working with Jude. Working *for* Jude?

"Ugh." No, she didn't want that. It'd have to be working *with*.

She couldn't be Jude's employee and she couldn't stay at the inn forever.

Helping her sisters and contributing to their investment was one thing. Being an event caterer and working in a bed-and-breakfast as her life's work for forty more years was another.

Honest and challenging work, sure, but her heart was in restaurants, not catering. Even in Texas, her dream would be to head up a restaurant. Preferably her own.

Even Jude's wouldn't be "her" restaurant.

But being here, having her sisters closer, permanently, warmed her heart. Helping them find a proper replacement at the inn, being nearby in case they really needed her or she needed them—the notion held a lot promise.

What if she got stuck here though? She could stay in Fredericksburg, Jude's restaurant could never happen or, worse, it would, but they couldn't find a way to work together. She didn't want to cater events for a lifetime and then, there she was.

No prospects, no hopes—her dream, gone.

Her head throbbed with too many thoughts. Maybe she should've stayed in the kitchen and cooked after all.

"Just stop," she admonished herself.

She was going to blow a gasket if she kept on.

Walking. All she needed to think about right now was walking without falling into a ditch somewhere.

She was almost a mile down the rural road when a familiar truck rumbled past her and hit the brakes. The driver's-side window came down as she neared.

"You resort to hitchhiking just to get outta here?" Jude asked.

Aurora smiled at the sight of him. His ropy forearms in short sleeves as he held the wheel. The way he'd held her last night.

The way he'd kissed her.

No one had kissed her the way Jude did. Like she was the air he breathed.

Aurora cleared her throat. "I'm taking a walk to clear my head."

"Tell me about it. I've been driving around for almost half an hour, doing the same."

And he'd ended up here.

Jude smirked. "It isn't working for me. How about you?"

She smiled despite herself and stared at her dusty shoes. "Not really."

"Want to jump in? Ride around for a bit?"

Her plan had been time alone. Time to think. Reflect. But this was Jude, looking yummy in his worn T-shirt and jeans, tousled hair and gentle smile. And, like Beth said, she needed to talk to him. Talking to him might bring clarity.

"Sure," she said.

His smile broadened. "Don't cross this road though. Let me U-turn up there and I'll come back down to get you."

Always cautious. Always thinking about the risks.

He drove on up and turned around using the closest driveway and pulled up beside her. "Hop in."

"We've done a lot of driving around together," she said as she climbed into his truck.

"It's the only way I get a moment alone these days."

Speaking of a moment alone—she grabbed her phone and sent her sisters a quick message, so they'd know where she was.

Jude cruised the country roads, his radio playing low, and they remained silent for an entire song.

"Were you headed anywhere in particular?" he finally asked.

"No. You?"

"Not at first. Getting out to clear my head was my only plan. Then I ended up on your street."

She fought not to smile at his honesty. Jude didn't know how to be anything but genuine. Zero poker face, terrible liar.

She loved that about him.

"Why did you need to clear your head?" she asked.

"Well...that's an interesting question. My dad found my notes on the restaurant."

Aurora pinched her lips together. Crappidy crap. Knowing how Mr. Jones was, that couldn't have gone well.

"And?"

Jude huffed a laugh. "Went over about as well as you'd think. He knows we want to open a restaurant, he knows we've been talking about it and making plans, and he ain't happy."

Aurora shifted to see his profile. "What did he say?"

"That we're trying to leave him out, go over him. He's against it, of course. Being completely unreasonable. He's made it clear he's not interested in anything new, from the beginning, but the fact that we kept pursuing new ideas sent him over the edge. Naturally, we weren't going to include him until we had a solid plan to pursue and propose to him, but he found out anyway and he's furious."

She studied a thread at the bottom of her shirt, picking at it, unsure of what to say.

John Jones's reaction was predictable and completely in character, but this sucked for Jude, and the prospect of a new restaurant. Plus, now it sucked for her too. "I'm so sorry."

"It's not your fault. I was the one who wanted to talk about it and take freaking notes. And it's not like we were trying to cut him out. We just know we can't talk to him about making changes."

"I'm sorry regardless. I know the last thing you wanted was to hurt your dad."

"Thanks." Jude got quiet and kept driving.

Aurora sat back. She wanted to open up, tell him all about where her mind was at the moment, that she was emotionally invested in this restaurant idea now, too, but now wasn't the time to pile on. He needed time to contemplate.

"I worry about him is all," Jude blurted moments later. "He's slowing down a lot. More so this past year. But that's normal, right? He's at retirement age. He should slow down. He's earned the right to take it easy and reap the rewards of all his hard work. Thing is, he doesn't see it that way. He's fighting what's natural because he doesn't trust me to take over. He doesn't think I'm capable, and he won't let go."

She studied his profile again, the strong jaw and straight nose that made him so handsome. His eyes were sad though. Jude loved his father, and no one could doubt he wanted what was best for his family and the farm.

John Jones couldn't seriously think that Jude wasn't capable. No one could.

"What if that's not it at all?" she asked.

"What?"

"What if your dad's…resistance isn't about your abilities. Maybe it isn't about *you* at all."

His gaze glanced off hers before his eyes went back to the road. "You think?"

"Your dad trusts you enough to let you run the day-to-day operations. He's around, but I've seen the way things work at the farm. It's all you, with Jenna by your side with Bonnie and Meredith helping. Your dad is a smart man. He sees this. He knows you're capable."

"But not capable enough to do anything without his oversight." Jude scowled at the road ahead. "Not capable enough to grow the family business."

Aurora shook her head, tugging at the thread of her shirt again. "I don't know. What if he's just scared?"

Jude glanced her way again, his brow furrowed.

"I think he might be scared of letting go," Aurora added. She knew more than a little something about how that felt. "Of trusting the unknown and jumping into something new and uncharted."

For the first time in her life, she could sympathize with what Mr. Jones must be feeling.

"I don't think it's because of you though," she continued. "Letting go means something new. If he retires, it means moving on and admitting he can't do it anymore, or even that he doesn't want to. Retiring, or leaving, stepping away means...well maybe he thinks it means quitting. And all he's ever known is the farm and fulfilling that dream."

Jude was quiet and still until they stopped at a four-way crossing. He turned to her, his eyes pleading to understand.

"Maybe he's just scared," she repeated, the truth of it echoing in her bones.

Jude bit at his bottom lip as he worked his jaw in thought. "I hadn't thought about it that way."

"I know your father trusts you. He has no reason not to. His issues are his own."

"You know..." Jude leaned his head back against the headrest with a sigh. "You might be right."

"I would know," she muttered.

"What's that?"

"Nothing." She dropped the thread she'd been picking. "Maybe try including your dad in the restaurant in some small way. I know he's against it *now*, but if he felt needed? Wanted? Maybe that would help him get on board."

Jude's brow furrowed as he considered this. "That's

not a bad idea. And let's be honest, it couldn't hurt at this point."

"I know, when my sisters were getting the inn off the ground, I wasn't actively involved beyond conference calls. Couldn't be helped because I was so far away, but it still stung a bit. I wanted to be involved, no matter how irrational it was to think that way."

"Yeah?"

"I craved our calls in those early days. I loved giving my input, and seeing the place grow into a real inn, with actual events."

Jude drove through the four-way stop, not another car in sight. "And when your sisters needed your help, you were there."

"Exactly." She smiled, remembering. "Happily."

When she'd first heard from Beth about what had happened, and how the whole wedding event and inn business might fall apart, Aurora hadn't thought twice about putting in for a leave of absence to help her sisters and set everything back on course. When family needed you, you showed up.

Truth be told, she had been eager to get away from what'd turned into a rat race and to work with people she loved and trusted.

Now the thought of going back was more bitter than sweet.

The promise of being head chef with control was gone. She wasn't sure she could go back to that pressure if the fulfillment and reward weren't there.

Aurora looked out the window, trying to shake off her maudlin thoughts. They were at Jude's farm, over by the refurbished barn.

"Not sure why I ended up back here." He slumped and killed the engine. "Power of suggestion? Since we were talking about it."

"Probably." She slumped back too.

It really was a stunning location. She could envision lights strung outside, over a patio for outdoor dining. Heating lamps for the winter months, casting a warm glow. Customers sipping wine and eating from a whole-food-, plant-forward-, locally-grown-based menu. Seasonal. Fresh. Simple.

Perfect.

"Hey, you want a drink?" Jude sat up. "I have some wine inside. Probably some bourbon, and this honey mead I bought in Austin that I've been wanting to try."

Aurora sat up as well. "I'd love to."

Jude unlocked the barn, and they entered the dim interior. She waited near the door as he turned on the lights.

Even empty, the inside was inviting. Warm, neutral colors. She pictured white tables and wooden chairs. More windows, open and airy, bringing the outside in.

"Drinks are up here." Jude stood at the bottom of a narrow ladder.

"There's a loft?" Aurora asked, following him.

"Well, it's a barn, so I left the loft."

She climbed up behind him and found a sitting area with a sofa and chairs, a small television, some shelving, and a row of three cabinets.

"Yes, I totally hide out up here sometimes," Jude confessed. "Have a seat. You want bourbon, wine—"

"Let's try the mead. I don't know that I've ever had it."

"Seriously?" Jude grabbed two glasses from the

cabinet and the bottle of honey-hued liquid. "Big-city girl like you?"

Aurora laughed, taking the empty glass he offered. "People in L.A. drink skinny margaritas and vodka with club soda. I'm going to guess this stuff has way too many calories for California drinkers."

"This is true." He opened the bottle. "It's sweet, and a sipper, but it makes for a nice drink when it's cool out, or you just want something sweet at the end of the day."

He poured them both a couple of fingers, and the scent of honey and something akin to mulled wine filled her nose.

"I can tell from the smell, it's strong."

Jude read the label and laughed. "Eleven percent ABV. So yeah, sip it." He clinked his glass to hers.

Aurora took a small sip, the sweetness hitting her tongue first, followed by the warm burn of the alcohol, finished with the smooth lingering taste of honey.

The result was a delightful drinking experience. "I like it," she announced.

Jude took a sip and closed his eyes with a low hum. "I concur."

The warmth spread to her limbs and Aurora settled back on the couch. It'd been a long week. For both of them.

She held the glass up to the light, turning it to catch the different amber hues throughout. "You could serve this at the restaurant," she said. "As a specialty. An aperitif."

Jude nodded and settled back beside her, mirroring her motions with his glass. "That's a great idea. Especially if I could find a local vendor."

"I'm sure you could, at least regionally."

"And if not, I could probably learn to make my own."

"It'd be a good skill to learn. Craft beer, mead. It's all the rage now." And she had no doubt he would and could learn both. From renovating the barn to running a farm to juggling his family and planning an expansion, she imagined there was little Jude couldn't do.

Outside of baking a pie and managing his father.

"So." He turned toward her and patted her knee. "What's going on with you? What had you walking the streets in thought this afternoon?"

Aurora debated telling him, and how much to tell him. Beth would say she should lay it all out, her opportunities, her emotions, her insecurities, and her feelings for Jude.

Self-preservation told her to stick with the facts.

"My boss called me this afternoon. I've been asked to open a new restaurant in Malibu, and I have to be back next week."

Chapter 19

Jude carefully kept his expression blank and remained silent, while his stomach fell through the floor.

Aurora turned the glass of mead in her hands. "It's all I ever thought I wanted. My dream come true, but... I don't know."

A surge of hope bolted through his limbs. "What do you mean, you don't know?"

She turned toward him, tucking one leg under her. "I'm not jumping at the opportunity like I thought I would."

"I'm guessing it's an amazing offer. The kind you've been waiting for?"

Aurora tilted her head. "It's an amazing offer, and I imagine most chefs in my position would be flattered and back in L.A. tomorrow, but..."

He nodded slowly. "Not you."

With a heavy sigh, she shifted. "This is what I thought I always wanted. It's why I moved to California in the first place and worked my fingers to the bone. This was the goal. To rise up through the ranks with a big restaurant group, get a head chef gig, and make a big name for myself."

He said nothing, but the doubt in her eyes pulled at his heart.

Those eyes. Aurora had always seen him for who he really was, the same way he saw her. She was a dreamer who needed to dream. He got it. He was the same. But sometimes you could focus so intently on the dream that you forgot to stop and ask if it was still what you wanted.

"I don't understand. Why do I have doubts? Why am I not more excited?"

He wanted to be supportive, and unbiased, even though his dream was to have her here. Someone who really cared about her would put her first and help her figure this out.

Jude shifted as well, to mirror her position. "Well, let's think about this. You've been back home for a couple of months now, were able to turn your family's business around and make a difference, work with your sisters. Do you really have a boss here like you did back west?"

Aurora quirked her lips. "No. Beth can be bossy, but she's not really my boss."

"So then you've had the freedom and control that working with family provides, and you probably put less pressure on yourself now that business is good at the inn. You feel supported. Maybe, deep down, you're happier here. Only you can answer that though. Maybe being here has made you question what's best, and that old dream in L.A. isn't what you really want anymore."

Her gaze locked with his.

That was precisely the issue. It was written all over her face.

"It's okay to feel that way." He reached for her free hand. "In fact, it's normal. You've been back and working with your sisters for a while now. You've been successful. The inn has flourished with you there. Everyone brags about you and your food. People see how amazing you are, and you're home. You're somewhere you feel comfortable and happy."

She squeezed his hand. "It's so weird, because I didn't feel comfortable about coming back here. I left home because I was hurt. I needed to get away, to find myself. Coming back, I was worried about facing the past, facing you."

A knot formed in his chest.

He nodded, knowing what she meant. He'd felt the same. Aurora left for good reason. He'd hurt her and, when she left, she'd hurt him too. Distance had helped them heal, and age gave them perspective.

"But I needed to go. Get out of the nest, away from my mom and sisters. Figure out what I wanted outside of you and find my own way."

"Which you did. Successfully." He intertwined his fingers with hers.

"I didn't know how it'd be to see you again."

"Weird, at first." He laughed.

"So weird."

He didn't want her to leave again. Not now. "Listen, I'm trying to remain unbiased here, and just be supportive. My sisters tell me all the time that sometimes I just need to listen and not try to solve everyone's problems, but..." He took a swig of his mead and set the glass down. "But screw it. I wasn't really kidding about you being chef at the restaurant. I just said that because I thought I'd stepped on my tongue while telling you about it and—"

"I knew you weren't kidding." Aurora squeezed his hand.

"You did?"

"Come on, Jude. I know your tells. I knew you were serious, but I...I'd frozen up by then. I didn't know what to say. A million thoughts were racing through my head when you said that and..." She let the sentence drift and shrugged.

"I know. It was a lot." And he'd been selfish enough once to try to decide things for her. He'd never make that mistake again. He couldn't ask her to give up what she wanted just for him. He wasn't sure what kind of future she wanted, but he knew he wanted her.

"Listen." He brought their hands to his lips and dropped a kiss on her knuckles. "I think you can do whatever you want, and you should follow the dream that makes *you* happy. Not because you feel like you have to accomplish something or risk being a failure, and not because you owe it to anyone else. Not out of fear or obligation. Do what *you* want. And I don't know what's going to happen with the restaurant as far as timeline and success, but if I can open a restaurant and you want the chef job, it's yours. Consider it a standing offer for whenever you decide."

Aurora smiled sweetly, and his chest ached at the sight.

"I think..." She swallowed hard. "I might like that."

His heart cut a backflip and it took every bit of his will not to attempt one himself. "Yeah?"

"I mean, I know there's still a lot to be decided, but I'm not freezing up or saying no. I'm saying maybe. Everything inside me is telling me I can't take that job in Malibu. It's all wrong. I just...I have to figure out how to tell them and, like you said, figure out what I want."

His heart was still busy dancing as he kissed her hand again. "Take whatever time you need."

"Are you going to talk to your dad again?" she asked.

"I am." He nodded, more determined than ever. "I'll try your advice and ask him to be involved. If he's still against it, I'll figure out another way. Maybe buy the barn outright and do it all on my own."

Aurora's face lit up at that. "You would do that?"

"I may have to." He chuckled. "I don't want to go that route, but the old man might not give me any other option."

She set down her glass and wrapped his hand in hers. "It wouldn't be the worst plan in the world. You could still make it work."

Pulse pounding in his ears, he dared to address the other piece of their future. "If you stay." He swallowed hard. "I'd like to..." He stopped and began again. "I don't want to just be friends."

Her eyes sparkled and her flushed cheeks glowed. "Being friends has been great and all, but me neither." She smiled.

That she would even consider staying here, give up Los Angeles and a head chef's gig for a future and a possible second chance—he was dreaming.

Jude leaned in, pulling her closer. His lips found hers and she wrapped her arms around his neck, in his favorite way. She tasted sweet, like honey, and she kissed him like she never wanted to let go.

He wouldn't.

He'd never hold her down, but god, he wanted her to stay forever. He wanted another shot. Wanted to be more than a friend or an old flame. He wanted to be hers. He longed to share dreams with her again, and this time, make them a reality.

Aurora kissed his jaw and whispered into his ear. "I want to stay the night. With you."

He leaned back, her breath warm on his skin, making his entire body thrum with life. "Here?"

She smiled at him, impishly. "It's what we would've done years ago."

Jude kissed her again, clinging to their past and praying they had a future.

Chapter 20

"Was that Jude?" Cece pounced on Aurora as soon as she walked into the inn.

It was barely six in the morning. "Why are you up so early?"

"That was Jude's truck. He's dropping you off and he was kissing you. Did you spend all night with him?"

Beth chose that moment to join them, her mouth hanging open. "*What?*"

She'd had zero coffee, and she'd finally slept with her high school sweetheart.

She couldn't deal with any of this just yet.

"I need to start breakfast." Aurora trudged past her sisters and reached what was normally the safety of the kitchen, but they followed her.

First, she poured herself a cup of coffee and took several sips. Then she got out a carton of eggs and some cheese, not completely sure what she planned to do with them.

"You need to answer the question." Cece dogged her every move.

"You were with Jude all night?" Beth's eyes were comically wide over her coffee. Like an overcaffeinated owl.

"I need to cook." Aurora picked up a skillet.

"You need to talk. Stop..." Cece grabbed the skillet and took it away. "Stop doing kitchen things and start talking."

"Fine. Yes, I was with Jude. Yes, that was Jude dropping me off after we spent the night together."

Cece's mouth fell open.

"Did you talk to him about being chef at the farm-to-table restaurant?" Beth asked.

"Did you not just hear the woman?" Cece spun on their sister. "The two of them had s-e-x. I think a restaurant is the least of their concerns."

"Actually." Aurora jerked the skillet away from Cece. "We did talk about the restaurant, and you don't have to spell *sex*. We aren't teenagers."

"I know, but you *were*. It's teenage love, rekindled. That makes it even more romantic." Cece clasped her hands together.

Aurora plunked the skillet down and turned on the burner. "Let's pace ourselves."

"What we need are details. How did this happen? Did he kiss you first or vice versa?"

"Did you tell him you're interested in being chef at his new restaurant?" Beth persisted.

"Beth," Aurora ground out, grabbing a spatula from the pottery canister of utensils.

"What? I think that's a very important bit of information that he'd be very interested to know."

"Okay, stop it. Both of you." Aurora brandished the spatula at her sisters. "I need to start on breakfast, and I can't concentrate with the two of you in my ear."

Cece looked offended, but Beth had the grace to look

properly censured. "Let's let Aurora fix breakfast, and we can continue this discussion while getting ready for Erica's visit."

Right. Erica Burr's wedding. Fun.

"Erica is visiting again?" Cece asked.

"Yes, it's on your Outlook calendar. She wanted to do a run-through of everything well before the wedding in case there needed to be any changes."

"What changes?" Cece chided. "There isn't much to it."

Aurora snorted with laughter.

"Don't be rude. We're going through the ceremony with the bride and groom and going over the details of the reception now that Aurora has them. We can talk about all of this later."

Except later came, and there was no time.

Aurora spent all day in the kitchen, juggling wedding cake ideas with how she was going to text her boss later and turn down the job offer. Refusing the Malibu chef gig would mean her termination, and then where would she be? Right here at the inn, making more wedding cakes.

Her situation could be worse, but it still astounded her to be in this position.

She wanted to be head chef at a farm-to-table in Texas.

Her *high school sweetheart's* farm-to-table, to be exact. A complete one-eighty from just a couple months ago. But so much had changed in those two months, not the least of which was reuniting with Jude.

Aurora smiled, her limbs warm with thoughts of last night.

"Stop it." She fanned herself on the way to meet

with her sisters. She couldn't show up all pink-cheeked and grinning or there'd be another round of rapid-fire questions.

Aurora joined them in the sitting room, cake details in hand. A classic white cake with buttercream frosting—baking cakes still wasn't her strong suit, but she could pull off a classic as needed—but with beautiful fondant frosted roses she'd taught herself how to make.

The finished look would be elegant and sophisticated. Both things that Erica prided herself on.

"How are we looking?" Aurora plopped down beside Cece.

Cece lifted an eyebrow. "Great, except for the lack of a bride."

"Excuse me?"

"Erica. She's over an hour late and won't respond to Beth."

Aurora searched Beth's face for confirmation.

"I've texted and called. No response. It goes straight to voice mail."

"You don't think...?"

A shadow passed over her sister's face. "I wish I wasn't thinking that."

"Thinking what?" Cece asked.

Aurora sat down next to Beth. "That Erica is running away from this wedding. Or worse yet, the whole thing was bull, meant to waste our time."

"*What?*" Cece joined them, sitting on the ottoman. "No way. Seriously?"

"It'd fit her character more than this simple wedding facade," Aurora snipped.

"I think it's more likely she's a runner." Beth clutched

her phone. "I hope anyway." She dialed Erica's number again on speaker but got no answer.

"Have you seen or heard from Ted?" Cece asked.

"No, but I rarely do, so that's not unusual. Erica is the primary for everything."

The coin dropped for Aurora. "Try Erica's mom," she suggested.

"You think she'd know, and talk to us about it?"

"Absolutely. They've always been close. Erica used to brag about it constantly, like she somehow knew my mom and I had a tenser relationship. I think she liked rubbing it in."

"That's so mean."

"That was Erica. Focus. And if she *is* legitimately running from this wedding, then I'll take back my hypothesis. Erica's mom won't be able to lie about what's going on, either way. That woman is a drama queen of the highest order. She's just waiting for someone to call so she can vent."

Beth picked up her phone again, nodding at the screen as she dialed. "It's worth a try." She held her phone to her ear. "Hello? Mrs. Burr? Yes, this is Beth Shipley, from the Orchard In—oh. Goodness. Okay, um." Beth's eyes went big as quarters.

Aurora could hear Erica's mom voicing her displeasure. So a runaway bride after all.

"Do you know how we could get in touch with her? Or where she might be?" Beth snapped her fingers toward a pad and a pencil. Aurora handed both over. "All right. Okay. It will be okay. Everything will be fine. We'll find her and talk to her. I'm sure it's only nerves. We see it all the time. Yes, ma'am. Okay, we will." Beth hung up. "Erica called the whole thing off and won't take her mom's calls either."

Cece gasped. "What are we going to do?"

"Let her go?" Aurora offered.

"Aurora," her sisters chirped in unison.

"I don't mean that in an ugly way. I'm saying, and I can't believe I'm saying it, maybe we take Erica's side. If she doesn't want to marry the guy, we can't make her. It's her life."

"I'm not suggesting we make her do anything." Beth planted her hands on her hips. "Her mom sounded really worried though. Said she's been acting weird the last few days and was probably wandering around downtown or in the parks. She won't answer her mom's calls, but apparently, she texted Ted earlier today and he called Erica's mom, none too pleased."

"Sheesh." Cece twisted a finger in her hair. "She could be really upset. I feel like we should try to talk to her. Emotions make people do crazy stuff."

Beth nodded. "We can't be all c'est la vie about her personal well-being."

Aurora grimaced. She hadn't thought about it that way.

"I need to see if I can get in touch with Ted." Beth scrolled through her phone. "I have his number in here somewhere."

"I can go look for Erica," Aurora offered.

Beth's gaze jerked to hers. "You can?"

Aurora shrugged. "My life is like a whole retrospective lately. I'm on a healing-old-wounds kick. Might as well go help my high school nemesis."

"I'll go with you." Cece got to her feet.

"Great." Beth took a breath, her wheels turning. "You two look around downtown. I'll call her mom again if I can't get in contact with the groom. If you find her, just make sure she's okay. This is her decision, and we respect it. We just want to make sure she's well."

"Got it, sis." Aurora waved as she and Cece left the inn.

They went up and down the long, straight roads of town. Past the shops and restaurants, German bakeries and small parks. No sign of Erica.

Cece let Aurora out at the corner of Main and Crockett.

"I'll check Old Fair Park and the Marktplatz. You keep driving around."

"Got it. Text me if you find her."

Cece pulled away and Aurora began walking. First to the gazebo, but all she found were a few couples strolling hand-in-hand. Then to Marktplatz von Fredericksburg. There were a lot more people there, milling about as they finished shopping or headed to dinner. Children ran around and played; a few tourists read the plaques for the town's replica Vereins Kirche, Fredericksburg's first school and church, built in 1847.

And on one of the benches around the octagonal building sat Erica, all alone, her knees pulled up to her chest, chin resting on them.

"Erica?"

Erica dropped her knees, sat up straighter, and jerked her face toward the sound of Aurora's voice.

"Oh, it's just you." She looked relieved. "Hey, Aurora."

Only Erica could manage to sound pleased yet dismissive all at once. Aurora approached slowly.

"I was worried you were my mother, and I was about to get the biggest lecture of my life."

Maybe things between Erica and her mom weren't so perfect after all.

"May I sit?" Aurora asked.

Erica scooted over, but her stare remained distant, on a far-off point outside Aurora's reach.

"Are you okay?" she tried.

"Sure. I'm supposed to be going through all my wedding plans and instead I'm sitting in the park with you." Erica snorted. "I'm fabulous."

Aurora bit back her retort. Erica was hurting. Maybe it was okay to let her have this one.

"I'm sorry." Erica shook her head. "That was really snide."

"No, it's fine. You're allowed. Besides, I have plenty of experience with you being snide."

"Ouch." Erica looked at her.

"Sorry. Now I'm being snide."

Erica lifted a shoulder. "No, it's okay. I deserve it. Kinda surprised you didn't give it to me when I talked to you at the inn the other day."

"I couldn't." Aurora managed a laugh. "You were being mostly polite. You threw me off and I didn't know what to say or how to act."

Erica chuckled. "Yeah. I threw myself off too." She brought her knees back up and wrapped her arms around them. "I thought polite and malleable was what a guy like Ted wanted in a wife. Agreeable, no ripples." Her derisive laugh chilled the air. "Turns out, being a doormat doesn't fit me."

"Yeeeeeah." Aurora drew the word out. "About that. I know it's not technically any of my business—but you are supposed to be getting married at my family's inn, so it's kind of my business—what the heck is going on there? What's going on with you?"

"Other than hiding from life right now?"

"Other than hiding from your life."

"I don't know exactly." Erica sighed. "But I do know, I don't want to marry Ted."

Aurora found her muscles relaxing, and her world, once again settling back on its axis. "Thank god."

Erica turned to her with a baffled expression. "I didn't know you cared."

"Well, I..." Wait, did she care?

Had she forgiven Erica? Let go of the past long enough to at least want her to be with a decent guy? What even was her life anymore?

Aurora shook her head, confounded by how the last few weeks had played out. "I guess I do care. Kinda. I know you and I aren't besties, but that guy..."

"Sucks," Erica finished.

"Yeah." Aurora chuckled. "And then, you wanted to get married all low-key and simple? None of it made sense. Low-key and simple goes against everything I know about you."

Erica laughed again, but this time joy threaded through the sound. "Right? All of that minimal and simple crap was his idea. His insistence. I am not minimal and simple."

"Exactly. I wondered if something had changed or this was a new you."

"It was all him," Erica ground out the words. "But there didn't need to be a new me. I was wonderful as is."

"See." Aurora held out her hands toward the woman beside her. "This Erica, I know. This makes sense to me."

"Plus, I'm not sure I want to marry anyone, any time soon."

Now that did surprise her.

"My mother, on the other hand, thinks I'm shriveling on the vine, and it's past time. Tick tock, tick tock, biological clock and all that nonsense."

"Oh."

"I think I knew the whole time that we were engaged that I was forcing myself to fit a mold made for someone else, but..." Erica let the sentence drag, but Aurora knew to be quiet and allow her the time to get this off her chest.

"Dating Ted was fine at first. Great even. We had fun. He's got money, so we traveled, we were always doing things, eating in the best restaurants, going to events. He courted me, hard, and really showed me how much is out there. Ted got me out of the bubble of this town, but turns out, he's a jerk."

"Wow." Aurora tried to sound surprised.

"All the money in the world doesn't make up for being a jerk. I know I can be a lot, but I'm not mean like I used to be. Once he won me over? Mean as all get-out. He's rude to everyone. And he's actually cheap."

She bet that didn't fly at all with Erica.

Erica shrugged. "He wasn't at first, but once we were together, he stopped trying. I got my real estate license and I've slowly been making my own money. Growing my brand. I kept hoping his bad attitude was just a phase. Nope. Just a cheap jerk once he thought he had me. I told myself it'd get better. He'd mellow out once we were engaged."

Mmm. In Aurora's dating experience, things rarely got better once the worst of a person came out.

Erica leaned toward her. "Spoiler alert, it never got better."

"It usually doesn't."

"Then, everything I wanted to do was suddenly vetoed. Mentioned an engagement trip to New York City, but no way was that happening. I wanted a big wedding and reception, and he's suddenly pinching pennies, even when my family offered to pay for a lot of it."

Aurora shook her head. "You sound pretty mismatched."

"I know." Erica groaned and buried her face in her knees.

"Then why force it?" Aurora asked.

Silence stretched out, but she waited patiently for an answer.

"I don't know," Erica finally answered. "I've wondered the same thing. But a lot of it was because this *is* what I've always wanted. Or what I thought I wanted. I've wanted to get married and be someone's wife since I was a little girl. The notion that I was wrong, that I'd made a mistake, or rather changed my mind, on something so important. I don't know. It took a while to comprehend."

Erica's words hung in the air, a reflection of Aurora's life.

The circumstances were different, their dreams distinctively their own, but a basic truth remained.

They'd both had big plans for what they thought they wanted. What they wanted was genuine and well-meaning, but life had a way of making you grow. Change. And if your dreams didn't change with you, they died.

"I'm not sure when I changed my mind or why," Erica continued. "But the idea of being trapped in a marriage right now makes me want to run and hide. I want to travel. I want to do things, go places, experience life. I want to see the world. And it hit me the other day, I'd rather go to some far-off country, all alone, than marry Ted."

Aurora nodded. "Being stuck in an unhappy marriage, in any situation you don't want to be in, all because you once thought it'd make you happy, would be a nightmare."

"I never again want a man to tell me where I can and can't go. I want to make my own decisions. Not my parents, not my fiancé, not my friends. Me."

Though hesitant to admit it, Aurora was proud of Erica. She was finding the strength to figure out what she wanted and the courage to go after it.

"Good for you," Aurora told her.

"Thank you." Erica smiled. "You know, I was so jealous of you when you moved away after school."

The admission caught Aurora off guard. "Seriously?"

"Very serious. I thought I wanted to be a big fish in a small pond, but I don't. It sucks."

Aurora wasn't sure she could agree. Being a small fish in a huge pond wasn't great either.

"I don't want to be with someone who doesn't love me. I don't want to be with anyone at all. At least not for a long time. And when I am, I want it to be someone who believes in me and encourages me."

Aurora thought of Jude, and his words to her last night. That she should follow her heart, and make her decision based on what she wanted—nothing else.

Erica's honesty and openness about her faults and where she'd failed showed her in a new light. She was another person, doing her best, trying to find herself.

Aurora never thought she'd have anything in common with Erica Burr, yet here they were.

There was pain in the history of Aurora's hometown, but there was also a lot of sweetness. People and places weren't all good or all bad. They were both, and she found she appreciated the good more because of the bad.

"Thank you for looking for me and talking to me." Erica sat up. "It's nice to know people care."

Aurora did care. She never would've believed it, but she wanted the best for Erica and hoped she found happiness. "You're welcome," she said. "I'm glad I found you."

"I should probably call my mom, huh?"

"Yes, and I was supposed to call my sister if I found you."

Erica opened her arms. "I'm sorry if I caused you guys any trouble. I can pay you for your time."

"It's okay, really. One of the benefits of planning a simple wedding." Aurora hugged her former enemy, wondering what other surprises her life had in store.

Erica stepped away to call her mom, and Aurora was in the middle of group texting Cece and Beth when her phone rang.

"Aurora."

"Hey, Beth. Good news. I've found the runaway bride and all is well. Better than well. Erica is the happiest and most authentically Erica I've seen since I've been home."

"That's good, but Aurora—"

"And she helped me realize that what you want in life changes, and that's okay. It's okay to drop back and rethink your options. Anyway, she's safe, and not marrying Ted. We should be headed home in a minute."

"Aurora."

"What?"

"Jude's dad had a heart attack."

The earth tilted beneath Aurora's feet and she grasped a light post to keep from stumbling. "*What?*"

"Cece is pulling back around to the park now to get you and take you to the hospital."

Her sister said something else. Something about where or when, but it was all static in her ears. All she could hear was Jude's voice, telling her how much family meant to him.

Chapter 21

Traffic lights flew by in a blur.

She and Cece made it to the hospital in mere moments and found part of Jude's family huddled in the ER waiting room. Jenna sat with their mother as Jude paced.

"Hey." Aurora rushed to his side. "What happened?"

Jude shrugged. "He was in the kitchen with Mom and just...collapsed."

"I'm so sorry." Aurora put her arms around him.

"He's in surgery now. I don't know what's going on," he said, the agitation rolling off him. "They haven't told us anything."

"I'm sure we'll hear something soon," his mother said. "He's in the best place to get help now."

"I know, Mom. But..."

"Please sit down," Linda urged him.

Aurora glanced at her sister. What should she say in a moment like this? She wanted to be there for Jude, without overstepping.

Rather than sit, Jude continued pacing.

Bonnie and Meredith arrived a moment later.

"Hey, Aurora." Bonnie sounded surprised.

"Where's Wyatt?" Meredith asked Jenna.

"Max kept him at home. Neither of us thought he needed to be in an ER waiting room."

"Agreed." Bonnie hugged her.

"I'm just so relieved to have Max home at a time like this. I don't know what I'd do if he was out on that rig right now."

Jenna caught Bonnie and Meredith up on what little they knew about their dad. Then the siblings all embraced and sat down, including, finally, Jude.

Aurora and Cece sat next to him, and he leaned forward with his elbows on his knees.

She wanted to comfort him, place a hand on his back, talk to him, but it might be odd with his family right there. They wouldn't know about her and Jude, how they'd reconnected or where they stood.

If she came across as too familiar, how would they react? Was it strange, her and Cece even being here?

Bonnie studied her closely, Jude's mom occasionally casting glances her way.

Next to Bonnie, Meredith gave her and Cece a small smile. Meredith wasn't technically family either, but she appeared at ease. At home. Maybe Aurora was missing something, because she very much felt like an outsider at the moment.

Jude sat back with a sigh.

Aurora leaned closer. "You okay?" she whispered.

"No, I'm not okay," he said, his voice clipped.

"Can I get you anything?"

He shook his head and dug a hand through his hair. "No. Answers about my dad?"

Aurora shot a glance at Cece, who gave her a slight shrug.

She should be better at this. She consoled her sisters all the time, so why did it feel like she was mucking this up completely?

"I'm sure they'll come out in a minute and let us know what's going on," Aurora tried.

"It's been minutes already."

She placed a hand on his shoulder, hoping to offer some comfort. If he felt her, he gave no indication.

They sat silently for a while, Aurora praying for the right words to say.

"Why can't they tell us what's going on?" Jude asked no one in particular.

"He's going to be okay," Aurora encouraged.

"You don't know that."

"Your dad is strong."

Jude sat back, shrugging off her hand. "I just...I should've been there. I feel awful, because the last time we spoke, we were arguing over a stupid restaurant."

Aurora bit her lips together, moving her hand back to her lap. She knew she shouldn't take his comment personally. He was upset and stressed. It didn't mean anything, and she shouldn't take it on board. But her heart still twisted in her chest.

The restaurant was far from stupid, but now wasn't the time to point that out.

Jude didn't look at her as he spoke. "I hate arguing with him."

"I know," she said quietly.

"What if our fight— You know? What if the strain from our fight and pushing the restaurant on him caused—"

"Don't say that." She made him meet her gaze. "Don't even think that. This isn't your fault."

"Pushing him about the restaurant and arguing certainly didn't help though."

"What are you two talking about?" Jude's mom asked.

"Nothing," he answered quickly.

"It didn't *make* this happen either," Aurora whispered, sitting back.

"I'll never forgive myself if he doesn't pull through. I can't lose him like this."

"I know." She tried to be soothing.

"Well, that decides it then." Jude clamped his lips together.

Another beat of silence passed, and she felt the nauseous foreboding of something awful. She'd seen that look on his face before. That locked jaw, the angry grinding of his teeth. She remembered another time when his open, affectionate gaze went blank. Hard and distant, determined to shut out everyone and everything, except one misguided notion he clung to like a lifeline.

"Decides what?" she dared to ask.

"We can't talk about the restaurant anymore," he bit off. "Not any of it, not anytime soon."

Aurora sat up and stared at him, the room and everyone in it falling away.

He was going to throw away this dream, his plans, this very real future, for both of them, out of...out of guilt?

"We can't," he repeated, his jaw set. "It's too much for him to handle. All that matters right now is my dad. Not some restaurant that might never happen. I'll never forgive myself if he doesn't pull through." Jude shot up from his seat and marched away.

Aurora's stomach plummeted.

Might never happen.

Why wouldn't it?

He'd offered her a dream. Not just the restaurant, but the two of them, together again. It wasn't just his dream to take or leave. She thought they had a future.

And the connection between the restaurant and his dad's heart attack was a stretch. John Jones had always had blood pressure issues, even ten years ago.

The line Jude was drawing was as ludicrous as the connection between her supposedly standing in the way of his future at eighteen.

"I need some air." Aurora blindly pushed herself to try to stand, but Cece stopped her with a hand on hers.

"Don't walk out of here," Cece murmured.

"What?" She eased back down and leaned into her sister.

"You can't leave. Not now." Cece's gaze went down the hall and back to Aurora. "Jude just stormed off. If you take off, too, it won't look good. Stay here. For his family. I'll go see if I can find Jude."

Her sister made a good point. As gut-wrenching as Jude's distance was, as easy as it would be to run and hide right now, she wasn't eighteen anymore. She was stronger than that.

"Thank you," she whispered.

Moments later, Jude's mom stood and stretched her back. "I need some coffee," she said, looking right at Aurora. "Come with me?"

"Okay." Aurora didn't particularly need caffeine at the moment. She needed Jude to explain how his mind worked, but Linda asking her to join her was more direction than question.

They walked down the hall and around the corner, into a vending area with a free coffee machine.

Linda Jones hit the buttons for a black coffee and waited while it brewed.

"I'm so sorry this happened." Aurora crossed her arms in front of her, hoping this exchange went better than the one with Jude had.

"Thank you." Linda frowned. "Oh, honey, you look ready to cry when I'm the one that should be bawling." She extended her arms and took Aurora into a hug.

"I'm sorry," Aurora said again, heat rushing to her face. "I'm here to comfort you. Not the other way around."

"Maybe we can comfort each other. How's that sound?"

Aurora breathed deeply. That sounded nice. "Thank you. And if there's anything I can do, I will. You guys have always been good to me."

"Thank you, dear." Jude's mom leaned away. "Did Jude say something to upset you?"

She brushed off the question, unwilling to bother his mom with everything else on her plate. "No ma'am. I'm just worried about Mr. Jones."

Linda chuckled. "It always tickled me how you called him Mr. Jones. So formal." She picked up her coffee and urged Aurora forward to get her own.

She hit the button for hot chocolate instead.

"You know, *Mr.* Jones is going to be okay," Linda stated, with no small amount of authority.

Aurora stood up with her hot chocolate.

"He was talking to me when they brought him in."

"He was?"

"He was in bad shape, granted, but the EMT told me I called in time. See, John's daddy had a heart attack, two in fact, and his granddaddy had a heart attack. All the Jones men deal with this. My Mr. Jones won't take his meds regularly and he doesn't eat right. He never has." She sipped her coffee like she'd seen the future and knew what to expect. "He says I harp on him, but after this, that man won't see red meat again except on Christmas Eve and his birthday. He calls vegetables, or anything healthy, rabbit food, but I can tell you one thing, he better strap on some big ears and a fuzzy white tail, because rabbit food is what he's going to be eating from now on."

Aurora couldn't help but smile.

"I kept telling him this would happen. I think I've mentally prepared myself for years. And while I'm worried, I'm less so after the EMT talked to me." Linda patted her arm. "So, try not to be so upset, okay?"

"I'll try." Aurora sipped her hot chocolate and decided to open up to the woman who was once like a second mother to her. "I was a little upset before, even though I said I wasn't. And, I feel bad saying, not just about your husband."

"I know. I have two daughters of my own and I used to know you pretty well, dear."

Aurora smiled, warmed by her words as much as the hot chocolate. "Jude can be tough to read is all. And he's upset about his dad, naturally, but he kind of... shuts down?"

"Not kind of. That's exactly what he does." Linda nodded and drank her coffee. "Just like his dad. Holding it all in isn't good for their health either. They can be the most stubborn, tunnel-visioned people you'll ever meet."

She was right. Aurora had never thought about it that

way, but Jude wasn't that unlike his dad when it came to shutting out people and ideas.

"I know Jude gets aggravated at how stubborn his dad can be. I tell John all the time, I love him, but he's like an old mule. But Jude is just as stubborn. They're very different in some ways, but exactly alike in others."

"Have you ever told him that?"

Linda stopped sipping her coffee. "Goodness no. Have you?"

Aurora shook her head.

"Can you imagine? Neither one of them would ever admit it and then they'd be mad at me for comparing them." Linda smiled. "But you know, our faults and flaws are often just the flip side of our strengths. You can't have one without the other. Every coin has two sides kind of thing."

Aurora thought about that for a second.

"You see, Jude and John, both so dang single-minded and stubborn, right? But that also means they're persistent. Driven and determined. If they set their mind on something good and worthwhile, then by gosh, they'll get it done and done well. On the other hand, if they decide they won't do something, then you'll have better luck moving a two-ton bull than getting them to change their mind."

Aurora laughed inside at the imagery.

"It can be done though." Linda grinned. "I've done it before, when Bonnie first told us about her and Meredith."

Aurora clamped her mouth shut and stared down into her hot chocolate, unsure of what to say.

For her, the love between Bonnie and Meredith was

obvious and lovely. But she knew not everyone looked at things the way she did. She'd wondered if Linda and Mr.—if John—knew.

"John struggled accepting it a little bit at first," Linda said. "Even though we wondered about it ages ago. A mother knows, and I reminded him he'd kind of always known too. In the end, his love for his daughter outweighed any nonsense in society. I just gently reminded him of that."

Aurora admired the woman before her so much.

"So, you see, they *can* be reasoned with. You have to lead them to it, not force it on them. Like I'm going to do with this so-called rabbit food. Just watch me."

Aurora had absolutely no doubts.

"All that to say, try not to worry about Jude or John. He and his dad will be okay. They just process things the way they process them, and sometimes the best thing you can do is be upfront with them, and then let them figure out the rest for themselves."

Linda made perfect sense, and Aurora appreciated the advice more than she could express. If anyone understood Jude, it was his mom.

"I'll be honest with you though," Linda said. "I do worry about one thing."

"What's that?" Aurora stood a little straighter.

"I worry about him when you head back to California."

The wind was knocked from her lungs. "Oh," she managed.

"I see how he looks at you, even now, when he's fretting over his father. He's thinking about you, too, regardless of how it may seem. The girls have told me how much he talks about you and…" Linda stared into her paper cup before throwing it away. "I don't want to see him get hurt again."

Aurora stood there, stunned.

Him get hurt again? He broke up with her. He ended their relationship. Jude had broken her heart. *She* was the one who got hurt.

But had she broken his heart too?

"He was devastated when you left for college," Linda said, as though reading her mind. "I know he ended things between the two of you, but I think he always regretted how your breakup played out. And I know he regretted losing you."

Aurora wrapped one arm around herself. She knew he hated his handling of the matter, but she didn't quite grasp that he'd regretted breaking up with her.

"I was proud of you for broadening your horizons, and look how well things turned out," Linda continued. "But I know Jude. Underneath it all, he's a big softie. He was heartbroken when you left, even if it was for the best."

So maybe she wasn't the only one who'd had to heal from their past. Thankfully, the two of them had been able to come together and repair their relationship. But now, they were back to where they'd been ten years ago.

Whether she wanted to admit it or not, her heart was already in this restaurant project and she had feelings for Jude. Again. She wanted a future with him, and he was shutting her out.

She'd already started dreaming, and this was too much like history repeating.

Was she supposed to completely throw away her chances in California for an opportunity here that Jude refused to pursue? She didn't want her old L.A. life back anymore, but she didn't want to stay here and long for something that'd never happen.

She'd been down that road already and she couldn't do it again.

A lump formed in her throat, tight enough to hurt and choke. "I'm going to go check on my sister." She gave Linda a small smile and walked away before the cracks began to show.

She hurried toward Cece and flashed her a look.

Recognizing an emergency eject when she saw one, Cece jumped up and met her halfway. "I can't find Jude."

"That's okay. We should probably go."

"You sure?"

"Yeah, I…I need some time and I think…I think I need to give Jude some time too? Maybe?"

Cece took her hand. "You'll tell me more in the car?"

"I'll tell you in the car."

They got in the car and Cece was gracious enough to wait a few blocks before speaking. "What happened back there?"

Aurora's lip trembled and her voice shook as she spoke. "Jude's mom basically told me I broke Jude's heart."

Cece's mouth fell open. "But he broke up with you."

"I know, but I think— I don't know, he was heartbroken, too, when I left."

"Because he regretted it. Because he wanted you back."

"Yeah, I…" Aurora shook her head. "But that was years ago. It doesn't make any difference now."

"It makes a huge difference! What if he was still in love with you, even after you left? What if he's always been in love with you?"

Cece was being a hopeless romantic. Aurora wanted

to cry and scream and run to Jude and for the hills, all at the same time. If he'd still loved her then, if he still cared now, why was he shutting her out and pushing her away again?

"There's something else though," Aurora added. "Jude said he was done talking about the restaurant. It's over because he thinks trying to push his dad about the project brought on the heart attack. He said we can't talk about it anymore."

Cece hit the brakes a little too firmly at the red light. "He did not."

A crack began to show as her voice broke. "He called the restaurant stupid. So that's it. I know he was upset, and some of what he said was only out of emotion, but not when he said we couldn't talk about it anymore. You should've seen his face, Cece. Hard and cold. I've seen that face before." The first tear welled up and rolled down Aurora's cheek and she swiped it away.

"When he broke up with you?"

She nodded. "I can't believe I'm seeing it again. I can't believe I'm in this position. Again."

"Aurora." Cece sat at the light, missing when it turned green, until the car behind them beeped.

They drove another block in silence as more tears fell. "I'd gone so far as planning to turn down the Malibu offer. I was going to be Jude's chef. I was going to leave my life in California. I'm such an idiot!"

"No." Cece reached for her. "You're not an idiot for believing in something."

"I was stupid for believing there was enough between me and Jude that things would be different this time. That we had what it'd take to make this work. I should've never gotten mixed back up with him and the past, all those feelings. I knew, going into it, this was a bad idea. But what did I do? I strolled right in like a glutton for punishment."

Cece pulled her car over on the shoulder and jammed it into park. "Now you listen here. I don't want to hear you putting yourself down, not one more time, you got it?"

Aurora blinked at her sister, caught off guard at her vehemence. "I mean it. If Jude doesn't open a restaurant, even if he never speaks of it again, so what? Supporting him when he did believe in it doesn't make you stupid. Just because he gives up doesn't mean you have to. If your dream is to be head chef of your own place, where you can run the show, then follow it. You could still stay in Texas and open your own restaurant."

Aurora gave her sister a dubious look.

"I'm serious. Why not? Why can't Aurora Shipley open her own restaurant?"

"Um, money, for one. The main one."

"Get investors. That's what all start-ups do. I could help. I've gotten very good at PR lately. And I know people. Just saying."

Aurora swiped at the corner of her eye and shook her head. "I think the best thing I could do right now is go back to L.A. Even if I turn down Malibu, I could probably keep my old job and live my life as I have for years."

"Now *that* is the stupidest thing I've ever heard. I know you're happier here. Long before you ran into Jude Jones, you were more at ease and happier than I've seen you in years. I know you don't want to plan wedding menus forever, so don't. Open your own restaurant."

Aurora shook her head. That was such a huge risk and responsibility.

"I know it's scary, but you're so much braver than you realize."

"I'm not."

Her sister huffed in frustration. "I never told you about the time I saw Erica and her friends at the lockers that day, did I?"

"What?"

"Your senior year, my sophomore. It was after school, you were at your locker, and Erica and her friends walked by. You remember?"

It'd been at least a week of the rumors swirling about her being easy as the only reason Jude was with her. She'd been exhausted from the slut-shaming, sick of the attention, and wanted to disappear. At the end of a long day, Erica was there with her friends to turn the knife a little bit. They'd loudly contemplated who all Aurora had slept with before Jude.

"You were there?" Aurora asked.

"I was at the end of the hall, in a doorway. But I could see you and hear them. I heard the names they called you. I wanted to run down there and throat punch all three of them."

Aurora could picture her sister, with her sweet blond curls bouncing as she stalked toward those girls, taking a swing at a few upperclassmen. The vision made her smile.

"But you finished up at your locker, closed it, and walked right by them. Head held high. They might as well have been invisible for all the attention you paid them. I'd heard the rumors and knew how mean those girls could be. I always admired you for handling that the way you did. Then you kept your head up after the breakup, you moved away for culinary school and made it, all on your own. You are the strongest person I know, Aurora."

New tears rolled down Aurora's face.

"You've always been my hero. Because of you, I became more determined. You're the reason I don't hesitate when trying new things and putting myself out there on social media. You helped me believe in myself because you believed in yourself. I know you can do anything you put your heart and mind to."

"Cece," she managed, probably smearing mascara as she wiped at her face.

Her sister reached over and hugged her. "So, no more talking down about yourself, okay?"

Aurora nodded.

Cece put the car back in drive and they made their way home in silence.

Maybe Cece was right. Maybe Aurora didn't have to give up on the dream of running her own restaurant, with or without Jude, with or without a restaurant group in California.

It might be terrifying, and she might fail, but how would she know if she never tried?

The advice she'd given everyone else recently, she needed to take herself. Aurora needed to follow her own dream, and not let fear or doubt or anyone else stop her.

Chapter 22

Jude hunched over in the chair by his father's hospital bed, praying over and over again that everything turned out okay for his dad. His limbs felt like bags of cement, his head a jackhammer. Wandering the hospital corridors hadn't helped, and now all he wanted was to have his family home, safe and healthy.

The doctor had come out an hour ago, informing them about his father's bypass surgery and allowing their mom to go back and see him. Jude and his sisters had waited impatiently for their turn.

His dad was asleep now, and while his sisters had gone to get something to snack on, Jude had stayed by his dad's side.

No matter what anyone said, he was responsible for his dad's heart attack, and he wanted to be there when his dad woke up again. He'd never forgive himself if there were long-term, lingering effects. He should've never pushed the restaurant idea.

Jude scrubbed at his stubble as he glanced around at all the monitors and IVs. He'd meant to shave last night but had spent the night in the loft with Aurora. No razors in the loft.

He dropped his hand.

Aurora.

He'd been short with her in the waiting room. Standoffish. Even rude.

He hadn't meant to be, but he couldn't even think about the restaurant or his future or anything else right now. Not with his dad's life in the balance.

Screw the restaurant. Forget about branching out. He'd give it all up if he could just have his dad back, healthy and whole.

He'd run the farm exactly like his dad wanted and handle the business the way John Jones intended. All that mattered was that his dad pulled through this. He'd bargain and barter his way through it if the outcome meant keeping his family intact.

"You look worse than I feel, son."

His dad's croaky voice startled him. "Dad." He scooted his chair up to the edge of the bed. "Hey."

"How long have you been here?"

Jude looked around for a clock. "I don't know. As soon as Mom finished seeing you and told me you'd come around. You fell back to sleep though. You want me to go get her?"

"No, no. I talked to her before." He held out his hand and Jude took it. "I want to talk to you now."

"Okay."

"How are your sisters? They here?"

"Yeah, they're with Mom. They're okay. We're all just worried about you."

His dad patted his hand. "I know, I know. Worried myself for a bit there too." He gave Jude a wobbly grin. "Your mom will never let up after this. I'll be eating rabbit food till the day I die."

"You'll do whatever you need to do to be healthy. We want you around for a long time, Dad."

His dad nodded, his gaze going to the industrial-tile ceiling. "You sure you wouldn't be better off without me?"

"*What?* No. Dad, stop that."

He patted Jude's hand again. "I don't mean it like that. Not dead, just...not pestering you kids. I know you and your sisters love me and want me around to be your dad. But I also know I can be an ornery cuss about the farm."

Jude schooled his expression to show no reaction.

"I know I can, son. You can say as much. Your momma says it all the time."

"Maybe a little stubborn is all."

"Aww, now, I'm a lot stubborn. Set in my ways. It's in our blood. Stubborn, hard-working, and prone to heart issues. You better start watching your cholesterol now, son."

Jude smiled despite himself.

"I know I've been down on you about wanting to expand things on the farm or, how do you say it? Diversify."

Jude opened his mouth, but his dad talked over him.

"Especially about that restaurant, I know I lost my cool—"

"Don't worry about that anymore." Jude shook his head, stopping his dad. "Forget I ever said anything about a restaurant. It was a crazy dream anyway. Just focus on getting better and stronger, and getting back home."

John cocked an eyebrow at him. "What if I don't want to forget about it, son?"

Jude ignored his father giving him that look. "It's not

good for you to get worked up. I'm not going to bring up the restaurant or any new ideas anymore. I just want you to be okay."

His dad pushed himself to sit up some and look Jude in the eyes. Jude got up to try to stop his dad from exerting himself, but his dad waved him off. "Stop fussing over me, boy. Let me just say this, and you sit your tail down and listen."

Jude sat down, all too familiar with his old man's tone, and buoyed by the fact he still had the spitfire to use it.

"Jude. I don't want you to stop talking about your crazy ideas, you hear me?"

Jude blinked. Had he heard what he thought he just heard?

"This farm, *our farm*, has been around for almost a hundred years. A hundred years, son. It's hard to believe. Generations have made a living off that land. But I know…or I guess I need to admit, that times are changing." He patted Jude's hand again. "Just because something worked fifty years ago doesn't mean it works now or that it's going to work forever. Profit margins ain't what they used to be and, if we keep on like we are right now…well, we might not be around for future generations."

His father's admission made his heart jump. Could it be? Would his father consider…change?

"I don't want that to happen. I want the farm to be there for you and your sisters, maybe for grandkids, I don't know. But I don't want to stand in the way of some things that might help us grow. I know the core of what we do works, and it will stand strong because it must, but…I don't know. Maybe we need to broaden our scope a little?"

Jude nodded, his legs going a bit numb. He was scared to hope.

"But I'll be real honest with you, son, that scares the pants off me."

The tremble in his dad's voice tugged at Jude's heart. That was a ginormous admission for a man like John Jones. To confess fear wasn't something his generation did.

"I don't like change."

No kidding, Jude thought, smiling to himself.

"And I know it scares *you* too. Yet you still believe in it. As thoughtful as you are, the way you like to plan things out and double-check daggum locks and lights and"—he chuckled—"all that stuff you do. As careful as you are, and you still want to make these additions and branch out...I have to believe you'd put a lot of thought and care into it."

Jude felt like his heart might explode. "I would, Dad. I *have*. I only want what's best for the farm. For our family. I wouldn't even consider it otherwise."

"And that's what matters, right here and now, for the farm. When I was in that ambulance with your mom, I realized that's all that matters. My family. And the future isn't about me working all the time and doing things my way. This is about you, and your sisters, and keeping the farm in the family for a hundred more years. It's about what y'all want to do going forward, and I don't want to run y'all off. Your mother would kill me." His father managed a grin.

Jude could've jumped up and hugged his dad around the neck if it weren't for the IVs and sensors.

"And listen, I don't want you to be just like me. You're your own man. You think big and outside the box. You always have, and you're always smart about it. What's more, you've got two whip-smart sisters who aren't afraid to let you know they think you're screwing up."

Jude laughed. They'd be very quick to point out if he was wrong.

"I want you to keep dreaming up ideas, and just know some are going to work and sometimes you'll fall flat on your keister. That's okay too. I need to let you know that." His dad shook his head. "You realize a lot of things, real clearly, when you think you're going to die."

"Dad." Jude gripped his hand that much tighter.

"I should've let you make your own decisions and mistakes years ago, and I can't stand in the way of you making them now."

Jude was stunned speechless. It was all he'd wanted to hear from his father, and then some. He swallowed down the lump in his throat and choked back the emotion.

"Speaking of standing in your way, what about that girl of yours? Aurora."

Jude had to work not to laugh or cry at the same time. "She's not my girl, Dad."

"Ah, hogwash." His dad grumbled as he scootched up in the bed. "You listen to me now. I know I was a big ol' monkey wrench between the two of you a long time ago. I'm sorry for that, I really am. But, I...ah hell, I don't know. I thought I was doing what was best for you. I don't know if I was though. Regardless, I never intended to do the same thing now."

Jude gazed toward the hospital room door. "Pretty sure I'm the monkey wrench this time, Dad. Not you."

"Why? What'd you do?"

"I don't..." Jude shrugged, figuring what was the

point in sugar-coating the truth now. "I think I told her the restaurant was stupid and I never wanted to talk about it again."

His dad's eyes went wide. "That was dumb."

Jude laughed as he hung his head. "I know. I thought I was going to lose you. I feel like I caused this, and I just wanted you to be okay. I'd give up all those ideas if it meant my family being okay."

"I am okay, son. But are you?"

He sighed, really considering his father's question.

He wasn't okay. Better, because his dad was going to be just fine, but he'd chased off the best thing that'd ever happened to him.

"No, I'm not," he admitted.

"Because of Aurora."

Jude nodded. "I think I might've run her off. Again." He hadn't meant to shut her out, but he'd done what he swore he'd never do. He'd pulled away, so caught up in making things right that he forgot to be true to himself.

"Not if you own up to your mistakes, you haven't. Remember what I said. You're going to fall flat on the ol' keister sometimes. That's unavoidable. It's how you deal with it that matters. If you want to make things right with your girl, then do exactly that. You're a good man, Jude. I know you can handle it."

And Jude's truth was he wanted to bring the farm into the future *and* have Aurora by his side.

He wanted both and having the farm and restaurant without her would be an empty life. A future without Aurora was no real future at all.

His dad nodded, as if reading his thoughts. "She'll understand what happened tonight, and what you're going through. But you let her decide what she wants as well. I know it's scary, but all you can do is speak your mind, and be honest about how you feel. You can't control her or what she wants. All you can do is love her true." His dad closed his eyes and laughed. "If you could control a woman, I'd make sure Linda didn't take my bacon and steak away, but I already know how that's going to go."

Jude gave his dad's hand a squeeze. "You get some more rest now, Dad. And thank you. For everything."

Chapter 23

The Stonewall Peach JAMboree and Rodeo was that weekend, and it'd snuck up on everyone. Aurora ran around the next morning like a headless chicken, her sisters doing the same.

She was almost busy enough not to think about Jude Jones every five seconds.

Almost.

"I still need to tie up all the little takeaway gift bags for the inn." Cece hurried into the kitchen. "But I can't find my scissors. Have you seen my scissors?"

Aurora tried to think back to the last place she saw Cece working on the one hundred cellophane gift bags that contained a delicious chocolate chip cookie—Aurora's secret recipe—a recipe card for a delicious dip—not a secret recipe, also Aurora's—a scented votive candle, and a brochure about the inn.

"You were stuffing cookies into bags in the dining room," she said.

Cece took off in that direction.

Beth scurried in next. "Did Cece have enough brochures for the gift bags? Because another box just arrived from the printer. I thought I'd take extras to the festival tomorrow."

"She had enough brochures but can't find her scissors and I bet she'll need help tying them up."

"Got it." Beth glanced around the kitchen. "How are you coming along with the pie for the contest?"

"Haven't even started yet."

"Are you..." Her sister approached her like she would've approached a sleeping tiger. Cece had come home and immediately told Beth all about what'd happened at the hospital. Aurora had filled in any blanks. "Are you still okay to do it?"

"I'm fine," Aurora insisted. "I'm not about to have a meltdown. I'm just...disappointed in Jude and upset about the whole situation. But Jenna let me know that Mr. Jones is going to be fine, and that's what matters. It is what it is with Jude. I can't force him."

"Have you talked to your manager from Malibu yet?" Beth asked carefully.

Aurora groaned and refolded the kitchen towel in her hands for the third time. "I was supposed to text him yesterday."

Beth returned her grimace.

"I need to call him today and tell him..." She wasn't sure what she'd say.

How did one turn down what once seemed to be a dream job? How could she best explain she was experiencing a quarter-life crisis and thought she might leave the security of her old job to dive, headfirst, into something brand-new?

Beth nodded. "You'll figure out what to say and how to say it. And just know, you always have a job here, no matter what happens. We're your family. We got you."

Aurora smiled at her sister, the support a warm comfort, even though she was so tired she felt it in her bones.

Cece rushed back in, breathless. "Mom is here."

Why was their mother dropping by on one of their busiest days?

"She called this morning and I told her I needed help with the gift bags, so she's here to help."

The anxiety that Aurora normally felt when facing her mother wasn't there. Their last visit together had gone as well as it could, and there was so much on Aurora's plate, she couldn't worry about her mother's judgment.

"Well, I'll be in the kitchen on pie duty if anyone needs me." Aurora shooed her sisters out.

Once she was alone, she stared at her recipe card for the honey-lavender custard she'd made days earlier.

When she'd first made it, the flavor was different. Exceptional.

Now it didn't hold the same interest for her.

This wasn't unusual for any chef. She became infatuated with dishes all the time, and sometimes grew disinterested if the mood of the dish changed.

No, a custard wouldn't do. She needed something with more...pizzazz.

Aurora paced the kitchen, pondering pie ideas that would win a contest.

She was still pondering when her mother popped her head into the kitchen.

"Hey, honey," she said. Her mom's long hair was pulled up into a ponytail, making her look ten years younger. She looked amazing. Happy, glowing. "I'm not disturbing you, am I? I know how you like to focus when you're in the kitchen."

"No, come on in. I'm having chef's block right now."

"Oh no." Her mom joined her, studying the kitchen. "Your sisters told me you're making a pie for the contest."

"That's the plan anyway. I thought I'd decided on a lavender-honey custard style, but I've scrapped that idea. I feel like I should use peaches or apricots. Something from the orchard to represent the inn. Now I'm just waiting for inspiration to strike."

"Hmm." Her mother leaned a hip against the counter and crossed her arms. "Anything I can do to help?"

"Asking if you can help helps." Aurora smiled. "But no. I think I've got it. Plus, Cece has a ton to finish for the booth at the jamboree."

Her mother nodded slowly, studying her. "I'll give her a hand. But I wanted to check on you first." She paused, studying her shoes before saying, "Cece told me what happened with Jude."

"Great."

"Don't be mad at her. I'm the one who asked how you were doing."

It was a new experience, having her mother interested and involved.

"I'm okay. I mean, I will be. Just...I got my hopes up thinking something was an option, that one thing was going to happen, and now it isn't, which also means..." What did it mean? "Which means Jude and I..."

"Had a falling-out?" her mother offered.

"For lack of a better word, yeah." And if she were completely honest, she was sadder about that than the restaurant.

No. That wasn't completely honest.

She was heartbroken. Again. She'd gotten her hopes up, her feelings involved. Then he'd bailed on her. Again.

"I thought I knew what I wanted, and I'd always intended to go back to L.A. Then I wasn't sure what I was going to do," Aurora admitted. "Later on, I thought I was closing in on an answer, but the rug got jerked from underneath me. Now I'm adrift again and figuring out what I'm going to do with my life." She forced a self-deprecating laugh. "It's been a crazy couple of months."

Her mom pushed away from the counter and moved closer. "It's okay to not have all the answers. To be undecided or to change your mind a hundred times. You're too hard on yourself. You always have been."

Aurora met her mother's gaze, caught off guard by her comment.

"I remember the first time you wanted to make homemade cookies for your sisters. I think you were twelve. They were good, but not great. It was a first effort. You got so mad at yourself and were in such a bad, a tween mood. I didn't know how to handle it, so I just let you be. Beth was still her logical self at twelve, so I had no experience. You were a lot more emotional. So was Cece."

Aurora thought back on the memory. She'd gone to her room, slammed the door, and stayed in there for a couple of hours. She'd thought her mother was mad at her for acting out.

Her mother placed a hand on her arm. "If you make a mistake, that's part of life. No matter how old you are. There's nothing to be ashamed of."

Warmth surrounded Aurora. It was the kindest, most intimate affection her mom had shown her in years.

Her mom rubbed her arm. "Trust me, I know. I spent so

many years being ashamed of my choices. Embarrassed because I'd fallen for your dad and didn't see him for who he really was. I was so bitter he left us in such a state. I swore off men, relationships. I spent way too much energy being angry and beating myself up, being resentful of everyone else and myself. I was my own worst enemy. I don't want you to do the same."

Unshed tears burned Aurora's eyes. She was turning into such a weepy baby lately.

"I was hard on you girls too," her mom added. "Especially you. I know that now."

A tear did well up then. The confirmation of what Aurora had felt was true, more than she could handle.

"Oh, honey." Her mom hugged her. "I'm sorry. I know I was tough, but I saw what you could do, the raw talent. You had such wild ideas growing up, of all these things you wanted to be and do, but I also saw you needed the push. You'd come up with ideas, and then that'd be it. You didn't fight for them or for yourself. You were so quiet and happy to just sit back and let others shine. You were so…agreeable. Maybe it's middle child syndrome, I don't know."

Aurora melted into her mother's hug. She wanted to savor this moment. The unfiltered honesty and emotion.

"You know, I was a middle child too," her mother spoke into her hair.

Aurora nodded. She knew but hadn't ever really thought about it.

"I wanted to have my own thing and be somebody. But the safety of home is…well, it's safe, and you can get bogged down in what's comfortable. I knew that wouldn't serve you well. I saw myself in you, and I didn't want you going down the same path as me. I wanted you to strive for more, so I was tougher on you."

Aurora leaned away. In a way, she was glad for her mom's toughness. She resented it, but it'd helped her be strong.

"I'm sorry I wasn't a softer mom," Anita said.

"You were a good mom. And you did your best. Raising all of us on your own."

"Yeah, but...I should've talked to you about what I was feeling after your dad left. I was dealing with a lot, and I didn't want to burden you all with it. I should've let you in though. Especially once you were older."

Aurora sniffed back more tears. "You're letting us in now. It means a lot." And she could appreciate it more than she would've as a teenager.

Her mom brushed back her hair. "Lyle has been good for me. He listens and helps. Even a year ago I wouldn't have given him the time of day, but my friends were like, when are you going to stop being so scared and start living for you? And they were right. I wasn't living for me. I *was* scared."

Aurora was scared too. As much as she denied it to herself, she was too frightened to admit the truth.

Aurora had chased her dream to California because chasing meant running away from Texas. From her parents, her broken heart, her hometown, and toward a different dream.

Her dream had changed once before, and she made it happen, so why couldn't it change again?

She knew she didn't want to follow the path she'd started in California anymore. She didn't want to be someone's chef and mere employee. She didn't want the grind and competitive hustle of big-city hospitality. She hadn't been happy the last couple of years. Anyone who paid attention could see.

She'd been happy the last couple of months here, at home. But she didn't want to cater weddings and be locked into the box of those events.

Cece was right. She'd given voice to Aurora's truth, because sometimes your sisters knew what you wouldn't say.

Aurora wanted her own place. Her own restaurant. Something she developed and believed in.

"I know what I want," she told her mom.

"I know you do."

"I think I've known for a while, but I keep…"

"Getting in your own way?" Anita asked.

"Yeah."

Finding the money and investors would be tricky, but she and her sisters had made it work for the inn, they could make it work for a restaurant. She had no doubt her sisters would be thrilled at the idea and do everything they could to help. Somehow, she'd figure it out.

Her mother gave her arms a squeeze. "You are going to be just fine, Aurora. I know it. And if there's anything I can do, or Lyle can do, to help, just say the word."

"Thank you," Aurora said, giving her mom another quick hug. "You have no idea what this means to me."

Her mom's eyes misted as they let go. "I know what it means to me."

They said goodbye as Anita went to help Cece get their gift bags ready for the jamboree.

Aurora grabbed her phone and stared at the dark screen. She needed to do this. She had to do this.

Unlocking the phone, she hit Mark's number and waited for him to answer.

After five rings, he finally said hello.

"Mark, hey, it's Aurora."

"Aurora." Wind blew loudly in the background, as though he were standing on a cliff to take her call. "I thought you were going to text me with your return date yesterday."

She took a steadying breath. "Yeah, about that. I don't have one."

"Excuse me?"

"I don't have a return date. I don't think I'm returning." Aurora bit her lip and tried again. "I mean, I'm not. I'm not returning to work. Or to L.A."

Silence roared through the phone.

"Mark?"

"Yeah, I…I'm here. I'm surprised to hear this. May I ask why?"

"I'm pursuing another option here in Texas. Something new and something of mine. I…I appreciate everything I've learned working out there, and I appreciate the opportunity of Malibu, but it's just, it's not me. I thought that's what I wanted, but it's not."

"Are you going to open your own restaurant there?"

Aurora stood a little taller and squared her shoulders. "I am."

Another beat of silence and then, "I was wondering when you might."

She blinked at his statement.

"It's our loss, but good for you. I commend you on striking out. Nothing risked, nothing gained, right? I had to start my first restaurant to be where I am now."

Aurora sighed with relief. This was not at all how she'd envisioned their conversation going.

"I... I didn't think you'd..."

"You thought I'd be mad?"

"Yeah."

"You won't be my competition if you're in Texas, so why should I be mad?"

"Because I'm turning you down."

Mark laughed. "You've been a good chef for us, for years. You always put in your best work, so I don't see this as you turning us down, like you're going to work for a competitor. I understand wanting to do your own thing."

"Thank you."

"Thank you too. And good luck. It'll be a lot of hard work. Let me know if you have any questions."

They ended the call and Aurora stood there, stunned, in the middle of the kitchen.

She'd done it, and it'd gone better than she could imagine. She'd cut the cord on her old career, and now there was nothing to do but pursue her dream.

She glanced around the kitchen, at the collection of pie dishes catching her attention.

The pie for the jamboree.

Okay, nothing to do but bake a pie for the contest and *then* pursue her dream.

Her mind buzzed with potential. This was the new era of Aurora. This pie needed to be special. Different. A unique combination of flavors that popped and stood apart.

At first, she hadn't even wanted to enter the contest, but now that she was in it, she wanted to win. Winning would get her name out. It could springboard something locally. It certainly couldn't hurt.

Ideas of her own restaurant spun her brain around. She needed to go sit down and start making notes, get the noise out of her head, but she couldn't. She had a pie to make.

Aurora went to the pantry and pulled out all of her herbs and spices. Then she grabbed the latest basket of fruit from the orchard. Peaches, plums, and apricots covered the kitchen island.

She'd thought she was tired of peaches, but she plucked a peach from the bowl, turning it in her hand. It was beautiful and bright. The scent was fresh, sweet, and undeniably a favorite in Hill Country.

But she couldn't just do a peach pie. Boring. There would be a dozen others in the contest.

It needed the right seasoning to make it next level.

She grabbed the flour, salt, sugar, butter, and eggs. She mixed the dry goods first, sifting her flour, pondering how to make a crust that was just a little bit different. Gazing across the field of herbs on the counter, the lavender caught her eye.

She wanted to ignore it. Lavender reminded her of Jude.

But what was wrong with thinking of Jude? She wasn't going to lie to herself anymore. She cared about Jude.

She loved him.

She'd loved him at eighteen, and she loved him still. No matter how frustrating and bull-headed he might be, no matter what happened or what paths their lives took, she loved him.

They might not share the same dream anymore, but that didn't mean she had to deny how she felt.

Aurora picked up the culinary lavender, crumbling a few buds in her hand. The soft sweetness was an instant comfort.

She sprinkled bits of lavender into the flour before adding everything else.

Once the crust was in the oven, she turned her attention to the peaches. Defuzzing and slicing, her fingers became a sticky mess. She ate a few slices of fresh peaches—because that was a rule of baking—and put the rest in a bowl.

In a smaller bowl, she mixed some honey, sugar, and lavender, and stirred.

"This isn't enough," she said to herself before picking through the rest of her herbs. What could she add to make it special?

Her hand landed on the thyme from Jude's farm. His pet project of adding herbs to the farm that'd become a huge success.

He was a smart businessman, if he'd only let go of his fear too.

"Thyme it is," she said to herself, sniffing the warmth and spiciness of the herb. It had some complexity and would balance out the sweetness with an earthy base.

"Love it," Aurora said, adding the thyme.

She stirred her mixture together and slowly poured it over the peaches, gently combining everything. The sharp sweet scent of peaches mingled with the warmth of thyme and the delicate touch of lavender. The combination was a love letter to the Orchard Inn and her sisters, to the farm and Jude's family. Aurora breathed deeply before pouring it into the cooked crust. Placing her pie in to bake, she set the timer and began tidying up her workspace.

Intently focused on the pantry, she was startled by a steady deep voice behind her.

"Aurora?"

Her stomach leapt. Jude had come to see her.

Aurora turned, schooling her emotion. He could be here for any number of reasons.

"Hey," he said, and strode toward her. He placed a basket on the counter as he passed it, cornering her near the pantry. "I wouldn't blame you if you threw me out, but please don't. I need to talk to you. I have to try."

Her heart hammered, her vision narrowing to only his face. "Try what?"

"To fix things." He motioned between them. "To fix this."

"Wha—" She tried to swallow, her mouth too dry. "What's there to fix?"

His gaze softened, his eyes wide as if taking her in. "You know what. I messed up. I messed *everything* up. I know I was short with you at the hospital. I shut you down. I pulled away because I was scared about my dad. I shut you out like I did senior year, and I'd sworn to myself I'd never do that again. But I…I realized, it wasn't just my dad and his health that scared me."

"No?"

"No. You scare me too. You and me. Us. I'm scared of getting close to you again. Scared of getting hurt." He shook his head to keep her from speaking. "I know I never told you that I was heartbroken, too, when you left after school, but I was. I knew I'd made a mistake almost as soon as I did it. I wanted you back. But I couldn't…I had no right to keep you from your dreams. Your plans for culinary school, and after. I couldn't stand in the way of that, especially not after what I'd done. So I let you go, but I should've told you I still loved you. And being with you lately, spending all this time together, realizing all those feelings are still there—I've been so happy. But I was like a scared kid again. Because I still love you, Aurora. I don't know that I ever stopped loving you."

Aurora's heart longed to hold him, to tell him it was okay, she felt the same, but she waited for him to finish.

"I talked to my dad, at the hospital, and I realized that fear, fear of failing, of disappointing my dad, and then fear of losing him, it's kept me from the best things in my life. It's stopping me from doing what I really want."

Her heart soared, high above the kitchen. Even high above the Orchard Inn. It's what she'd longed to hear ten years ago. Two days ago. Two minutes ago.

"And what do you really want?" she dared to ask.

Jude smiled, his blue eyes like the deepest, warmest ocean. "*You*, silly. I want you." He took her hands in his. "I want to be with you, open a restaurant with you, make plans and dream big dreams with you. I love you, Aurora."

She swallowed hard against the knot in her throat, the swell of emotions threatening to overwhelm her. "I love you too," she managed.

Jude kissed her.

Hard and fast, sweeping her up against him and holding on to her like he was holding on for life.

"I'm not going to cry," he muttered against her hair.

The big softie.

"That's okay, because I think I am." Truth was, she was a big softie too.

After a long moment, he leaned back to study her face. "I want to open that restaurant. I'm *going* to open that restaurant." He spoke with full confidence and all the authority in the world. "And I'd love to have you as the chef. I want to support you in your dreams and help make them come true. I never want to lose you again and I know I screwed up. Maybe I lost your trust and you might want to go back to L.A., but that doesn't matter. This is still how I feel, and I owe it to myself and to you, to tell you the truth. To put it all out there on the line."

Aurora smiled, her cheeks tired from smiling and crying and the flurry of emotions that'd swirled around her all day.

"I'm so happy to hear you say that," she said. "But I can't be your chef."

His face fell, those deep eyes sorrowful. "You can't?"

"No. Because I realized something, too, just in the last twenty-four hours. I don't want to be *anyone's* chef or employee. I want my own restaurant, or least equal partnership in it."

His sad eyes crinkled at the corners. "I'm listening."

Aurora cleared her throat. "I could be your partner."

A smile broke out across his face as he swept her up again with a whoop. "I love that idea. Yes!"

She couldn't say another word for the next minute, while he spun her around the room, dropping tiny kisses onto her cheeks.

"This is the best idea anyone's ever had," he claimed.

Aurora giggled until her sides hurt. "Put me down before you hurt yourself."

Once she was back on her feet, she took his hands in hers. "I'll find a way to pull together my part of the investment. I don't know how, exactly, but I believe in myself. I know I can do it. And obviously I'll put in the sweat equity. I'm ready for my own place, and I can prove it."

Jude glowed, radiating like he'd just won a million

dollars. "I know you are, and I know you can. Let's do it. Let's make our dreams come true."

He kissed her again, so deeply and slowly that she almost forgot about her pie.

"Oh my gosh!" Aurora jumped away from him and hurried to the oven.

The latticework crust on top was just starting to golden. "Whew. Needs a few more minutes."

"Is that the contest winner?" Jude asked.

"It's the trial run. I'll bake the real one right before the jamboree. By the way, what's in the basket?" She nodded toward the counter.

"Oh. That." His voice was flat, no inflection. "Well. I brought you something. It's not a gift. I wanted it to be a gift, but it's— I think I did something wrong."

"What is it?"

She opened one end of the picnic basket to find a pie inside.

His lemon icebox pie.

"Aw, you baked! Kind of."

"I destroyed it. I tried a bite of it and..."

Aurora pulled the pie from the basket and got a knife. "It looks okay. Can't be that bad."

"Trust me, it's worse."

She cut a small slice and placed it on a plate. Carefully, she tried a bite.

The tartness hit her salivary glands like a Mack truck. "Oh!" She puckered, swallowing it down. "That's..." She reached for a glass of water. "That's lemon pie all right."

"See?" He groaned. "I might kill someone with that pie!"

"How much lemon zest did you use?"

"Um..." He scrunched his brow. "I thought it called for lemon juice."

"Oh no." Aurora pushed the pie to the side. "That... we're going to forget about that. I have a better recipe for you anyway. A honey-lavender custard."

"Yeah?" He stepped closer again, sweeping her hair back from her shoulders. "I like both of those things."

"So do I," she said. "And I'll even show you how to make it as soon as mine is done."

"You'd do that for me? The competition?"

Aurora raised up on her tiptoes, wrapping her arms around his neck before kissing him gently on the lips. "What's a little competition between partners?"

Chapter 24

The morning of the jamboree, Jude drove Aurora, her destined-to-win pie, and his honorable mention to the grounds where the annual event was held. He parked them as close as he could and escorted her toward the baking contest tent.

"You got this in the bag." He squeezed her close, carrying both of their pies in his picnic basket.

"Why am I nervous? This shouldn't make me nervous."

"Because deep down you're as competitive as Beth, but you try to deny it. Relax though, no way anyone can beat your pie."

"I don't know, there are some folks here who have been cooking for a lot of years."

Jude brushed off the thought as blasphemy. He didn't care what anyone else brought to the table. Aurora was taking home that trophy.

They passed the rodeo area, finding Cece, Beth, and Sawyer.

"Hey." Sawyer shook Jude's free hand and gave Aurora a hug. "Y'all headed to the big contest?"

With an arched brow, Aurora asked, "The *big* contest?"

"Yeah, apparently it's all the buzz today. Big baking contest, they've got a publisher here as one of the judges. Winner might get in a cookbook."

Aurora tensed next to him. "That's right. In the tornado that's been my life lately, I forgot all about a publisher judging the contest."

"What have you got to worry about?" Jude asked. "You're a pro. I'm the one entering a serious contest with no clue how to bake."

She patted his arm. "I helped you. You'll be fine. I'm nervous though. That's a serious judge."

"You guys coming?" Jude asked the others.

"Wouldn't miss it." Cece grinned, staring back and forth between him and Aurora.

They made their way to the contest area, weaving through pockets of people, when a blur of brown and speckled white whizzed past Jude's peripheral.

"Dog!" Cece blurted.

"Well, hello." Aurora stopped in her tracks, blocked by an eagerly nudging, waggling nub-tailed German pointer. "It's Roscoe." She reached down to scratch his ears, much to Roscoe's delight.

Roscoe's leash lay stretched out on the ground behind him.

"Did you escape Mrs. Watterson again?" Jude asked the dog.

Cece scratched him on the shoulders. "Is this the baby chicken dog?"

"This would be him," Aurora answered.

"Roscoe made you talk to me that day."

Aurora rolled her eyes. "He did not *make* me talk to you. I was going to talk to you."

Jude scoffed before laughing. "Sure. You were all kinds of chatty."

"Okay fine. Roscoe broke the ice."

"Thank you, Roscoe." Jude patted him on the head.

Cece picked up the leash. "Y'all are so weird. I'll take him back to Mrs. Watterson."

"Bye, Roscoe." Aurora waved. "Are we weird?" she asked as they kept walking.

Jude shrugged, scanning above the crowd for the right tent. "Maybe. But I'd be weird with you any day."

Aurora smiled up at him. "Me too."

He spotted the pie contest tent, and they found it filled with people and excited chatter.

"Looks like Sawyer was right, this is the place to be."

Jenna found them, rushing up with Wyatt in his wrap. "I can't wait to see how you two do. There are thirty entries. *Thirty*."

Jude's mom was several steps behind Jenna, Bonnie and Meredith with her.

"Aurora." His mom opened her arms as they approached, hugging Aurora. "Jude told me how you helped him with that pitiful pie of his. Thank you for making the farm look good."

He'd told her more than that; he'd also said they'd talked about the restaurant and their plans. Maybe she'd play it cool though.

"And he told me you two are going to be partners in opening a restaurant on the farm. John and I are so excited to see it come to life."

Nope. Not playing it cool at all.

"That's the plan." Aurora smiled. "How is Mr. Jones?"

"He's doing very well." His mom sighed. "He wanted to be here, but he still tires really easily. The doctors said while he heals up from the stents, he has to stay close to home. Then, he'll be able to get out and about more and more."

"Well, please tell Mr. Jones I'll bring him by some of my best rabbit food next week. I'm determined to find a plant-based meal he loves as much as country-fried steak."

Linda laughed. "From your lips to the Lord's ears. And you know, at some point, you're going to have to stop calling him Mr. Jones."

Aurora smiled. "I promise I'll try."

"Y'all better get your pies to the check-in guy." Bonnie pointed to a table with a stern-looking sort holding a clipboard.

"I'll go with you," Meredith said with a smile. "I want to find out how one becomes a judge of these things."

Jude and Aurora entered their pies and received pieces of paper with their entry numbers. Now all they could do was wait.

Meredith and Bonnie busied themselves interviewing the various contest admins about how one got involved in such a gig. Beth, Sawyer, and Cece joined them just as the judges got seated and, one by one, slices of pie were presented to them.

There were five judges in all, and Jude tried to determine which one was the big-shot publisher.

"Have they tried yours yet?" A tall man approached Aurora, a petite, familiar-looking blonde beside him.

"Hey!" Aurora hugged them both, and a lightbulb went on for Jude.

That was Aurora's mom.

"Jude, you know my mom, and this is her boyfriend, Lyle."

"I almost didn't recognize you," Jude admitted, hugging her mom. She looked younger than she had ten years ago. "Nice to meet you," he told Lyle.

"Your mom told me you're staying in town," Lyle said, his happiness evident. "And you're going to open a restaurant. That's awesome!"

"Thank you." Aurora's cheeks deepened in color. "This is my business partner and..." She looked at him, a giant question mark looming.

Jude nodded, not quite satisfied with that introduction either. He didn't want to be her business partner first, boyfriend second. There was nothing like the present to make it official.

"Boyfriend," Jude said. "Boyfriend and business partner."

Cece grinned from ear to ear. "Yeah, you are."

Aurora's color deepened even more.

"I wanted to talk to you about the restaurant later too," Lyle said. "Your mom mentioned start-up money and maybe an angel investor or some seed money to back you as partner?"

Aurora blinked. "Yeah, I want to contribute my share. I have some savings and Cece has found one investor already, but I'm still figuring out the rest."

"Good." Lyle nodded. "Let's talk. I was once a start-up myself and now I have my own contractor company. I might be interested in making an investment."

She beamed. "Really? That'd be...yes! Let's talk."

"Oh my gosh." Cece elbowed Jude, hard. "I think that's your pie."

Jude checked his number and, yep. Pie number 12 was up.

The judges each took a bite or two, but he couldn't tell a thing from their expressions.

"At least none of them spit it out," he said.

"Oh, stop," his mom said.

Jenna bounced Wyatt. "Yeah, have some faith."

Aurora's was up next. "Ugh, lucky number thirteen," she said.

"Now this one, I have faith in." Jude wrapped his arm around her. "It's a winner. You'll see."

Almost an hour later, they all milled about, still waiting for the contest announcement.

Sawyer had gotten restless and already had gone to look at the horses *and* returned.

"I never thought I'd be this anxious about pie," he said to Jude.

"Tell me about it." Jude shifted on his feet.

Finally, someone tapped on a microphone.

"If we could have your attention, please. The judges have reached a decision." The man with the clipboard had the mic and fumbled with the envelope. "The winner of this year's Stonewall Peach JAMboree and Rodeo's first annual pie contest is...contestant number thirteen! The lavender-peach pie!"

Aurora screamed.

Her family screamed. Jude's family screamed. Everyone was clapping and hollering, like they were surprised.

He didn't get it. He'd figured it was a foregone conclusion. This was Aurora after all.

Jude scooped her up into a hug. "Congratulations," he said, kissing her on the temple. "I knew you'd win."

She was shaking with excitement as she left him and went to get her trophy.

He stood there, grinning.

"You look like you knew she'd win," the woman next to him said.

"I did. I know her cooking."

"It was actually a close one though," the lady said.

He turned toward her, shocked. "It was? *How?*"

"There was a custard that was divine, too, a lavender-honey."

Jude chuckled. "Oh, that was hers, too, actually."

The lady seemed alarmed. "It was?"

"No, no," he backtracked. "It was my entry and my pie, but the original recipe was hers. Because I botched a lemon one completely."

The lady hid a giggle behind her hand.

"Wait, you... you judged this."

She nodded. "I did." The lady held out her hand. "Madeline, with Beardsley Books."

"Oh." Realization dawned. "*Oh.*"

"I was going to talk to the creator of that pie about featuring a recipe in one of our books. But... considering she's the mind behind both the first- and second-place pies, maybe we need to talk more."

He didn't care how he came across or what this Madeline person thought of him. Jude jumped at the opportunity. "You do. You definitely do! She's an amazing chef. She does more than just pies too. In fact, she's going to open a restaurant. Soon. And she's catered events, and brought, like, I don't know, nouveau southern cuisine to the West Coast. I think that's what I read one time, and—"

The lady—Madeline—laughed again. "You certainly know a lot about her."

"She's my girlfriend," he told her proudly.

Madeline nodded. "Then you could introduce us."

"I could. I mean I would. I will. Let me get her. You stay right there. I mean, please. Don't move."

Jude rushed off, his heart pounding. A publisher wanted to talk to Aurora about her cooking. Her recipes. This could really happen.

No. This *would* happen.

No more fear or doubt. He and Aurora were together again, and nothing was going to stand in the way of their dreams.

"Hey." He rushed up to her, kissing her congratulations on her win. "I have some good news," he blurted.

"I know, I won." She held up her little gold pie trophy.

"Yeah, but more than that."

"Your face is all flushed, what's going on?" She put her hand on his cheek.

"I need to introduce you to someone. You're not going to believe it."

"Okay?" She tilted her head, obviously baffled.

"But first, I love you."

She pressed her lips to his. "I love you too."

"I know," he said, his heart about to explode. "Here's to making our dreams come true."

Epilogue

Six months later…

Aurora brushed off one of the outdoor tables and straightened the table setting.

The utensils weren't crooked, but she couldn't help herself. She wanted everything to be perfect for the soft opening.

"How many times are you going to fix that table?" Jude hugged her from behind.

"I need something to keep my hands busy."

"Well in that case." Jude turned her around and wrapped her in his arms.

"What if people hate it?"

He rested his chin on her head. "Would you stop? No one is going to hate it. You're an excellent chef, the author of your own cookbook—"

Aurora squealed, still trying to accept that reality. She'd landed a cookbook deal with Madeline and Beardsley Books, with an option for more if sales went well.

"And my dad loves your plant-based dishes. That right there is the highest praise ever bestowed upon a chef. John Jones willingly eats plant-based food."

Aurora laughed. "Very true. I'm glad we added more

options for vegans and heart patients who need to eat rabbit food."

"That lentil soup with saffron? I think he'll eat that every day this winter."

Jude dropped a kiss on her forehead and began walking them backward.

"What are you doing?"

"Turning on one of these heat torch thingies. It might get chilly out here as the sun goes down."

He adjusted the flame to mid-height.

"You think it's okay, opening up in the winter?"

"I think it's perfect. Holiday season. People are all out and about, shopping and too tired to cook dinner. I predict we'll have a great month."

"I hope so."

Jenna stepped outside to join them. "Max finally got that last beer tapped. He wanted me to let you know."

In the midst of all their restaurant prep, Max had come to Jude and laid everything out on the table. He couldn't work on the rig anymore.

Jude had filled her in later that day over a glass of mead.

Max hated being away from Jenna and Wyatt, he saw how hard his absence was on both of them, but he worried about finances and wanted to support his family.

Jude immediately hired him at the farm.

"My dad is retiring, and I need more hands on deck," he'd said. "With the restaurant opening, there's going to be more hours of work than we have people."

"Count me in," Max had replied. "And not for nothing, but I bartended for the few years I tried college and after. Before I hit the rigs. So, you know, if you need a hand there."

Turned out, Max was a whiz at plumbing and pipework. He helped outfit the place under the guidance of Lyle, who had stepped in as their contractor and gotten the barn up to code in record time, allowing Aurora and Jude to focus on the business and food side of things.

"Okay, I'm all done with the bathroom lighting." Lyle joined them, adjusting his tool belt. "Nothing like the last minute."

"Thank you so much." Aurora hugged him.

"No worries. It's all in the family, right?"

Between Lyle, Aurora's savings, Cece's angel investor, and her sisters gathering some money—which she insisted was a loan that she'd pay back—she had her half of the start-up money to make her a partner. Of course, they all said she didn't need to pay them back any time soon, but it would be her first priority.

"I better go wash up before I pick up your mom." Lyle waved goodbye for now. "See you both in a bit."

They all needed this to be a big season. They needed customers and money coming in. Aurora needed this to be a rousing success for her family as much as Jude's.

Cece joined them, a tablet in her hand like she was doing her best Beth impersonation. "Look at you," Aurora teased.

Cece had sworn she had the publicity in the bag. Aurora wasn't sure how much of a dent she'd make with mainly social media, but then again, Cece knew a lot of things that went over her head.

The soft opening was just friends and family. The grand opening was tomorrow night, and Cece kept the reservation list.

"You wanna guess how many reservations we have for tomorrow?" she asked.

"Please don't torture me."

Cece grinned. "We're booked solid."

Aurora's jaw hit the floor.

"No availability. Walk-ins for the bar area only."

"You're joking." Jude clapped his hands together. "That's what I'm talking about." He high-fived Cece.

"I'm only the best amateur publicist ever, I think." She flipped her hair. "Oh, and temporary hostess. That too."

Aurora nibbled at her bottom lip. Now they had a full house tonight *and* tomorrow night.

Jude put his arm around her again. "Stop stressing."

"What if I mess everything up? What if I'm off my game and the food is garbage?"

"What if pigs fly? You've got this. You're going to knock it out of the park."

Aurora turned and met his gaze. His complete faith and belief in her melted away her anxiety. "I love you so much," she told him. "You're the best."

"I know." He grinned cheekily before kissing the tip of her nose. "I love you too. Now, and I say this with the utmost respect and adoration, go get in that kitchen and start cooking."

She kissed him goodbye and went inside *their* restaurant.

Warm lighting made the inside glow, and honey-oak chairs sat around crisp ivory-cloth-covered tables. The combination was inviting and classic. The food was authentic and uncomplicated, but exceptional in its careful preparation and freshness.

And she was doing this with Jude.

It was everything she'd ever wanted, even before she knew it and could admit it.

Aurora stepped into her kitchen and donned her apron.

"You ready, Chef?" Sloane grinned at her from the other side of the counter.

Her best friend and roommate had come to visit in the fall, immediately falling in love with the food and culture of Texas...and the men. She'd left L.A. last month, eager to join Aurora as her sous chef on this venture.

"I'm ready." I think, Aurora thought to herself, sharpening the first of her knives.

"I hope that's not for me?" John Jones stood at the end of the prep counter.

Aurora set down her stone and knife and hugged him tightly. "How you doing, Pops?"

She'd finally stopped calling him Mr. Jones.

"Better than ever. I get to have my weekly red meat tonight. It's a red-banner day all around." He chuckled.

"I'll give you a very lean, but slightly bigger cut too." She winked at him.

"That's my girl." He patted her shoulder. "Do you say break a leg to a chef or...?"

"Break a leg works," Sloane chimed in.

"Then y'all break a leg."

"Dad? Mom got you a table outside." Jude came in to retrieve his dad, giving Aurora a smile.

She'd grown so close to his dad in the last several months, helping him figure out a nutritional plan that worked with his high blood pressure and cholesterol, but also—as he put it—didn't mean a miserable existence on rice cakes. Trial and error over many meals, all of which he was happy to enjoy as guinea pig, meant hours and hours together, talking.

John Jones was a gem, not unlike his son. And once he decided he loved you, he loved you for life.

"You good?" Jude approached, checking on her one last time.

"I'm great."

"Good. Me too."

Sloane smiled and rolled her eyes at them before busying herself elsewhere.

"I'll be at the front of house if you need me," he said. "Hey, and after we close tonight, maybe we can go for a drive?"

She arched an eyebrow at him. "A drive, huh? Where to?"

He shrugged. "I don't know. To McGregor's lake? Maybe go for a stroll, do a little stargazing, a little day-dreaming."

Her smile began in her bones. The twinkle in Jude's eyes and the sly grin on his face warmed her heart. "It'll be nighttime, silly," she said.

He brushed his lips against hers and pulled her in close. "You want to go or not?"

"Of course. I'd love to dream a little more with you."

Excerpt from Restaurant Review:

Local farm-to-table restaurant LAVENDER breathes life into Fredericksburg's restaurant scene

The chef, Aurora Shipley, spent five years as sous chef at Brio in Los Angeles. There, she learned how to accentuate the freshest of vegetables, the tenderest cuts of beef, and take pure, honest ingredients and create something out of this world. Most recently, she's been the chef at the Orchard Inn, thrilling brides and grooms and guests with menus that match their wishes, then elevating each item to something beyond expectation. Texans who care about their dining experience should give thanks for everything she's learned. For all of it, and more, is now here at the newest Fredericksburg farm-to-table restaurant, Lavender.

A plate of pasta becomes so much more when seasoned with local herbs, lemon, and freshly grated Romano from a farm not five miles away. And clearly Aurora's kitchen isn't afraid of bold flavors. Gulf shrimp are tossed in a tornado of spices that leave you salivating for more while ordering that second locally brewed Hefeweizen or neighboring-winery Riesling to quench your thirst.

You won't find anything puzzling on Lavender's menu. Nothing you can't pronounce or some wayward ingredient you've never heard of before. These dishes are familiar, comfortable, and comforting. A taste of home, but as exquisite as the rarest of menus.

Lavender isn't pretentious or self-important. Ms. Shipley and her team are your neighbors and your friends, preparing the best Texas has to offer with an unfussy, genuine approach. The result allows the ingredients to speak for themselves. Make a reservation and find out for yourself.

Lavender is great food, done extraordinarily well.

Don't miss the next book
in the Orchard Inn series!
Coming Summer 2024

About the Author

Heather McGovern writes contemporary romance in swoony settings. While her love of travel and adventure takes her far, there is no place like home. She lives in South Carolina with her husband and son, and one Maltipoo to rule them all. When she isn't writing, she enjoys hiking, scuba diving, going to Disney World, reading, and streaming her latest favorite on television.

You can learn more at:

HeatherMcGovernNovels.com
Facebook.com/Heather.McGovern.Author

For a bonus story from another author that you'll love, please turn the page to read

ONLY HOME WITH YOU

by Jeannie Chin.

Zoe Leung allowed her mother to pressure her into a safe, stable career path, but her job search has hit a dead end, and now she doesn't know what to do with her life. She fills her days with waitressing and volunteering at Harvest Home, her uncle's food bank and soup kitchen, while waiting for inspiration to strike. And if she also flirts with fellow volunteer—and her older brother's best friend—Devin James, who can blame her? He's only the subject of her lifelong crush. And finally looking at her like he returns the sentiment.

Construction worker Devin James has always thought Zoe was gorgeous, but he doesn't want to jeopardize his friendship with her brother, or her family, who all but took him in when he was younger. But as much as he plans to stay focused on building his dream house, he can't stop thinking about Zoe. And the more time he spends with her, the more he realizes that the only home he wants is one with her.

Chapter One

Twenty-eight more months.

Devin James silently repeated it to himself with every crack of his nail gun. He moved to the next mark on the beam, lined up his shot, and drove another spike of steel into the wood.

Based on the numbers he'd rerun over the weekend, twenty-eight months was how long it was going to take him to save up for a house of his own. Still too long, but he was on target, putting away exactly as much as he'd budgeted for, paycheck after paycheck.

"Take that," he muttered, sucking in a breath as he kept moving down the line.

His dad had told him enough times that he'd never amount to anything. Devin tightened his grip on the nail gun and sank his teeth into the inside of his lip. What he'd give to get that voice out of his head. To show his dad he wasn't too stupid to do the math, and he wasn't too lazy to do the work.

He'd buy those three acres of land from Arthur. His mentor—and his best friend Han's uncle—had been saving the lot for him for three years now, and he'd promised to sell it to him at cost. Once Devin had the deed in his hand, he'd start digging out the foundation the next day. Between the buddies he'd made at construction sites and the favors folks owed him, he could be standing in his own house within six months. A quiet place all to himself on a wooded lot five miles outside of town. He'd get a dog—a big one, too. A mutt from the animal rescue off Main Street.

He'd have everything his useless old man told him he could never have. All he had to do was keep his head down and keep working hard.

He finished the last join on this section of the house's frame and nodded at Terrell, who'd been helping him out. The guy let go, and they both stood.

Adjusting his safety glasses, Devin glanced around. It was a cool fall day in his hometown of Blue Cedar Falls, North Carolina. The sun shone down from a bright blue sky dotted with wispy clouds. The last few autumn leaves hung on to the branches of the surrounding trees, while in the distance, the mountains were a piney green.

He and his crew had been working on this development for the better part of a year now. It was a good job, with good guys for the most part. Solid pay for solid work, and if he had a restlessness buzzing around under his skin, well, that was the kind of thing he was good at pushing down.

"Hey—James."

At the shout of his last name across the build site, Devin looked up. One of the new guys stood outside the trailer, waving him over. Devin nudged the protective muffs off his ears so he could hear.

"Boss wants to see you before you clock out."

Devin nodded and glanced at his watch. The shift

ended in thirty. That gave him enough time to quickly clean up and check in with Joe.

He made a motion to Terrell to wrap things up.

"What's the hurry?" a voice behind him sneered. "Got to run off to Daddy?"

Devin pulled a rough breath in between his teeth. Head down and work hard, he reminded himself.

No punching the mayor's son in the face.

But Bryce Horton wasn't going to be ignored. He stepped right in Devin's way, and it took everything Devin had to keep his mouth shut.

"Isn't that what you call old Joe?" Bryce taunted. "*Daddy?* You sure come fast enough when he calls."

Devin's muscles tensed, heat building in his chest.

He kept himself together, though. Bryce had been like this since high school, putting everybody down and acting like he was the king of the hill. The entire hill was all sand, though. The guy never did any work. If *his* daddy didn't run this town, he'd have been out on his rear end ages ago.

As it was, Bryce'd been hired on as a favor to the mayor's office, and getting him fired would take an act of God. Didn't stop Devin from picturing it in his head. Daily.

Devin ground his molars together and brushed past him.

"Oh, that's right," Bryce called as Devin showed him his back and started to walk away. "Your real daddy left, didn't he?"

Red tinted Devin's vision. He flexed his fingers, curling them into a palm before taking a deep breath and letting them go.

It'd be so easy, was the thing. Bryce wasn't a small

guy, but he wasn't a particularly strong one, either. Two hits and he'd be on the ground, snot-faced and crying. That was how bullies were.

That was how Devin's dad had been.

Without so much as a glance in Bryce's direction, Devin shucked his glasses, muffs, and gloves, stowed his stuff, and headed over to the trailer. As he walked, he blocked out the sound of Bryce running his mouth. He blocked out the surly voice in his own head, too.

By the time he got to the door, his blood was still up, but he was calm enough to show model employee material, because that was what mattered.

With a quick knock, he tugged open the trailer door and poked his head inside. Joe was at his desk, big hands pecking out something or other on the keyboard.

"Hey." Devin kept his voice level. "Heard you wanted to see me?"

Joe glanced up and smiled, the lines around his eyes crinkling. "Yeah, hey, have a seat."

Devin closed the door and sat down. While Joe finished up what he was working on, Devin half smiled.

Joe was a good boss because he was one of them. He'd worked his way up the ranks from grunt to site supervisor over the last twenty-five years.

Didn't make the sight of his giant frame squished behind a desk any less funny, though.

After a minute, Joe squinted and hammered the return key before straightening and turning to Devin. "James. Thanks for coming in."

"No problem, boss."

"I'll cut to the chase. You're probably wondering why I called you in here."

Devin shifted his weight in his chair. He'd been so distracted by Bryce and then by watching Joe pretend he didn't need reading glasses that he hadn't given it that much thought. Business had been good, and Devin never missed a day. He hadn't screwed anything up that he knew of. Which left only one thing.

Something he'd dismissed out of hand, even as he'd thrown his hat in the ring.

"Uh..."

"You know Todd's retiring at the end of the month."

Devin nodded, his mouth going dry. He fought to keep his reaction—and his expectations—down. "Sorry to see him go."

"We all are, but he's earned it." Joe let out a breath. Then he cocked a brow. "Big question of the day is who's going to fill in for him as shift leader for your crew."

"You made a decision."

"Sure did." Joe kept a straight face for all of a second. When his face split into a wide smile, Devin mentally pumped his fist. Joe extended his hand across the desk. "Congratulations."

Devin didn't waste any time. He shoved his hand into Joe's with fireworks going off inside his chest.

Yes. Holy freaking hell, yes.

"I won't let you down, sir."

"Oh, believe me, I know it, or I woulda picked somebody else."

As he pulled his hand back, Joe started talking about responsibilities and expectations, and Devin was definitely listening.

He was also mentally updating all the numbers in his budget.

He'd never really expected to get the job of shift leader. There were older guys who'd put their names in. Heck, Bryce could have gotten it, and then Devin would have been looking for another job entirely.

But he knew exactly how much his pay was going to go up by. Every cent of it could go into savings. Twenty-eight months would be more like fourteen. Maybe even twelve.

One year. One year until he'd have enough for the land and the materials.

He couldn't wait to tell everybody. Drinks with his buddy Han would be on him tonight.

Arthur was going to be so proud.

Joe paused, narrowing his eyes at Devin and making him tap the brakes on his runaway thoughts. "It won't be an easy job, Devin."

Devin swallowed. "I'm up for the challenge."

"You don't have to convince me," Joe repeated, holding his big hands up in front of his chest. He set them down on the desk and fixed Devin with a meaningful look. "Just. Stand your ground, okay? Do that and I have every confidence you'll be fine."

Right.

Moving up would also mean being responsible for an entire shift crew of guys.

Including Bryce Horton.

That same hot, ready-to-fight instinct flared inside him, followed right after by the icy reminder to push it down. He smiled tightly. "Not a problem."

"All righty, then." The matter seemed settled as Joe stood. "I'll get the paperwork sorted. You start training on Monday."

Devin rose. "Thank you. Really."

Joe gestured with his head toward the door. "Go on. Have a beer or three to celebrate, you hear?"

Devin had no doubt he'd do exactly that—eventually.

With a spring in his step, he headed for the parking lot. He smacked the steering wheel of his beat-up bucket of bolts as he got in and slammed the door behind him. As the old truck lurched to life, he cranked the stereo and peeled out, triumph bursting inside him.

This was it. The break he hadn't dared to hope for but that he needed, the thing that was going to get him on the fast track to his goals.

And there was only one place he wanted to go.

The Harvest Home food bank and soup kitchen stood in a converted mill on the north end of town. Business in Blue Cedar Falls was generally good, and it had only been getting better since tourism had picked up on Main Street.

Main Street's cute little tourist district felt a long way away, though. Devin's wasn't the only rust bucket truck parked outside Harvest Home. On his way in, he held the door for a woman and her four kids who were coming out, each armed with a bag. He didn't need to peek inside to know they were filled with not just cans but with fresh food, too. The kind of stuff that filled your belly *and* your heart.

Goodness knew Devin'd had to rely on that enough times when he was a kid.

He ran his hand along the yellow painted concrete wall of the entry hallway, his throat tight. He couldn't wait to tell Arthur.

But when he turned the corner, it wasn't Arthur standing behind the desk. Oh no. Of course it wasn't.

Devin's blood flashed hot. For one fraction of a second, he let his gaze wander, taking in soft curves and softer-looking lips. Dark eyes and long, silky, ink-black hair.

A throat cleared. A brow arched.

Like he'd been slapped upside the head, he jerked his gaze back to meet hers. She smiled at him mischievously, and he bit back a swear.

"Hey, Zoe," he managed to grit out. Silently, he said the rest of her name, too.

Zoe *Leung*. Devin's best friend Han Leung's little sister. Arthur Chao's beloved niece.

The one person on this earth he should *not* be getting caught checking out. Especially by her.

"Hey, Dev." The curl of her full lips made his heart feel like a puppy tugging at its leash to go run off into traffic. Only a semi was barreling down the road.

The past few months since Zoe had moved back home after college had been torture. Fortunately, he had lots of practice keeping himself from doing anything stupid around her. He'd been holding himself in check for years, after all. Since she was eighteen and he was twenty-two.

Because if he ever let go of that leash on his control? Gave in to the invitation in her eyes?

Well.

It'd probably be a whole lot easier if he just got run over by a truck.

Chapter Two

Zoe Leung's heart pounded as heat flared in Devin's eyes.

Only for it to flicker and then fizzle in about two seconds flat.

The whole thing made her want to tear her hair out.

Because she was a realist, you know? Sure, she'd had a crush on Devin since she'd realized that not all boys were slimy and gross (her brother Han definitely excluded). But she'd never expected anything to ever come of it.

To him, she was the bratty kid who used to follow her brother and his friends around all the time. Skinned knees and messy ponytails and oversize hand-me-down T-shirts did not bring any boys to the yard, and she'd made her peace with that.

Right until her high school graduation, four and a half long years ago.

Her mom had made such a big deal of it. Her last kid graduating from high school had combined with menopause in some pretty unpredictable ways. Finally, the nagging about wanting a good picture had gotten to be too much. Fed up with it all, Zoe had gotten her sister Lian to help her figure out how to do her hair and her makeup, and she'd actually worn a dress for once. It'd been a big hassle, but she'd had to admit that she felt and looked great.

At the party after, while Han and Devin and a few of their friends were tossing a football around in the backyard, she'd gone up to them to let them know the pizza was there.

She could see it all in her head so clearly. Devin had looked up. His eyes had gone wide.

Only to have a football smack him right in the head.

He'd never looked at her the same after that. Every time his gaze landed on her, it would darken. His Adam's apple would bob, and that scruffy jaw would tense, his rough, hardworking hands clenching into fists at his sides.

Exactly the way he'd been looking at her about two seconds ago.

An angry flush warmed her cheeks as he jerked his gaze away—probably checking to make sure her overprotective big brother, Han, wasn't going to materialize out of nowhere and throw another football at his head.

It was infuriating.

When he didn't have any interest in her, she could totally handle it. But now? This weird, intense game of sexual-attraction chicken he was playing?

What a bunch of bull.

The last time they'd run into each other at the drugstore, he'd done the same thing, heat building in his gaze right until the moment she'd stared back at him. She'd played it cool, hoping he'd say something. Instead, he'd grabbed the first thing he saw off the shelf and darted toward the checkout. Either the guy was super eager to get home with his novelty sunglasses or he was avoiding her.

After months of being back home spinning her wheels on her doomed job search, she was tired of spinning her wheels on whatever was going on between the two of them, too. She wasn't expecting him to drop down on one knee and ask her to marry him or anything. But she was into him, and it sure seemed like he was into her. While she was here, couldn't they, like, *do* something about it?

Enough playing it cool. Clearly she was going to have to be the one to make the first move.

Abandoning subtlety for once, she sauntered over to him. She put a little swing in her hips, just for fun. She'd come out of her shell a lot during the four years she'd been away. She could still rock a messy ponytail and an oversize T-shirt, but the snug top and short skirt she was wearing in preparation for her shift at the Junebug tonight were just as comfortable—and she knew how to use them.

"How's it going?" she asked, coming to a stop a foot away. Too close, for sure. The air hummed. He was tantalizingly warm, pushing heat into the tight space between them and making her skin prickle with awareness.

Licking her lips, she gazed up at him. She was all but batting her lashes here.

The darkness in his eyes returned as he stared down at her.

He had always been good-looking. Back in the day, it had been in a loping, gangly teenage way. His spots on the baseball and football teams had put some muscle on him, but whatever he'd been up to at his construction job had done even more. Under his jacket and tee, he rippled with muscle. His jaw had gone from soft to chiseled, and he kept his golden-brown hair shorter, too.

"Uh." He swallowed. "Good. Great, actually."

"Yeah?"

He still hadn't backed away. That was a good sign, right?

"Yeah." He nodded almost imperceptibly.

Something turned over, low in the pit of her belly. He smelled so good, like man and hard work and wood shavings.

She wanted to ask him what was going on that was so great. She wanted to sway forward into him, tip her head up or put her hand on his broad chest and find out if it was as hard and hot as it looked.

He swallowed and shifted his weight, edging ever so slightly closer to her. Her heart thudded hard. Maybe he wanted her to do all those things, too. Maybe…

"Devin? What are you doing here?"

Crap.

The instant Uncle Arthur's gently accented voice rang out, Devin jumped back as if he'd been burned. The hot thread of tension that had been building between them snapped. A flush rose on her cheeks, almost as deep as the disappointment flooding her chest.

"Arthur! Hey, um." Devin glanced around wildly, looking at everything but Zoe. Honestly, it would have been less conspicuous if he'd come over and put his arm around her. "Do you have a second?"

"For you?" Uncle Arthur smiled, pleased lines appearing around his eyes and mouth. "Of course." He looked to Zoe. "You don't mind?"

Zoe forced a smile of her own. "Of course not."

With a smile of thanks to Zoe, Uncle Arthur led Devin back to his office. Zoe was tempted to follow and listen at the door, but that would be childish.

Instead, she sighed and retreated to the front desk. This was a slow hour. All the appointments for people to pick up goods from the food bank were over, but the soup kitchen hadn't opened for dinner service yet. Down the hall, pots and pans banged, though, so Harvest Home's two staff cooks, Sherry and Tania, must already be at work.

That didn't mean there wasn't anything to do, of course.

Ever since she'd slunk back to Blue Cedar Falls with the useless accounting degree her mom had talked her into, she'd been splitting her time between scrolling social media, waitressing at the new bar in town, and helping out here. Working at Harvest Home barely paid a pittance, of course, but she didn't mind. Uncle Arthur might be her mom's brother, but he was her exact opposite in terms of how he treated Zoe. He was cool and relaxed, and he trusted Zoe with real responsibilities. Watching him work his rear end off here—even though he was in his sixties and on three different high blood pressure medications—made her want to live up to his example.

She liked helping people. Sending folks off with whatever they needed to help get them through tough times gave her a warm feeling inside. Even the boring administrative stuff felt important.

With a sigh, she plunked behind the desk and got to it, confirming pickups, arranging deliveries, and checking in about volunteer shifts. When the crew of said volunteers helping out with supper tonight showed up, she showed them to the kitchen and placed them in Sherry's and Tania's capable hands. On the way back, she definitely did *not* linger outside Arthur's office, staring at the closed door as if she could burn through it with her laser eyes and find out what he and Devin were going on about.

Okay, maybe for a minute, but that was it.

As she returned to the front room and started in on labeling bags for the next day's pickups, the door swung open.

A telltale *tutt*ing sound announced who it was before Zoe could so much as look up.

"Zhaohui." Her mother came in carrying a box of extra produce from their family restaurant, the same way she did every Tuesday—the one day of the week the Jade Garden was closed. She set the box down and came straight over, her tone as disapproving as ever as she snatched the marker from Zoe's hand. "You know Arthur likes black ink."

Zoe rolled her eyes. "Well, I like purple, and do you see Arthur doing the work?"

"I think the bags look great." Han had come in behind her, hauling another crate of soon-to-expire vegetables.

"See?" Zoe told her mom.

Her mom made that noise in the back of her throat that said nothing and everything as she waved a hand at Zoe and let her grab the marker back. She drifted away, and Zoe met her brother's gaze over her head.

"Hey." Han wrapped an arm around her shoulders to give her a quick squeeze in greeting. She rolled her eyes the way she was contractually obligated to as his little sister, but she appreciated the affection all the same. "How's it been today?"

"Not bad." Zoe finished labeling the bags—in dark, entirely legible purple—as she gave him a general rundown. She glanced at the clock. She didn't need to leave for her shift at the Junebug for another few minutes. Normally, with Han and her mom here to take over, she'd head out and get a few minutes of quiet in her car to decompress, but she eyed the back office again.

Before she had to make a decision, the door swung open, and her breath caught. Devin came out first. Uncle Arthur followed, patting his back. Both of them were all smiles.

As Devin spotted Han, his grin grew even wider. "Dude, I didn't know you were going to be here."

"What's up?" The two traded bro-hugs and smashed their fists together, and for a second it was like being twelve years old again, watching them and feeling completely outside it all.

Devin stepped back. "Guess who's moving up to shift leader next week."

"Whaaaat?" Han held his hand out, and they high-fived.

"That's awesome," Zoe interjected.

Devin's gaze shot to hers only to dart right back away.

Uncle Arthur clapped Devin's shoulder. "I knew it would happen."

The corners of Devin's mouth curled up, even as he shrugged and looked down.

Zoe's ribs squeezed. He might be trying to act cool, but Devin had been following her uncle around for even longer than Zoe had been following Devin. She knew the praise and faith meant the world to him.

"Your company hiring?" her mom asked Devin, her tone way too innocent. "Maybe in accounting department?"

Zoe glared at her.

"What?" Her mom put her hand over her chest. "I'm just asking." She raised her brows. "Someone has to."

Sure, sure. So helpful. Zoe clamped her mouth shut

against the instinct to remind her mom that she'd been the one to push Zoe into accounting in the first place. Well, that or medicine or law, and accounting had definitely been the easiest option of those.

Zoe hadn't exactly had a strong sense of what she wanted to do, but it wasn't sit behind a desk crunching numbers all day. The fact that she hadn't been able to find a job in the field was salt in the wound. Did her mom really need to remind her of it constantly?

"I'll check, Mrs. Leung," Devin promised. He cast Zoe a sympathetic glance, and she couldn't decide if that was better or worse than him totally ignoring her.

Her mother cocked a brow, silently saying, *See?*

Zoe huffed out a breath.

Defusing things the way he always did, Han turned back to Devin. "We *have* to celebrate."

"The Junebug does two-for-one drinks before eight tonight," Zoe blurted out. Self-consciousness stole over her as all eyes turned to her, but screw it. She doubled down. "Plus, you know." She pointed her thumbs at her chest. "Employee discount."

Han looked to Devin, brows raised.

"Sure," Devin said slowly. He let his gaze fall on her for all of a second. There was that flare of heat again. But as fast as it had come, it disappeared as his eyes darted away. "Who doesn't like cheap beer, right?"

"Right," Zoe agreed. She smiled tightly.

Thanks to her entire freaking family showing up, this round of "Poke Devin Until He Cracks" was a stalemate.

But the good news was that she'd just earned herself another shot.

Chapter Three

So, how's it feel?" Han asked. "Mr. Fancypants promotion."

Devin shook his head. "I'm still having a pretty hard time believing it."

After a brief stop at home to change, he'd met Han at the Junebug on Main Street for the cheap drinks Zoe had promised them. Add in some burgers and the owner Clay's famous cheese fries, and this was basically Devin's ideal night out. He snagged another stick of greasy goodness from the basket in front of him and popped it in his mouth. It tasted like victory.

And cheese.

But mostly victory. After years of careful planning, everything he'd been working for finally felt like it was within his grasp. Arthur'd taken the time to rerun the numbers with him in his office, and twelve months was a solid projection. For years now, Arthur had been holding on to that lot on the outskirts of town for him. It was one of a handful of shrewd real estate investments he'd made decades ago. He'd been slowly selling off the rest of his plots as Blue Cedar Falls had grown and tourism had boomed, but not that one. It made Devin's throat tight, just thinking about it. The guy had so much faith in him.

Sure, he'd also somehow gotten Devin to commit to mustering up a volunteer squad from Meyer Construction to serve Sunday supper at Harvest Home—some church group had apparently made the finals in a choral competition and had to pull out at the last minute. But that was just more evidence of how much he trusted Devin.

Well, Devin was going to show him that he'd put his faith in the right man. He'd get enough guys from work to show up on Sunday—no problem. And twelve months from now, he'd make good on his promise to buy those undeveloped acres.

His own land, away from the crappy apartments where he'd grown up. Someplace quiet just for him, no nosy roommates or noisy neighbors upstairs. A home he'd build with his own two hands.

Just don't screw it up, a voice in his head whispered.

Devin bit the inside of his cheek. Ignoring the doubt in the back of his mind, he reached for his beer and took a good swig.

"How're you boys doing?" Zoe appeared at the side of their table in the corner. Heaven help him. She'd put on some lipstick or something since he'd seen her at Harvest Home. He couldn't stop looking at her red mouth, and his best friend was going to *murder him.* Oblivious, Zoe glanced between the both of them. "Y'all ready for another round?"

Devin drained the last gulp from his glass and thunked it down in front of her. "Sure am."

"Awesome."

Devin should probably be pacing himself. He had an

early shift in the morning. But he was celebrating. Letting loose for one night wouldn't hurt.

Just so long as he didn't slip up and let himself look at Zoe's chest.

Crap. Too late.

He jerked his gaze away. "Maybe some water, too," he croaked.

Zoe nodded. "Probably a good call."

"Whatever he's having, put it on the house." Clay Hawthorne, owner and proprietor of the Junebug, wandered over. He clapped Devin on the shoulder, then shot a narrow-eyed glance at Han. "Not this guy, though."

"Hey," Han protested. "After all the free food I give you."

"Fine, fine." Clay held his hands up in front of his chest. "It's all on the house, but, Zoe, don't give them any top-shelf stuff, you hear?"

"Only the worst for my brother," Zoe agreed. "Got it, boss."

"You know I'm just giving you free stuff because it means I don't have to write a receipt, right?" Clay told them.

Han shook his head. "You have really got to figure that stuff out, man."

"I know." Clay scrubbed a hand through his red-brown hair. "But math is hard."

Devin gestured around. "When you get to big numbers like this it is."

"Doomed by your own success," Han sympathized.

Clay was a relative newcomer to Blue Cedar Falls, but you'd never know it. Devin didn't make it out to Main Street all that often, but whenever he did, the Junebug was hopping, drawing in the tourists that flocked to the area and locals alike. Clay seemed to know everybody on a first-name basis—or if he didn't at the start of the night, he did by the end.

He'd become good friends in particular with Han, which was great to see. Han had been Devin's best friend since they were kids. He was a good guy—maybe the best. But he was so serious, carrying the weight of the world on his shoulders. He didn't get out a lot. The guy could use another friend in his corner.

"Tell me about it," Clay grumbled. "This place was supposed to be small, you know. Just a hole in the wall for me and maybe ten other people."

"Guess you should have told June that." Han tipped his head toward the front door, which had just swung open to reveal the lady in question.

Clay's complaining ceased, his whole demeanor changing as he lifted a hand to her in greeting. She smiled, too, broad and unreserved, as she crossed the space toward him.

Devin shook his head, rolling his eyes fondly as Clay swept June up in his arms. He'd never get over a big, gruff guy like that turning into a teddy bear whenever his girlfriend was around.

As they kissed, Devin looked away, because wow. They were really going at it. He happened to meet Zoe's gaze, and they shared a stifled laugh at the PDA.

Then Devin had to look away all over again, because sharing anything with Zoe—especially something related to kissing—was a terrible idea.

"Get a room." Han threw a napkin at Clay and June, and they finally broke apart.

Zoe swatted lightly at Han. "Don't listen to my brother," she told June. "He's just jealous."

"Ew." Han recoiled. "I definitely am not."

And okay, yeah, considering Han had dated June's sister May for approximately all of high school, that made sense.

"How's it going?" June asked, ignoring him.

"Fine," Zoe told her. "Just commiserating with Clay about how you ruthlessly turned his dive bar into the most popular spot on Main Street."

June shook her head and patted his arm. "Pretty sure that was mostly your doing." She gestured around. "Everything here was your idea. I just helped you put it all together."

"Okay, fine, it was a group effort," Clay said, his smile wry. He then pointedly steered the conversation away from how business was booming—and, Devin noticed, away from the jabs Han had been making about how he needed to get his accounting figured out.

If anybody else noticed, they didn't make a big deal of it, so Devin kept mum, too. They all made small talk for a few minutes. Inevitably, Zoe had to excuse herself to go check on her other tables. "You got everything under control?" Clay asked.

Zoe gave him a thumbs-up as she walked away. "On top of it all, boss."

"Guess we should head out." To Han and Devin, he explained, "Date night."

"Have fun," Han told them.

"And thanks again for the grub," Devin said.

Clay tipped an imaginary hat at him before turning and steering June toward the back.

Devin returned to his burger, but after a minute, it registered with him that Han's attention was decidedly elsewhere. And that he wasn't happy.

He followed his buddy's scowling gaze.

And kind of immediately wished he hadn't.

Zoe stood over by a table on the other side of the bar, her head tipped back in laughter as a group of guys gave her their orders. One of them had sidled his chair awfully close to her. Another winked.

Devin fought not to sigh.

"Don't do it," he warned.

Han's voice came out gruff and pinched. "Do what?"

"Whatever it is you're thinking about doing to those jerks."

The guy next to Zoe leaned over as if to pick something up off the ground, only there was nothing there.

Han bristled.

Zoe neatly sidestepped the creeper, but none of the tension left Han's frame.

"Seriously, dude." Devin shifted his chair to block Han's sight line. If it also meant he couldn't see Zoe anymore, well, that was just a bonus. "She can handle herself."

The opening night of the Junebug had proven that. Han had lost it on the guys leering at his little sister, and she'd put both them—and her brother—in their places.

"I know," Han grumbled. "But those guys are out of line."

He wasn't wrong, but still. "When it comes to Zoe, you think everyone is out of line."

"I do not."

"You absolutely do." Devin's throat tightened.

Han had always been overprotective. When they were kids, it was cool. No one at Blue Cedar Falls Elementary could mess with either Zoe or their middle sister, Lian. But as the girls had gotten older—and after Han's father died—Han's overprotective instincts went out of control.

"I just..." Han picked at his fries before pushing them away. "I know she's an adult, okay?"

"You sure about that?"

Han ignored him. "She's an adult, but she doesn't act like one. At her age, I'd taken over the restaurant. I was paying the mortgage, you know? She's living in the basement."

Ouch.

That wasn't exactly fair, though. Their father had died during Han's first term at the Culinary Institute in Raleigh. It'd been his decision to leave and help his mom out after.

It'd also been his decision to make sure Zoe and Lian wouldn't have to make the same sorts of sacrifices.

Devin raised a brow. "You think she shouldn't have gone to school?"

"Of course not." Han blew out a breath. "It's not even that I mind her living in the basement. It's just—those guys are dirtbags."

"Maybe dirtbags leave good tips."

"It's more than that," Han insisted. "It's like she *likes* dirtbags. You remember all the losers she brought home in high school. And none of them lasted."

"So she dated a few guys." Devin stared at Han pointedly. "*Most* people did."

Han narrowed his eyes right back. "This is not about me. Or May."

Han had been practically married to May Wu for the entirety of high school, and everybody knew it.

As Devin saw it, Han had never gotten over her, either. Just because he'd mated for life didn't mean he should expect everybody else to.

"Uh-huh."

"I didn't go nuts on Lian, did I?"

Lian had also been a lot less of a wild child than Zoe growing up.

"I'm telling you," Han insisted. "You know how Zoe and Mom would go at it. She's always been rebellious. Mom says turn left and Zoe heads right. Mom says get a job in your field, and Zoe ends up waitressing in a bar."

"In a job you got her."

"Beside the point—I just wanted to get her out of the house, and Clay needed the help." Han picked up a fry and pointed at Devin with it. "The guy thing is just a part of it. She'll bring home anyone she thinks will piss Mom off."

Was that it?

Devin fought not to squirm. If so, how far did it go? Their mom had her opinions, and yes, she and Zoe bumped heads about them. But was Han any different with his overprotective crap?

Would Zoe do something just to piss her brother off, too?

Suddenly, Zoe going all seductive temptress on Devin back at Harvest Home that afternoon took on a whole new light.

Something in his stomach churned. He'd known better than to act on her flirtations—for a whole host of reasons. But if she'd been doing it to get a rise out of Han?

Devin took a big gulp of his water to wash down the bitterness creeping into the back of his throat.

It didn't matter. Han was Devin's best friend. If he didn't want anyone dating his little sister, Devin would respect that.

That didn't stop him from asking one final question.

"So what if she brought home someone you *did* like? Someone with good intentions, a decent job. Treated her well." Devin's voice threatened to tick upward, but he wrestled it down. "What would you do then?"

Han chuckled. "Sure. That'll be the day."

"For real, though."

"Look, I just want her to be happy. She brings home someone great, fine. But I don't see it happening. She's immature and messing with fire just to see if it'll burn. I'm protecting her from douchebag guys at bars, sure. But I'm also protecting her from herself."

"Who are you protecting from herself? Someone new?" Crap, where had Zoe come from? She set a fresh beer down in front of Devin. She snagged the other one off her tray and held it over the table like she was seriously considering throwing it in her brother's face. "Or just me, like usual?"

Han reached out and grabbed the pint glass, but she pulled it away, keeping it out of his grasp.

"Way to prove how mature you are." Han stood.

She set the glass down with a thud. Beer sloshed right to the edge, but it didn't spill over. Clenching her jaw, she asked, "Anything else I can get you gentlemen?"

"Zo, don't be like that."

She ignored Han. "Devin?"

"Nah," Devin said carefully. "I'm good."

"Great, well, anything you need, you just let me know." She smiled at him way too sweetly.

He swallowed hard, his heart pounding. The full force of her attention on him affected him way more than it should. He didn't want Han getting a whiff of him being interested. He didn't want her getting an inkling about it, either.

Maybe her earlier flirting had been genuine. But her being sunshine and roses to him now?

Yeah. That was definitely for Han's benefit.

Which cast everything else in doubt, too.

Chapter Four

Stop."

Zoe screeched to a halt with her hand mere inches from the knob on her family home's back door.

So close.

Her mother cleared her throat, and Zoe prayed for strength before turning around. "Yes, Mother?"

Her mom stood in the kitchen, brows raised, arms crossed. Ling-Ling, the shepherd mix Han had adopted after Zoe left home, sat at her heels. If it was possible, the dog bore the same judgmental glare. "How many résumés did you send out today?"

"Mom—"

"How many?" her mother repeated, firm.

Zoe blew out an exasperated breath. "I didn't, like, count."

"And why not? We paid for a degree in *accounting*, did we not?"

"Would you like me to send you a spreadsheet?"

Her mom scowled, and Ling-Ling made a little growling sound. "No need to take that tone."

Zoe could say the same herself. "Look—"

"You remember what we talked about earlier, right?"

How could Zoe forget?

"Yes, Mom." Zoe wasn't applying herself enough, wasn't taking her future seriously, wasn't considering enough options, blah, blah, blah. "Can I go now? I promised Uncle Arthur I'd open up Harvest Home for him."

The severe line of her mother's frown finally softened. "Fine." She made a little shooing motion with her hand. "Go, go."

Zoe turned to leave. "I just fed Ling-Ling, so don't let her con you into a second dinner."

Her mom never cut Zoe an inch of slack, but the dog walked all over her.

"You send me that spreadsheet tomorrow," her mom called.

"I was *obviously* kidding about that," Zoe cast over her shoulder, opening the door.

She kept walking right on through it, too, blocking out any further replies from her mother by swiftly—but gently!—closing the door behind her.

Still annoyed by the whole thing, she got into her sensible pre-owned Kia and started it up. Her fingers itched on the steering wheel, and the urge to put the pedal to the metal as she pulled onto Main Street tugged at her. She mentally shook her head at herself. The last thing she needed was Officer Dwight pulling her over and giving her a lecture, too.

As she begrudgingly maintained the speed limit, she ran over her mom's words again in her head. With every iteration, she got more worked up. Wasn't it bad enough that her mom had pressured her into going into accounting in the first place?

"Think about your future," Zoe mumbled, imitating her mother's voice. "You want good job, right?"

Fat lot of good the accounting degree had done her in that respect.

To be fair, Zoe hadn't exactly had a better idea about what to do with her life. But it would have been nice to have had some options other than doctor, lawyer, or bean counter.

She chewed on the inside of her lip. At a stoplight, she impulsively hit the button on the dashboard to make a call.

Her sister, Lian, picked up on the second ring. Long and drawn out, her voice came out over the car's tinny speakers, "Yes?"

"How did you know what you wanted to do with your life?"

"Well, hello to you, too."

"I'm serious," Zoe insisted.

Despite facing more or less the same pressure from their mother, Lian had forged her own path. She had a job as a teacher in the next town over, with a 401(k) and health insurance and everything and an apartment where no one harassed her every time she tried to get out the door.

Basically, living the dream.

"I can tell," Lian said dryly. There were rustling noises in the background. "Give me a second to think."

Zoe didn't have a second. The drive to Harvest Home took only ten minutes, and she'd squandered at least seven of them stewing. "I mean, you must have felt pretty strongly about it. Goodness knows it wasn't Mom's idea."

Lian laughed. "No, that it was not." She hummed in

thought, then said, "I guess... When you know, you just *know*. You know?"

"Clearly not." Zoe groaned.

"Sorry, that's what I've got."

"You are so useless."

"Uh-huh. Which is why you always call me first when you're stuck."

"I'm not stuck." Okay, she was. Kind of.

She just didn't know what to do with her life or how to get her mother off her back. But other than that, she was fine.

No, she hadn't made any progress on Operation: Seduce Devin Until He Breaks, but she had her job at the Junebug, which was fun and paid well. Her left-over free time—when she wasn't applying for jobs or making pointless spreadsheets for her mother—she spent at Harvest Home, and it was... well, great.

She sighed. If only she could convince Uncle Arthur to take that well-earned trip to Fiji he was always talking about and let her take over there full-time. She'd miss him, sure, and it wouldn't exactly be a fancy corporate accounting job. But if she could rustle up enough grants to pay herself a salary, even her mother couldn't give her a hard time about that.

As she turned into Harvest Home's parking lot, she finished up her conversation with her sister. Sherry and Tania arrived just as she was heading toward the door.

"Good afternoon, ladies," Zoe said, swinging her hair out of her face as she found the right key.

Sherry grinned. She was an older white woman who'd been cooking for Harvest Home since Arthur had founded it back in the late nineties. "Hey, Zoe."

"Arthur finally take a day off?" Tania asked. Tania was newer, hired when the place had expanded a few years ago, but now it was hard to imagine how they'd gotten along without her. She was Black and maybe twenty years younger than Sherry, and the two were a powerhouse team.

"Fingers crossed."

Tania threw her head back and laughed. "I give it an hour."

"Swear I'm going to tie that man to his recliner." Zoe shook her head and pushed open the door.

Uncle Arthur was tireless, and getting him to take an entire day off—much less a trip to Fiji—was a rare victory. She swallowed hard. The only person she'd ever known who worked harder was her dad, and everyone knew how that had ended. If he'd rested and relaxed more, would that have prevented him from dropping dead of a heart attack at forty-eight?

Who knew. Probably not.

But Uncle Arthur was sixty-five with high blood pressure. The guy deserved a break.

Heading inside, Zoe flicked on the lights and fired up the computer to check messages at the front desk. Sherry and Tania made their way to the kitchen. Absently, Zoe pulled up the volunteer schedule. It took its sweet time loading, so she called, "Any idea who's serving tonight?"

As paid employees, Sherry and Tania were the backbone of the organization's meal service, but they couldn't pull off feeding fifty people a day without an equally dedicated crew of volunteers. Businesses, churches, and schools fielded teams that came out to make the magic happen every night.

Sherry and Tania must have been out of earshot. Frowning, she wiggled the computer mouse and reloaded the schedule. Before it could come up, the door swung open. Zoe darted her gaze toward the entryway.

Only to be met with a pair of gorgeous blue eyes, a broad set of shoulders, a trim, muscular frame, and a bright smile.

"Meyer Construction, reporting for duty," Devin said.

Zoe's heart did a little jump inside her chest as she straightened up. "Oh, hey!"

"Hey." Just like he had the last time he strode through that door, he raked his gaze over her. She swallowed. She wasn't dressed to get good tips at the Junebug today. A flannel shirt over a T-shirt and jeans was hardly what she'd call sexy, but it didn't seem to matter, based on the way his eyes darkened.

"I didn't know you all were serving today."

Devin moved forward into the space, making room for a half dozen folks to file in after him. He shrugged, tucking his thumbs into the belt loops of his dark-rinse jeans. "Arthur talked me into it when I was here telling him about my promotion." One corner of his mouth curled upward. "Said it'd be a good use for my new leadership skills."

The last guy to come in groaned. "Are we ever going to hear the end of that?"

Devin stiffened and flexed his jaw. "I haven't even started yet, Bryce."

Ah, okay, now Zoe recognized the guy shouldering past Devin. The mayor's son, Bryce Horton, had been a couple of years ahead of her in school, but Lian had complained about him plenty at the time. He'd been a royal jerk, and it didn't seem like much had changed.

"Then why am I even here?" Bryce asked, pulling out his phone and plunking down in one of the chairs meant for patrons.

Devin's whole frame radiated tension, but however angry he was, he kept it out of his tone. "Come on. Kitchen's in the back."

Bryce rolled his eyes, even as he kept his gaze glued to what sure looked like a dating app he was swiping through. Zoe resisted the urge to sneak a peek at his username—just so she could avoid it if she ever ended up on the same site.

Devin's voice dropped. "Now."

Grumbling, Bryce lurched out of the chair and followed Devin down the hall.

"Right behind you," Zoe called. She just had a couple more quick things to take care of out here.

Bryce looked over his shoulder at her and made a super-gross kissy face. Glancing back, Devin caught him, and his eyes narrowed, his hands curling into fists at his sides.

Interesting. When her brother shot his death glare at guys who were hitting on her at the bar, it made her want to strangle him. But when Devin did it?

A warm little shiver ran up her spine.

She probably shouldn't like it so much, but she did.

She swallowed, fighting to calm the flutters in her chest as she shot Bryce a glare of her own. No matter how much Devin's protectiveness gave her the warm fuzzies, she could handle herself. "Wasn't talking to you," she informed Bryce.

"Sure." He clicked his tongue and brought his hand to his ear like a phone and mouthed, *Call me.*

Devin bustled him along, thunderclouds in his eyes. The coiled strength in him gave her even more little flutters inside.

As soon as they disappeared around the corner, she put her head in her hands to muffle her groan. Getting the butterflies over this guy was pathetic. She was acting like a swooning schoolgirl with a crush again.

Sucking in a deep breath, she dropped her hands from her face. She was too old for this pining nonsense.

Resolve filled her. Devin showing up to volunteer tonight might have taken her by surprise, but it was a golden opportunity. Han was working at the restaurant tonight, so he couldn't appear from out of nowhere, football in hand or no. Devin would have his guard down.

With so many people around, Zoe couldn't exactly seduce Devin. But maybe this was her chance to show him that she was so much more than a kid with a crush now.

And that the spark between them was real.

"Need any help?"

Zoe sighed and cast her gaze skyward but didn't stop busing dishes. "I thought you were taking the day off."

Uncle Arthur smiled. "Was just in the neighborhood and thought I'd stop in." He craned his neck to peer into the dining room. "Decent crowd tonight."

"Fifty-seven."

"Impressive." He pursed his lips. "Terrible, but impressive."

Nobody wanted to be put out of business more than Uncle Arthur. When his family had landed in this country nearly sixty years ago, they'd relied on soup kitchens.

He'd come a long way since then, and he'd had some good luck with investments that had allowed him to found this place. He loved having a way to give back to the community here in Blue Cedar Falls that had taken him in. But if hunger and unemployment just disappeared, he'd be delighted to be out of a job.

Stir crazy and climbing the walls, looking for his next venture, but delighted.

"Late fall is always tough."

The weather here was warm enough that construction and tourism carried on year-round, but whenever the weather turned chilly, the number of people showing up at Harvest Home climbed.

"True." Uncle Arthur came over to squeeze her arm. "Knew you could handle it, though."

Her chest contracted. With no one else in her life trusting her to handle anything more than her TikTok account, that was way too nice to hear. She chuckled to hide the tightness behind her ribs. "Which is why you felt no need to check up on me at all."

"He's not checking up on you," Tania said, coming in from taking a load to the compost pile out back. "He just can't stay away from me," she teased.

"You know me," Uncle Arthur agreed indulgently, dropping his hand.

Sherry was right behind Tania. She shook her head at Arthur. "Held out longer than I thought you would."

Ignoring her, Uncle Arthur gestured toward the dining room. "I'm just going to quick make the rounds."

Zoe waved him along. On his way out, Arthur nearly bumped right into Devin, who had a crate filled with dirty dishes in his arms.

Devin's eyes lit up. "Thought you were taking the night off."

"Don't you start in on me, too." Uncle Arthur waggled a finger at him.

"You're working yourself to an early grave," Zoe called after him.

Uncle Arthur's finger shifted to point at her, but she just shrugged. She wasn't going to apologize for trying to remind him to take a break once in a while. He continued out to the dining room to do his usual thing, thanking volunteers and checking in on the guests. Sherry and Tania followed him with more milk crates to help with cleanup.

Rolling her sleeves to her elbows, Zoe started running the water.

Devin brought his crate of dishes over to her. "He's unstoppable, huh?"

"Seems it." She frowned. Her uncle definitely gave that impression, but he was getting up there, and she did genuinely worry about him.

"He's fine. There's a reason he showed up at the last possible second." Devin tipped his head toward the dining room. "He's not going to do any work. He just likes talking to everybody."

His voice was soft and full of affection.

"Right." Sometimes Zoe forgot that Devin's road to practically becoming a member of their extended family began right here at Harvest Home. Uncle Arthur didn't like to talk about it, but Devin had started out as a guest, coming by with his dad every week. Then by himself even more often than that. Sure, he'd become best buddies with Han by then, but it went deeper than that. Devin knew better than anyone how dedicated Uncle Arthur was to making people feel welcome here.

As he started unloading the dirty dishes, Devin's arm brushed hers, and a shiver of warmth ran through her skin.

Her throat went dry as she glanced up at him. They'd been working in close quarters all night, but any efforts to either seduce him or change his impression of her had taken a back seat to the task of getting dinner on the table for almost sixty people. In the end, this was the closest they'd really gotten, physically.

As if he could feel her gaze, he looked down. When their eyes met, heat flushed through her. How could a person's eyes be so blue? She got lost for a second, just staring at the gold-brown scruff on his sharp jaw, the soft red fullness of his lips, when everything else about him was chiseled and hard.

"Do you—" The huskiness of his voice only distracted her more.

"Huh?"

He pushed a plate toward her more insistently.

A different, embarrassed flush rose to her cheeks as she grabbed it and ran it under the water. "Right, right. Sorry."

He didn't need to stand so close as he passed her the next one, but she didn't tell him that. Wasn't she the one who'd started the game of trying to make him break? With the way he'd been looking at her, she'd taken it as a personal challenge to get him to make a move or at least admit that there was something brewing between them.

Now here she was, right on the cusp of cracking herself.

What would he do if she did? If she made the real

first move and turned to him. Reached up to graze her fingertips along his cheek.

If she leaned forward on her tiptoes and tugged him down so she could taste his mouth…

She shuddered inside, blushing furiously as she placed another plate on the rack inside the dishwasher. She'd been harboring these kinds of fantasies since she was a teenager. It was hard to tell how much was actually possible and how much was just the same nonsense she'd been imagining for years.

Unwilling to shatter the moment, she set it all aside and concentrated on cleaning up. He seemed content to do the same. Even if his presence was making her heart do weird flips behind her ribs, she tried not to let it show.

They fell into a rhythm, like they'd been working together like this forever. That made sense—they'd both been volunteering here for years, but it still felt unfairly kismet, somehow.

"Thanks," she said after a couple of minutes. "By the way. For bringing in the folks from your company tonight."

"Happy to do it." He let out a rough sigh. "Well, for the most part."

It was clear who he was talking about.

Chuckling quietly, she shook her head. "Yeah, Bryce is still a piece of work, huh?"

"You have no idea."

The guy had barely lifted a finger the entire time he'd been here, and he'd eaten a solid dinner's worth of food meant for the guests.

"How does he get away with it?"

"You know." A dark undertone ran through Devin's words.

She shivered, reminded again of how much strength Devin kept contained inside himself. He never used it, though, no matter how frustrated he got.

It made her feel...safe. It always had. Even when they'd been kids messing around in Uncle Arthur's basement. Any time the other boys his age had gotten too rough around her, he'd stepped in and said something.

Which was probably part of how she'd ended up with this stupid crush on him in the first place.

"Yeah, I guess I do."

People filed in and out of the kitchen, bringing new loads of dishes through. Zoe was indulging herself, spending this time rinsing plates when she should be out there directing traffic, but between Uncle Arthur, Sherry, and Tania, there were enough people running the show for her to dawdle a little longer. And the chance to stand so close to Devin was just too good to pass up.

"So you've really gotten involved here, huh?" he asked, moving to her other side to help her start loading the second washer.

She shrugged and passed him a stack of silverware. "I have the time right now. And I like helping out. Working with the guests. Getting to spend more time with Uncle Arthur."

A smile stole across her face as she talked about it all. She'd missed everyone in her family while she'd been away at college, but her uncle was the only one who didn't carry any baggage—or seem to have some sort of agenda for what she should do with her life.

Devin hummed in acknowledgment, giving her space to keep talking. It was refreshing.

"This place," she continued, trying to sum it up. "The work we do here, the people we serve. It feels important."

"I get it," Devin said quietly.

He would.

But then one corner of his mouth tilted down. "You said you have the time 'right now.' You see that changing soon?"

"Ugh." Zoe huffed out a breath as she scrubbed at a particularly stubborn spot on a plate. "I don't know. Apparently, at some point I'm supposed to get a real job."

He chuckled and passed her another dish. "What? Overrated."

"Says the guy who just got the big promotion."

"It's not that big a deal," he said, rolling his eyes, but his posture straightened slightly. It was definitely at least a medium-size deal. Humble as he might be, she hoped he was getting some satisfaction from his work.

She considered for a second before asking, "How did you know? That construction was what you wanted to do?"

It was the same basic question she'd asked Lian earlier—unhelpful as that conversation had been.

"I don't know," he answered slowly. "I didn't exactly have a ton of options."

"Smart guy like you?"

He laughed, only it didn't entirely sound funny. "I like working with my hands. Got a decent eye for it. Pay's good, relatively speaking. Arthur was able to help me get my foot in the door when I needed—when I decided it was time to find a place of my own."

There was something he wasn't saying, his voice dipping low and pulling at something in her chest. Before she could probe any deeper, though, he looked at her.

"So, how are things going with the whole real job thing, then?" he asked.

Well, that was certainly a way to kill the mood.

"Ugh. Terrible." Her mom had laid into her just that afternoon, telling her she wasn't sending out enough résumés or casting her net wide enough, prompting her to waste a good hour or two rage-scrolling Monster. "I'm putting in applications for jobs pretty much all over the state at this point. A few in Atlanta, too."

His eyebrows pinched together. "You'd really go that far?"

"I don't want to." She liked it here. She always had. Things here were easy. Comfortable. Being close to her family—when they weren't driving her up a wall or dictating her love life and her job search, anyway—was nice.

But she'd do what she had to do. She'd always wanted to get out on her own, and this extended period of being between things was making her itch to be independent again.

It wasn't like it was with her brother. Han had come home when their father died and had taken over—well, everything. His sense of duty was giving him white hairs.

She'd choose to stay here, too, if it worked out. But she had to keep her options open. She couldn't just be *stuck* here because she couldn't make it on her own.

"We'll see how things go." She shrugged. It was such an annoying platitude, but that was her life now.

"Well, I hope you stay close." The way he said it was so genuine, she jerked her gaze up to meet his, but he was pointedly studying the dishes. After a second, he smiled, his tone lightening as he darted a teasing glance her way. "I mean, how can Han kill anyone who dares to look at you if you live far away?"

That was it. She shoved him, and he laughed, plates clanking together as he bumped into them where they were so neatly stacked in the racks. He playfully pushed back, and then what choice did she have, with her wet hands and all, but to flick some water in his face?

He sputtered, the droplets clinging to his skin in interesting ways, and her breath sped up. She went to do it again, but she must have telegraphed her intentions too clearly, because he grabbed her wrist before she could. Her heart hammered in her chest.

She stared up into his eyes, and for a second, everything around them faded, because she had seen that look before.

About two seconds before he got hit in the head with a football.

"Someone wanna tell me why we're out there doing all the work while these two are messing around in here?"

Devin straightened, pulling away from her so fast, she had to catch herself from falling over.

Apparently, playing the part of the football tonight, Bryce came over holding one measly dish, which he popped—still caked in drying potatoes—straight into the dishwasher. Struggling not to let on how flustered she was by the unwelcome interruption, Zoe plucked it out and set it in the sink, shooting him a glare.

"Thank you, Mr. Horton," Arthur said delicately as he

hauled a crate in and set it on the counter. He caught Zoe's gaze, and she huffed out a breath.

Bryce's dad was the mayor. The town gave Harvest Home a bunch of money and support every year. She would do well to remember it.

But wasn't that just how a jerk like Bryce got so... jerk-y? Everyone giving him a free pass because his father was a powerful guy?

She glanced at Devin. How did he do it? Constantly keeping a lid on himself when the guy kept asking to get punched in the face?

Before she could suss it out, a few more of the Meyer Construction volunteers came in with the last of the supper service cleanup.

Bryce gawked at the towering piles of dishes. "How are we supposed to get all this done? Some of us have places to be tonight." Winking, he elbowed one of the other guys, who subtly moved to put more distance between them. Not that Bryce noticed. With a leering smirk and a waggle of his phone, he added, "If you know what I mean."

Devin exhaled roughly. He threw his shoulders back. Instead of answering Bryce, he looked around and held his hands out expansively. "With a crew like this? We all pitch in and we'll have it done in no time."

"Uh-huh." Bryce kept scrolling on his phone.

"What do you say we put a little wager on it?" Devin's smile rippled with challenge. "We get out of here within the hour, and the first round at the bar is on me."

Chapter Five

This was going to cost Devin a small fortune.

It was worth it, though. At the hour mark, pretty nearly on the dot, his team had put the last clean pan on its shelf. The fact that Arthur, Sherry, Tania, and Zoe had thrown their backs into it, too, had helped a ton. Heck, even Bryce had cleaned a few tables. Free drinks were some powerful motivation.

Powerful, expensive motivation.

As the last guy put in his order, Clay whistled, punching in the numbers on the register.

"This sure seems like a nightmare for the bookkeeping," Devin tried in vain. "You should probably just give them to me for free."

"Nice try." Clay printed off the bill and handed it to Devin. "You wanna settle up now or start a tab?"

"Settle up now." Passing over his debit card, Devin eyed Bryce, who was standing by the pool table in the corner. Devin had promised the first round, and he was going to see it through, but he wasn't going to make it easy for anyone to try to turn it into two.

"Good choice."

He signed the slip, then joined the rest of his crew. He

tried to pay attention to what they were saying, but his gaze kept drifting to the table in the corner where Zoe sat with Arthur, Sherry, and Tania. All four of them had been only too happy to take him up on the free drink offer, too, and he was happy to have them.

Probably too happy.

Working side by side with Zoe tonight had been an eye-opening experience. While her sexy waitress outfit had bowled him over the other day, this afternoon it had been her maturity—the way she'd known how to handle every situation that arose as they'd cooked and served. Even now, while he and his buddies from work stood around, shooting pool and playing darts and talking about yesterday's game, she was engaged in what looked like a deep conversation with Arthur, Sherry, and Tania. They regarded her with all the respect she deserved. Which he was starting to realize was a heck of a lot.

She'd really rolled up her sleeves tonight. She knew Harvest Home as well as he did, and despite mostly working in the front office, she wasn't afraid to get her hands dirty. Her eyes went all soft when she talked about the place, too. She might be the only person besides him and Arthur who understood it for the miracle it was.

She was funny and smart and beautiful and...

He cut off his train of thought before it could pull any farther out of the station. Jerking his gaze away from her mouth as she laughed at something Tania was saying, he took a big gulp of his beer.

Han wasn't here tonight, but the two of them had been friends for so long that the guy lived rent-free in his head. If anybody else was staring at Zoe the way Devin had been just now, Han would've been ready to deck him. Devin wasn't some dirtbag trying to get a peek up her skirt, but he needed to do a better job keeping his eyes to himself.

Before too long, Bryce gave one of the other guys a noogie before sauntering Devin's way. Devin crossed his arms over his chest, but his body language wasn't enough to keep Bryce from coming over and slapping him on the biceps.

"See you tomorrow, *boss*." He said it like an insult, but Devin wasn't going to take it that way.

"Bright and early."

The instant Bryce was gone, it was like someone had undone one of the knots in Devin's back. A few others filtered out not long after, and he thanked them each for coming out and giving a part of their day to volunteer.

Eventually, he and what was left of his crew drifted toward the pool table. They played a couple of rounds, but it was tough to focus. Every time he lined up a shot, he either had to face Zoe or put his back to her, and he had to get this under control. Being this aware of her wasn't right.

But it did give him a heads-up when she and the others started to gather their things.

Arthur was the one to approach first and clear his throat. Devin turned to find him jacket in hand.

Arthur clapped him firmly on the shoulder. "Good work tonight, Devin."

"Anytime." Then he remembered how Arthur had somehow managed to get him to agree to find a crew for this afternoon without his even fully realizing he'd committed until it was too late. "I mean, not *any* time, but..."

"I know what you mean."

Devin nodded at Sherry and Tania, who stood behind Arthur, clearly ready to go, too. "Glad you all could come out."

Tania grinned. "Any time you feel like footing the bill, you let us know."

They said their goodbyes, and the three of them made for the exit.

Which left Zoe. He scrunched his brows together. She wouldn't have just snuck out, would she? He would have noticed.

"Boo," she said from just behind him, poking his shoulder.

He didn't jump, but it was a near thing.

"Oh, hey." His voice came out rough. God, she smelled good. She was doing that thing again, getting up in his space, but unlike the other day, it didn't feel forced or unnatural. It felt like where she was supposed to be. Half hopeful and half ready to be disappointed, he asked, "You taking off, too?"

She had her flannel shirt draped over her arm and her bag slung across one shoulder, but there wasn't any sign of her keys. She cocked a brow and glanced behind him. "Actually, I was about to call winner."

Oh.

Oh, okay. This he remembered.

Devin and Han and some of the other guys used to play pool in Arthur's basement, days they couldn't mess around outside. Zoe would hang out there, too, and of course they couldn't tell Arthur's niece to scram. They only ever let her play if they needed an even number for a team. She was short and she scratched half her shots, and when she called winner, everybody had to pretend not to groan.

Unconsciously, he flicked his gaze over her form. His throat bobbed.

She was still short, but the confidence in her expression told him she'd learned a couple of things since she was twelve.

It was late. He should probably tell her he was just wrapping up here and ready to call it a night. If he was serious about not jeopardizing his friendship with Han, spending more time with his baby sister was *not* a smart strategy.

But there was something about the challenge in her eyes that was too enticing to resist.

For old times' sake…

Before he could second-guess himself any further, he lifted a brow to match hers. Without a word, he turned. He surveyed the table. His team was in good shape—just the eight ball left to sink, while stripes had three balls on the table. Sucking in a deep breath, he pointed toward the corner pocket.

He could feel her behind him as he lined up his shot. His skin tingled with awareness, but his vision went sharp. He pulled his cue back and nudged it forward, once, then twice.

The cue ball went spinning off across the felt, straight as an arrow. It rebounded, narrowly missing the ten before smacking straight into the eight. The eight shot toward the corner pocket, where it hovered for half a second on the edge before sinking right in.

He couldn't have done it better if he'd tried.

His partner held out his hand, and Devin slapped their

palms together. He nodded at the guys he'd beaten. They shook their heads, but they took it just fine. He grabbed his beer and swallowed the last of it down.

Then he turned. He met Zoe's gaze again, and the heat in it went straight to the center of him.

"You want winner?" he asked, throat raw.

Her head bobbed up and down, her pretty pink mouth parted just the tiniest bit.

"Well." He swallowed deeply. This was a monumentally stupid idea. But he was in it now. "What're you waiting for?"

Zoe was seriously starting to lose track of who was egging on who. After she'd called winner, the other guys Devin had been playing with decided to head out. At least one of them had shot him a knowing look. Another had patted him on the back and winked at her. She'd rolled her eyes and sent them on their way.

Was the tension between them as obvious to the people around them as it was to her? If so, it was a good thing her brother wasn't around. She glanced toward the bar. Clay didn't seem to be paying them any attention. His girlfriend, June, had shown up a little while ago with her friends Caitlin and Bobbi, and between pouring drinks for everyone and chatting with them, he had his hands full.

Zoe still didn't completely trust him not to rat her out to Han—intentionally or otherwise.

Whatever. All along, she'd said her brother should mind his own business. She was a grown woman, and she could do as she pleased.

And at the moment, what she wanted to do was Devin.

Only it wasn't quite that simple anymore, was it? Her advances had sort of been a lark at the beginning, but after spending time talking to him while cleaning up tonight, she was starting to wonder if there might be more between them than simple attraction. This wasn't a schoolgirl crush, and it wasn't leading to just a single night of fun.

As to what it was leading to?

Little sparklers fired off inside her. She'd love to have the chance to find out.

After she schooled him at pool.

She took a second to select a cue and chalk the tip as he went ahead and racked the balls. The sight of him in those jeans had her sucking her bottom lip between her teeth.

The guy was really just unfairly handsome, with that golden tan skin and clear blue eyes. The short-cropped hair that shone under the hanging lights and the scruff on his deliciously sharp jaw.

He smiled at her and gestured toward the table. "You wanna break?"

"Be my guest." That had been her plan, right? Getting him to break.

He grabbed his cue from where he'd leaned it. He set the cue ball down just to the right of center, leaned over, and lined up. She let her gaze move over his entire body as his muscles tensed.

With a sudden surge of motion, he fired off his shot. The crack of the cue ball hitting the one dead center rang out through the air. Balls scattered everywhere, while the cue ball spun in the middle of the table before coming to a halt.

"Nice."

He winked. "I've been practicing a bit."

Oh, she liked him like this. She'd always appreciated his serious side, but seeing him loose and playful and—dare she say flirty? It warmed her insides, even as it ratcheted up nervous anticipation about where this evening was going.

He called a shot and made it with ease. He sank two more before finally missing.

Zoe gripped her cue more tightly as she walked the perimeter of the table. Devin's gaze on her was distracting as hell, but she kept her focus.

He might have missed, but he'd done a good job setting her up for failure. Nice to know he wasn't going easy on her. She finally selected her shot and grabbed a bridge off the rack.

"You don't need that," Devin told her.

"Speak for yourself, tall person."

"Seriously." Then he was there, wrapping his hand around hers. "May I?"

Heat zipped up her arm. His warm scent surrounded her, and she got dizzy for a second, having him so close.

Which was her only explanation for why she let him take the bridge away. He guided her to the other edge of the table. She lined up her shot, and sure, she was closer to the ball now, but she didn't love the angles.

"I don't know." She shook her head, ready to stand and go back to her original plan, but he stopped her.

"Let me show you?" he asked.

Her whole body locked down as he stepped up behind her. He was so hot, bracketing her frame. His height swamped her, making it hard for her to breathe, and she was going to die before she even so much as managed to seduce him.

"See?" he asked.

Did he know what he was doing to her? She clenched down inside against a powerful wave of desire.

But he was still talking about pool. He placed his hand over hers on the felt, realigning her shot a few degrees to the left. Her breath caught.

Seriously. She was Going. To. *Die.*

She hovered there for just a second, soaking in the feeling of his body blanketing her, fluttering her eyes shut to bask in his closeness.

But as good as it felt—and as much as she never wanted to move again, ever in her life—she couldn't stand there and take a crummy shot just because a hot guy was scrambling her brains.

Carefully, she stood up again. He moved with her. She glanced at him over her shoulder, and his face was inches from hers, his kissable mouth *right there*.

She stepped away. She got the bridge down from the rack. Her face flushed hot as she set up her original shot again. If she missed, she was going to feel like twice the idiot now, but she knew herself, dammit all. She knew her own mind, and she knew her body and her abilities.

No guy was going to waltz in out of nowhere and try to tell her differently before he'd even seen her play.

She ignored the pressure of his gaze. Then, with a breath and a prayer, she pulled the cue stick back.

The ball careened forward, banking off the far rail before heading straight for the nine. Everything in her tightened as the nine rolled toward the side pocket, slower than she would have liked. It hovered on the edge for an agonizing instant.

And then it tipped right on in.

She wanted to shout and scream—maybe jump and dance. As it was, she restricted herself to a single pump of her fist before locking her gaze with Devin's.

"Watch out," she told him, breathless—and not just from the score. "I've been practicing, too."

Chapter Six

Okay, for real, though, where did you learn to play like that?"

Zoe laughed as she braced her elbow against the bar. Devin settled onto the stool beside hers. His knee rested against hers, and she shivered.

They'd been getting closer and closer all evening. She wasn't complaining, but there was a tension inside her chest. This didn't seem like it could last. A half dozen games of pool and almost as many drinks between the two of them had them both loose-limbed and happy. After their last match, when someone else had asked them for the table, she'd kind of expected him to call it a night. It was late, after all. But when she'd started making her way over to the bar, figuring she'd check in with Clay before heading out herself, Devin had come on over, too.

Now here they were. Sitting together, fresh drinks in hand.

Zoe shrugged and took a sip of her cosmo. "There was a pool table in the basement of my dorm my first year of college."

"And a shark there to teach you all?"

"Don't underestimate bored teenage girls trying to avoid writing term papers."

He chuckled. "Fair enough."

She stirred her drink, probably a little too forcefully. "Turns out, hustling pool is one of the most useful things I learned at school."

"Oh?"

"I mean..." Releasing the tiny straw, she gestured around. She couldn't quite keep the sour note out of her tone. "See how far that degree has gotten me?"

"I don't know. Doesn't seem so bad."

She shook her head. "Try telling that to everyone else."

"You mean your mom?"

"Among other people. Han and Lian don't seem super impressed, either." Sighing, she looked away, to the bottles of liquor on the shelf, the taps, the specials she'd written on the big black board the day before. "I mean, I had a great time at college—don't get me wrong. But the whole grand compromise of it all—me going so far away, to a school that cost so much..." Even with aid and a bunch of money from her mom, she was going to be paying off loans forever. "Mom let me follow my dream, but she hammered home that if I didn't pick something practical, I'd end up penniless in a gutter somewhere."

"And that's how you ended up going into accounting?" Devin asked, leaning his elbow on the bar.

"Pretty much." She pinched the little straw from her drink again and stabbed at an ice cube. "I'm good at math, and after the first year, none of the courses were before noon. Seemed like a good deal at the time."

"What if you could do it all over again? Without your

mom hanging over your shoulder. Would you pick something different?"

The question barely computed. Zoe's parents had always had strong opinions about her life. After her dad had died, her mom had become even more aggressive in trying to control Zoe's future. She'd clearly been grieving. Zoe had been, too. She'd fought back about some things, but on others, she got worn down and just got used to going along.

"I don't know," she said quietly. "Maybe? There wasn't anything I was super passionate about at school."

"Was there anything you were passionate about outside of it?"

"Not really." Usually, when people asked her questions like this, it made her uncomfortable, but Devin's expression was so open as he gazed at her. He'd known her practically their entire lives, but it felt like he actually wanted to know more. So she dug deeper. "I liked normal stuff—hanging out with my friends, watching TV."

"Making friendship bracelets."

"Shut up." She flapped a hand in his general direction as if to swat at him. Her cheeks flushed warmer.

One corner of his mouth lifted. "I still have mine."

"You do not." Oh wow. She'd made them for everybody one summer. She'd found a ton of old embroidery floss from some kit her mother had never finished. Bored, she'd gone to town.

She'd picked the colors for the one she'd given to Devin so carefully. Blue for his eyes, orange and brown for the Blue Cedar Falls team colors. Red for the hearts she secretly drew around his name in the back of her diary. Because she was super, super cool and not a dork at all.

"I do," he promised, and for some reason, she actually believed him.

Her throat tight, she looked down at her drink again. Silence held for a second. Then she continued. "But yeah. Just normal teenager stuff, mostly. I mean, I liked volunteering at Harvest Home, too, but if I'd told my mom I wanted to work at a nonprofit or go into social services or something, I think she would have flipped her lid."

"Did you ever try?"

"What? No." The idea had never occurred to her.

But maybe it should have.

That was too much food for thought for this late into the night, though.

"How about you?" she asked. "You said construction was sort of something you fell into. Did you ever think about doing anything else? Going to school?"

The question seemed to take him off guard. Furrows appeared between his brows. She wanted to reach over and smooth them out, but even with the soft intimacy that somehow surrounded them now, it felt like too big of a line to cross.

"You mean college?"

She nodded, sipping at her drink.

"Sort of?" He lifted one shoulder before setting it back down. "Mrs. Jeffries in the guidance department thought I should, but it was never in the cards for me."

"How come?"

"Money." He said it without any bitterness to his tone. "There's a reason I started going to Harvest Home, you know."

Right. Crap. "Sorry—"

"It's fine. I could have maybe gotten financial aid or something, but I needed to be out on my own."

"I can drink to that." She lifted her drink, and he clinked his glass against hers before taking a deep pull at it and setting it down.

He still seemed calm, but a familiar stiffness settled into his shoulders. A far-off look came into his gaze. "My mom died when I was young, you know. Really, really young. I don't even remember her. But my dad—he was..."

As he searched for words, Zoe sat up straighter. A girl couldn't hang around her big brother and his best friend all the time without overhearing some stuff. She knew Devin's home life wasn't great, but he'd never talked about it in front of her directly.

"Yeah?" She held her breath and reached out, brushing her hand against his. His skin was warm and rough, and she wasn't oblivious to all the other, different ways she wanted to touch him. But she dropped her hand away after one quick, encouraging squeeze.

The point of his jaw flexed. His bright eyes met hers for a second, shadows forming behind his irises. Then he looked away. "He wasn't a good guy—let's just leave it at that."

He picked up his glass again. Zoe bit her lip. She should probably leave well enough alone.

But the book he'd started to crack open didn't feel shut quite yet. She couldn't shake the sense that he *wanted* to talk about this. How many times had she caught him holding himself back? Was this just more restraint?

What would it be like if he let go?

And honestly. Poking the bear had gotten her this far.

"You don't have to."

He lowered his drink and stared at her in question.

She took a deep breath. "You don't have to leave it at that. If you don't want to." Her face warmed, but she wasn't backing down. "I'm happy to listen."

He regarded her for a long, silent moment. The sounds of the bar around them filtered in. It had felt like they'd been in their own little world this whole time, but there were other people here. Not many. It really was late. But a few. Clay was still kicking around here somewhere.

No one else mattered, though.

As the moment stretched on, she held her ground, waiting patiently.

Finally, he grabbed his beer and tossed the rest of it back. He gestured at her drink. She was tempted to finish it, too, especially when he put on his jacket. The taste of it soured in her mouth. She'd pushed too far, huh? Sometimes she did that. She set her half-full glass on the bar.

But then he tipped his head toward the door.

"Come on. Let me walk you home."

The offer took her by surprise. Neither of them had had so much to drink that they couldn't drive. She probably *should* drive. Getting her car in the morning would be a hassle.

But walking home... walking home was good.

Letting *Devin* walk her home. Well, that was downright great.

When he extended his hand to help her up? No way that was an invitation she could refuse.

His calloused fingers were warm against hers. He gripped her tightly as she popped down from the stool. Was she imagining it when he held on for a second even after her feet hit the floor?

He let go, and she dropped her gaze. She untied her flannel from around her waist and shrugged it on.

Then she followed him out into the night.

It was chillier than she was prepared for, but between the Asian flush from the little alcohol she'd had and the heat Devin radiated at her side, she didn't mind. She crossed her arms over her chest.

Devin didn't have to ask where she lived, of course. He'd been hanging out at the Leung house for a decade or two. They were both quiet as they headed north on Main Street.

The crisp air smelled like fall, the last few leaves of the season just clinging to the trees. She hugged herself more tightly. The dark sky above shone with stars and a half-full moon. Twinkling lights draped over the white fences all along Main Street gave everything a cozy feel.

She sighed. When she'd first realized she'd have to move home, she'd spent most of her time thinking about how annoying it would be to have to camp out in her mom's basement. She'd been right about that. Her mother's constant, snide comments about her prospects had only added to the ambience.

She hadn't been thinking about this, though. Blue Cedar Falls was beautiful by day, with the bright blue sky above and the mountains all around them. At night it was quiet and still, and it just felt like...

Home.

A tiny shiver racked her, followed by a pang. Getting a real job would be great, but the more time she spent here in Blue Cedar Falls—and with Devin—the less eager she was to leave.

Misunderstanding her shiver, Devin glanced down at her. "Cold?"

"I'm fine."

Stupid, chivalrous boy. He whipped off his jacket anyway, leaving his arms bare. Really hot, sexy, muscular arms, but it still seemed unpleasant for him.

"I'm fine," she protested again, but he was having none of it.

He draped the jacket over her shoulders. Instantly, heat blanketed her. Oh wow. His delicious scent wrapped around her even more thoroughly, making her whole body come into another, deeper level of awareness.

"Looks good on you," he said, his voice rough. He snapped his mouth closed as if he hadn't meant to say that, but it was out there now.

There was clearly no point arguing anymore, and anyway, now that she had his jacket, it wasn't as if she wanted to give it up. "Thanks."

"No problem."

They hit the end of the downtown strip and turned right together. As the businesses faded away into little houses, the quiet grew. She glanced up at him.

She met the soft blue gaze staring back down at her, and warmth fluttered inside her chest.

"Thanks," he murmured. He pointed with his thumb in the direction of the Junebug. "For what you said back there."

Right. Talking about his not-a-good-guy father.

She got her head out of the clouds of teenage crush land and mustered a smile. "I meant it."

"I know." He directed his gaze forward, ducking to avoid a couple of low-hanging branches on an old oak.

"Sorry it took me by surprise. I work with too many guys. Some women, too, but they act even tougher than the men. Nobody gets touchy-feely on the job site."

"What about friends?"

"You mean your brother?"

"Okay, yeah, never mind."

Han was a cool guy, deep down. To hear Clay talk about it, he'd offered all kinds of great relationship advice back when he and June were getting their act together. But Han had never gotten over their father. He'd died suddenly, almost ten years ago. All Han's plans for his life had gone up in smoke when he'd rushed home, eighteen years old and determined to take up the mantle and become the man of the house.

The loss still hurt in Zoe's heart, too, of course. She missed her dad. Losing him had changed the entire family. It had harshened her mom and aged her brother. Fortunately, she'd had Lian and Uncle Arthur to lean on, both during that first tough year and after.

But Han hadn't seemed interested in leaning on anyone. He was too busy taking over the business and the house. Deep down, though, she knew her brother too well. He'd been devastated.

Talking about someone else's issues with their father? He couldn't have handled it. He probably still couldn't.

Devin's gaze focused on something far off in the distance. His jaw hardened before going soft—like he was building walls around himself only to have to consciously decide to let them down.

"He was a bully," he said quietly. "A mean old drunk who told me I'd never amount to anything in my life."

Zoe's heart squeezed. "Devin... That's awful."

"When high school graduation came around, I still half believed him." His smile was pained. "I told myself I didn't, but asking for people to give me money so I could go fail out of college just the way he always told me I would? Nah."

She shook her head, but he kept talking. As they turned onto her street, his pace slowed.

"It was all stupid head games, I know. In the end, it didn't matter. The best route to getting out of his house was getting a job." The sharpness in his gaze finally eased. "Arthur hooked me up, actually."

"Sounds like him."

"Yeah, it does." Unguarded affection colored his tone—with maybe a little hero worship mixed in there, too. "I was always handy. He got me an interview at Meyer, and the rest is history. I got a good-paying job and an apartment." His jaw flexed. "And I never looked back."

A different kind of darkness shadowed his eyes now. He clenched and unclenched his hands at his sides.

"Devin..."

"It's for the best. I'm saving up for a house of my own, too. In another year, it'll be just me and some mutt out on the edge of town, and no one will ever be able to bother me like that again." He looked down at her and blew out a breath. "I'm glad. Honestly."

"Okay." There was more to the story than he was telling, but even she knew when a bear had been poked too much. "Well, I'm glad you're glad, too." With a soft smile of her own, she bumped her elbow against his arm. "For what it's worth, I think you turned out pretty great."

His lips curled upward. "You didn't turn out so bad yourself, Itch."

"Hey!" She swatted at him. That's what he and Han and their friends had called her when she was really bugging them.

"Sorry, sorry!" He put his hands in front of his face as she swung at him again.

And she was just goofing around—really, she was. He was, too. But she rose onto her toes and reached up, aiming for a good smack upside his head. "Take it back."

"I take it back. I take it back." He grabbed her wrists in his big, strong hands. He held on to her, stopping her from taking another shot at him.

He was breathing hard. She was, too.

Suddenly, it dawned on her exactly how close they were standing. Her chest was practically brushing his. Heat radiated off his body, soaking into hers, and out of nowhere, she couldn't get enough air.

She darted her gaze to his. Surprise colored his eyes, like he'd just realized the position they were in, too.

But he didn't let go.

Forget fluttering. Her whole chest was on fire. She was dizzy with the unexpected rush of contact.

Of his gaze darting down to her lips.

A pang of wanting hit her so hard it took her breath away. She looked to his mouth, too, red and soft. She'd been dreaming about this since she was twelve, but this was real. Devin James was really standing here with her, looking at her.

"Zoe..."

Before he could move, a bright light suddenly blinded them. Devin jerked away, shielding his eyes. Zoe cursed.

Right. Without her even really noticing, they'd arrived at her house.

And the floodlights outside had just turned on.

Humiliated anger swept across her cheeks. She looked at Devin, but he was backing up—fast.

"Sorry. Good grief, Zo."

"What—"

"You should go in." His throat bobbed as he gestured at the house.

And it was hard to make out, given the glare of the lights. But yeah. That was her mom standing just inside the door.

She cursed beneath her breath. "Look—"

"You should go," he said again, firmer.

She wanted to laugh. Almost as much as she wanted to cry.

Five seconds ago, he'd been looking at her like she was anything but the little girl she used to be. His gaze had been hot as fire, his hands grasping at her wrists like he had no intention of letting go. He'd been about to kiss her.

Her. A grown woman, fully capable of making her own decisions.

"Devin." She hated the shakiness in her voice.

"Keep the jacket," he told her, backing away. "I can grab it from Han. Later."

"Devin," she called again.

Regret flashed in his eyes.

And that was what did it.

She couldn't decide which was worse—him regretting getting caught or him regretting almost letting it happen in the first place. Either way, if he regretted it already?

It didn't matter how much she liked him—how

much she had liked him since she was twelve freaking years old.

She deserved better than that.

He turned and walked away. She watched him go for a long minute.

Fuming, she turned and stormed toward the house. The door swung open before she could get to it, which only pissed her off more. With her mom holding the thing, she couldn't even slam it behind her.

"Late night," her mom observed.

"I've been home later." She worked at a bar, for Pete's sake.

"*Zhaohui*..."

She rounded on her mom. "Save it."

Her mom regarded her. Zoe was vibrating with anger. At her mom for interrupting. At Devin for walking away.

At every freaking person in her life who treated her like a kid, who didn't trust her to know her own mind.

Her mother made a soft *tutt*ing sound in the back of her throat. She let the door swing closed. Lifting one brow, she leveled Zoe with her most skeptical gaze. "I hope you know what you're doing."

"Believe it or not, Mom," she gritted out, "I usually do."

Only in this case, even she wasn't sure that was true.

Chapter Seven

"You want to talk about it?"

Devin looked up to find Arthur gazing at him across the worktable in the back of Harvest Home. He fought not to snap at him. Arthur didn't deserve any of his crap.

The only one who deserved that was himself.

"About what?"

Arthur just raised his brows, shifting his gaze pointedly to the mangled box Devin had been destroying in a vain effort to rip it open with his bare hands.

Okay, yeah, fine, so he was acting a little off.

Scrubbing his hand across his face, he grabbed the box cutter from the other side of the table and got back to work.

But Arthur wasn't going to leave this one alone. "Let me guess. Girl trouble."

Devin narrowly avoided slicing his finger off. Stupid. More carefully, he started again. "No."

"Boy trouble, then?"

Devin scrunched up his face in confusion. "What?"

"Never hurts to ask," Arthur said, waving away Devin's reaction. "Zoe yelled at me the other day, saying I'm too"—he snapped his fingers a couple of times before finding the word—"'heteronormative.'"

"Believe me, I still like the ladies." There was nothing wrong with being gay, obviously, but Devin had known from day one that he was into women.

And what he was into right now, apparently, was a girl who was too young for him, a girl who got under his skin like nobody else. A girl who made it easy to talk about things he never talked about. His dad, his life, everything.

A girl with dark, sparkling eyes, silky hair, and the softest hands. A girl he'd come so close to ruining everything with on Sunday night.

He swallowed hard, putting down the knife and clenching his hands around the edges of the box. Ever since he'd been a kid, this place had been a second home to him. The Leung house had become a third. Arthur, Han, and everyone else in their family trusted him. How would they look at him if they found out he was having wildly inappropriate thoughts about the youngest member of their family?

What would happen if he got with Zoe for real? Even if everyone accepted it…if it didn't work out, if their relationship hit the rocks or went down in flames…

Arthur and Han cared about him. Deeply. But at the end of the day, faced with the decision, they'd choose their flesh and blood over some stray they'd taken in.

Acting on his attraction to Zoe was a nonstarter. It couldn't happen.

So why couldn't he stop thinking about it?

Even a couple of days later, he could feel her skin, smell the sweet scent of her wrapping around him and turning him inside out. In the driveway of the Leung house—right where he and Han used to hang out when they were kids, when Zoe was *literally* a kid—he'd been inches from kissing her. The moment they'd shared kept playing in his head on repeat, and all he could think was, what if those lights hadn't gone on? What if Zoe and Han's mom hadn't caught him ready to claim those soft, rose-colored lips?

When would he have stopped?

How much would he have risked?

He shook his head. Fury burned in his chest, almost as hot as his arousal whenever he let his mind drift back to that almost-kiss. He was an idiot to be even thinking about it, much less actively imagining it.

So why was he torturing himself like this?

And why was Arthur just sitting there instead of trying to get him to talk?

"Okay, fine," he exploded. He glared at Arthur. Patient bastard had always been good at waiting him out until he finally told on himself. "Let's say there is a particular lady in question."

Arthur set aside the inventory sheet he'd been working on and gave Devin his full attention. "Okay."

"But it's a terrible idea."

"Most love usually is," Arthur said with a sly smile.

Devin shook his head, gesturing wildly with his hands. "Like, natural disaster kind of terrible."

Arthur just raised his brows.

"Okay, fine, maybe not that bad, but bad. It would cause big problems."

"What sort of problems are we talking about? Legal trouble?"

"No." Though a half dozen years ago, it would have.

"Work trouble?"

"No."

"Then...?"

Devin cast about for a second before landing on "Her family."

Of which Arthur was a member. This was so messed up.

"I can't believe they wouldn't approve of you."

"It's more complicated than that." Devin raked a hand through his hair. "But they'd have good reason to think it's a bad idea."

The Leungs had welcomed Devin with open arms. Here at Harvest Home, Arthur had taken Devin under his wing. As Han's best friend, Devin had free run of the Leung house. Sleepovers, afternoon hangouts. They trusted him.

Han trusted him. Han, who was so obsessed with keeping his family safe and secure. He'd always been protective of his baby sister. How many times had he confided in Devin about wanting to basically go check Zoe into a convent?

Devin hadn't been lusting after Zoe that entire time, but his attraction to her had grown and grown, from the spark he first felt at her high school graduation to this inferno now. The other night, first at Harvest Home and then later at the bar, he'd kept losing sight of who she was. She stopped being his best friend's sister or Arthur's niece. She'd become just...Zoe. Gorgeous, easy-to-talk-to, smart, funny, empathetic Zoe.

While Devin's thoughts spun out, Arthur kept regarding him with that steady, patient gaze of his. Finally, he sat back and exhaled long and low.

"Have I ever told you the story of how I ended up here?"

Only about a million times.

Devin managed not to thunk his head against the table. "Yeah."

"All of it?"

"I don't know," Devin said carefully.

"My family, when we came over, we started in San Francisco."

"Right."

"Moved to New York from there. It was crowded. Dirty. We worked hard, lived in a tiny apartment. Huilang and David and me with our parents." Huilang being Han, Lian, and Zoe's mom, and David their distant uncle.

"Okay..."

"I was the one who decided to set out and go somewhere else. Not an easy decision."

"I'm sure." There was no stopping Arthur now, so Devin strapped in for the ride.

"My father. He told me it would be big trouble if I left."

Devin perked up. This was a part of the story he hadn't heard before. "Really?"

Arthur nodded. "He had so many reasons it wouldn't work. He thought I was betraying the family by leaving them behind." He smiled, knowing and maybe just a little smug. "But I knew. There were more reasons to go. And you know what?"

"What?"

"I was right." He waved a hand around. "Look what I've been able to accomplish. I had a great career." He had, starting the Jade Garden restaurant. Socking away cash and making a whole series of unlikely investments that had enabled him to open this place and grow it year after year. "Brought my sister and her husband down here with me, and they've had happy lives. We all have."

"Okay..."

Arthur fixed him with a gaze like he could see right through Devin. Could he? Did he know more than he was letting on?

If he did, he kept it to himself. "You can't let fear push you around. Worrying about what other people will think, what other people will do. It leaves you miserable. This girl—if she means enough to you, you go to her. You find a way to make it work. No matter what anybody else says, you hear me?"

For a split second, Devin considered it. He let go of all his concerns about Han and Arthur and Zoe's mom.

He let himself imagine going for it. Being with Zoe. Having her in his arms, talking to her the way he had the other night. Celebrating a great game of pool with a kiss.

Taking her to his bed.

A jolt of electricity zipped down his spine.

Yeah. He wanted that. All of it.

But before he could really talk himself into believing he could have it, a deep voice broke in.

"Wait—Devin's got a girl?"

All the hope that had started to rise in Devin's chest came crashing down. He turned to find Han in the doorway.

Right. Crap. It was Tuesday. Han or his mom or both—they always came by in the late afternoon.

Stupid. How could he have forgotten? How could he have asked Arthur of all people about Zoe—even in the most veiled of terms?

How could he have imagined this could work?

He forced out a laugh, but it was hollow to his own ears. "Nah, man. Me and Arthur—we were just talking."

Devin stood up, anxious, restless energy making it impossible to sit.

"Really?" Han asked, setting down a crate of left-over produce from the restaurant before wiping his brow. "Because it sounded like—"

Mercifully, Arthur stepped in to save him. "Your friend. He was talking in"—he cleared his throat—"hypotheticals."

Devin directed an appreciative glance his way. Leave it to Arthur to make Devin sound innocent without telling a single untruth.

But Han wasn't going to be deterred. "I don't know, man." He sized Devin up. "You have been a little weird lately."

"Work stuff." That wasn't an untruth, either. Taking over as shift leader had been great, but it had come with all the headaches he'd assumed it would.

Namely managing Bryce Horton.

But he wasn't here to complain about Bryce. Especially when Han was still regarding Devin with suspicion, and Devin was trying not to sweat.

Finally, Han gave him a playful shove on his shoulder. "Well, whoever the *hypothetical* girl is, I hope you win her over. Your dry spell has been going on for *way* too long."

"Like you're one to talk."

Han's gaze darkened. The fact he hadn't had a serious long-term relationship since he and May broke up after high school was a sore spot, and Devin had aimed right for it. "Whatever. Keep your secrets."

"No secrets to tell." And he was going to make sure it

stayed that way. Needing some air after that close call, he grabbed a stack of inventory forms they'd already gotten through. "Gotta hit the head. I'll swing these by the front office."

"Thanks," Arthur said.

Han got to work. Relieved there wasn't going to be any more third degree, Devin headed out.

He had an ulterior motive for swinging past the office anyway.

The second Zoe came into view, his heart did something funny in his chest. She looked as beautiful as ever. She had when he'd first arrived, too.

She'd avoided his gaze in a way that was new, though. There'd been no flirty banter. She hadn't gotten in his space. She definitely hadn't come close enough for him to slip up and almost kiss her, and that was a good thing.

So why did it feel so awful?

Arthur hadn't known all the facts, so his advice hadn't been right, but there was one area where he'd been on the nose. Zoe did mean something to Devin. That meant he had to make this work between them. Not the kissing part, but the rest of it. He'd really started to think they were becoming friends. He wanted her, sure, but he also just plain liked her.

If almost kissing her meant losing her smiles and the way she looked at him and talked to him, then he'd screwed up worse than he'd realized. He had to make it right. Fast, before he messed this up for good.

He walked right up to the desk and put the inventory sheets in the bin. She glanced up at him. Her eyes sparkled for a second before darkening. Glowering, she looked away.

No smile. No "hello," even.

Guilt churned in his gut. She really was mad, and she had every right to be.

"You have a minute?" he asked. He couldn't keep the urgency out of his tone.

"Nope."

"Come on, Zo." He reached for her hand, only for her to snap it away.

"Uh-uh. No way." She darted her gaze around, but they were definitely alone out here. She still lowered her voice. "You of all people do not get to do what you almost did on Sunday night and then 'Zo' me."

Anger flashed in her gaze, only it was more than that.

She was trying to hide it, but she was hurt.

Was it possible to feel even worse?

"Just hear me out," he begged.

She narrowed her eyes. "Fine."

Crossing her arms over her chest, she stared up at him, fire and defiance in her gaze, and that really shouldn't get him feeling hot under the collar, but it did.

He didn't care that she'd just verified that they were alone. He did the same thing she had, glancing around, but he couldn't talk to her like this, one eye constantly looking over his shoulder.

"Come on."

He tipped his head toward the spare office behind the desk. Keeping her feet planted, she cocked a brow at him, and he shot a glance skyward before holding out a hand. "Please?"

With a gruff sigh, she rolled her eyes but then consented to follow him. Once they were both inside, he closed the door and flipped the lock.

He turned to look at her. Her posture was still closed and defensive, and he hated that. But what could he do? How could he get them back to the place they'd been the other night—all smiles and quiet confidences—without going too far?

"Look, Zoe." He was making this up as he went along, barreling ahead without a plan. "I'm sorry. Really."

"For what?" She tipped her chin up, the stubborn set to her jaw driving him to distraction. She started counting things off on her fingers. "For almost kissing me? Because if so, screw you. Or for jumping away from me like I'm a leper? Because if so, also screw you." She started advancing on him, her voice rising. "Or for treating me like a freaking child, the way everybody in my life does?" She was right in his space again, her eyes on fire. "Because if so"—she reached out and jabbed him in the chest—"screw"—she did it again—"you."

He grabbed her by the hand, and oh no. This was too much like the other night. She'd been swatting at him for his teasing then. She was righteously angry now. Guilt churned in his stomach, but his skin was prickling, her hand warm in his. He stroked his thumb over her palm, holding on even though he should let her go.

He should walk right out of this office. Out of this building and maybe off a short pier, but her cheeks were flushed, her eyes bright, and her soft red lips so wet and kissable, he was losing his mind.

"I can't," he said. "Your brother—"

"Isn't my keeper." She went softer against him, some of the anger fading out of her.

And it was like he couldn't stop himself.

He drifted closer to her, erasing the gap between them,

licks of flame darting across his skin. "I don't want to be a bad guy."

He didn't want to take advantage. He didn't want to mess things up between them and lose the fragile friendship they'd been building—the one that had already come to mean so much to him.

What could they even have together besides friendship? Her time here in Blue Cedar Falls was clearly a stopgap. She was on her way to bigger and better things. His biggest goal in life was a house in the woods alone. If they crossed this line, it would change things forever. With her. With her family.

Keeper or not, he didn't want to violate Han's trust.

She gazed up into his eyes. The liquid brown of her irises melted something inside him. Reaching up, she grazed her fingertips across his cheek.

"You're not a bad guy, Devin." Her hand settled tentatively on the side of his neck, and the intimacy of it was almost too much. "I've been back home for months, and I swear you're the first person who's made me feel like you're actually listening to me. You care. A lot." She shook her head gently. "Bad guys don't do that."

He swallowed, scarcely able to think with her so close. Without his permission, his arm moved to wrap around her, and that felt so good. She was practically flush against him, warm and soft and smelling like heaven.

All his resolutions went up in smoke.

"This is a terrible idea," he rasped.

"Probably."

Then she rose onto her toes.

He was going to hell, because he met her halfway. Their mouths crashed together, and that was it. Something snapped inside him. Hauling her in against him, he let himself really feel her. Light exploded behind his eyes. Forget all his worries about the fact that she used to be a kid to him—Zoe Leung was all woman now. Her soft curves fit to his body like they were made to press together. She kissed like the spitfire she was, opening to him, nipping at his lips with her teeth, sucking on his tongue.

Groaning, he picked her up and sat her on the edge of the desk. This whole place was a disaster—the place they put stuff when they didn't know where it should go. Something clattered to the floor, but he didn't care. With a hand at the back of his neck, she reeled him in, and he went so happily. He lost his mind to the heat of her mouth, the warmth of her hips in his hands. Scooting backward on the desk, she folded her legs around him.

Alarm bells went off in his head.

What was he doing?

He tore himself away, only for her to drag him back in.

"Zoe," he gasped, kissing her again, but he had to stop.

She raked her nails through his scalp. "If you say one word about my stupid brother, I swear—"

"No." He laughed. "Just no."

But as he drew away, the kiss-bitten redness of her lips, her tousled hair, and her flushed cheeks told him the truth. They'd crossed a line. He knew how she tasted now, how perfectly she fit in his arms.

There was no going back.

But he wasn't a complete idiot.

"My place," he panted. "Not here."

She hooked her ankles behind his rear and pulled him in, and he saw stars.

He pulled away again and fixed her with a gaze that brooked no argument. "Not here."

She pouted, breathing hard, but she released him. He stepped away, and she hopped down off the table.

"Fine," she relented. She narrowed her eyes at him, but her voice shook. "No take-backs, though, okay?" She reached up to tap him on the head. "Don't overthink this."

Yeah. Like that was going to happen.

He grabbed her hand again. But instead of brushing her away, he held her gaze and brought the back of her palm to his mouth.

"No take-backs." He kissed the soft skin of her knuckles.

And seriously. He was going to hell.

But if the smoldering look in her eyes was any indication?

It was going to be worth the ride.

Chapter Eight

Nervous anticipation and wary disbelief warred in Zoe's gut as she pulled up to Devin's building an hour later. Staying at Harvest Home and finishing the tasks she usually enjoyed had been pure torture—especially when Devin had slipped out. The dark look he'd given her on his way to the door had made her clench down deep inside.

But he'd been hot and cold over the past few days, to say nothing of the past few years. She had no idea what she was walking into here.

Still half expecting him to have changed his mind again, she got out of the car and headed up the walk. Bubbles formed and popped inside her chest. She was trying to keep her expectations in check, but his kiss had set her on fire. An hour of waiting had only stoked the flame. By the time she hit the top of the stairs, she was a riot of desire and nerves—if he turned her away after all that, she really was going to deck him. She reached the apartment number he'd given her, lifted her hand, and curled it into a fist. She took a deep breath, then steeled up her nerve and knocked.

The door swung open instantly.

Behind it stood Devin, and Zoe's stomach did a loop-the-loop.

Good grief, he was gorgeous. His sandy-brown hair was all mussed, exactly the way she wanted it to be after she'd been raking her hands through it all night. If it was possible, his jaw was sharper, the scruff there even more masculine. He stood there in a T-shirt and jeans, his feet bare on the hardwood.

His eyes shone midnight black with want, and just like that, all the doubt disappeared from her mind.

"Devin—"

"C'mere."

He reached into the space between them to drag her in.

She crashed into him with the same passionate, desperate need that had overcome them in the back office of Harvest Home. The kisses were just that bright and stinging, and she couldn't get enough. The door slammed closed behind her. With all his bulk, Devin pressed her into it, and oh *God*.

She'd known he was ripped, but feeling all that hard muscle awakened a need inside her. Wrapping her arms around his neck, she used what leverage she had to climb his body, and he helped her, lifting her up. She curled her legs around him.

The hot bulge of him against her center sent fireworks off inside her. He let out a noise that was pure sex as they ground together. She'd never gone from zero to sixty so fast. She was dizzy with it, barely able to think.

He moved them away from the door, holding on to her as he turned to carry her through his apartment.

She got only the most glancing impression of the place. It was neat but spare, no pictures on the wall. A plain beige couch, a glass coffee table, and a sage-green rug.

And then she didn't have time to even think about his

interior decorating, because that was his bedroom door he was hauling her through.

She pulsed deep inside as he practically tossed her down onto the big bed. He stood over her for a long moment, breath coming hard. Her entire body flushed. She liked being seen like this, liked the dark glint in his piercing eyes as he ran his broad hands along the tops of her thighs.

But the moment stretched and stretched. That same nervous flutter from earlier returned. "No take-backs?" she reminded him. She hated how it came out like a question.

He inhaled deeply. Then he nodded. "No take-backs."

Resolved, he climbed on top of her. As he kissed her again, slower this time, she wanted to pinch herself. There was no hesitation in him, and when she put her hands on his skin, under the hem of his shirt, he pushed into her touch. This wasn't some frantic, impulsive rush.

This was real.

Savoring every moment, she opened to him, curling her legs around his hips. The hot weight of his body settled over her. Every lick of his tongue and scrape of his teeth across her lips set her ablaze. Molten desire bubbled up inside her, and she wanted to take her time, but she couldn't wait.

She pushed his shirt up. Rising onto his knees, he grabbed the fabric by the back of the neck and tore it off, and holy crap. His muscles had muscles, all of him golden tan and smooth. A trail of hair led down to the button of his jeans, and she had to stop herself from ripping those open right away, too.

When he kissed her again, it was with a new intensity. A flash of burning arousal shot through her when his rough hands dipped beneath her top. She helped him take it off. Her bra followed, and he groaned.

"I've been trying not to think about these for so long." He buried his face in her breasts, and she laughed.

It didn't stay funny for long. Not when his hot mouth sealed over that tender flesh. Aching for more, she arched into him, running her fingers through his hair. Everything he did felt so good. Triumph had her flying high.

Until he started kissing lower down her abdomen.

"Devin," she moaned when he got to the waistband of her leggings.

Staring her straight in the eyes, he pressed one firm kiss to the very center of her through the fabric, and she practically came right then and there.

She reached for him.

He raced back up her body, sucking and biting at her all the way. As soon as he was close enough, she kissed him hot and deep, scrambling at his fly. She finally ripped it open and pushed his jeans and underwear down. The hot, hard length of him sprang free, and they groaned as one. He was huge in her hands, and she still couldn't believe this was happening.

As she stroked him, he tore at her clothes, too. She kicked off her boots, and it was all a mad dash until they were both naked. He paused just long enough to get a condom on. When he lined himself up, she had no doubts.

Still, he paused. "Zo..."

She sucked in a breath. Cupping his face in her hands, she brought his lips to hers for another, softer kiss.

"I want this," she promised him, and it was too true. With emotion she couldn't name, she told him, "I want you."

He closed his eyes.

His body sinking into hers turned her inside out. He felt so perfect as he ground against her, sending sparks surging through her.

"Zo," he repeated.

"I'm here." She was babbling. What was she saying? "I'm here, I'm here, I want you. I want this."

He pulled back, and she pushed into him until they fell into a rhythm. Pleasure started at the apex of her thighs, spreading outward until all she could see and feel and touch and taste was him. Over and over he drove into her, faster. She scrabbled at him, running her hands all up and down his back and shoulders.

"Zoe, Zo, I can't—you feel so good—"

"Devin, come on, please, I want—"

He slammed into her another half dozen times.

Her climax tore through her out of nowhere. Her vision flashed to black, and she squeezed every part of herself around him. Driving in deep, he called her name a final time. He pulsed inside her, and her entire world shattered.

Because this was *real*. She'd had sex with Devin James.

What had started as a challenge to see if she could get him to break had turned into a breaking down of her conception of the natural order of the universe.

She still had no real delusions that this could be more than a fling, but the impossible had already happened the instant he'd touched his lips to hers.

As she stared up at his ceiling in wonder, she pressed a hand to the center of his back.

Who knew? Maybe all her notions of what she could and couldn't have in this world were wrong.

Chapter Nine

Watch out!"

At the sound of Terrell's shout, Devin jerked his gaze up from his clipboard.

Half his people were raising a section of the house's frame, Terrell and Gene up on ladders while the rest supported and spotted from below, only something wasn't right. Devin shot to his feet, gaze swinging wildly, the entire site going into slow motion. There—crap.

Off to the side, Bryce had let go prematurely, and Devin lurched forward, calling his name, but it was too late. Terrell's grip slipped without anyone to back him up.

The whole thing came crashing down.

Devin raced over. "Is everybody okay?"

"Yeah." Terrell scrubbed a hand over his face.

Devin checked in with everybody else, and no one had gotten hurt, thank goodness. He appraised the rest of the scene. The damage to the section that had fallen wasn't that bad, either, but it was still going to set them back a couple of hours—and that was before the headache of writing this up.

"I swore I had it," Terrell said, climbing down. His eyes narrowed as he glared silently off to the left.

Following his gaze, Devin flexed his jaw. He patted Terrell on the back. "It's just about lunch time anyway. Take a break, and then we'll get this cleaned up afterward."

He and the rest of the crew nodded.

Reassured that they were all okay, Devin stalked to the other side of the building, grinding his teeth together hard enough to crack.

A week had passed since he'd moved up to shift leader, and for the most part it had been going great. The team listened to him, and he'd handled the couple of issues that had arisen without much trouble.

Except Bryce.

Mostly it was little things like unauthorized breaks or screwing around on his phone when he was supposed to be working. Some of it was more serious, like using inappropriate language when talking to the women on the crew. Devin had documented it all, slowly building a case that even the folks who protected him couldn't ignore.

But this?

"Horton," he growled.

Bryce looked up from his phone. "What?"

"Don't 'what' me." Devin wanted to grab the guy's phone and chuck it in the cement mixer, only that would make a defect in the next house's foundation. Workers on the site weren't forbidden from being on them or anything; this wasn't high school. But when your eyes and hands needed to be on the job, they needed to be on the job. "Where were you?"

"Right there." He gestured toward where the crash had happened. "Weren't you watching?"

Old anxiety rose in Devin. His dad used to do that, too—reframing everything to make it out like Devin was the one to blame. He had to remind himself that wasn't true today. Devin had been doing his job, keeping an eye on his team while also seeing to the rest of his duties. "You weren't paying attention, and somebody could've gotten hurt."

Bryce rolled his eyes. "Terrell's butterfingers aren't my fault."

Forget a headache; the incident report was going to be a full-on migraine. Enough other people would back Devin and Terrell up that Bryce had been the one to let go, but the fact of the matter was that this never should have happened in the first place.

"You not doing your job is your fault." Devin kept his voice restrained but barely. "I'm not going to turn a blind eye to this BS."

"Sure you won't." Bryce's smile was mocking as he patted Devin on the shoulder.

Devin shoved him off automatically. He clenched and unclenched his jaw.

He walked away, hating the hot feeling in his chest and the hotter one in his face. The sense of helplessness ate at him, making him feel like he was twelve years old all over again.

Sure, he'd document this entire thing, but there was no satisfaction in that.

How did he protect his people? Stop giving Bryce any jobs where he could put the other members of his crew at risk? Stop giving him jobs at all? Bryce would love that.

The unfairness made him want to punch something.

Instead, he drew in a few deep breaths, trying to calm himself down before getting back to it.

On impulse, he popped his phone out of his pocket for the first time all morning. A handful of alerts greeted him, and he scrolled through them. When he got to the couple of texts from Zoe, the remaining tension bled out of his body, and he couldn't hold back the warm smile that curled his lips.

Ugh, remind me why I'm shacking up with a morning person again? I need coffee and it's all the way over theeeeerre

A photo came with the message, showing her in his bed, her hair a mess where it lay splayed out across his sheets, and he had to suck in a breath. There wasn't a single inappropriate thing about the shot, but it didn't matter. The sight of her, all rumpled and gorgeous and soft from sleep... It did things to him.

He just wished he could be there to take advantage of it. To roll her over and kiss that red mouth until they were both breathless.

Or maybe—if it was a day when he wasn't working... to go make her coffee. Pancakes. Breakfast in bed.

He mentally shook his head at himself. What a sap.

A week now they'd been doing... whatever it was they were doing together. Giving in to the overwhelming force of attraction between them had been the easiest thing in the world. When she was around, it was like all his worries disappeared.

He'd thought it would be weird, going from her brother's best friend to her friend to maybe something more, but it hadn't been. At all.

They'd never had to have any intense conversations

about what was going on between them, either. Even that first time, when he'd been nervous about risking everything for a night of fun, it was like she'd been able to see right through him. Proving just how well she knew him, she'd just climbed right back on top of him and kissed him senseless, then wandered naked into his kitchen to fix herself a sandwich. She'd called out to ask if he wanted anything, too. Casual—like it was the most normal thing. And you know, he had been kind of hungry after working up an appetite like that.

So she'd just slipped into his life. When they weren't having mind-blowing sex, they were sharing takeout pizza or introducing each other to their favorite shows. He still wasn't quite sold on *The Bachelor*, but watching her yelling at the TV made him grin, and she was surprisingly receptive to reruns of *This Old House* playing in the background the rest of the time.

His crummy, boring apartment felt warm when she was in it. So warm that he almost forgot for hours at a time that his entire goal in life was to build his house in the woods and get out of here.

His only regret was the same one she had. She worked nights and he worked days, and so there she was waking up at—he checked the time stamp on the message—ten in the morning, while he was up at six.

Shaking his head at himself, he tapped out a quick reply. *Wish I could've gone and grabbed you one.*

Her answer came seconds later. *It's ok, I managed.*

The picture that followed was of her at Bobbi's bakery on Main Street. She was seated at one of the little tables inside, a latte and an empty plate set next to her open laptop.

His smile faded slightly. She'd kicked it up a notch on the job search of late. That or, now that he got regular updates about her life, he was just more aware of it.

Every time she talked about it, a little pit formed in his stomach. Which was stupid. He'd known from the minute she moved back home that it was temporary. She was only here until the right opportunity came along, and he could be a big enough man to hope it showed up for her soon.

Even if, deep down, he never wanted her to leave.

"Hey, James." Bryce's voice had Devin jerking his gaze up. "Your girlfriend's here."

For a second, Devin's heart lurched into his throat.

No way. Zoe had just texted him from the bakery, and even if she hadn't—they hadn't exactly talked about it, but the one time he'd tried to bring up how he'd prefer to keep whatever they were doing together quiet, at least for the time being, she'd just rolled her eyes.

"Don't worry. Your secret is safe with me," she'd said before kissing his cheek. "My brother murdering you would be a real bummer."

And then she'd started kissing *other* parts of him, and well, that'd been the end of that.

Long story short, she wouldn't just show up at his work unannounced, and Bryce wouldn't know to call her his girlfriend.

Before he could work himself up any further worrying, he spotted Han's car in the lot—not Zoe's. Relief swept over him, even as a new kind of nervousness started to intrude.

Flipping Bryce off for being a homophobic prick, he started crossing the site toward the lot. As he approached,

Han got out of his car and held up one of the same chopped-up liquor boxes he used for Jade Garden deliveries, and Devin managed a smile.

"Hey, buddy," Han said as he hauled the food over to the picnic table by the trailer, where they usually ate.

"Hey."

He and Han did this once a week or so. Their schedules didn't match up much better than Devin's and Zoe's. Lunch on the job site was one of the easier ways to get together most weeks.

As Han started unpacking the containers he'd brought, Devin pulled apart a couple of paper plates. His stomach growled as the mouthwatering scents of whatever Han had cooked up today hit him.

"The mango pork's new," Han said. "And I tweaked the ginger on the veggies."

"Yeah?"

Han might've had to drop out of culinary school when his dad died, but you'd never know it. He cooked all day, and then he cooked some more on his days off. He tried out new recipes—fancy "fusion" stuff that he and his mom had agreed didn't fit with the Jade Garden's brand, though he did manage to sneak a few of the tamer test recipes into the Chef's Specials "secret menu" now and then.

As Han plated up the food, he tipped his head toward the guys eating sandwiches and leftovers at the other tables. "So, how's it going?"

Devin rolled his eyes. "Same as usual."

"AKA, Bryce is being a jerk?"

Devin glared, but he knew there had been no one close enough to hear Han. "Yeah, pretty much."

Han scooped meat and vegetables onto a bed of noodles, then went ahead and sprinkled sesame seeds and scallions and drizzled some sort of orange sauce over it all, because the parking lot of a construction site was a five-star restaurant in his eyes. He passed the plate over, and Devin smacked his lips.

"I'm telling you." Han opened a set of wooden chopsticks and pointed them at Devin. "You gotta stand up to guys like him."

The same old discomfort churned in Devin's gut, but he pushed it down. "Sure, just like you did with all the mean kids back in high school."

"Shut up, man."

Neither of them had gotten picked on too badly when they were kids. Han stuck out, one of maybe four Asian kids in the school at the time, but he'd been as charming then as he was now—the bastard. Devin had held his own. He never started any fights, but when any came his way, he finished them. The two of them and the rest of the gang they ran with—they were fine.

But Han's girlfriend, May, had gotten savaged by the mean girl squad. She acted like it was no big deal, but whatever had happened, it had been bad enough that May had taken off after graduation. She'd come back for Han's dad's funeral and a visit or two here and there, and that was it.

Han scowled and nodded at Devin's food. "So? You gonna eat or just give me crap about things that happened a decade ago?"

"Like I can't do both." He tore open his own chopsticks. He'd never be as good with them as Han was, but he managed okay. He eyed the food. "Nice presentation."

"Obviously."

He tried the pork first, because how could he not.

"Get some mango with it," Han urged him.

Devin raised a brow. He didn't ignore the advice, though. He scooped up a noodle for good measure and shoveled the whole thing into his mouth.

His eyes slipped closed and he thumped his fist onto the table.

"Uh..."

"Shh." Devin put a finger to his sealed lips as he chewed. Once he swallowed, he opened his eyes.

"Well?"

"Man, that's good." Salty and sweet, rich but not heavy.

"The mango really makes it, huh?"

"Yup."

"You getting the garlic?"

"Uh-huh."

"But not too much."

"Close—I wouldn't do any more. But seriously. It's a keeper."

"Try the veg."

Devin forced himself to stop cramming delicious, delicious pork in his face. The vegetable was some weird green thing Han had been messing around with. It'd been a little bitter for his taste last time, but it'd probably go pretty well with the pork. He gave it a shot and nodded. "Yup. Cutting the ginger helped a lot."

"Thought so." Han flashed a smug, ever-so-slightly-secretive smile as he dug into his own plate.

"What're you up to?"

"Nothing."

"Yeah, I don't buy it."

Han had always had fun messing around with new recipes, but he'd been more intense about it of late. There was definitely something going on.

"You don't have to." Then his smirk deepened. "But maybe someday someone will."

Devin put down his chopsticks. "You aren't finally doing it."

Han had always idly talked about opening his own restaurant. It never came to anything, though. He was too busy at the family business.

"No." Han shook his head. "Not yet. But let's just say I'm working on something that might be a first step."

"Okay, you keep your secrets. As long as you keep the awesome grub coming, too."

Chuckling, Han nodded. "That I can do." He took a bite of his own lunch and seemed pleased. "Speaking of which, I've got a few other things I'm ready to guinea pig. Dinner at my place tomorrow?"

Normally, Devin would jump at the chance, but heading to the Leung house made all the hairs stand up on the back of his neck. He cleared his throat. "Who all's going to be there?"

"Does it matter? Free grub, remember."

"I know. I'm just asking."

Han shrugged. "Bobbi and Caitlin probably. Clay if I can pry him away from the Junebug for a minute, and you know he'll want to bring June." He listed the names of a couple of other guys they hung out with regularly. Then he grimaced. "I think Zoe has the night off, so she'll probably invite herself."

"Oh?" Devin's voice came out strangled to his own ears.

"Maybe. Who knows."

Not good enough. But he couldn't probe any deeper without sounding suspicious. He rummaged around in his brain, trying to think of excuses why he couldn't go, but he came up with squat.

Zoe was a firecracker. She said their secret was safe with her, but she loved to push him, and he had to admit it—he kind of loved it when she did. But interacting with her at their family home, with Han right there? What lines would get blurred?

It wasn't just her he didn't trust. His fingers twitched. He was getting too comfortable hanging out at his apartment with her. They spent half their time naked or snuggled up or both. Reaching out and putting his hand over hers and pulling her into him was becoming second nature.

Would he be the one to slip up and give them away?

Oblivious to Devin twisting himself into knots, Han pursed his lips. "Then again, she's been going out a lot recently."

"Yeah?" Devin's throat threatened to close again.

"It's super weird. She bummed around the house all the time when she first moved back in, but now it's like she's never there. I think she's sneaking out at night, too."

Devin tried not to choke on a piece of mango and pork. He coughed into a napkin.

"You okay?" Han asked.

No.

"Yeah, yeah." Fighting both to breathe and to come off as casual, Devin asked, "Is it really sneaking, though? She's in her twenties, right?"

"Fine, fine, whatever. It's still weird. I didn't think she had a lot of friends around here." He narrowed his eyes. "I'm pretty sure she's not dating anybody."

"Maybe she's just working late? The Junebug is a bar."

"Maybe." Han frowned. "You're right—it's none of my business. I just hope she's not doing anything stupid."

Devin's stomach flopped around inside his abdomen.

She was doing something stupid all right.

Namely him.

"I'm sure it's nothing," he lied.

Only he wasn't so sure of that.

He wasn't so sure at all.

"So...do you want me to stay away?" Zoe had her back turned to Devin as she brushed her hair, but her gaze flicked to his in the bathroom mirror.

He was a little groggy, still splayed out on the mattress, naked and boneless. She hadn't had to close the bar tonight, so she'd come over after her shift, which was great—he loved seeing her. But it was past his bedtime, and that last round had been particularly athletic.

There was something in her voice that told him he needed to pay attention, though.

He rose onto his elbows and rummaged around in his skull for enough brain cells to rub together. "What do you mean? It's your house."

Their pillow talk had inevitably turned to a discussion of the dinner party Han was holding at the Leung house. She'd seemed surprised to hear he was trying to find a way out of it.

"Yeah," she allowed. She set down her brush—one of a couple of her things that had somehow found a home for themselves in his bathroom this week—and came back over to the bed. As if she could tell that he wasn't at his best when she wasn't wearing any clothes, she pulled the covers up over her chest. "But Han is your best friend. I don't want to get in the way of that."

He wasn't quite tired or stupid enough to laugh. He'd only resisted her as long as he had because he hadn't been willing to risk Han's friendship or Arthur's welcome. Of course his being with her now was going to affect his relationship with her family.

He reached for her hand and held it in his, running his thumb along the lines of her palm. He should be stressing out right now, but it was hard to be anything but relaxed when it was just the two of them. She made talking about his feelings easy in a way no one ever had. "You aren't in the way. I'm just nervous he'll catch on to something being weird between us."

"Yeah..."

He closed his fingers around hers more firmly. "You know I don't like keeping this secret, right?"

"I know." She wasn't looking at him, though.

"It's just..."

"I get it. I'm probably not going to be here for long." She huffed out a breath and pitched her voice higher, putting on the fake-happy smile she always used when talking about her job search. "Fifteen more applications submitted today." She deflated back to a more natural tone. "No point rocking the boat for something temporary, right?"

Sourness coated the back of his tongue. This was good, them being clear with each other like this. It was smart and mature.

So why did he hate it so much?

He couldn't bring himself to agree with her, so he barreled on. "Look, I don't want you to feel like you have to stay away."

"And I don't want you to feel like you do."

"So we won't," he decided. "We'll both go—if that's what you want to do. And we'll just try to be normal. It'll probably be fine."

Her expression finally brightened. "Sure. We can do this."

"Of course we can."

"So, what do you think?" She scooted closer to him, and he breathed a little easier. "Does Han just keep living with our mom out of sheer martyrdom? Or is it because he's using her for her kitchen?"

Devin tipped his head back and laughed. Leave it to Zoe not to mince words. "He'd probably say it's to take care of your mom and save money."

"Martyrdom." She poked his arm with her index finger.

He took her hand in his and kissed her knuckles. "But you might be onto something with the kitchen." Devin had helped them redo it back a few years ago. "He'd never find an apartment with one as nice."

Gazing down at their joined hands, Zoe asked, "What about at your loner house in the woods? Any plans to build a giant kitchen there that he can use?"

"It'd be worth it just for the free food," he mused. But he shook his head. "I don't know. It's going to be a small place. Just me kicking around it."

"You don't think there'd ever be anybody else?" she asked quietly.

The question settled on him heavily. She was still studiously looking down. He brushed her hair back from her face, but it didn't let him see her eyes any better.

The answer should be simple. His whole life, he'd been dreaming of the day he could have a home of his own.

He glanced over at the bathroom, though. At the hairbrush and the toothbrush and the little bottles of lotion and soap.

He shrugged, noncommittal. "How about you? Gorgeous kitchen a must-have for your Realtor when you land your dream job?"

He kept his voice light, but forget heavy. This question sank inside him like a stone.

"Nah." She put her head on his shoulder. "It's not like Han would ever leave to come visit me."

I would, Devin didn't say. But her kitchen wouldn't have a thing to do with it.

Silence hung between them for a minute. He twisted his neck to press a kiss to her temple, but before he could come up with anything smart to say, a yawn snuck out of him.

She laughed and kissed him back before ruffling his hair. "Come on. Let's get you to bed. You have incident reports to write in the morning."

"Don't remind me," he groaned, flopping backward into his pillow.

She got up and turned off the lights, and wow, she was so great. As she slipped back into the bed beside him, he curled his arms around her. Even the prospect of dealing with more paperwork and more people letting Bryce off the hook couldn't bring him down.

Nope. Apparently, the only thing that could do that was the reminder that his time with her was temporary.

Which sucked. Because he was pretty sure he was going to get even more of those when he was pretending not to be sleeping with her at Han's party tomorrow night.

Chapter Ten

Y'all—don't even get me started on weird customers." June held a hand in front of herself, palm out.

Zoe raised a brow and took another sip of her wine.

Ten minutes into Han's dinner party, she, June, and June's friend Bobbi were standing around the island in the center of the kitchen, trading work stories. Over by the stove, Han prepped ingredients while trying to keep Ling-Ling from stealing any of them—with mixed success. Between fond rebukes to the dog, he kept a light conversation going with Clay, Bobbi's girlfriend, Caitlin, and a couple of guy friends.

"Ooh." Bobbi rubbed her hands together. "This is going to be good."

June smiled. "Let's just say there's a reason the Sweetbriar Inn now has an official policy prohibiting birds."

Zoe snickered, but before June could dive any deeper into whatever guest at her family's B&B had prompted that new rule, the doorbell rang, setting Ling-Ling off.

Zoe's pulse raced, and she put her glass down with a thunk. "I'll get it!"

"Seriously," Han called after her, "nobody's fighting you for it except the dog."

And okay, yeah, she was a little eager, racing to get the door each time a new person arrived. But this time, she had extra reason to run. Devin was the only person they were still waiting for. This had to be him.

She skidded to a stop in the entryway, making sure her body was blocking Ling-Ling from getting out before flinging open the door.

And there Devin was. All six foot something glorious inches of him, his cheeks flushed from the chill outside, his blue eyes sparkling, and what was it about the way he lit up when his gaze fell on her? Her heart pounded, her ribs squeezing around it.

Her over-the-top reaction made no sense. He was just a guy, and she was in a weird, temporary place in her life. They'd basically agreed that whatever they were doing together was just for fun. The very sight of him shouldn't turn her to goo.

But she liked him so much.

She cast one backward glance over her shoulder before closing the door and launching herself at him. He caught her in his arms. Pausing only to set down the six-pack he'd brought, he pressed her into the freezing-cold siding of the house, and she didn't care about the temperature or the fact that he was so worried about getting caught.

His mouth was hot as it covered hers, his tongue commanding. She kissed him back with a hunger that had nothing to do with the promise of the upcoming meal. Running her hands through his hair, she soaked up every second of contact with him.

It wasn't enough. He jerked away, his breath coming fast, the darkness in his gaze pure torture considering what was coming next. "We should—"

"Go make out some more in your truck?" she suggested helpfully.

He buried his face in her shoulder, and she wrapped her arms around him as tightly as she could. "Don't tempt me, woman."

"Why not?" She gazed up at the stars and breathed him in. "It's so much fun."

"For you, maybe," he said, but there was a hint of darkness in his tone.

The corners of her mouth turned down. "I was just messing around."

"I know." Did he, though?

The mood broken, he gave her one last quick peck before letting go.

Stepping away, he gestured at his face. "Do I have any...?"

"Just—" She reached up on her toes to swipe at the little smudge of lipstick at the corner of his mouth. Considering how they'd just been sticking their tongues down each other's throats, it wasn't bad. This long-wearing stuff was the best.

"Thanks."

"No problem."

He picked up the beer he'd set down and they headed inside. She stole another glance at him under the entryway light as he stopped to give Ling-Ling a quick scratch behind the ear. There was no sign that anything was amiss. The way she'd run her fingers through his hair could have easily been the wind. No one would know.

She tried to remind herself that that was a good thing.

"I'll, uh, show you where to put your coat." She started to lead him down the hall.

"Please," her brother scoffed, appearing at the top of the half flight of stairs. "It's just Devin. He knows." Han smiled at Devin. "What's up, man?"

"Nothing," Devin replied.

"Was starting to think you'd gotten lost out there."

"Nah." Devin brushed past her. Out of her brother's sight line, he gave her fingers a reassuring squeeze before continuing on. He held up the six-pack. "Almost forgot these in the truck and had to run back for them."

"Nice." Han accepted the beers.

But as Zoe followed Han and Devin into the kitchen, she caught June gazing at her appraisingly. Crap—she'd checked Devin for lipstick smudges but she hadn't checked herself. She casually glanced at her reflection in the hallway mirror. Nope—she was basically okay.

Well, whatever. June could give her weird looks if she wanted to. Zoe wasn't going to act like she had anything to hide.

To prove it, she snagged a fried wonton strip off one of the appetizer plates. She dragged it through the plum sauce dip and popped it in her mouth. She really didn't know what that was supposed to prove, but it was freaking delicious, so it didn't matter.

Around her, all signs showed this to be a successful dinner party. Han was doing his thing, cooking and putting on a show. If it weren't so clichéd—and if they were Japanese instead of Chinese—he could've had a heck of a career at one of those hibachi places.

Zoe shook her head, trying not to stare at Devin, who had joined the loose cluster hanging out over by her brother. Han's parties were never formal or anything, but people usually put in a little effort. Devin had traded in his work clothes for a sharp blue button-down that made his eyes look even brighter.

She wanted to peel it off him.

"So, you wanna talk about it?"

Zoe tried not to jump when June spoke from right beside her. "Talk about what?"

June's friend Bobbi snickered.

Zoe's face went warm. Crap. She was really bad at this secretly banging her brother's friend thing, huh?

"There's nothing to talk about," she said, more firmly this time.

June didn't seem convinced. "Uh-huh."

"He's one of Han's friends." Zoe swallowed past the lump in her throat. "Gross."

"Gross? I mean—" Bobbi gestured with her wineglass at the guys. Her girlfriend, Caitlin, stood over beside them. "I don't even like dudes, and I can admit he's hot."

"They're all hot," June said.

Zoe recoiled. "Ew. My brother is not hot."

Shrugging, June took a sip of her wine. "May would kill me for saying it, but it's true."

"Seriously, though," Bobbi said, leaning in. "Devin's been sneaking looks at you almost as much as you've been sneaking looks at him."

"Really?" Her voice came out too high. She retreated to the side a bit to reclaim her wineglass and took a gulp.

"Really," June confirmed.

Zoe had to stop herself from glancing over at him to verify. "It doesn't matter. Even if he weren't gross." He was so, so not gross. "It's like I said—he's my brother's best friend, and you know how Han is." Her mouth felt dry despite the wine. "If either of us made a move, he'd flip his lid."

"I don't know..." June mused.

"Well, believe me, I do."

Devin and Han had both been plenty clear. A bitter taste formed at the back of her mouth.

At first, the whole off-limits thing had been kind of fun. But the more time they spent together, the more it twisted her up inside.

Being someone's dirty little secret wasn't great for the ego.

Not that that was stopping her from developing—ugh—*feelings* for the guy.

Yeah, she might be in denial about a lot of things, but that was a tough one to get away from. She wasn't an idiot. The way his touch made her feel all warm and squishy inside, the way her thoughts kept drifting to him throughout the day...It was like her teenage crush, only times a million, because now she knew he liked her, too.

Maybe not as much as she liked him, but more than enough to keep throwing gasoline on the fire in her chest.

She was saved from having to downplay things to June and Bobbi any further by Han flicking off the burners with a flourish. "Okay, y'all, grub's up."

Zoe downed another gulp of her wine before excusing herself. This was old hat. Positioning herself at her brother's side, she passed him plates, and he portioned out the food.

Her mouth watered. Han had been refining his stable of experimental dishes for ages, and they just kept getting better. Tonight's menu included a rice dish with pickled ginger and edamame, plus seared scallops in a basil sauce she never would have thought would work, but it did. Baby bok choy that he'd cooked over a little electric grill, and some mystery egg tarts he'd done in the oven. He scattered the lot with a drizzle of vibrant green and white sauces, chopped nori, and sesame.

Devin stepped in to pass the completed dishes out.

"Wow," Caitlin said as she received the first plate.

"Let me know what you think."

Zoe frowned at her brother. His voice had a different pitch to it. He was always proud of his cooking, but the nerves jangling around in there were new.

She didn't have much time to think about it. Before she knew it, everyone had a plate in hand. As they found places to sit or stand, appreciative moans and compliments sounded out around the room. Han shone a sly smile as he started eating, too, Ling-Ling parked hopefully at his feet. He made a running commentary—he always did. What worked and what hadn't, though as far as Zoe was concerned, it was all a hit.

The regulars in Han's guinea pig squad were easy to spot as they echoed Han's comments. Devin was a down-to-earth guy, but he'd been hanging out with Han long enough to mention something about the butter-to-shortening ratio in the crust of the savory egg tart. Zoe shook her head and just kept shoveling it in.

One of Han and Devin's buddies, Terrell, snapped his fingers. "I know what this reminds me of. That thing you made for my sister's wedding."

Han tipped his head to the side. "Did I do shrimp for that?"

"No, but the sauce."

"That was totally different," Han said.

Devin scrunched up his nose. "It was kind of the same."

"You know what it reminds me of?" June interjected.

"What?" Han asked. "And please tell me you have a better memory than these guys."

"She usually does." Clay chuckled, and Devin elbowed him in the ribs.

"Graduation," June said, sure of herself. "Your year. That meal you did at our place."

"Oh." A shadow crept across Han's gaze.

Right. Any meal he would have made at the Wu-Miller house would have been because of May.

Devin looked at Han with the same concern Zoe felt.

As if realizing her mistake in bringing that up, June continued. "Though this is way better. I mean, the graduation meal was amazing, but these egg tarts are next level. What's in them again?"

Han rattled off some of the ingredients.

Devin cleared his throat. "I think it's more like that Thanksgiving you cooked—what was it? Twenty seventeen?"

Han pulled a face. "That menu was totally different."

"Yeah, but the basil—"

"Oh man," Terrell said, elbowing his buddy. "New Year's Eve, like, five years ago."

"Yeah!" The dude's eyes lit up. He waved a hand at Han. "The one you did at the park."

"Fried turkey," Han agreed. "Seriously, guys, that was nothing like this."

"Didn't you have little pastries? I swear there was, like, basil in them like this."

"The basil is in the sauce." Han was smiling again now, which was something.

“Oh! Oh!” Terrell held up a finger. “Wasn’t that the year we were picking gravel out of the cupcakes?”

“Man, who baked those?”

“Pretty sure it was me.” Bobbi grinned.

“They were so good, it was totally worth it, even when—”

Devin slammed his plate down on the counter. His fork clattered against the china. Ling-Ling whined.

Suddenly, everyone got quiet.

Zoe sucked in a breath. Devin’s face had turned a shade of purple. Thunderheads colored his eyes.

“What?” she asked.

Devin’s gaze connected with hers for a fraction of a second, and it was like an iron band closed around her heart.

Devin glanced away. “Excuse me.”

He stalked off. Zoe put her plate down. The band around her heart released, but it was replaced by a freaking jackrabbit, jumping up and down on the insides of her chest so fast, she could hardly breathe. She gripped the edge of the counter she’d been leaning against until her knuckles turned white.

Everything in her told her to follow him. His gaze was seared into her. His eyes had looked so *angry*.

But more than that, he’d looked so…

Lost.

A door slammed in the distance, and Zoe squeezed the counter even tighter. Han smacked himself in the forehead, then reached over to cuff Terrell on the back of his head, too.

“Ow—”

“Devin’s dad,” Han hissed. “Remember?”

"Wait." Zoe should shut up, but she couldn't. "What—"

Han shook his head.

Wincing, Terrell scrubbed at his face. "Oh, right. Crap."

Quietly, Bobbi turned to Zoe. "Devin's dad showed up drunk. He knocked over the cupcakes."

"Said some really awful stuff, too," Han added.

Zoe stared toward the corner Devin had disappeared around. It was like she was being yanked in that direction. He'd told her the other night that his dad wasn't a good guy, but seeing his reaction to someone bringing up that memory now...

She bit the inside of her lip.

Was he okay? No, of course not. How could he be?

She wanted so badly to chase after him. If she were really his girlfriend, she would do just that. She'd put her arms around him and hold him tight, and maybe—maybe he'd even let her.

Her stomach plummeted to the floor.

The only problem was that she wasn't. If she gave them away, he'd be even more furious—furious at her.

But she couldn't ignore this *pull*.

"Shouldn't someone go after him?" she asked.

Han shook his head. "Just makes it worse."

Everyone seemed to take that as definitive.

Slowly, people started eating and talking again, but Zoe couldn't hear any of it. She was listening so carefully for any sort of sound from the hallway. When she heard the bathroom door open, her heart leaped.

Speaking to no one in particular, she said, "I have to..."

She pulled out her phone as if that would explain her needing to step away.

June gave her a knowing glance that bordered on

encouragement. Accepting that unexpected morsel of support, she took off down the hall at a measured pace, but as soon as she was out of sight, she couldn't help it. She broke into an all-out sprint.

Only to almost crash into Devin. His jaw was set, storms still brewing in his eyes, and she'd just come out here to check on him.

But she couldn't stand this.

She grabbed him by the wrist and hauled him down the hall.

"Zo—"

He resisted, but he finally let himself be dragged into the next available room with a door. It was Lian's old room—now her mother's sewing room, but it would do. Her mom was working at the restaurant tonight, so she wouldn't notice.

As soon as the door was closed behind them, she launched herself at him. She wrapped her arms around his chest, but he was stone.

"You don't have to—" he gritted out.

"Shh."

He shook his head, but she wasn't having any of it.

She shushed him again. He stayed as stiff as a board for a long moment. Crap. Maybe she'd misread this entire thing. Maybe he didn't need comfort.

Maybe he didn't want any from her.

Well, too bad. She was giving it to him anyway.

She'd give him anything.

She clenched her eyes tight. That was probably so stupid of her. He wasn't in this with her for real. Even if he were—what kind of future could they have? He'd never be willing to face Han's wrath or risk Arthur's judgment. There wasn't any place for her in his lonely loner's house in the woods. Who knew how long she'd be staying in Blue Cedar Falls anyway? Getting invested was a waste, but she couldn't seem to fight it anymore.

Finally, Devin let out a sigh. He curled his arms around her, too. His posture softened as he pressed a kiss to the top of her head. "I'm fine," he told her.

"I know." People banging dishes on counters and leaving in a huff—that was always a sign that they were fine.

"I just..."

She leaned back so she could look him in the eye. The anger had faded from his gaze, replaced by something that made him look tired and older than he was. She sucked in a breath. "Han said it was something to do with your father?"

Devin nodded grimly. He pulled her back into a hug, her face pressed to his chest. Normally, she wouldn't mind being snuggled up with his firm pecs, but it was clearly a way for him to avoid her gaze. She allowed it for now.

Exhaling, he said, "Yeah. Told you he wasn't a good guy."

"You didn't tell me he was the 'shows up drunk to parties and knocks over cupcakes' kind of bad guy."

He shrugged, but she could practically feel his wince. "They told you that, huh?"

"Yup."

"They tell you the part about him smacking me around?"

She drew back. "No."

His grimace deepened. "Can we forget I just admitted it, then?"

"Seriously?"

"He was a jerk," he said, as if that were some kind of explanation.

"But he hit you?" More rumors and hushed conversations floated into her memory. She hadn't understood them then. But Devin telling her this...It slotted an awful lot of things into place.

Devin rubbed his hands up and down her arms, and she didn't need him to comfort her. Not when he was telling her about his pain. "It's okay. I'm fine now."

"How?"

His throat bobbed. "I got out."

"How?" An intense need to understand this man clawed at her. She shouldn't pry, but she wanted to know everything. "I mean—if you don't want to talk about it—"

"Your family, for one." His gaze connected with hers, a little light coming back to his eyes. "There's a reason I was always at your place or hanging out in Arthur's basement."

"Right."

"And then, as soon as I was out of high school, I packed my bag. Started working. Got an apartment. The rest is history."

Was it, though? The pain of it still seemed to live inside him.

She put her hands over Devin's chest, trying to take in the breadth of him. This strong, incredible man, who'd dealt with so much and who still stayed open and kind.

It occurred to her again, just like that night he'd walked her home after they'd hung out at the bar. Did he ever talk about what had happened to him? How did the pressure of keeping it all inside not make him explode?

Gazing up at him, she took a deep breath. "What happened to him?"

"I have no idea," he said quietly, ghosts in his eyes. "I assume he rotted in that house for a while. I never went back. He never came looking for me except a couple of times when he was trashed." He shrugged. "When he did, I just called Officer Dwight to take him home. Otherwise, I had nothing to do with him. Year or so after I left, I got a drunk dial from him. Said he was set up in a trailer park in Florida."

"You think he'll stay there?"

"Honestly, I don't care."

He meant it, too. The pain in his voice was like a hand reaching into her chest and squeezing.

Zoe's family was her bedrock. She defied them and fought with them, but deep down she loved them fiercely. She never in a million years could doubt they loved her, too.

Devin... he didn't have that.

Slowly, she skated her hands up his chest. She took his face between her palms. His scruff was rough against her skin. She stroked her thumbs just beneath his eyes. "I'm so sorry," she told him quietly.

"It's nothing. Old history."

She repeated it. More firmly this time. "I'm sorry." She reached up onto her tiptoes, pulling him down to meet her. She kissed his lips. "I'm sorry."

"Zo..."

"I'm sorry." She kissed him again, soft and slow.

He melted into it, wrapping his arms around her. Holding on to him, she tried to pour everything she was feeling into the motion of their lips. He didn't want her to comfort him or to let her tell him how her heart ached for him, and that was fine. She'd make him understand like this.

Because any of her ideas about not getting invested? Not growing *feelings* for this man?

They were out the window. She'd tossed her sense of self-preservation right along with them.

All she could do was hang on.

And wait for the crash when they all hit the ground.

Chapter Eleven

A couple of weeks later, Zoe sat on the kitchen counter, texting with June about grabbing coffee, Clay about whether or not she could open the bar tomorrow, Lian about how she wanted to bang her head against the wall over her job search, and a group of high school friends about a time to meet up for drinks later that week—all without accidentally sending any messages to the wrong person. She snickered to herself as she sent a reaction gif to Lian. Take that, accounting firm looking for "attention to detail."

No sooner had the thought occurred to her than her screen went blank, a call from an unknown number appearing over her fifteen messaging threads.

Her first impulse was to ignore it—she'd talked to quite enough people excited to offer her a free time-share or help her with a problem at the social security agency. But one of the worst things about being on a job hunt was having to answer every call.

Bracing for the worst, she tucked her hair out of the way and brought the phone to her ear. "Hello?"

A male voice replied, "Good morning. Is this Zoe Leung?"

She sat up straighter. "It is."

"Hi, I'm Brad Sullivan from Pinnacle Accounting, following up on a résumé we received."

"Oh, hi!" She scrambled down off the counter and over to her makeshift office set up on the end of the dining room table. Pinnacle, Pinnacle—oh, right. It was a firm in Atlanta she'd applied to last week.

"I was hoping to talk to you about your interest in the position. Do you have a few minutes?"

She blinked about fifty-seven times. "Of course."

"Great." With that, he launched into a quick overview of the job she'd applied for as well as a series of questions about her experience and training, which she somehow or other managed to string together coherent answers to.

Slipping back into the accounting persona she'd honed during her coursework and internship was harder than it used to be. Once upon a time, it had felt like a second skin. Now it felt like a wet suit that was three sizes too small.

"All right," Brad said, "sounds to me like you're an excellent candidate. Let me just talk to a few people and we'll get you set up for an interview with the rest of the team."

It was a good thing the chair she was sitting on had a back, because otherwise she might have tipped right out of it. "Oh wow, okay, great."

"Just one last question—this job does require you to be on-site in our Buckhead office. Looks like you're in North Carolina right now, but I'm assuming you're prepared to relocate?"

"Yes," she said, but as she did, a stone lodged in her throat.

"Perfect." He rattled off a few more details, and they said their goodbyes.

The whole while, the tightness in her windpipe grew and grew.

Atlanta was a four-hour drive from here. A few months ago, she might not have cared. She'd lived away from home when she'd gone to college. She'd always assumed she'd have to leave again to get a decent job that was in her field.

But her time back here in Blue Cedar Falls had changed her perspective.

She liked being home. She liked seeing Han all the time and being able to meet up with Lian now and then. She liked Clay and June and working at the bar. She loved getting to spend time with Arthur and helping out at Harvest Home.

She loved...

She clenched her phone so tightly she worried the screen would break.

She and Devin had told each other that their time together was limited. He wasn't interested in anything serious; all he wanted in this world was a house of his own outside of town, and he never imagined sharing it with anyone, least of all her. He definitely wasn't interested in upsetting the balance of his relationship with her family.

Ever since Han's dinner party, when he'd opened up to her about his dad, she'd known that eventually he'd break her heart.

She just hadn't been prepared for it to happen so soon.

Maybe it didn't have to. A bubble of hope filled her chest. Maybe she wouldn't get the job. Maybe she could just stay here forever, working at the bar and helping Arthur run the food kitchen and sleeping with Devin and it would all be okay.

Right.

The bubble popped almost instantaneously. She needed this job. If it was offered to her, she'd have no choice but to take it and go. This was the moment she'd been waiting for, working toward, training for.

So why did everything about it make her feel so terrible?

Before she could even begin to get it all sorted out, the front door opened.

"Crap."

Instinctively, she scrambled to look busy, but sitting at her laptop with her spreadsheet open was about as busy-looking as she could get.

"Oh, look, you're awake," her mom said, deadpan.

Zoe drew in a breath and forced herself to smile. She hadn't gotten home until two a.m. yesterday after closing up the Junebug. The fact that she was up before ten was a miracle.

Try telling her early-bird mother that, though.

"Han went to the restaurant already?" her mom asked.

Zoe shook her head. "Took the dog for a hike first."

"Good. Ling-Ling needs more exercise."

"Ling-Ling needs you to stop slipping her extra treats."

"Me?" Her mother put her hand to her chest dramatically. "Never."

Right. "How was brunch?"

Zoe's mother ate with May and June's mom and a few other old ladies almost every morning down at the Sweetbriar Inn on Main Street.

Her mom waved a hand dismissively. "Same as ever." She headed into the kitchen to start a pot of tea. Managing to sound both casual and pointed, she mentioned, "Mrs. Smith's son got a big promotion. Branch manager."

"That's great." Zoe dug her nails into the meat of her palm.

The competitive instinct in her told her to brag about the interview she'd just landed, but she knew better. Her mom would get obsessed with it and have her cramming for it like the SATs. Better to keep mum.

But as her mother puttered around, getting everything together for her tea, Zoe kept running around in circles inside her head. She wanted to talk this out with someone. Devin, namely. He was so grounded, and he asked her questions that made her see things in a new light. Could she bring up her mixed feelings about moving without letting on that she was getting too attached to him? Probably not. He was working right now anyway. So were June and Lian and pretty much all of her other friends she might try to talk to about this.

Which left her with her mom.

With her teapot and little porcelain cup and saucer balanced on a tray, her mother returned to the table and took her usual seat at the head. She put on her reading glasses and opened up the newspaper.

Zoe fidgeted, glancing between her open laptop screen and her mom, but she couldn't quite figure out how to open up her mouth and say what was on her mind.

Talking—really talking—with her mother had never been easy. Her mom had this unique way of shutting Zoe down and making all her ideas seem foolish.

Sometimes Zoe had enough force of will to barrel right through.

And sometimes she ended up picking a stupid major she didn't even like anyway.

She still couldn't decide who she was more upset with about that—her mother or herself. Clearly her mom wasn't entirely to blame. Yeah, Zoe had gotten a different version of her mom's weird guilt-trippy style of parenting, considering how much younger she'd been than her siblings when their father died. But Han and Lian—they were doing what they wanted to do. Or at least some variation on it. They were happy.

"Something on your mind?" her mother asked, not looking up from her paper.

So many things.

But the one she ended up blurting out was, "How come you always rode me so much harder than Han and Lian?"

Her mother's rapid blinking was the only sign that the question took her by surprise. With deliberate slowness, she set her teacup down and dabbed at the corner of her mouth with a napkin.

Stalling. Zoe was used to it.

That didn't make it any easier to wait her mother out. Chewing on the inside of her lip, she put her hands under her thighs, literally sitting on them to try to give herself patience.

Finally, her mom put the napkin down. She fixed Zoe with an appraising stare that lasted way too long for comfort. Inside, Zoe squirmed a little, but she remained firm.

Shaking her head, her mother let out a breath and looked away. "I ever tell you about the first day I picked you up from nursery school?"

Zoe deflated. She pulled her hands out from under her legs. "Probably."

"You were a mess. Glitter everywhere. Your teacher apologized, but I knew. It wasn't her fault."

Great, so Zoe had been a disaster since she was four. Good to know. "Look—"

Her mom talked right over her, slow and steady. Like a Zamboni. "Whole ride home, you never stopped talking. Told me all the friends you made, everything you did. You couldn't decide if you liked Joey best or Kim. Or costume party or building with blocks. Everything was your favorite."

"Right, right. I was a happy kid. I know."

Her mom's lips curled into a smile. "Ray of sunshine." She turned her gaze from the past and back to the woman in front of her. Her smile faded. "You remember what you told me you wanted to be when you grew up?"

Had she ever known? "No."

"I remember. Clear as yesterday. 'Princess astronaut veterinarian ballerina.' "

Zoe's face flushed warm. "I mean, I was, what? Four?"

"But you believed it. With all your heart."

"Mom..." She was beginning to lose her patience.

Her mother's voice rose by a fraction, her tone growing serious. "Your brother, Han. Only thing he cares about besides his family is cooking." Her mother jabbed her pointer finger into the table. "Han is easy."

Zoe frowned. She wasn't so sure about all that.

But her mom was on a roll now. She tapped the table hard again. "Lian wanted to be a teacher since she was six. Easy."

"But what about all the stuff you told me?" Zoe asked. Bitterness seeped into her tone. "Pick any career you want, just make sure it's comfortably middle class."

How many times had Zoe come home from school excited about some project in her communications elective or jazzed about a fundraiser Uncle Arthur was going to let her help out with at Harvest Home, only to be met with her mother's dismissive *tut-tutt*ing?

"You." Her mother shoved that finger in Zoe's direction this time. "You were never easy."

"Great," Zoe grumbled.

"You weren't. Still aren't."

Zoe's cheeks warmed, and she squirmed inside. Clearly she'd been selling her mom's passive-aggressive streak short, because this direct insult approach was no peach. "Okay, okay, I get it."

Her mother shook her head. She was fluent in English, but she still muttered a few words to herself in Mandarin. It was one of her only tells that she was getting flustered.

"That's not a bad thing, Zhaohui. You always make it out like I'm attacking you."

"Uh, you kind of are." How else was she supposed to interpret her mom telling her to her face that she was, always had been, and always would be difficult?

"You were not easy, because you actually wanted to be princess astronaut veterinarian ballerina!"

"Who wouldn't?" That sounded awesome.

"You have your head in the clouds. Someone has to help keep you here. On earth where you belong." Fire burned in her mother's gaze.

And okay, Zoe knew her mom loved her and that she'd

fight off an invading horde for her. But she occasionally forgot that the overbearing stuff was love, too.

Annoying, frustrating, occasionally infuriating love.

"You don't have to," she insisted.

"I do." Her mother reached across the table, and for the first time in what seemed like a long, long while, it felt like she was looking at Zoe. Not past her. No snide remarks, no judgment. She held out her hand. "I know it, because that's what your father did for me."

Zoe's eyes flew wide. Her mom almost never talked about her dad. "Wait—"

Her mother shook her head, her whole expression softening. "So like me, sometimes, my Zhaohui. I don't want you to learn lessons the hard way like I did." She extended her hand an inch farther, and Zoe slipped her fingers into her palm. "You have to be practical. You have to survive."

And Zoe would probably never fully understand her mother, but for one moment, she wondered if maybe she was right. If maybe they did have more in common than had ever been keeping them apart.

Her mother gave her hand a gentle, reassuring squeeze. "Look. I make you a deal."

"Okay..."

"You ever find job opening for princess astronaut veterinarian ballerina *with* pension and health insurance? I promise I stop riding you so hard."

Zoe laughed, and she swabbed at her eyes. This was making her way too emotional—especially considering her mom had basically just promised to never, ever give her a break.

She had about a bazillion other questions, but before

she could figure out a way to give voice to them, the actual, honest-to-goodness phone on the wall started ringing.

Her mother patted Zoe's hand before letting go to stand and answer it.

"Hello—" She barely got through the word. A muffled voice came over the line.

Then all the color drained from her face.

"For crying out loud, James." Bryce looked up from the same set of joists he'd been supposedly assembling for the last hour now. "Your mommy calling you or something?"

"Mind your own business." Devin ignored his phone buzzing in his pocket again. This was the third time, and no, it wasn't his mommy. Dead women didn't call.

He was starting to get a little worried, though.

He drove the last nail home in his set and looked up, meeting Terrell's gaze. "You got this for a second?"

"Sure, man."

"You heard him," Bryce said, dropping his nail gun. "That's five, everybody."

"You already had your break, and you don't have time to take another." Devin gestured at the work still to be done.

Bryce pantomimed a yapping mouth, and Devin gritted his teeth.

The guy had been giving Devin a hard time since high school. Ever since Bryce had come on at Meyer Construction, it had been the same—like Bryce resented that a guy as powerful as the mayor's son had to stoop so low as to be working alongside schlubs like Devin. Devin's promotion had been salt in the wound. The backtalk had gotten worse and worse, and Devin had tried to turn a blind eye to it. He'd focused on the job and the work and let the personal stuff slide.

Goodness knew there was enough to focus on work-wise. Ever since the disaster the other week when Bryce had let half a wall collapse, the higher-ups had taken a personal interest in Devin's crew. Devin had shown Joe all the documentation he'd been gathering about Bryce's sloppy work, and Joe had been clear that Devin had his support. He just needed to keep collecting evidence to build a case that could hold up against whatever scrutiny they might get if and when the time came to finally give the boot to the mayor's son.

Ignoring Bryce, Devin made sure he was out of every-body's way before pulling out his phone.

Only to find three missed calls from Zoe.

His heart thunked around in his chest, thrown by a whole warring set of reactions. Pleasure at hearing from her. Surprise, because she never called unless it was too late to come over and she still wanted to tell him some-thing dirty.

Worry.

He tapped on her number and brought his phone to his ear. As it rang, he glanced around. The rest of his crew was still working. Bryce was continuing with his little tantrum, but he'd actually nailed two pieces of wood together, so who cared.

On the third ring, Zoe picked up.

"Hey—" he started.

"Devin."

He straightened, adrenaline rushing his system. Her voice was all breathy and watery and wrong. "What happened."

"Uncle Arthur. He had a heart attack."

A ten-ton weight fell right on Devin's chest. He changed direction midstride. "Where is he?"

"Pine Ridge."

"I'll be there in ten."

"You don't have to." She sniffled. "I just—I thought you should know. Arthur—"

Arthur was like a father to him. A better one than his own had ever been, but Devin couldn't focus on his own concern right now.

Zoe put on such a front. She acted carefree, like nothing could touch her, but under all that she was tender and soft, and he knew her well enough now. The raw emotion in her voice reached into his chest and squeezed.

"Who's there with you?"

"Just my mom. She's trying not to freak out, but it's not working. Han's on his way, but Lian's car broke down, so he had to drive out to Lincoln to get her."

Right. "I'll be there in ten."

"Devin..." The way her voice broke made him stop.

He exhaled out, deep and rough. He covered his eyes with his hand. "Do you not want me to come?"

Everything in him was itching to go. A crisis demanded action. This was Arthur they were talking about.

"I just...If you don't...You're working."

She'd called him three times. She'd reached out.

"Tell me not to come."

"I—"

"Tell me explicitly, specifically, that you do not want me there, or I am getting in my truck."

Silence held across the line. A sob broke it.

"I want you to come," she whispered.

He dropped his hand from his face. "Ten minutes." His voice was still too hard. With a deep breath, he forced himself to be soft for her. "Hang on, baby."

Then he hung up.

It was fifty yards to the trailer. He crossed it in big strides.

"Hey, James, you okay?" one of the guys called.

"Family emergency," he barked out. He tossed open the door to the trailer, but it was empty. He backed right out. "Where's Joe?"

The couple of guys gathered around shook their heads and shrugged. "Maybe down at corporate?" one of them offered.

Devin shucked his safety gear. "When he gets back, tell him I had to go."

"Okay..."

"Terrell? You're in charge."

And then a voice came from behind him. A stupid, teasing voice. "What did your mommy want, James? Need you to come home and have your bottle?"

Devin ignored Bryce. He didn't have time for this.

But as he headed for his truck, Bryce followed him. "Real nice, ignoring your employees while you're running out the door halfway through your shift. Super responsible. I can see why you got the promotion over me."

Real nice, ignoring your father. Worthless sack of—

Devin's father's words had no place in his head. Not now when he was on his way to help Zoe, to help her family, who had been better to him than his own flesh and blood had ever been.

"Maybe I'll fill out one of those write-up forms you

keep doing for me—not that anybody reads them." Bryce leaned against the side of Devin's truck as Devin went to open the door. "You know that, right? That nobody listens to you?"

Just try to report me. Devin's dad had been stumbling, slurring. *Nobody's going to listen to you.*

"Get out of my way." Devin managed to keep from growling, but it was a narrow thing.

"Make me."

Devin hauled open the door of his truck and got in, but when he went to pull it closed behind him, Bryce was still there.

"Seriously, James. I want to see you do it." Bryce was in the way now, making it impossible to close the door. "Or are you too weak? Weak guy trying to boss everyone around." His voice dropped. "Not a great look. Think all of them will still respect you when they see me walk all over you?"

Devin looked past Bryce's shoulder before he could stop himself. Terrell and the rest of the team were back at work, but people were looking. Was that Bryce's angle? Trap him like this? Make him back down? Rub it in his face the next time Devin tried to call him out?

When would it end?

All Devin's life, he'd tried to keep his head down, work hard, stay out of trouble, and for the most part, it had panned out just fine. He had a great job, great friends. For the moment, at least, he had Zoe.

But what if it wasn't enough to keep quiet and do things the way they were supposed to be done?

What if he'd stood up to his dad a long, long time ago?

Righteousness surged through Devin's veins. "Move."

When Bryce didn't budge, Devin turned. He got out of the truck, and that put him right in Bryce's face, and he didn't care. "Go back to work now or pack up your things."

"Whatever—"

And that was it. Devin was done. "You're fired."

For the first time, Bryce flinched. "Wait."

"Get off my site. Don't come back."

"You can't—"

"I can." Devin took a step forward, and as Bryce retreated, power filled Devin's chest. He didn't have to keep his head down. He didn't have to stay silent when people were treating him like crap. He was in charge. People trusted him to make the right calls.

And this was one of them.

"Terrell?" Devin shouted.

"Yeah?"

"Call security to escort Mr. Horton off the property."

"With pleasure."

"My father—" Bryce tried.

"Doesn't have any authority here. And if he shows up and tries to pretend he does, then I'll stand up to him just the same."

Devin had heard enough. This guy didn't deserve his time. He had to get to the hospital, had to find out if Arthur was okay. Zoe needed him.

He climbed back into his truck and slammed the door shut behind him. He put the key in the ignition, and the engine roared to life.

From the other side of the window, Bryce shouted, "My dad is going to destroy you. One word from me and you can kiss this job goodbye. That little piece of land you've been saving up for? You can forget it. My father—"

Terrell appeared behind Bryce, two security officers in tow. "Oh, shut up already, Bryce."

One corner of Devin's lips curled up. They'd all been tiptoeing around Bryce forever, but a dam had just broken.

He should have told Bryce off years ago. It hadn't even taken a punch or a shove. Just evidence and words and an unwillingness to be pushed around anymore.

But he didn't have any more energy to waste on that guy now.

Arthur was in trouble. Zoe was reeling. Han was on his way.

The most important people in his life were waiting for him.

And he'd do anything for them.

Anything.

Chapter Twelve

O*k, class is covered, Han's here, be there in 20*

The text from Lian allowed Zoe to let out a sigh of relief.

Drive safe, she replied. She trusted her brother and all, but the look in his eyes as he'd taken off to go get their sister had shaken her.

It was the same look he'd had after their father died. Devastated. Determined. Hard.

She put her phone away, only to pull it back out again two seconds later. She couldn't focus on anything. The waiting room wasn't big enough for her to properly pace, and if she drank another cup of stale coffee, she'd shake right out of her skin.

The elevator at the other end of the room dinged, and she looked up. This was getting ridiculous. She'd been snapping her gaze to see who was arriving every time, but inevitably it was a group of doctors or nurses. Maybe another worried family with food from the cafeteria, a bouquet of flowers, or balloons.

Except this time, when the doors slid open, they finally revealed the face she'd been waiting for.

She leaped to her feet as Devin scanned the area. He spotted her immediately. Their gazes connected, and something inside her broke down. He ate up the space with huge strides and pulled her right into his arms.

A sob erupted from her. She clung to him, which was stupid—everyone could see.

When she started to pull away, he only held her tighter, though, and she couldn't help herself.

She'd been trying to keep it together since the moment the phone had rung.

Uncle Arthur was in his sixties. He had high blood pressure. He was fit enough, but he never stopped, never took care of himself. Others always came first.

"Shh, I got you," Devin murmured.

Tears were leaking down her face. She breathed through them. "He's fine. He's going to be fine."

So why was she losing it like this?

Maybe it was because she finally had the option to.

On the way to the hospital, she'd had to be the one to drive. Her mother had been even more of a wreck than her, so Zoe had been strong. It made sense. Uncle Arthur was her mother's big brother, after all. They'd been through so much together.

Devin rocked her back and forth, whispering reassurances into her ear the entire time, and she melted into him.

It seemed like it took forever, but Devin's steady strength slowly seeped into her. The tears ebbed. She pulled away, reaching into her purse for yet more Kleenex. Dabbing at her eyes, she shook her head. "Sorry."

"Don't be."

She blew her nose, but her mouth started wobbling all over again. He was being so nice to her, when he must be all shaken up, too.

Sitting back down, she beckoned him to take the seat beside her.

"What happened?"

"Heart attack. Partial, they said?" She gestured at the door her mother had disappeared behind a few minutes before. "They let my mom go see him before he heads up to surgery. They're doing that—that balloon thing." Angioplasty? "And a stent. They think his prognosis is good." She waved her hands at herself. "I don't know why I'm freaking out."

"Hey, hey." He grabbed her hand out of the air and squeezed it. "It's okay."

"I just—" She forced herself to stop and take a few deep breaths. As she stared up into his eyes, an unshakable sense of safety wrapped around her. It made her mist up all over again, but it was better this time. Shaky, she buried her face in his shoulder. "I'm just really glad you're here."

Too glad. Good grief. She needed to pull herself together. Han would be back with Lian soon. Her mother would be coming out before she knew it. The moment any of them returned, Devin would pull away. The idea of having him so close but unwilling to actually touch her made a fresh wave of misery crash across her chest.

"Come on." He held her close, rubbing her back. "You said it yourself. He's going to be okay."

"I know," she said, but the reassurances rang hollow. The only thing that helped was him holding her, so she clung to him, trying to soak in his strength while she could.

Far too soon, the elevator let out another chime. When

she looked toward the opening doors, a different sort of nerves stole over her.

There they were. Han and Lian. Ten minutes ago, she would have been trembling with relief.

Ha.

She dropped her face into Devin's neck for one last breath. Then she tore herself away, and it actually hurt. She met his concerned gaze, and she hated having to do it, but she nodded toward her brother and sister.

Devin glanced in the direction of the elevator. He had to see them, but he didn't let go. Instead, he turned to Zoe. He stared deep into her eyes. A dozen emotions flashed across his face.

But the last one—the one that remained…

It was resolve.

Enough.

It was the same feeling that had come over Devin back at the construction site. When he'd been pushed too far, and he finally pushed back. He'd made himself heard.

And it had worked.

A strange, ringing silence eclipsed the riot of voices in his head.

He wasn't powerless. He wasn't unworthy of love or acceptance.

He wasn't going to hide what he wanted. How he felt. From anyone.

Least of all his best friend.

Least of all when it was going to hurt someone he cared about, someone he…

Well.

For a long moment, he gazed down into Zoe's deep

brown eyes. She was shaking. Just minutes ago, she'd been crying. She'd gone soft in his arms, molding herself to him, leaning into him, and this wasn't about sex anymore. This wasn't some game to her. All his doubts about what she was doing with him finally melted away.

He held out his hand to her.

Without hesitation, she slipped her fingers into his palm, her eyes going wide as she sputtered, "But—"

He shook his head and raised his brows.

Her mouth snapped closed.

Like she understood him, she wordlessly rose to stand beside him. Their gazes held, and the rightness in his chest was so hot it burned. He curled an arm around her. Bending down, he pressed his lips first to her forehead. Then to her mouth.

He turned forward.

Lian spotted them first. Her eyes flew wide, and she started to divert Han, but Devin shook his head.

The second Han caught sight of them, he waved. A relieved grin crossed his face, only to fade in the next instant. His pace slowed, his brows furrowing.

A few feet away from them, Han came to a stop. "Devin." His mouth drew into a frown. "Zoe."

Zoe fidgeted the way she did when she was nervous, but Devin felt steady as a rock. He gave her fingers a reassuring squeeze.

"Hey there, Han."

Slowly, deliberately, Han darted his gaze between the two of them and their joined hands. "What's going on?"

Lian practically bounced up and down.

Maybe that shouldn't have given him confidence, but it did.

"Before you say anything," he started.

Han's complexion darkened. "Say anything like what?"

"We're in a hospital," Zoe interjected. "You try to murder us and they'll fix us up." She snapped her fingers. "Like that."

"Devin."

And Devin was standing his ground. He was refusing to let anyone push him around anymore. He wasn't going to live in fear of his best friend, and he wasn't going to hide the way he felt. He couldn't.

"I didn't mean for this to happen," he prefaced.

The vein in Han's temple started to bulge. "She's my *sister*, man. You were supposed to help me protect her."

"I am," Devin said helplessly. "I will." A lump formed in his throat.

Because he would. He'd protect her from anything that could possibly threaten her.

Even Han.

"I don't need protecting," Zoe insisted, because of course she'd never step back and let two men argue about her.

In the far reaches of Devin's brain, he registered the sound of Han laughing, but he couldn't focus on that right now.

This was Zoe he was talking about. The little girl he'd bickered with as a kid and the feisty, incredible, kind, wonderful woman he'd come to know since. She'd drawn him out of his shell over these past few weeks. She'd helped him let down his guard and see the world beyond the little piece of it he'd carved out for himself.

She made him happy. She made him want things he'd never even considered before.

He wanted them all with her.

"I love her," he blurted. The pressure behind his ribs popped, and he could breathe again.

Lian squealed, her hands over her mouth. Han looked like he might need heart surgery, too, but they were in a hospital. He'd be fine.

Zoe whipped her head around to gawk at him.

This wasn't how he'd wanted to tell her. He hadn't realized he wanted to tell her how he felt in the first place, but now that it was out there, he wouldn't take it back. Its truth radiated through him.

"I do," he confessed. "Sorry, but—"

"Oh my God, shut up, I love you, too, you idiot." Zoe flung herself at him, and if Han murdered them this second, it would be worth it.

Devin caught her in his arms and kissed her hard and deep. All this time, they'd been acting as if they were both okay with being casual, but apparently the only person he'd been fooling had been himself. Nobody made him laugh or turned him on or pulled him out of his head like she did.

For years now, he'd had dreams of building a house in the middle of nowhere, but those dreams had been about running away from the unhappy home he'd grown up in.

He wasn't running away from anything now.

At the sound of Lian clearing her throat, Devin tore himself away from Zoe. All around them, people cheered. Zoe hid her face in Devin's shoulder, blushing but happy.

He looked to Han.

The man had been Devin's best friend since they were in elementary school. They'd been through everything together.

But Devin had never seen Han's jaw come unhinged like this before.

"Wait—" Han held up a hand in front of himself. "Who said anything about love?"

"This guy." Zoe jabbed a finger into Devin's chest.

"Ow." He caught her hand and brought it to his lips.

He couldn't quite get a real lungful of air, though. Not while Han was looking at them like this.

"How long has this been going on?" he finally asked.

Devin looked to Zoe, who lifted a brow. "About a month?" he answered.

"Or maybe forever," Zoe said.

"Uh, but not like creepy forever, right?" Lian asked.

Devin scrunched up his face. "No."

"No." Zoe rolled her eyes. "Definitely not 'creepy forever.'"

He'd never laid a hand on her until this fall. But the truth of what she was saying smacked him upside the head all the same. He'd been looking at her differently since her high school graduation. Every time they'd hung out in the years since, he'd enjoyed her company more and more. The way they felt about each other now—yeah, it had been building for a lot longer than a month.

"I'm not even going to touch that one with a ten-foot pole." Han scrubbed a hand over his face. Then he let out a rough breath. "You're both happy."

"Yeah," Devin answered, automatic and sure. He glanced down at Zoe, and she nodded.

"Really, really happy," she promised.

"Well, that's good enough for me." Lian broke the tension by swooping in and hugging them both. She whispered something to Zoe that made her blush deeper.

Pulling back, she smiled at Devin. "Welcome to the family."

Oh wow. That part hadn't even occurred to Devin. He'd been too busy worrying about how pissed Han would be.

His gaze shot to Han. It was too early to be thinking about this stuff, but if he and Zoe worked out...if they went the distance...

They'd be brothers. For real.

Han shook his head. As Lian backed away, he held out his arms. There was still a certain wariness to him, but any fury had left him. "Dude. You've always been family."

With that he came in and awkwardly hugged them, too, and it was like a ten-ton weight suddenly floating off Devin's chest.

Zoe squirmed away from her brother, leaving Devin and Han in a weird side-to-side bro-hug. Han took advantage of the opportunity to haul Devin down into what Devin was going to choose to assume was a joking headlock. He ruffled Devin's hair, and yeah. He was definitely playing at the edge between teasing and menacing.

"Seriously, though," Han muttered under his breath as he let Devin go. "You ever hurt her, and I will kill you."

Devin straightened up and cleared his throat. Han's smile was warm, even as he cocked a brow in genuine warning.

Devin looked at Zoe. It was so clichéd, but his heart swelled.

Beautiful, incredible Zoe. Whom he loved and who loved him. He couldn't help but smile.

Devin bumped his hand against Han's. "I'm going to hold you to that."

Something in Han's gaze shifted. His mouth curled at the corners. He bumped Devin's hand right back, and even more relief flooded Devin's chest.

They were going to be okay.

It wasn't going to be easy, but for the first time since Zoe had arrived back home...Devin was starting to think this all just might work out.

Chapter Thirteen

"Read 'em and weep." Zoe laid her cards down on the table, showing her three of a kind.

"Ugh." Han tossed his cards aside.

Devin groaned and pushed the impressive pot of five sticks of gum and a half dozen of the wrapped hard candies her mom kept in her purse Zoe's way.

"Your deal." Her mom nudged the deck toward Lian. The two of them had been smart enough to fold as soon as Han and Devin started raising each other peppermints. Knowing exactly what she had in her hand, Zoe had stayed quiet and let them bid each other up.

Uncle Arthur had been in surgery for an hour or so now, and they'd had to dig deep into the well of ways to distract themselves—if for no other reason than that their mom was going to get herself kicked out if she bothered the nurses station any more.

As Lian started shuffling, Zoe's phone buzzed in her pocket. She pulled it out.

Oh crap. "Sorry, gotta take this."

"Sure, sure," Han said. "Wipe us out and then walk away."

"I'll be right back."

Devin tilted his head in question, but she shook her head, telling him that everything was okay.

Despite the thread of dread spinning in her gut, she was even pretty sure it was true.

Demonstrating exactly how distracted she was, her mom didn't even question her retreating toward the elevator bank. Zoe turned away from her family before accepting the call. "Hello?"

"Hi, Zoe. It's Brad from Pinnacle Accounting again. I just reviewed your file with the team, and we're excited to get you scheduled for that interview. How does Thursday morning work for you?"

Zoe opened her mouth. All the mumbo-jumbo accountant-drone speak she'd managed to summon to the tip of her tongue while talking to him earlier that morning was right there, ready to come spilling out again.

But she closed her mouth.

She turned, looking back across the waiting room at her mom eyeing the clock, her brother and sister fighting over a couple of Werther's.

Her Devin, who was holding his cards close to his chest, literally. But figuratively, he was staring right at her with all of them right there for the entire world to see.

Sudden certainty filled her chest.

"Zoe?" Brad asked. "You still there?"

"Yeah, Brad." She gripped the phone more tightly. "I'm right here."

Still holding eye contact with Devin across the space, she took a couple of deep breaths.

Every time she'd discussed her job search with him, he'd asked her questions she hadn't been ready to answer. Questions about what she wanted, what she loved, what had motivated her to go down the roads she'd chosen. She'd answered the best she could, but deep down, she'd known that she'd been hiding the truth, both from him and from herself.

She didn't care about some big corporate accounting job. She didn't want to go to Atlanta or Charlotte or Savannah.

She wanted to be here. With him. Working with Arthur and Clay and just living her life. Not the one her mother had charted out for her the second she'd been born.

She may be a dreamer, just like her mom said, but her head wasn't in the clouds. Her feet were firmly planted on the ground, and she was ready to stand tall.

"I'm sorry, Brad," she said. "But I've decided not to pursue this opportunity after all."

As she said the words, the rightness of them sank into her bones. There'd be consequences to this decision, but she was prepared to face them.

If Devin could stand up to Han for her, then Zoe could stand up to her mom. She could fight for her own happiness—and for a chance at a future for the both of them, here in Blue Cedar Falls, where they belonged.

"How is he?" Zoe practically bounced to her feet as Han and Lian returned to the waiting room after getting to go in and see Uncle Arthur in person.

"He's good," Han assured her.

"If already getting annoyed at Mom." Lian rolled her eyes.

Zoe could only imagine. She'd spent enough sick days at home with her mom—and her delightful bedside manner—to empathize.

"Can we...?" Devin asked, standing and gesturing toward the door. Zoe's mom had wrestled her way back to sit with Uncle Arthur the second he got out of recovery, but outside of her, they were only letting folks in one or two people at a time.

Han nodded. He reached for his jacket. "I should go check on the restaurant."

Thank goodness they had employees who could open the place.

"Call if you need anything," Devin told him.

"Will do." Han looked to Lian. "You want to stay or go?"

"I'll stay awhile." She tipped her head toward the door before sinking into one of the seats near where Zoe and Devin had been sitting. "Go on."

As he pulled out his keys, Han paused for a moment. "Hey, Zo?"

"Yeah?"

"Thanks." His gaze met hers, and it wasn't as if it was the first time he'd made eye contact with her since he'd found out about her and Devin, but there was something different about the way he regarded her. Like he was acknowledging her as an equal and not some kid sister he had to protect. "Mom told me how you held things together this afternoon, when I was off picking up Lian."

Zoe smiled. "No problem."

Han nodded, new respect in his eyes, and it was too much to hope that he'd start letting the rest of his family help carry some of the responsibility he was always lugging around with him. But a girl could dream, right?

As Han took a backward step toward the elevator, Devin held out his hand. Another little thrill ran through Zoe as she slipped her palm into his.

And hey, the vein in Han's temple bulged only a little, so that was progress, right?

A nurse was kind enough to show Zoe and Devin to Uncle Arthur's room, but they didn't really need the guide. Her mother's voice rang out as clear as day the moment they rounded the corner. "*Jeopardy!* gets you too worked up."

"*You* get me too worked up." Her uncle muttered a more colorful rebuke in Mandarin.

Zoe shook her head and sighed. Well, at least it was good to know he was feeling better.

She knocked on the door, eyebrows raised. "You two playing nice in here?"

Her mother and her uncle both looked up and smiled. Zoe didn't miss the way they were still silently wrestling over the remote, though.

"Zoe," Uncle Arthur said, swatting at his sister's hand. "Devin." Then he seemed to notice the fact that they were holding hands, and his head tilted in question.

"Uh..." Devin rubbed the back of his neck.

Her mother followed his gaze and did a double take, though she recovered quickly. Letting Uncle Arthur have the remote, she stepped back, one brow raised.

With Han finally in the know, Zoe and Devin hadn't held back on the casual PDA while they'd been hanging out in the waiting room, but they hadn't made an announcement or anything, either. Her mom was usually uncannily observant, but apparently she'd been too busy pacing a hole in the carpet to notice all the shared glances or the occasional moments when Devin would put a hand on her back or her knee.

Zoe's face warmed, but she held her head high, meeting her mother's gaze.

Her mom clicked her tongue behind her teeth and shook her head fondly. "Guess you did know what you were doing after all."

Zoe huffed out a breath. "Sure did."

"Good," her mom said, firm. A sly smile curled her lips, and Zoe's throat went tight.

It would scarcely count as approval from anybody else's parent, but for Zoe's mom? She might as well have thrown her a "Congratulations on Nailing the Hot Guy" party.

Uncle Arthur's reaction wasn't nearly as subdued, his pale face eclipsed by a bright grin. "About time."

"Hey," Devin protested.

"'Theoretical,'" Uncle Arthur scoffed, tucking the remote under his leg to make air quotes.

Zoe didn't know what they were talking about, but that was all right. Letting go of Devin's hand, she stepped forward to kiss her uncle on the cheek.

He squeezed her palm and winked. Quietly, he murmured, "Good choice."

"I know."

She moved aside, and Devin took his turn giving Arthur a careful hug.

Her mom slung her purse over her shoulder. "I'll give you two a minute."

"Really?"

She patted Zoe's hand. "Just a minute. I'm starving. Did you know vending machines here charge two dollars for a Kit Kat bar?"

Okay, yeah, her mom running to the car to grab a free snack from the stash she kept there made a lot more sense than her actually giving them privacy. "Outrageous."

Her mom made a disapproving sound in the back of her throat, calling out Zoe's sarcasm, but with a quick pat to Zoe's shoulder, she kept walking.

Zoe turned her attention back to Devin and Uncle Arthur, who were engaged in a little sidebar of their own. She rolled her eyes. "You don't have to threaten Devin if he hurts me. Han's already got that covered."

"You?" Uncle Arthur huffed out a breath and waved a hand dismissively. "You can fend for yourself. I was telling Devin that if you hurt him, you'd have to deal with me."

Devin looked kind of embarrassed about it, if secretly pleased.

Good. He deserved someone looking out for him.

Zoe dropped into the chair her mother had set up on the other side of Arthur's bed. As she did, Arthur struggled to sit up. She shook her head at him. "Relax."

"Your mother wouldn't let me have my phone."

"Nor should she have."

"I have to call Sherry." He scrubbed a hand across his forehead. "Ten people had appointments at Harvest Home today. Supper service—"

Zoe grabbed his hand and held on tight. "Is handled."

"The key—"

"Sherry already came by to pick up mine."

"Deliveries—"

"Have been postponed until tomorrow. All today's pickups, too."

"But—"

"Uncle Arthur." She gripped his hand in both of hers. "I've got it."

She sucked in a deep breath. Instinctively, she glanced up at Devin, but he just stood there, silently supportive. Because he was the awesomest dude in the world, and she was so freaking glad to have him at her side.

"Zoe..." Uncle Arthur started.

"Trust me." That's what she'd been asking everyone in her life to do since she graduated.

She could make her own decisions about who she wanted to date.

And about what she wanted to do with her life.

"I've been doing a lot of thinking." She stopped her uncle before he could interrupt again. "Not just today, but for the past few months. About my future."

That finally got him to let her speak. His mouth drew down into a frown, but she had his attention.

"You've been doing too much."

He shook his head, but she looked pointedly at the hospital bed he was all but strapped into.

"You do too much," she insisted again, "because you care too much. You take care of everyone all the time. Well, it's time we all took care of you." She cleared her throat. "It's time I did."

"Zhaohui?"

"I'm taking over Harvest Home." She kept going, putting it all out there before he could try to contradict her. "You'll still be in charge, obviously. It's your baby. But from now on, the day-to-day operations are on me."

"But your job—"

"Will be fine." She'd already talked to Clay about adjusting her schedule. It wouldn't be a problem. And she had some other ideas she was going to run past him, too.

Arthur started again. "Your job *search.* You had all those leads in Atlanta, Charlotte—"

Zoe shook her head. "My job search is over."

"But—"

"I don't want to be an accountant. And I don't want to leave Blue Cedar Falls," she said firmly. She looked at Devin, asking him to hear the weight of her words.

She was done worrying about what everyone else expected her to do.

Devin's own actions, telling Han about them, had been an inspiration. He wasn't going to let other people's opinions hold him back anymore. So neither was she.

"I like it here." She squeezed Uncle Arthur's hands. "I'm happy here. I have friends, family." Leaning in conspiratorially, she murmured, "And a really nice boyfriend."

Devin smiled, and her heart glowed. He wasn't going to fight her on this. Good.

Because she would fight. For her family and for her future and for her vision of how she wanted to spend her life, now that she'd finally figured it out.

"You don't have to..." Uncle Arthur put his other hand on top of hers.

"I want to. So you just focus on getting better. Leave all the worrying about Harvest Home to me."

Uncle Arthur finally smiled. "I wouldn't trust it to anyone else."

The warmth in her heart only grew.

"There are some grants we can apply for," he said, that gleam appearing in his eyes, exhausted as they were. "So we can get you a salary. If you go to my desk in the back office—"

"After you get out of the hospital," she assured him, reaching in to fluff his pillows. "Until then, you just rest." She nodded, both to him and to herself. "I've got everything under control."

Epilogue

One month later…

So, as you can see in Figure C in your handout." Zoe clicked a button on the remote for the LCD projector she'd borrowed from Lian. She arched a brow toward her audience as the spreadsheet she'd meticulously compiled came into view. "Taking into account average rent for a one-bedroom apartment, food, gas, personal expenses, and an acceptable rate of savings for a person in my age bracket…"

At the back of the room, June silently wiggled her hand, reminding Zoe about the laser pointer in her other hand. Right. Thank goodness the two of them had practiced this together last night.

She aimed the little red dot at the total at the bottom of the column. "Projected monthly expenses can be satisfactorily accounted for with projected earnings."

"Hold on a second." Clay held up his hand.

"I know exactly what you're going to say, Mr. Hawthorne." Zoe flipped to the next slide. "Income is broken out in Figure D." As the assembled crowd all turned the pages in their handout, she moved the laser pointer to highlight each number as she explained it. "Earnings fall into two major categories. The first is the modest salary

I'll be able to begin drawing from Harvest Home once our grant applications to expand our staff are accepted."

Uncle Arthur nodded, leaning forward to agree. "The grant proposals are very good."

"Thank you, Mr. Chao." Zoe shifted the pointer. "The second category is income from my part-time position in the hospitality industry."

"You mean waitressing," Clay said.

"Waitressing, hostessing"—she set down the pointer and remote to begin counting on her fingers—"bartending—"

"Okay, okay," Clay interrupted. "You're good, but—"

"And bookkeeping."

His mouth snapped closed. "Wait."

"Admit you need the help," June said from the back.

"Hey—"

"With these additional responsibilities, I've determined that I'll be earning a twenty percent raise."

"Twenty percent!" Clay balked.

Zoe's pulse ticked up, but she had full confidence in her value to him. She arched a brow. "You think you can find a new server who's as good as me *and* who can start doing your books for you?"

"She's got a point, man," Han agreed.

"This is a setup." Clay looked around at everyone with suspicion in his gaze. There wasn't any malice, though. The guy had been to war and ended up with a knee full of shrapnel and so many trust issues he might as well have gotten a subscription, but he knew he was among friends here.

"Of course it's a setup," Zoe's mom agreed. She gazed at Zoe with a knowing curl to her lips. "But you're not the one she's setting up."

Zoe's heart pounded harder as she met her mother's gaze.

Oblivious, Clay continued, gesturing at the screen. "She just gave herself a twenty percent raise."

"That I'm going to earn," she promised, still looking at her mom.

"You sure about this, Zhaohui?" her mother asked.

Clay sat back in his chair, arms crossed. "I'm not sure about it."

"Yes, you are," Zoe and her mom both said as one.

"I guess that settles that," Clay said.

June stepped forward to put her hands on his shoulders. She pressed her lips to his temple. "Accept when you're beaten, dear."

"Fine, fine."

As they spoke, Zoe and her mom continued their silent staring contest. Zoe could hear all her mother's doubts, and she expressed her confidence back to her, even as neither of them said anything at all.

This plan was going to work. She'd draw a low but respectable salary managing the day-to-day operations of Harvest Home. She'd augment it by continuing to work at the Junebug and taking over Clay's accounting. She liked both jobs. Her work at Harvest Home fulfilled her, while waitressing at the bar was both lucrative and fun. Doing a little bookkeeping would maintain her skills and her résumé in case she ever changed her mind. Uncle Arthur would be less stressed, and if he ever decided to retire, she'd be ready to step up and slide right into his place. It was a win-win-win-win.

Finally, Zoe's mother raised a brow. "Princess astronaut veterinarian ballerina?"

"Princess astronaut veterinarian ballerina." Zoe let out a rough breath as lightness filled her chest.

"Well, then." Her mother smiled. "I suppose I can't argue with that."

"Hey—James!"

At the sound of his last name, Devin looked up. Joe stood outside the trailer, waving him over.

"Got a sec before you head out?"

"Sure." He finished the last couple of joins he'd been working on before nodding to the crew. It was a few minutes early, but they'd made good progress today.

He helped with cleanup, but once it was all in hand, he patted his buddy Terrell on the back and gestured at Joe's office.

Terrell nodded. "See you in the morning, boss."

Devin took off, a spring in his step.

It still amazed him how peaceful the entire site felt now that Bryce was gone. The guy had talked a big game about getting his father to retaliate, but it had been precisely that: talk. Sure, the mayor's office had made a few overtures, hoping to get management to reverse his dismissal, but Joe had stood behind Devin's decision. In the end, Bryce had been more of a liability than he'd been worth. Last Devin had heard, the guy was heading back to community college. Devin hoped he learned some things while he was there, but as long as he didn't show up on Devin's job site again, he honestly didn't care.

Inside the trailer, Joe was perched behind his computer, same as always. He smiled when Devin knocked and let himself in, gesturing for him to have a seat.

Joe folded his big hands on top of the desk. "Just wanted to ask how things are going."

"Good." Devin pointed his thumb toward the door behind him. "We're on schedule out there, maybe even a little ahead."

"I know that. I meant with you."

"Me?" Uh... "I'm good."

Great, actually. He couldn't stop the little smile that curled his lips.

Work was less stressful. The bump in his pay from the promotion had finally started showing up in his bank account. Arthur's recovery was going well.

And then there was the conversation he and Arthur had had the other night.

His leg bobbed up and down in anticipation.

He couldn't wait to tell Zoe about it. He was leaving after his shift to go pick her up, and he was going to do just that.

It had only been a month since he and Zoe had gone public, but it had been the best month of his entire life. It was like the thing with Bryce; Devin hadn't grasped how much strain all the secrecy and sneaking around was putting on them both.

But that was behind them now. They were happy and in love. Han was still his best friend—even if he did look at him kind of funny now and then.

Well, he'd get used to it. Devin was in this for the long haul.

And after what he planned to show Zoe this evening, hopefully by the end of the night he'd know she was in it for the long haul, too.

"All right, all right." Joe shook his head. "I get it—

you're a private guy. Well, I just wanted to let you know that we're real pleased with how you've taken over as shift leader. Your crew's doing good work. Word on the street is you've really turned things around."

"Oh. Thanks."

Joe's raised brows were pointed. "Wasn't an easy situation you inherited with Horton on your crew. But you handled it like a pro." With that, Joe pulled open the top drawer of his desk and fished out an envelope. He passed it over. Nodding at it, he said, "Little token of our appreciation."

Devin blinked in surprise. He glanced at Joe, who motioned for him to go ahead and open it. The check inside stared back at him, and his jaw dropped. "I—I mean—"

People got bonuses pretty regularly around here when things were going well, but this was generous, to say the least. He sputtered for another few seconds before Joe took mercy.

" 'Thank you' is the phrase you're looking for, I think."

Right. "Thank you."

"You earned it." Joe closed the drawer and gestured toward the door. "Now get on out of here."

"Will do." Devin tucked the check in his pocket. He rose, turned to leave, then stopped and twisted back around. More fervently, he repeated, "Really, Joe. Thank you."

Devin didn't think he'd ever fully get rid of his old man's voice in his head, telling him he'd never amount to anything. But he had a lot of evidence to say otherwise of late. This bonus... the pride in Joe's eyes... They were the icing on what was already a pretty flipping amazing cake.

By the time he got back outside, the cleanup job was basically done, and folks were getting ready to head out. Devin gave everything one last check over before making his way to his truck. He drove the familiar route to Harvest Home, where Zoe stood outside waiting for him.

She hopped in the cab of the truck and leaned over the gearshift. He threaded his fingers through her silky hair, closed his eyes, and kissed her, and he was really never going to get over that, was he? How good she felt, how sweet she tasted.

How much he loved her.

"Hey," he managed when she pulled away.

"Hey, yourself."

The flush to her cheeks and the glazed darkness in her eyes almost derailed him, but he managed to keep his focus. "How'd it go?" he asked. "Your presentation?"

"Good. Really good." She rolled her eyes. "Clay's on board with the promotion, and Uncle Arthur was super supportive."

"And your mom?" That was the part she'd been worried about.

"I'm going to go with 'begrudgingly accepting.'"

"Hey!" Devin grinned. "So basically wild enthusiasm?"

"Next best thing."

"Good." He leaned in and pressed another firm kiss to her lips. "Knew you could do it."

Curling a hand in the collar of his shirt, she kept him close for a second. "Thank you," she said quietly. "For believing in me."

They kissed again. He tucked a bit of hair behind her ear. "Always."

She let him go and settled back into her seat. "So, what's the plan?"

The nerves he'd felt earlier while thinking about this moment melted away. "You mind going for a drive?"

She scrunched up her brows at him. "Uh...okay?"

Once she was buckled in, he put the truck back into first and steered toward the road. While he drove, he asked her about her day, and he told her about his. They commiserated over how tough it was to get Arthur to delegate and rest. She spoke with pride about her juggling act taking over for him.

But she had good people with her. Sherry and Tania had been only too happy to start managing the supper service by themselves most nights. Volunteers had come out of the woodwork to lend a hand, because that was what people in Blue Cedar Falls did. They took care of one another.

As he glanced over at her, warmth grew in his chest.

He was so glad to call this place home.

He was so glad she was going to stay. Here. With him.

Clearing his throat, he forced himself to focus on the road. Before long, he turned off onto the country route leading out of town.

Zoe shifted beside him. "You're not taking me out into the middle of nowhere to act out some weird serial killer fantasy, are you?"

Devin laughed. "Is that really the first thing to pop into your mind?"

"I mean..." In his periphery, she waved a hand at their surroundings.

"Not much farther," he promised.

Five minutes outside town, he put on the blinker.

"Wait—isn't this... ?"

Zoe held her tongue as they took the gravel road he'd been imagining driving down for the last three years. He came to a stop where the road ended.

It wasn't much. Just a small clearing in the wooded lot. He pulled the keys from the ignition and reached behind his seat for the camping lantern he stowed there. He turned it on and flicked his headlights off. Twilight settled over them, quiet and peaceful. Exactly the way he liked it.

He opened the door on his side. For a second, Zoe sat there, gazing out the front windshield.

"You coming?" he asked.

She looked at him. "This is Arthur's place, right? The old lot he snatched up in his real estate phase."

"None other."

"What are we doing here?"

"Just come on."

She followed him out, wary but smiling. Maybe she had a clue. They went to the center of the clearing. He breathed in the woodsy scent of the air. Tipped his head up at the stars just beginning to come out.

"I know you've been doing a lot of soul-searching lately," he told her. "I did some of that myself a while back."

"Yeah?"

"You know about my dad. I was... kind of directionless for a long time after I got out of his house. Just so glad to be on my own, I wasn't thinking about what I really wanted, you know?"

"Sure," she said slowly. "I can see that."

He held out his arm, and she came into his embrace.

The warmth of her against his side heated him all the way to his core. "Your uncle Arthur—he was a big part of helping me figure it out. I decided my goal was a place of my own. Not just a roof to live under that wasn't my old man's. A home."

His pulse sped up a tick, his mouth going dry. Getting nervous talking about this didn't make sense, but he couldn't seem to help it.

"Arthur promised me then and there that as soon as I could save up the money, he'd sell me this lot—at cost."

Zoe scrunched up her brow. "But he bought it twenty years ago. He must've paid, like, nothing for it."

Devin let out a quiet laugh. "It was a little more than nothing." A lot less than it was worth now, but on Devin's income, it was still a chunk of change.

A chunk of change that had taken him three whole years to save.

He was still a little shy, even with his promotion and his bonus. But that didn't matter.

"The other night, when I was keeping him company, he changed the deal."

"Yeah?"

Devin shrugged. "Apparently a heart attack gave him some new perspective. He doesn't want to make me wait anymore. He trusts me. Knows I'm good for it."

And he was. With the new promotion and the bonus he'd earned this afternoon, he'd be paying Arthur everything he owed in six months.

Pulling Zoe closer in against his side, he looked around. "He's signing it over to me next week."

"Devin. That's amazing."

It was. A kid like him who'd grown up with nothing,

living off what he could get at the local food bank. Cowering in a dark house with a dad who made him feel like dirt.

And now he was here.

He had the Leungs for his family. He had Zoe tucked beneath his arm.

He had this land.

His voice went hoarse. "This weekend, I was wondering if maybe you'd want to look at some building plans with me."

"Sure, I mean—"

"For when you move in here with me." He didn't want her mistaking him. He wanted to be clear. Looking down at her, he swallowed back his last remaining doubts. "I know it's soon, but I know what I want."

Her bright, beautiful gaze met his through the dimness. Her lips curled into a smile, and her eyes shone. "Devin..."

"Building a house. It'll take time. This isn't right now, but—"

"Yes," she said. She rose onto her toes and kissed him. "Of course, absolutely, yes."

He clutched her in his arms as tightly as he dared, returning the kiss with all the wonder in his heart. "I love you," he managed to get out.

"I love you, too." She pressed her mouth to his once more before pulling back. "There's just one tiny thing you're wrong about."

"What's that?" He was having a hard time concentrating. She felt so good pressed against him.

But then she grinned. "The soul-searching. The figuring out what I want with my life."

"Oh?"

"I'm done with that." Her smile widened, and he felt it in the center of his chest. "I'm exactly where I want to be."

And just like that, so was he.

Here. In this home that they would build.

Together.

About the Author

Jeannie Chin writes contemporary small-town romances. She draws on her experiences as a biracial Asian and white American to craft heartfelt stories that speak to a uniquely American experience. She is a former high school science teacher, wife to a geeky engineer, and mom to an extremely talkative kindergartener. Her hobbies include crafting, reading, and hiking.

You can learn more at:

Website: JeannieChin.com
Twitter @JeannieCWrites
Facebook.com/JeannieCWrites
Instagram @JeannieCWrites

For more from Jeannie Chin,
check out the rest of the
Blue Cedar Falls series!

The Inn on Sweetbriar Lane

Return to Cherry Blossom Way

The House on Mulberry Street

Can't get enough of that small-town charm? Forever has you covered with these heartwarming contemporary romances!

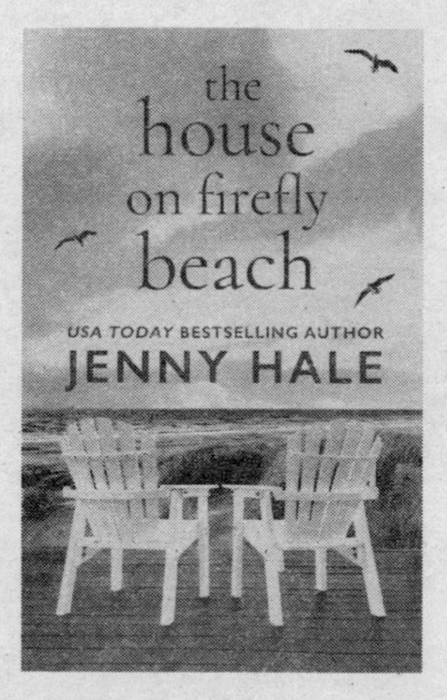

THE HOUSE ON FIREFLY BEACH
by Jenny Hale

Sydney Flynn can't wait to start fresh with her son at her sanctuary: Starlight Cottage at Firefly Beach. That is, until she spies her childhood sweetheart. Nate Henderson ended their relationship with no explanation and left to become a successful songwriter—only now, he wants to make amends. But when a new development threatens her beloved cottage, can Sydney forgive him and accept his help? Or will the town they adore—and the love they once had for each other—be lost forever?

Find more great reads on Instagram with @ReadForeverPub

THE GETAWAY
by Emily March

Jake Prentice has built a career out of being dependable. But when his widowed mother, Genevieve, shocks the family and moves to Lake in the Clouds, Colorado, in search of a change, he decides to heed her advice and find what makes him happy. Genevieve didn't expect her son to follow *her* to her new home, but when Jake's former colleague Tess Crenshaw appears, he'll finally have to assess what—and whom—he really wants.

ALL FIRED UP
by Dylan Newton

As much as book publicist Imani Lewis loves her job, she happily accepts a break to stay with her grandmother as she recovers from surgery. But being back in the same small town as Zander Matthews, with whom she once enjoyed a one-night stand, may not be quite as relaxing as she envisioned. When Zander begins to help fix up her grandmother's house, what starts out as friendly banter grows ever flirtier. But since Imani's stay is temporary, will she be able to handle it when things get all fired up?

Follow @ReadForeverPub on Twitter and join the conversation using #ReadForeverPub

RETURN TO HUMMINGBIRD WAY
by Reese Ryan

Ambitious real estate agent Sinclair Buchanan is thrilled that her childhood best friend is marrying her first love. But the former beauty queen and party planner extraordinaire hadn't anticipated being asked to work with her high school hate crush, Garrett Davenport, to plan the wedding. Five years ago, they spent one incredible night together—a mistake she won't make again. But when her plans for partnership in her firm require her to work with Rett to renovate his grandmother's seaside cottage, it becomes much harder to ignore their complicated history.

HER AMISH PATCHWORK FAMILY
by Winnie Griggs

Martha Eicher, formerly a schoolteacher in Hope's Haven, has always put her family first. But now everyone's happily married, and Martha isn't sure where she fits in…until she hears that Asher Lantz needs a nanny. As a single father to his niece and nephews, Asher struggles to be enough for his new family. Although a misunderstanding ended their childhood friendship, he's grateful for Martha's help. Slowly, both he and Martha begin to realize that she is exactly what his family needs. Could together be where they belong?